The Commandant's Daughter

BOOKS BY CATHERINE HOKIN

The Fortunate Ones

What Only We Know

The Lost Mother

The Secretary

The Commandant's Daughter

CATHERINE HOKIN

The Commandant's Daughter

bookouture

Published by Bookouture in 2022

An imprint of Storyfire Ltd.
Carmelite House
50 Victoria Embankment
London EC4Y 0DZ

www.bookouture.com

Copyright © Catherine Hokin, 2022

Catherine Hokin has asserted her right to be identified as the author of this work.

All rights reserved. No part of this publication may be reproduced, stored in any retrieval system, or transmitted, in any form or by any means, electronic, mechanical, photocopying, recording or otherwise, without the prior written permission of the publishers.

ISBN: 978-1-80019-701-5
eBook ISBN: 978-1-80019-700-8

This book is a work of fiction. Names, characters, businesses, organizations, places and events other than those clearly in the public domain, are either the product of the author's imagination or are used fictitiously. Any resemblance to actual persons, living or dead, events or locales is entirely coincidental.

To Veronica

for all the years of friendship

CHAPTER 1

30 JANUARY–9 FEBRUARY 1933

'It's the procession! It's coming!'

The sound rushed through the open glass doors, rolling round the crowded reception room in a deep-throated roar as if the sea had hurled itself inland. Hannelore drank it in, her heart hammering as a second, steadier thud pounded through the first wave. She closed her eyes, picturing the scene her father had promised – the heads thrown back, the voices swelling, the uniformed ranks marching step by perfect step through the wooded darkness of the Tiergarten – and shivered.

'Can you hear it?'

Hannelore whirled round as she spoke, expecting to see heads turning, eyes as wide with excitement as her own. Not one conversation skipped a beat. She stretched onto her toes and tried again.

'Isn't it time to go out onto the balcony? Isn't it time to watch?'

Nobody stopped talking. Nobody remarked on how delightful, or even how annoying, her enthusiasm was. Nobody took any notice of her or the commotion outside at all. Hannelore's voice floated away, sucked up into the never-ending swirl of chatter and the clink of brimming glasses.

What's wrong with them? Why aren't they racing to the windows?

Their lack of interest made no sense. Why else were they here if not to watch the parade? Her father had said that it would be the most wonderful celebration to ever take place in Berlin. That anyone who saw the massed ranks of the *Sturmabteilung* and the *Schutzstaffel* and the *Stahlhelm* veterans all marching together would never forget it and that nowhere would have better views than the Adlon Hotel. He had talked about nothing else since Adolf Hitler's appointment as Chancellor had been announced to the faithful that morning. Reiner Foss had gone straight into speech-giving mode then. Even though the household was barely awake, he had puffed up his chest and gathered the family and the servants together and he had sung the praises of the National Socialist Party and the 'new hope of Hitler' as if he was leading the worship in church.

He had, to Hannelore's ears at least, sounded rather ridiculous, although everybody else had clapped politely on cue. And when he repeated the same sentiments later that day, at a lunch as hastily convened as tonight's parade had been, his guests had greeted his words with thunderous applause.

So why doesn't anyone care about the march now?

The change in mood was impossible. It made Hannelore want to stamp her foot, even if that was a thing toddlers, not ten-year-olds, did. The evening reception was turning out to be as dull as the speech-laden one which had almost bored her to tears at lunchtime. Parties, or so Hannelore had always thought, were supposed to be fun; they definitely weren't that anymore. They hadn't been fun for the last two years, not since her father had stopped being Reiner Foss the wealthy businessman and had become SS Obergruppenführer Reiner Foss instead.

Her life had been happier before her father's had changed – Hannelore was certain of that. And her mother had definitely smiled more.

Before Reiner had started working for Hitler, parties had meant *Sahnetörtchen* on the lawn at their home in Lietzenseeufer in the leafy Berlin suburb of Charlottenburg, and treasure hunts and swimming in the lake that their elegant villa sloped down to. And her mother had definitely laughed more at those too.

Parties now, however, meant dull men in dark uniforms, and the best fun was had when Reiner was away and 'the women of the house' – as Grandma Alice called their little unit – were left to their own devices. Grandma Alice, Hannelore's adored mother Talie, and Hannelore, had been for years a cosy little group of three. The birth of baby Luise the previous year – after what Grandma Alice had described as 'far too much heartbreak' and then refused to explain herself – had made that group into an even happier four. As far as Hannelore could see, the 'women' formed a complete world, which Reiner's newly fault-finding presence invariably ruined. Fault-finding was apparently something which went hand in hand with her father's new uniform: Hannelore hoped it wouldn't be turned her way today.

The voices and the tramping feet were growing steadily louder. Hannelore stopped worrying about what might or might not irritate Reiner and inched a little closer to the billowing curtains, convinced she could hear the trees shaking as the marchers swarmed along Charlottenburger Chaussee towards the Brandenburg Gate.

The Gate: they must have almost arrived at it. Whatever else I miss, I can't miss that.

Ever since Reiner had described the route the procession would take, Hannelore had pictured every stage of it, especially the effect of the torches. How their flames would set the trees in the Tiergarten dancing; how they would turn the four giant horses charging over the gateway from dull grey into gold. That was a spectacle she was desperate to see, but how could she when no one else was moving and her father's 'you are not to go outside until you are summoned to do so' had left no room for argument?

Hannelore glanced round the bustling room. Her mother was caught between two plump, shiny men, her eyes glazing as they talked over her. Her father was locked in an intense-looking discussion. Nobody was interested in her. Nobody would notice if she turned a cartwheel, never mind slipped quietly outside. Hannelore had had enough of rules and waiting and adults who couldn't remember how to have fun. She pulled her cape tight, slid across the floor and stepped out.

The snow had stayed away that day – 'on Hitler's orders', or so her father had announced to great gales of laughter – but the cold was a slap and the frost had made an ice rink out of the stone balcony. Hannelore wobbled across to the ornately carved edge and peered over.

It was almost seven o'clock. The January sky should have been black, dusted with moonlight at best, and yet the view was carnival bright, the night bathed in a halo of yellow and red she hadn't expected. When Hannelore had imagined the torches coming, they had bobbed through the woods the way fireflies flickered through the shrubs in the Fosses' lakeshore garden. The rich glow spilling out below her, however, was a far more substantial thing: it moved in great sweeps, turning the streets into molten metal. The voices too were thicker, their roar more musical now that the singers were closer. Hannelore was transfixed by their tune, her skin fizzing, oblivious to anything but the excitement rising up to greet her.

'It's quite something, isn't it? And Minister Goebbels pulled the whole thing off in a day. I don't know whether to be thrilled by that or terrified.'

The voice came from the balcony's darkest corner. Its suddenness made Hannelore reply without thinking.

'I thought I was the only one out here. I thought nobody else cared.'

The man who had addressed her stepped out of the shadows and smiled. 'I doubt that's true. Everyone in there is as desperate to be out here on the balcony as you.'

He clearly hadn't been in the reception room and felt its indifference. Hannelore rolled her eyes, a habit she'd copied from

Grandma Alice and one which angered her father too much to risk using it at home.

The man laughed. 'A cynic allowed in the Adlon tonight? Well, that is unexpected. As is you standing out here. Are you supposed to be outside yet?'

Hannelore shook her head. 'No, not really. But nobody noticed me come out.'

The man's laughter stopped as quickly as it had started. 'Don't rely on that, not nowadays. Don't ever assume that there's no one watching.' He glanced at the window. 'Maybe you should go back in. It's not a good idea to get caught breaking the rules, not in this company.'

Going back inside was the last thing Hannelore wanted to do, although she knew the advice was well meant.

'I'd rather not. I'd rather know why you think they're desperate when they're behaving like they don't care. Grown-ups are always saying one thing and doing another – it's not very helpful.'

The man didn't laugh again, but he didn't chase her away either.

'No, I don't suppose that it is.'

He paused and glanced back at the rippling curtains. No one was looking their way.

'All right then, I'll explain what I meant if you want me to. But you tell me something first: have you heard of Joseph Goebbels?'

'Yes, of course I have.'

Hannelore didn't dare add 'and I wish that I hadn't', although from the way the man had said *Goebbels,* she suspected he might feel the same way. Hannelore found the Minister's eagle-eyed stare frightening. Her father, however, thought Goebbels was a marvel, which was why he was a regular visitor to their house. She decided not to mention that either.

'That's good. We're all going to be hearing a lot more about him and it's best to be forewarned. Now, what you might not know about our new Propaganda Minister is that everything he does has meaning. This whole night, for example, has been care-fully orchestrated to show the world how popular Herr Hitler is, and it's set to a very precise timetable. That's why all the guests are waiting inside: it isn't their time to appear yet, and if anyone messes up Goebbels' precious timings, he'll have their skin.'

He nodded to the lights which were quickly approaching. 'Very soon, the procession will turn onto Wilhelmstraβe and march past underneath us. Shortly after that, Hitler will step onto the balcony of the Reich Chancellery as humbly as if he hasn't been waiting to do it all day. And then, like clockwork, his adoring supporters will swarm out from the hotels and the ministries to greet him and the crowds waiting down there will go wild.'

He paused and looked out at the torches which were now blazing beneath the Brandenburg Gate. 'Everyone together, cele-brating a *united* new Germany. If I was Adolf, I'd be looking over my shoulder at Goebbels for stage-managing it so brilliantly. No one needs a rival on their first day out.'

He suddenly seemed to remember where he was. 'And now I have probably said far too much, and I should stop.'

Hannelore couldn't argue with that. It had been a longer explanation than she'd expected and a lot to take in. And never mind Goebbels, her father would have his skin for saying *united* as if he didn't mean it, and for using the name *Adolf* as if they were friends, and for daring to speak about *rivals*. At ten years old, politics was a mystery Hannelore was barely unravelling, but she was beginning to learn what kind of person made her father angry and this man, with his mocking tone, would definitely do that. Anyone who said anything negative about the National Socialists and their policies did that. Reiner wasn't just an admirer of Hitler's, he was... Hannelore cast round for the word her grandmother had used about her son – that was it: a *devotee*. He had put on his SS uniform, swapped *hallo* for *Sieg Heil* and become a new man. Hannelore wasn't at all sure that she liked that. The change in him was too harsh.

Her father – like her cuddle-filled mother – had always been a constant and affectionate presence in her life. All through her childhood, he had been easy to please, quick to reward, happy to indulge her with his time and with treats. He wasn't like that anymore. He was stern and humourless, and the further he rose in the Party, the sterner and more rigid he grew. Nothing pleased him anymore, including Hannelore. He had become obsessed with appearances and status. He criticised Talie because she was 'soft-hearted' and didn't measure up to the more 'Party-focused' wives, like the swastika-waving Magda Goebbels. He criticised Hannelore because she was a girl, not the son he openly longed for. And anyone who wasn't completely in step with his new allegiances was completely out of step with him. Reiner had changed – and had forced the house to change round him. Now he judged everything he, and therefore his family, did on how it reflected 'Hitler's vision for Germany' whose rules had become the family's new bible. Life in the Foss home had become a lot less pleasant and a lot more complicated.

Hannelore was still unsure what this shifting world meant. She did know that it hurt not to be her father's darling anymore and that the list of things that were no longer acceptable to him kept growing. Friends she had played with since babyhood were suddenly unsuitable. Servants who had served her family since the days when her grandfather had owned the house were dismissed overnight. Nothing was requested or explained; everything was an order. When Reiner began using the peculiar phrase 'bad blood' as casually as if it had always been part of his vocabulary, Grandma Alice – who had initially refused to hide her contempt for the Party, no matter how much that angered her son – began slamming doors. Someone who spoke as bluntly as the man on the balcony would not, therefore, be allowed within a mile of her father, never mind this close to Hannelore.

She shifted from one cold foot to the other. She knew that she should go back inside, and she was almost sure she should report him, but... He was different and that intrigued her, so she stayed.

'How do you know all this? About Goebbels and the timings, and how everyone is supposed to behave? And why are you out here if no one is meant to be?'

'Because it's my job to, or it is for now. Who knows what tomorrow will bring?'

He moved aside and gestured to a tripod set up behind him in the far corner. 'I should have introduced myself. My name is Ezra Stein and I'm not a guest, I'm a photographer. I'm here to record this display of spontaneous celebration for posterity, or for tomorrow's newspapers, which may or may not be the same thing.'

Hannelore was starting to get a little tired of his convoluted way of speaking, which seemed to be full of hints she wasn't sure how to pick up. She also couldn't tell if the mockery laced through it extended to her.

'Why do you have to speak in riddles? You sound as if you don't like anyone here, or your job either. If that's true, why not say so? Why do it?'

Herr Stein suddenly seemed less sure of himself. 'I don't hate my job. The people here tonight are one thing, but my job is another. It lets me see things…' He stopped and leaped over to the camera as a drum crashed into life not far below.

Hannelore leaned back over the balcony, her senses as alive as his. The procession was moving quicker now, its first ranks already spilling through the Gate. The marchers were densely packed, their pounding feet echoed by the beating drums whose deep vibrations shook the air. Hannelore stretched forward, her hand unconsciously reaching out for the flame-topped torches.

'Do you want a closer look?' Herr Stein stopped snapping and waved Hannelore towards the tripod. 'It's set for shutter speed and light. All you have to do is look down through the top and find the right picture.'

Hannelore glanced back at the window. No one was looking. She moved closer to the camera and bent over the viewfinder, trying not to flinch as the dazzling torches sprang up towards her.

'I don't understand. Isn't the picture whatever the camera shows me?'

She waited while the photographer took her place for a moment and reset the equipment, his fingers flashing from one button to the next. When he gestured her to step back behind the tripod, the flames had dipped out of view and faces filled the frame instead.

'No, not at all. You choose what you see. With your eyes, of course, but with your feelings too: your heart, or your gut – whatever you want to call it. Maybe that's the confusion you heard in me: I might not always like the subjects I'm paid to portray, but I love what I do, and what comes out of it.'

He guided her hand, first to a button and then to a lever.

'Press there when you have your image, pull that to move on to the next. Don't overthink it, then the real story will come.'

'I still don't understand…'

Hannelore stopped. She might not fully understand what Ezra had said, but she could feel in her bones what he meant. The world had suddenly shrunk; the photographer and the balcony had disappeared. All that mattered was the face turned up towards hers. A blonde boy in a Hitler Youth uniform, singing his heart out as if he was determined that every word of his song should reach his new Führer. The rapture shining from his eyes and powering his open mouth filled the lens and pulled at the hairs on her arms. His voice was in her head: she could see each note soaring as pure and clear and bright as her father had promised her the night's music would be. But it was his face that was caught in the camera, and that was a very different thing: that was twisted and contorted and furious.

Hannelore gasped and pressed down the way Ezra had shown her, although the skin on her neck had started to prickle and every instinct told her to stop looking and step back. She couldn't do that, however – her fingers wouldn't let her. They clicked on, reaching for the buttons and levers as if grabbing hold of the boy's image was their only purpose.

Good girls have quiet voices.

Reiner's new mantra – the one he berated her with every day – jumped into Hannelore's head. She could never be like this boy, roaring her beliefs to the sky, or not in her father's world anyway. Her opinions, which had once entertained him, were 'unladylike' now. Her thoughts held no value and were meant to be kept to herself. Reiner had been forcing her for months into a silence which chafed. Hannelore had endured that because she thought she had no other choice, because she had hoped her father would turn back into himself again. Tonight – watching men and boys as zealous as him marching in their thousands below her – she no longer believed that: she knew that if she was to play the part he had thrust on her, she would be the one who was forced to bend.

But what if that isn't true?

A new voice crept into her head. One that pushed away Reiner's, one that whispered, *Perhaps there is another way to be heard.* Hannelore shivered as her fingers carried on working. Once that thought caught hold, others rushed in behind it. What if he couldn't stifle her? What if there was a way of speaking he couldn't so easily control?

She refocused the camera as the column marched on without even realising she was doing it. If she had tried to describe the boy and all his contradictions to her father, Reiner would have told her – using more polite words perhaps but meaning the same – to shut up. He couldn't say shut up to a picture.

Hannelore stared through the lens, her eyes so alive it was as if she had never properly used them before. There was another face staring up at her now, as distorted with anger as the first. She clicked the shutter again and again, her fingers dancing. She was still clicking when the crowds started cheering and the balcony filled.

.   .   .

The parcel arrived on the Saturday after the victory parade, but it wasn't delivered by the usual boy. This one lurked, peering out from behind a tree on the other side of the road until Hannelore's curiosity got the better of her and she slipped outside. She was very glad that she had. If the boy had been challenged and the parcel hidden behind his back had been taken straight to Reiner, as the post usually was, the combination of *Fraulein Hannelore Foss* and the sticker advertising *Stein and Sons' Photographic Studio* would have brought another whirlwind down on her head.

Hannelore had been spotted on the balcony. Worst of all, she had been spotted talking to a stranger whose dark looks and 'unacceptable name' had infuriated her father. Herr Stein had been ordered to leave the hotel. First by Reiner, who had lost his temper when Ezra refused to apologise for the 'sin' of addressing his daughter, and then very roughly by the hotel manager. Hannelore had been forbidden to say goodbye to him and the 'I'm sorry' she had shouted across the room had sent her early to bed for the rest of the week. 'He was showing me how to take photos' had fallen on deaf ears and – beyond Reiner's catch-all 'I won't have you mixing with unsuitable people' – no one would explain what had caused such an upset.

But he didn't forget me and he can't have been cross, not if he's sent me a parcel.

Hannelore raced upstairs to her bedroom and ripped the thin paper away from the package. When she opened the cardboard box waiting inside, it was all she could do not to shout. Herr Stein had sent her a camera. It had clearly been well-used – the body was a little battered and the casing was chipped – but it was a camera, and it was beautiful.

Hannah eased the metal body out of the layers of tissue paper as gently as if it was made out of porcelain. Unlike the heavy double-lens model she had used on the tripod, this camera was lightweight and compact. Its buttons and levers were arranged in a neat formation across the top where they were easy to get at, and there was a carrying strap attached to its sides. It looked as if it was made for speed, ready to jump into action.

Hannelore put it to her eye and pointed the lens, her fingers itching to start pulling and pressing. She didn't, however, have a clear idea where to start.

There must be more. He spoke like he was teasing me, but he wouldn't be mean enough to send me something I couldn't use.

Laying the camera gently down on the bedspread, she tipped the rest of the box out. There was an elegant brown leather carrying case, a stack of black canisters labelled 'Film' and – joy of joys – an instruction manual. There was also a copy of the picture she had taken of the boy, with his teeth bared and his eyes blazing. It was a good photograph – even with her limited experience, Hannelore could see that she had framed the shot well and she had definitely captured her subject's fury – it did not, however, make for easy viewing. She put it aside and picked up the last item, a slip of paper which opened into a note.

6 Wassertorstraße
Berlin Kreuzberg

Dear Fraulein Foss,
What a lively evening! It was a delight to meet you, and a more pleasing experience, I confess, than meeting your father.
I have sent you a copy of one of the photographs you took. I believe that you may have a talent for this work, if you nurture it carefully. I hope that you will: Germany is going to need a brave new breed of story-tellers in the years to come. Your picture tells a version of that night that very few of the people who witnessed it would have seen. I think it is the more honest one, but that is a conclusion which you must come to yourself. Herr Foss, I know, will not agree with me, but whether you discuss this with your father or not is also a conclusion for you. I cannot, and would not, ask a young girl to keep secrets from her family. Perhaps, however, this is one which does not need revealing

until you have made up your own mind what it might mean – or might cost.

As you can see, I have also sent you a camera, a Leica. It is an old one of mine and a good starting tool for a beginner. Practise a little with it, and then – if my words haven't scared you and there is an adult you trust to act as your chaperone – come and see me at my studio. Perhaps you would like a few lessons? I have a feeling that there are pictures you could take whose subjects I wouldn't get close to, if you really have an appetite, and a voice, for telling the whole story, that is.

With best wishes,

Ezra Stein

The note was as cryptic as the way he spoke, full of the layers Hannelore suddenly realised were also in her photograph.

A voice for telling the whole story. It was as if he had looked into her head.

She picked the print up and scrutinised its details again, trying to find a match between what she had been told about the joyous nature of the night and what she had actually witnessed. There was a disconnect, but how deep it ran wasn't clear from one image. The boy could have been angry at something she couldn't see, or perhaps frightened by the noise around him. Hannelore didn't know what the *honest* story of the celebration parade was, but the photograph confirmed the gossip she had overhead about how Goebbels had restaged parts of the procession because the crowds in the first pictures weren't enthusiastic enough. That the truth of the night wasn't as simple as the 'great triumph' her father and his cronies had called it. That, as she now realized Ezra had been trying to teach her, there was never only one way to view the tale being told.

Hannelore stared at the boy's face again, wishing that she had other pictures to compare it to. She didn't fully know yet how photographs were taken, or how they could be used. She was, however, beginning to learn that they had a value which went beyond the annual family portraits her mother delighted in and she was determined to understand more. Which meant she needed Ezra Stein – and a trusted adult.

'Where are we meant to turn next?'

Hannelore looked at the city map spread out across her knees and prayed that her grandmother would keep her own eyes on the road. Alice Foss's driving skills were rusty at best; at worst, they were terrifying. Alice had refused, however, to involve the family chauffeur in the scheme to visit the Stein Studio, on the grounds that 'if I do that, your father will only ask all the questions I assume you're trying to avoid'. Her assumption was, of course, correct. It was why Hannelore had gone to Alice in the first place.

Like everyone else in the family, Hannelore's grandmother had been reduced to obedience by her son's new career path. That not only sat badly with her, but she was convinced that Reiner's father would, as she had muttered more than once, 'have been thoroughly ashamed of his son'. Hannelore barely remembered her grandfather – she and her parents hadn't lived in the Lietzenseeufer house when he was alive – but she had an impression of a lively man, full of laughter, who strode round waving a newspaper and demanding a 'debate', and of a wife he adored and treated as an equal.

Grandma Alice was a more subservient woman now, and Reiner was unkinder than an only son should be. Hannelore had heard his veiled threats about widows clinging to houses they no longer owned; her grandmother had shrunk from them. Slamming doors had given way to shut lips and subjects to be avoided, although Hannelore saw the fight rise in Alice's eyes when Reiner was in full rule-setting flow, and she knew that Alice itched to argue with him. That was why she had gone to her grandmother with the contents of the parcel. Alice might not dare to pick fights with her son anymore, but Hannelore was certain that didn't mean she shared his beliefs.

To her relief, when she'd showed Alice the photograph, her gamble had paid off. Hannelore had been grateful for that until the moment Alice launched the Mercedes into Berlin's speeding traffic. Now she was wondering if her father's anger might have been a safer thing to negotiate. She gritted her teeth and folded the map up a split second before Alice could grab it and black out the car's windscreen.

'The studio is on Wassertorstraße, Grandma. If you take the next turn onto Prinzenstraße, it's a block after that.'

The car shuddered as Alice spotted their turning and stamped on the brake.

'Here we are. Look out for the number, while I find a place to park.'

Hannelore peered out at a street that was drabber than she was used to and clutched the camera she had spent every private moment learning her way around. She had practised loading and unloading film spools until she could almost do it in the dark. She had driven herself mad with the mathematics of shutter speeds. She hadn't, however, dared take a picture: she was too worried about giving Herr Stein something to develop that turned out to be ordinary and dull and making a fool of herself.

'That's number two, so number six must be over there. I hope he doesn't mind that we didn't telephone first. I didn't want anyone to overhear...' She stopped as the car pulled up. 'This can't be it. Not in this state.'

Alice switched the engine off. She looked at the studio for a long moment and then she turned to Hannelore. 'Maybe you shouldn't get out, sweetheart. I doubt your photographer is here. And it may not be safe to go looking for him, not if the idiots who did this are still around.'

It wasn't an order; it was a plea: Alice sounded as shocked as Hannelore. Given the state of the building, it was probably good advice. Hannelore, however, didn't take it. She stumbled out of the car and across the litter-strewn pavement to the studio's vandalised door.

The damage was worse close up. The wood was splintered and covered in red paint and cruel words – *Dirty Jew, Parasite*. The same paint had been slopped in long streaks onto the window, which was open to the wind and the rain. It too had been deliberately ruined, the glass smashed, the photographs which had stood on display there ripped out of their frames and covered in boot marks.

'Who would do this, Grandma? Why would anyone do this?'

Hannelore fought not to cry as Alice's hands steadied her shaking shoulders.

'The who is easy.' Her grandmother's voice was far harder than it had been in the car. 'The thugs who follow Adolf Hitler. As to why, presumably because poor Herr Stein has the thing the National Socialists hate most: bad blood.'

Hannelore whirled round. That was her father's phrase, the one her grandmother hated; the one nobody would explain. 'What on earth does that mean? How can anyone's blood be *bad*? And why would having it get your shop smashed to bits?'

Alice shook her head. Her face had fallen into all the lines powder and lipstick normally hid. 'Because people are ignorant and easily fooled and happy to blame their problems on lies, which is a tragedy not an excuse. Of course there's no such thing as "bad blood" – that's one of our new Chancellor's inventions. Here at poor Herr Stein's shop, what it means is Jewish. Everywhere in Germany, if Hitler gets his way, it will mean *other*. People who are not, in his party's eyes, "properly" German and who are responsible for all its ills. People who have no place in his version of our country. God help us all if that works out the way that he wants it to.'

She took Hannelore's hand and tried to ease her back into the car. 'We should go – there's nothing to be done here. I'll tell Reiner I bought you the camera. I'll arrange lessons myself, if that's what you want. It's best that you forget about Herr Stein.'

Hannelore wasn't sure how she could do that. She was certain that she didn't want to do that. And she wasn't ready to leave the broken shop, not until she had captured all it was saying.

'Hannelore, sweetheart, we need to go.'

Hannelore wasn't listening. She was watching a ray of weak winter sunlight skim across the shattered window and catch on a jagged hole smashed deep through its centre. The shape left by the fist or the brick or the boot looked like a star, a many-pointed, angry star. Hannelore lifted her camera and pressed.

CHAPTER 2

2–5 MARCH 1945

If he sees me, he'll push me on board too.

Hannelore flattened herself against the wall surrounding the Theresienstadt station platform, looking for a gap in the chaos to run away through. It was too late. Reiner was coming, slashing a path with his whip, forcing his way through the passengers who had realised too late that this wasn't the journey they had been told they were taking.

'Give it to me right now or I swear I'll break your arm.'

He thrust past a woman holding a crying child, his hand stretched out towards the camera Hannelore was holding. She handed it over before he could snatch it, praying that she hadn't torn the film when she had ripped it out in the seconds before he came for her, or exposed it to light. That the image she had taken of him was safe.

My father the family man. Cramming children onto a train on its way to the ovens.

When he threw the Leica onto the ground and crushed it under his boot, she bit down tight on her lip and refused to flinch.

'What are you doing here? Who let you in?'

She wasn't going to give up the guard who was so susceptible to a smile, who had let her in to the hell that was Theresienstadt today and before. And she wasn't going to pretend with her father anymore either.

'I'm watching you. I'm remembering.'

His bark of a laugh made the man stumbling past cower. 'And then what, Hannelore? What are you going to do next? Run crying to the Allies about your beast of a father? They'll shoot you before you get close, or they'll wait for you and do worse.'

The crowds were still coming. There wasn't a hand's space between the passengers already packed on to the train, but the soldiers pushed, and the carriages kept filling.

'How can you do it? The war is almost lost and yet here you are, still killing. Still telling them that they are being sent to "family camps" when there is no such thing.'

Her fury bounced off him.

'I am doing my job. Protecting Germany from' – he glanced round the platform – 'vermin. Something you've never bothered about before.'

'That's not true! I've always hated this; I've always been disgusted by this.'

This time, it was Hannelore's shout which made people cower and flinch and look for the bullet or the whip. It had absolutely no effect on Reiner.

'Oh, Hannelore, how hard it must be to be you. Yes, I know: you've cried yourself to sleep at the "cruelty" you think that you've seen here, and you have, no doubt, taken dozens of pictures of "the terror of Theresienstadt", as you so dramatically put it. But have you ever sent those pictures anywhere? Have you ever tried to run away and join the resistance? Of course not. I'd probably admire you more if you did. You said it yourself: you "watch". But you don't act, do you? You "see" everything, and you "know" everything, but that's it. You're a coward, Hannelore, and you'll never be anything more than that.'

It wasn't true. Hannelore had decided – she had promised – months ago that she was going to tell Theresienstadt's real story, that she was going to tell her father's real story. She wasn't going to break that pledge: it was the whole point of all the pictures she had taken.

But I haven't honoured it yet and I don't know how to. So what if he's right?

The thought hit her like the blow Reiner intended it to be.

He was talking again before she could pull herself together and fight back.

'None of it matters anyway. I'm sending you and your mother back to Berlin. The enemy is close, so I need to focus on my future and that will take a little reinventing. I can't do that with you hanging like a millstone round my neck.'

'Good. I'll be glad to be away from you.' Her fury barely got his attention. 'I'll tell the truth there; I'll tell the Allies all about you.'

He had turned away again to the train waiting to leave for Dachau and to the challenge of how to cram more bodies onto it. He threw his parting shot over his shoulder and didn't bother to turn back.

'No you won't. With the state Berlin will be in when you get there, you'll never survive long enough.'

They weren't the last words he said to her. His last words – which had been tossed across the dinner table during an otherwise silent meal on the last night she and both her parents had spent together – were worse.

'This one's blood is on your hands, Hannelore, not on mine. You forgot that the men are more frightened of me than they are taken in by you.'

He had given her the photograph then – the first one she had taken in Theresienstadt a week or two after the Foss family had arrived in 1943. An image snapped with shaking hands when she had stumbled into an attic full of the dying that she wasn't meant to see. And the one she had pulled out of her camera bag and forced into the young guard's hands as she ran away from the train station and out of Theresienstadt, begging him to give it to the advancing Russians along with her father's name.

'He handed it straight over to me. I shot him anyway. Oh, Hannelore, how hopeless you are. You don't think, you don't plan. You could never be a danger to me. If you were, you can be sure this would all have played out very differently.'

His blood is on your hands.

Hannelore could still feel it staining them, burning them as she sat in the car carrying her away from the camp and her father. She might be leaving Theresienstadt, but that didn't mean she would ever be able to get herself clean.

'I don't know what to do. I'm responsible for that boy's death and I don't know how to make it right.'

She stopped. Talie was staring out of the window. Hannelore knew she hadn't heard her, that she couldn't see the scenery passing by. She scooped up her mother's thin hand and patted it. Talie turned and gave her a vague smile. It wasn't the response Hannelore needed, but there was as much love in it as Talie could give. Her mother was ill and had been since Hannelore's little sister Luise had died in a scarlet-fever epidemic in 1938. Talie had disappeared then. The woman who had once spent her days devising adventures for her girls, who was never too busy for them, who was filled up with love for them, had retreated into a world of shadows and silences. Hannelore knew that she couldn't help it: at twenty-two, she understood what she hadn't at ten, that the heartbreak before Luise's birth which her grandmother had refused to explain, had been a string of miscarriages. Hannelore also knew that she couldn't reach her mother, no matter how hard she tried, and that Reiner would never try at all.

Which is another good reason to hate him.

The car which Reiner had ordered to take his 'millstones' back to Berlin bumped over the cobbled streets, finally speeding up as it approached the bridge that would carry them over the River Elbe and towards... Hannelore supposed the word in her head should be *home*, but it was hard to visualise what that word now meant.

For the last fifteen months, it should have meant the Bohemian town of Leitmeritz, or so Reiner had promised them, but that had turned into a nightmare. She knew what *home* meant to her father and his kind: they used it and *homeland* like magic talismans, not to describe actual places, but as a shorthand for a concept of blood purity that was sick to its soul. She wished it meant the comfort and safety of childhood, but those days were long gone.

Hannelore pressed closer into her mother's side and clutched tight to her camera bag. It contained her spare camera, along with the dozens of photographs she had taken of Theresienstadt, the rolls of film she still had to develop and the chemicals which she doubted she would be able to replenish in bomb-battered Berlin.

It contains the truth.

Truth was a word Hannelore needed to cling to as hard as her bag. Fifteen months in Theresienstadt had taught her even more than Ezra Stein had done that the truth could wear very different faces.

Images crowded her head as the car sped on. Leitmeritz and Theresienstadt appearing as she had first seen them in December 1943 when Reiner had been appointed to oversee what he described as 'a series of projects' in the garrison town and the nearby work camp. Leitmeritz with its snow-capped mountains and then with the green meadows and pink-blossom-decked fruit trees which covered the slopes when the snow melted and spring came. Theresienstadt with its towering red walls and its chequerboard black-and-white entrance arch and the grass-covered ramparts which were twice as wide at their tops as the Brandenburg Gate. Those images were beautiful. They were what Reiner had wanted her to see.

And then the other sights, the ones that he had meant to stay hidden, came crowding into her head. The attics and the trains and the bodies, the sights it had sickened her to photograph, but

the ones that had to be preserved. The other truth of Theresienstadt, the one which proved that the public face the town wore
was a lie.

Hannelore had dozens of those. Images held not only in her
head, but on the reels of film still to be developed and in the
photographs she had printed and packed. Her father thought she
was a coward. Maybe she had been, maybe she still was. She had
certainly been foolish. Whether Reiner survived the Russians or
not, there were hundreds of others who had committed the same
crimes as him and the guard's death was a warning about the
dangers to be faced if she made what she knew about those sins
public.

*But that has to change. If the regime is beaten, if men like my father
are beaten, that surely has to change.*

She had to believe that a reckoning was coming. A day when
evidence would be asked for, evidence which would put her
father and all the men like him – who had divided people into the
ones who deserved life and the ones who didn't according to
some formula based on their own hatreds – behind bars.

Hannelore stared out of the window as the world flashed past
in dull shades of brown and grey which held no promise of
spring.

I will stand up then; I will be brave then.

And God help Reiner Foss when she did.

CHAPTER 3

2 OCTOBER 1946

***Nuremberg Verdicts Announced: Twelve Hang, Seven Imprisoned,
Three Free to Walk Away***

Gerhard folded the newspaper into a neatly creased rectangle and
dropped it into the wastebin at the side of his desk. He had no
desire to reread it. The report beneath the stark headline was
exactly the disappointment he had expected it to be.

He checked the room to make sure that no one was looking
his way. That done, he closed his eyes and let his mind scroll back
through the article whose key details he had memorised. Gerhard
had not found doing that a difficult task: he had an excellent,
almost photographic, memory for facts and figures, not that any
of his colleagues knew or cared. His co-workers had grown deaf
to anything Gerhard had to say, and the Americans who ran the
facility he worked in had no interest in him at all.

Gerhard snapped his eyes open. Instead of focusing on the
disappointment of the trials, he had slipped into worrying at the
disappointment which was himself.

How did you permit this? How were you reduced to this?

The criticism came first in his father's voice, then in his mother's – the usual pattern. He didn't want to hear it, especially not today, although he knew it was true. *Reduced* was the reason why nobody listened or looked at him. *Reduced* meant that Gerhard – for all his years of training and service and all his innumerable talents – was not employed in a court or in a lawyer's office where his talents would be best used, that he was no more nowadays than a filing clerk. The only skill anyone required from him was a menial one: transferring information onto index cards, putting them into alphabetical order and then sorting them into the correct cabinet before they went on to the final stage of processing. It was a job a child could do. It was, however, the only one the Americans who controlled the sector of Berlin Gerhard lived in and who – despite their smiles – continued to regard German men of military age as the enemy, had finally permitted him to hold. Even at his lowest points, Gerhard refused to be grateful for that. Even though he had been told at his interview – where the officer in charge had barely looked up at him – that grateful was exactly what he should be.

Gerhard was no fool: he knew filing was demeaning work for a man of his intellect; he also understood he was meant to know that. The word *nobody* was never explicitly used, but the glances that flickered over and never registered him, and the constant failure to remember his name, spelled it out. All Gerhard's German colleagues were, it had to be said, treated with the same levels of polite disdain as he was, but none of them seemed to care. Not that Gerhard had asked them how they felt, or that they had asked him. His co-workers rarely socialised with him; they preferred conversations about beer and sport and nothing that mattered.

Which is a good thing today.

He picked up his pen and the next card from the pile. What his mother and father didn't know was that *reduced* could be useful, when it brought with it the kind of access to information Gerhard now had. And that *overlooked* could be useful too. Especially when he needed to get his plan started and, for once, did not want to discuss any aspect of the trial. He did not need a comment from his colleagues about how 'obsessed' with it he was. He did not need to listen to anyone else's opinions on the verdicts or have them refuse to listen to his. The judgements, for what little they were worth, had only just been handed down; his feelings – and where those feelings would now have to take him – were too raw to expose.

Why does nobody care but me?

The question niggled at him like a flea bite.

As did the judgements. The newspaper had reported those as if they were a triumph of justice. As if it was now time for the world to move on from the horrors committed during the war. Gerhard knew better. Gerhard knew that the verdicts, and the trials, were a travesty. Scratch under the headlines and there wasn't an inch of substance in any of it.

Martin Bormann, Hitler's private secretary who had been condemned to hang, was still on the run. Karl Dönitz – who had succeeded Hitler as Head of State in the last days of the war – had been sentenced to a jail term of less than ten years, which put him on a par with a repeat offending burglar. Three of the defendants – including Franz von Papen, who had collaborated with the Führer to crush Austria – had walked away with no consequences at all. And none of the ringleaders had faced the punishments they deserved for destroying Germany's good standing. Hitler, Goebbels and Himmler had taken what Gerhard viewed as the coward's way out and killed themselves. Of the whole Nazi inner circle, only Reichsmarschall Göring had been captured, and he had treated the trial with the kind of contempt only a fool would show for the law. Gerhard knew nothing could be done about them, but as for the rest… He despaired of those, there were so many. Too many, apparently, for a toothless trial to deal with.

Gerhard did not need to look up the numbers of the unnamed and faceless men and women who had committed the atrocities the world now shuddered at: he was surrounded by them. He spent his days sorting them. He was perfectly, precisely aware of how many National Socialist Party members there had been in Germany once Hitler came to power and it was far more than the newspapers, or the trial, wanted to admit.

He busied himself with the pile of cards on his desk as if he was sorting them. What he was actually doing, however, was running through a list of statistics in the way he had learned to do whenever he needed to push away his emotions and anchor himself.

Ten million Party membership records and almost a quarter of a million more covering the SS; 61,465 officers' files; another 238,600 which included the general ranks; 7,837 from the Women's Division. They weren't numbers Gerhard wanted to forget. There was also an as yet uncounted wealth of SS paybooks and health records and personal profiles. Hundreds of thousands of SS members. All identified and described in minute detail. All, in Gerhard's eyes, if not in their own, potentially guilty of far overstepping their military lines. All waiting to be filed. And then?

He shuffled another batch of cards and splayed them out across his desk. Before the Nuremberg Trials began, eleven months ago in November 1945, Gerhard had believed in their power to do good and redress the wrongs that had been done in Germany's name. He had welcomed them. His homeland was a nation marked by shame, and all its citizens, whatever they had or hadn't done during the war, were tarnished by the crimes whose discovery wouldn't stop. Murders running into the millions. Numbers of the dead and the disappeared too big to comprehend for anyone who, unlike Gerhard, hadn't witnessed the killing machine in motion. Some people, admittedly, had wished the investigations away, arguing that the past was the past and better forgotten. Others had shouted for a swift spate of revenge shootings and be done with it. Not Gerhard. A trial in plain sight was the right thing, the honourable thing, to hold. His legally trained mind appreciated the subtleties of that.

Gerhard had, it was true, been disappointed that only twenty-two men were initially indicted to appear before the court. Twenty-two – as he had explained, quite forcefully, to any colleague he could persuade to listen to him then – was much too small a number to stand for the thousands of officers who had handed out orders which breached any kind of military code. He had hoped, however, that the pitiful charge sheet was merely an opening gambit: seven organisations were, after all, also on trial, including the SS, the SA and the Gestapo. Gerhard had hoped that more individuals would be brought forward as proceedings continued. He had continued to remain hopeful when it had taken a whole day to read out the indictments. As soon as those were published, Gerhard had scoured every word of them – all twenty-four thousand in fact, as he informed his dumbfounded co-workers – searching for the legal wins as well as the pitfalls, and he had found more to feel positive than negative about. Once the trial itself started, however, it hadn't taken him long to lose heart.

Gerhard realised he had crumpled the card he was holding. That kind of carelessness was not acceptable behaviour, but it was hard to keep himself in check when the humiliations wouldn't stop flying into his head. The beatings and the torture depicted in the films and described in the testimonies; the never-ending mass shootings; the selections and the gassing. All the things ordinary soldiers had been instructed to do, which went far past the things they had trained for or had expected when they put on their uniforms. The real culprits, however – the officers who had disregarded military honour in their bloody pursuit of a new Germany – never appeared. Their names remained buried beneath the organisations they had, apparently, blindly and silently participated in. The trial dragged on and none of them paid.

Every new piece of evidence blackened his country's reputation. Gerhard's German colleagues wanted the whole thing over and done with and a line drawn in the sand no one could step back across. His American colleagues might talk about their 'mission' to help Germany, but they still saw punishment as part of that mix. As for Gerhard, who loved his country far more than the men who had ruined it, he wanted...

Something more.

He stopped fiddling with the cards and turned the top one over. The SS officer's profile he was holding was a bulky one with a fan of papers clipped to the summary sheet. There was a list of his scientific qualifications and promotions and the camps and chemical plants he had worked at. There was his last address in Berlin. It was perfect.

Gerhard opened his desk drawer and slipped the card inside, ready to properly memorise the details on his break. Gerhard had a plan. A carefully thought-out one he wouldn't have had to carry out if the trial had shown more bite. If the prosecutors and the judges had shared Gerhard's deep understanding of honour and loved Germany as Germany ought to be loved. The judges, however, had failed in their duty. Gerhard therefore would not.

This officer whose details were now tucked in his drawer had still been alive in February 1945; with a little luck, he would still be alive now and easy to find. According to his card, he had possessed a skill which could have seen him plucked out of the humiliation of the post-war internment camps and dropped into a job with real value. Plenty had been favoured like that; plenty hadn't been *reduced* to filing clerks. Gerhard had stood on the filthy parade ground and watched them get chosen while he was ignored, their talents mattering far more than his honesty. Denazification – the purge of German society which was meant to enable all its corrupted institutions to start again fresh and new – had proved to be little more than empty rhetoric. Instead, a talent for chemistry or medicine or logistics, or some other skill the broken industries and the greedy Allies prized, had, apparently, been enough to wipe out past sins. Well now it was time to make the purge stick.

Gerhard patted the drawer and permitted himself a small

smile. If this man was dead, it didn't matter: there would be another one. There would always be another one. One thing, however, was certain: this man, and all the men like him whose records Gerhard had at his fingertips, had ruined Germany's past and Germany's future and walked away from the stain of it.

Not anymore.

CHAPTER 4

20 NOVEMBER 1946

She was the newspaper kiosk's first customer, hopping from foot to frozen foot as she waited for the delivery van to arrive. When the bundles finally dropped, the copies were so fresh off the press, the ink still smelled warm. She grabbed one off the top pile and tore through the pages, ignoring the delivery boys who had stopped their work to watch her and whistle. Then she finally found what she had been looking for and her overexcited squeal turned their whistles to laughter.

Picture credit: Hanni Winter

The photograph was buried in the middle of the morning's edition, not splashed across the front page, but it was there, it was a start. It was the first step towards the future she had promised herself when the war had finally ended and she was still standing. To be out in the world with her camera, finding her own voice, telling her own stories. Not being quiet anymore.

'That's me! I took that!' Hanni grinned and waved the tiny black-and-white square at the boys.

Her photograph – a group portrait of a dozen newly commissioned German police officers accepting their certificates and armbands – had made it into the morning edition of the *Berliner Zeitung*. It wasn't, admittedly, one of her favourite shots – the men had proved difficult to pose and looked stiff – but it was hers. And it was her name beside it. Or, more accurately, the one she had taught herself to wear.

Hanni Winter. Her given name Hannelore cut in two and Foss replaced by her mother's maiden name. Seeing it spelled out in black and white, even though she was glad to be someone new, was a jolt. The switch from being one girl to being another had not been a planned one. In the first few weeks trying to adjust to the broken shapes of Berlin, Hanni had continued to be who she was: Hannelore Foss, a privileged girl with – thankfully, given the hollow and hungry state of the city – enough of a home and enough food stored away to still live what passed for a privileged life. And then Reiner had reappeared without warning and Hannelore Foss was the last person she wanted to be.

'Hannel— Hanni. Winter. My name is Hanni Winter.'

The first time Hanni had tried on her new self, in June 1945, she had stumbled and stammered and expected a challenge. She had expected to be challenged about a lot of things that day. Instead, her name and her story had been accepted at face value and had stuck.

And now I don't know how to change it back to the one I should have told.

It wasn't as if she had concealed herself out of choice: Hanni knew that if she had given her real name when she had tumbled into the Stein Studio and the warmth that was Natan, Reiner might have tracked her down. The possibility of that was unthinkable. And if she had told the truth about who she was, Natan would have sent her away, which was as bad. She wouldn't have the job, or the friends she had now, or a picture in the paper, without Natan Stein. And maybe she didn't deserve those things, maybe she shouldn't have told the lie that got her them, but her deception was never a deliberate one.

If it had been Ezra I found that day, I would have done what I intended to do and told him the truth.

That had been her only plan when she had fled from Lietzenseeufer: to find the photographer she had always associated with kindness, to denounce the returned Reiner and to ask for help. But the man she had encountered in the dark shop wasn't Ezra. If Hanni had been rational, she would have known that the chance of finding him so easily after so many lost years was the kind of miracle the war and its ending didn't deal in. Hanni, however, wasn't being rational: she was caught up in a panic. Hannelore Foss was impossible; Hanni Winter was the first combination that came out of her mouth. She regretted a lot of the silences and omissions that had followed that lie, but the name had hidden her, and she couldn't regret that.

It's been eighteen months and he hasn't found me, or he isn't looking, and I don't care which.

In the first weeks of her return to Berlin in March 1945, faced with the frightening realities of her and Talie's new existence, it hadn't been Reiner's crimes which had kept Hanni from sleep; it was surviving the imminent arrival of the victorious Allies. The Russians – whose country had suffered so badly at German hands during the middle years of the war – were rumoured to be the closest army to the beleaguered city. Everyone in Berlin was terrified by that: there were as many citizens packing their bags ready to leave as there were refugees pouring in. On the rare occasions Hanni left the house to scavenge for food to supplement their dwindling stock of tins, the shops and the street corners had been thick with whispers. All anyone could talk about was the revenge that the Russians had promised to unleash the moment Berlin was taken. Hanni had been as frightened by the prospect of that as anyone else. In the end, however, the danger she faced turned out to be closer to home.

Her mother, who had locked herself away from the world whenever she could in Leitmeritz, now threw herself into it. Although the Foss family villa had still been standing when they arrived – and not as stripped of the food stores tucked away in the basement as Reiner had supposed it would be – Talie behaved as if its walls were a prison, not a promise of safety. Despite Hanni's pleas, despite the bombing raids daily pummelling the city and the shells exploding too close outside it, Talie fled from the house, and she roamed.

Hanni knew she couldn't help it. She knew that her mother's mind had finally fractured, that she went out into the streets and the parks looking for Luise; that she was caught up in a fog of long-ago days.

She also quickly learned that she couldn't stop her from doing it. No matter how hard Hanni tried to keep watch, Talie slipped away. From the house, from the queues. She would be there one moment and gone the next. At first, her vanishing had left Hanni distraught. She had run all over the neighbourhood, knocking on doors that wouldn't open, combing through the ruins that had remade the city. No one was deliberately unkind; no one could help her. A missing grief-stricken woman was just another missing grief-stricken woman.

Talie wandered and yet, despite Hanni's fears, she had somehow always found her way back. When she did, Hanni held her and bandaged her blistered feet and dried her tears. She convinced herself that her mother's childlike innocence and her own unwavering love for her mother would keep Talie out of harm. That when the war was finally over and the world was mended again, there would be a doctor and a cure. And then, on the twenty-fourth of March, a wave of planes crested over Berlin and Talie didn't come home.

Hanni had searched through the chaos, as countless other white-faced women had searched. None of the splayed bodies she was led away from were whole. Nobody was digging beneath the rubble anymore. Berlin was a city of ghosts, its buildings and its people buried together. After three fruitless days of fingertip searching, and three sleepless nights crammed into a shelter, Hanni had given up hoping and gone back to the silent house. She found hiding places tucked deep into the basement and high in the attic, places she could run to when the shells stopped falling and the armies marched in. She filled them with food and water. She packed her case and her camera bag, and she had waited for the end, determined, whatever her father had hoped, to survive it.

Berlin fell in a blaze of bullets and hatred. As April turned into May and spring shrank from the fires and the snipers and the street battles, Russian soldiers swarmed through the streets, drunk on victory and vodka, determined to revenge their own ravaged country.

Hanni had locked herself away from the chaos and willed herself invisible. She had woken once from a troubled sleep to the certainty of invaders in the house below, to the crash of tramping feet and smashing glass. She had curled then into her attic corner, closed her eyes and her ears, become as tiny as a dust speck. No one, thankfully, came near. She had stayed wrapped tight in her eyrie until the screams and the shooting finally stopped and the streets had lain silent for a week. Then she had crept downstairs and repaired what damage she could, but she had stayed inside the house far longer than that. When she eventually emerged on a nameless, timeless day – sleepless and aching with hunger, lured out by loudspeaker announcements which promised food and calm – the Russians were in charge and Berlin was devastated.

Buildings had crumbled into a dust that blurred the air and scorched eyes and throats. Bridges choked the rivers they were supposed to span. Bodies poked out from beneath fallen walls, their bones as smashed as the bricks. The streets stank of sewage. The water was unsafe to drink without boiling it, but there was no electricity or coal, or kettles, to boil it with, so people kept on drinking, and sickening, and disease spread out its poison until the only things thriving were the rats. Berlin had been ripped out of the twentieth century and flung back a thousand years.

Hanni had wrapped her face in rags against the stinging wind and scurried through the streets, avoiding the shadowy people who avoided her, trying to believe the world could pick up its shattered pieces and go on. The city was quieter than she expected it to be, muffled by dust and without the savagery that had so recently filled it. The Russians, it seemed, had decided to drop a blanket of civility across Berlin, softening the hard edges of their occupation with promises of order and bread; burying the atrocities they had unleashed on the terrified population along with the bodies.

Hanni, like the rest of the starving scarecrows crawling out of their hiding places, had no alternative but to trust them. She took her place in the food and the fuel queues she had never had to endure in the war and kept that fact firmly to herself. She learned to regulate her days by Soviet timekeeping and clocks that were set two hours ahead of where German ones ached to be. She registered for work. Not as a photographer – that wasn't yet an option, even though her fingers itched to capture the splintered state of the city. Germans were forbidden to own cameras, or telephones, or radios, or anything that might connect them to the world outside the one they had been permitted to live in. There were rumours, however, that the Russians were about to restart the newspaper industry as further proof that they were a more civilised people than war had made them. Hanni had hope, therefore, that the prohibition against cameras might not be a lasting one and that she might be able to carve herself out some purpose.

As the days passed, it gradually dawned on Berlin's exhausted residents that none of the prohibitions and rules they were slowly learning their way around would be lasting ones. New rumours spread. That the American and the British and the French armies were finally coming. That the city was about to be remade again, its governance not a matter for Russia alone but for all four Allied powers, who would divide up the city between them.

The Russian soldiers began to move out of Charlottenburg, but Hanni kept her bags packed anyway. She assumed that the Foss property, like more and more of the area's large villas, would be requisitioned for some army's use. She no longer, however, woke in a sweat in the night, her body tensed to run. She started to edge round the idea of a future. As part of that, she left cards filled with her mother's description at every train station within an hour's walk, tacked to the boards groaning with the countless numbers of the disappeared. In her heart, Hanni knew that Talie somehow still being alive was a fiction, but it was easier to take her first steps forward clinging to a fiction than under the weight of her mother's death. Her father, however, was a harder prospect to deal with.

The Russians had begun a purge, a denazification so complete they promised that it would purify Germany – or the Russian sectors of the occupied country at least. The slightest scent of the Third Reich lingering around anyone meant imprisonment, or deportation to work camps far away in the East, which rumour turned as savage as the ones the Nazis had run. Or, if not either of those, a bullet.

Hanni read the proclamations along with the rest of the silent crowds, exhorting anyone with evidence of fascist leanings to come forward and denounce their families and friends. She had got as far as the Soviet district office, determined to give up Reiner's name and point the Russians towards his crimes. And then *what if they take me and my mother comes back* had stopped her. Her plan became to wait for the British or the Americans instead. Her hope was that Reiner was dead.

Then she looked through her bedroom window early one sunny July morning and her plans and her hopes turned to dust.

Reiner wasn't dead. He had, improbably, impossibly returned. He was standing outside the house, on the opposite pavement, looking up, searching its grime-stained and newspaper-patched windows. His hair was longer. He had grown a thick beard and he was wearing a shabby suit not a uniform, but it was unmistakeably him. He was pressed into the shadows of the street corner, keeping his distance.

Hanni had been as certain as she could be that he couldn't see her. Her stomach had still plummeted, her bones had turned soft. She had still flattened herself against the wall, her heart pounding so hard she was convinced he would hear it. From the way he was hunched into himself, Hanni guessed that he was checking the house for movement and waiting for the few neighbours who were outside to bustle away. Whatever his motives, that he was there meant that he hadn't been caught. That he was looking for a way back into his life again.

You could never be a danger to me. If you were, this would all have played out very differently.

Hanni hadn't waited to see if he was going to come closer. Every instinct had told her he wouldn't want to see her; every instinct had screamed that she didn't want to see him. She had grabbed her suitcase and her camera bag, and she had fled. She had sprinted along the winding path that led from the back of the house and edged the lake and hadn't stopped until she reached the safety of the subway platform at Sophie-Charlotte-Platz. And then, because she had no other addresses or names at all in her head, she had searched the stained and torn city map until she found the route to Wassertorstraβe and the Stein Studio.

Where I was met with the kindness I'm still hiding behind.

An angry car horn pulled Hanni abruptly back to the present. The delivery boys had gone; customers were starting to queue. Hanni waved at the kiosk owner who had refused to take her money and put the newspaper carefully into her bag. It was almost eight o'clock. She hadn't yet solved the problem of Reiner and, as guilty as she felt about that, she wasn't going to solve it today. She had a piece of work to complete, and she was already at risk of missing the best of the morning's early light and, more importantly, its solitude. By nine o'clock, the rubble-women, who were still at work clearing the debris from this part of Berlin, would be in place, lined up with their sledgehammers and picks. Hanni had photographed them before, fascinated by the co-ordinated way the women worked. She had shot a series of pictures that turned their swinging arms balletic. Today, however, it was the buildings themselves that she wanted.

Tightening her scarf against the wind that barrelled down the area's wide boulevards whatever the season, Hanni hurried past the Unter den Linden's already bustling cafés towards Wilhelm-straße. The old government district – the Third Reich's one-time nerve centre – was still a wasteland no one knew quite what to do with. The division of Berlin between the four Allied powers in August 1945 had put the area's once elegant palaces under Soviet control. In reality, however, the strip of bombed-out ministries was so close to the British sector that the boundaries were blurred. No one seemed to want to take responsibility for repur-posing the tainted buildings. Few people other than the clearance teams and the scavengers went voluntarily near them. Hanni, however, couldn't keep away.

She had been chronicling their collapse for months, photographing their deterioration at different times of the day and across the changing seasons. She had floated the idea of holding an exhibition featuring the series to Natan, who was, very slowly, coming round to the idea, provided that she told the horror of the buildings as well as featuring their beauty. Hanni hadn't disagreed with that. And she hadn't told him that the story she was cataloguing was partly hers – that her father had worked in one of the buildings in the 1930s and 1940s and that she had visited him there and drunk tea inside its swastika-draped extravagance. If she had, her job and her home would be gone in an instant.

And he would hate me. And I can't live with that.

Pushing thoughts of Natan Stein aside for the second time that morning, Hanni turned the corner onto Wilhelmstraße. Her subject today was the gaping wreck that had once been the Reich Chancellery. If she could get the angles right, Hanni knew that the toppled walls in its courtyard would transform into cloisters. As eager as she was, however, to get started, Hanni paused as she always did opposite the ruins of the Adlon Hotel. The balcony she had leaned over thirteen years earlier to watch Hitler's triumph was gone. The once majestic hotel was now a blackened, eyeless shell, destroyed at the end of the war in a fire set by a mob of drunken soldiers looting its wine cellars.

Although she had already taken a dozen of them, Hanni snapped a photograph of the broken Adlon sign, which hung cracked and gaping over the hotel's bricked-up entrance, and the giant portrait of Stalin that stood next to it and dwarfed its exhausted façade. She had never described that night in 1933 to anyone, not even – especially not even – when she had told Natan about her long-ago meeting with his father. The Adlon wasn't the Adlon anymore, and she wasn't a little girl fooled by torches and pageants.

The clouds had cleared and finally let the wintry sun through. There was no warmth in it – its cold disc better resembled the moon – but it was awake, pushing through the gaping stonework of the ruined palace behind her, turning the flecks of glass embedded in its brick dust diamond bright.

Hanni glanced at her watch, glad of a distraction from the hotel and its memories. She still had two hours before she was due at the studio, which gave her time to photograph the building whose nooks and crannies were now beckoning her and to also visit the remains of the Reich Chancellery. She pulled her recon-ditioned Leica out of her bag, popped the strap around her neck and followed the sunlight's path into the ruin, her camera raised and ready.

The sun had found a window opening which still held most of its shape; its rays fell through the spaces where the panes should be and split into beams as broad as searchlights. Hanni snapped without thinking, tracing the arcs of pale light from their start to their end as if she was following a watered-down rainbow. Like the Chancellery, this building had decayed to thin walls and deli-cate arches and taken on the hushed aspect of a monastery.

Hanni clicked away, her skin tingling as she felt her exhibition theme developing. She was so absorbed in the play of shadows and light, she didn't at first notice the figure stretched out across the stone floor. When she did, it was through the camera. The shape it made perfectly fitted into her vision of churches and cloisters.

She closed in on it, tilting the lens to catch the texture of the wood she assumed the effigy was nailed to. The workmanship that had gone into the face and the limbs was incredibly lifelike, almost heartbreakingly so. The skin tone had been painted the perfect shade of blue-tinged grey to capture the last minutes of life, the transition from that into death. The features had been carved with such realistic precision that the eyelashes, arranged in a delicate fan on the cheek, looked a moment away from lifting. A figure as eloquently captured as this would move even an atheist's soul to pity, which Hanni assumed was the point.

She stopped, her finger hovering over the lever that would load the next frame. She lowered the camera and blinked. The building resettled itself. She wasn't in a church. There wasn't a cross lying under the body. This wasn't a wooden figure breathed into life by a skilled craftsman. And the man – because it was, to her horror, a man, not a semblance of one – wasn't in the crucifixion pose her overactive imagination had put him into. His upper body was bare, that much was true, but only one arm was splayed out, not two. There was no crown of thrones cresting the dark hair, just a light dusting of frost, and the circle surrounding the man's head was far too dark and sticky-looking to be a halo.

Hanni moved closer, her breath catching in the chilly air. There was a sign of some kind resting on his chest, the thin rope that held it circling the man's sinewy throat. It was a white card with a message printed on it. She hesitated, her throat tightening as the sunlight splashed across the spilled blood, and then her photographer's eye kicked in, dropping a screen between the details she needed to capture and the horrible shock of them.

Hanni stooped and scanned the thickly inked capitals. She raised the camera and took a carefully positioned shot to give herself time to think. She had seen the wording before, a year and a half ago, pinned on another corpse. She had – although she didn't want to remember it – seen the same wording more than once, and all of the dead bodies displaying it then had been hanging from lamp posts with their necks stretched.

THOSE WHO BETRAY THEIR HOMELAND MUST DIE

She lowered the camera, blinking as the swinging corpses danced through her head. The sign on the body in front of her was the one which had been displayed on the men and women who had spoken out against Hitler in the dying days of the war, put there after the SS had cut out their victims' tongues and lynched them.

A rush of sour liquid filled Hanni's mouth; her lungs burned as if she was drowning.

Keep a clear head; think logically. You've seen worse than this before.

That thought brought other images with it, filled with stinking attics and starvation-shrunk bodies. Hanni swallowed hard and forced herself to push those away – focusing on those deaths, as terrible as they had been, wouldn't help her or the man lying at her feet. This wasn't a murder she had to witness in silence. This was a killing she could do something about.

Hanni stepped back. She didn't know anything about crime scenes, but she doubted anyone was meant to disturb them. She focused on her surroundings as they actually were, not as her imagination had made them, her senses sharpened by the body's discovery. There were noises coming from outside in the street, a distant clinking Hanni assumed was the clearance women coming. She couldn't let them pour in: whoever, or whatever, this man had been, he surely deserved better than a gawping crowd.

Taking more care than she had coming in, Hanni made her way back to the building's crumbling entrance. There were two boys of about ten or eleven loitering on the pavement. There were always boys loitering on Berlin's pavements nowadays, looking for someone to separate from their money. They were lost souls. Too small for the manual work they queued up and pretended they were ready for; too big to believe that a classroom held any use for them. Whatever their size, few of them looked like children. The war which had filled and warped their short lives had wiped any innocence from their thin faces. They were, however, as Hanni had discovered when she was trying to take photographs of the men running the black market, useful: they knew their way round the city, and they knew all its unwritten rules.

She called the pair over, gave the smaller of the two a coin to find a policeman and the other, who was burly and rather fearsome looking, a coin to stand guard against the approaching women. The boys swaggered into action the moment they pocketed the money.

Hanni tightened her camera strap, reloaded the Leica with a fresh spool of film and went back inside to the body.

CHAPTER 5

20 NOVEMBER 1946

Freddy Schlüssel sat in the Unter den Linden's newly refurbished Café Schön, sipping his coffee and missing his mother. She would have adored the café; she would have savoured the darkly roasted blend it was famous for. He wished knowing that brought him more comfort.

Ever since Freddy could remember, coffee had been Rosa Schlüsselberg's favourite treat. There wasn't a perfume that better conjured her up than the smell of it brewing: the scent had been baked into the language of the Schlüsselberg home. Rosa had bought small quantities of the best beans she could afford and stored those up for what she referred to as 'her moments'.

At five o'clock on a Saturday evening, its rich nutty warmth meant, 'Don't disturb me, my week is done.' At eleven o'clock on a Wednesday morning, it heralded the arrival of her 'sisters' and their offspring, the friends she had gathered around her since Freddy's birth. They were a formidable group of women who burst into the Ritterstraβe apartment armed with honey cakes and Mandelbrot and primed for gossip. Freddy couldn't recall a week in his childhood that had passed by without their chatter. The first trick he had taught his younger brother Leo was the art of sweeping leftovers from the women's plates before the other children spotted them. And on a Sunday afternoon, it had meant a coffee shop like this one, all white linen tablecloths and best behaviour.

Until the new laws that turned Jews into demons swept in and all the best cafés closed their doors to her.

Rosa had found the loss of that pleasure hard, although she had pretended not to. She had, as Freddy, if not her younger children, had always known, done a lot of pretending. As the Schlüsselbergs' world had narrowed, she had kept up the pretence that everything would be fine. She had wrapped that certainty like a shield around her family, insisting that none of the National Socialist Party's restrictions could hurt them. More than her words, however, what Freddy remembered best was her smile. She had held that in place even when the shopkeepers turned their backs and the 'Jews Forbidden' notices spread like weeds across Berlin and the increasing unkindness from one-time acquaintances had chipped away at her soul.

Freddy put his cup down unfinished, suddenly loathing the taste. He hated these moments, when the past rushed in and swallowed the present, but they couldn't be stopped once they started. He closed his eyes against the café's breakfast bustle. It had taken him a long time, but he had finally learned that the only way to manage the echoes was to let the memories come, for a few brief moments, and then parcel them back up again and get on with his day.

He had also learned that, wherever the echoes took him, the images they conjured up always began the same way. Evening in a fire-warmed lounge. Rosa's darting fingers busy with her needle. His father Jakub dozing in his armchair, worn out from early-morning starts in the family bakery, his dark beard speckled grey, not with age but with flour. Sometimes the location was the spacious Ritterstraße apartment where Freddy had been born, and his brother Leo was there playing, lining up his soldiers on the braided rag rug. Sometimes it was one of the two cramped rooms they had been forced to move into in the Bachstraße tenement and this time Leo was as speckled with flour as Jakub, and baby Renny was gurgling in her crib. Wherever they were gathered, whether they had chosen the home they lived in or not, it was family.

What would they make of me now, their son the detective?

Freddy couldn't bear that thought either, although it was another that wouldn't keep away. He hated the pointless hope in it. The *Would they be proud of me?* buried inside the question that would never be answered.

Proud or not, he had no doubt they would be surprised. The life he had managed to carve out from the war's wreckage was not the one he, or his mother, had imagined for him. Sitting in a courthouse in a judge's robes and handing down the law as he had once pictured his future was one thing, but getting his hands dirty with it by joining the police, the collaborators? Even Freddy wondered sometimes at the choice he had made.

The newly reformed and supposedly denazified German police force had seemed a place full of fresh starts when he had joined after the war, although Freddy was still uncertain enough of the world to enter its ranks warily. He was still wary over a year on.

There were older men returned to the service now whose dubious pasts had kept them away in 1945. There were rumours about his boss, Chief Inspector Brack, whispers that he had learned his criminal investigation techniques at the notorious *Führerschule* set up by Reichsprotektor Reinhard Heydrich to train the Third Reich's police. That Brack's *Fragebogen* – the hopelessly unwieldy questionnaire which the Allies had introduced to try to weed the 'good' German public servants from the 'bad' – had been lost, or rinsed clean, to entice him back to the force when it became clear how desperately inexperienced the post-war recruits were.

Nothing he had experienced while working with Brack had put Freddy's mind at ease. He had, however, stayed in his job, although some days his reason for joining – the desire to play a role in recreating a fair society out of the one that had destroyed all he loved, and the belief he could do that – bemused him.

She would understand the need to build something better. She would help me wade through the confusion.

Freddy pressed his eyelids tighter. This was going to be a bad one, a remembering in which the pain of loss stung like a fresh ache. When it hurt to recall that it was Rosa who he had shared his dreams with, who had best understood him.

He couldn't remember a time when the two of them hadn't been in step. It was Rosa who had recognised that an apprentice-ship in the bakery would make Jakub happy but Freddy miser-able. It was Rosa who had tried to keep his dreams alive when Hitler's 'pure blood'-obsessed government had crushed them. She had found him a position as a clerk in a Jewish legal firm when the schools and universities closed their doors on him and had kept his ambitions to be a lawyer and then a judge at least breath-ing. Rosa Schlüsselberg hadn't let any opportunity she could grab go to waste. She had been the wisest woman Freddy had ever met.

And she may as well have been the stupidest, for all that wisdom mattered.

He snapped out of the trance the memories had plunged him into. Anger swirled through his stomach, souring the last drops of coffee. There were times when anger felt like his lifeblood. It was always there, scratching at him on some days worse than others. He worked very hard to control it, because he couldn't afford to let the fury rise. He couldn't follow where it wanted to lead, into that darkness filled with dreams of avenging them all: Rosa and Jakob, Leo and baby Renny. He wouldn't, therefore, let it consume him, but, dear God, it was a hard potion to swallow.

'Inspector Schlüssel? Did you hear me?'

Freddy blinked and stared blankly at the black-aproned waiter hovering at his elbow.

'Sir? Excuse me, but are you feeling all right?'

Freddy didn't know how to answer. How could he explain that, no, he wasn't all right at all because a moment ago the café had been thronged with ghosts who were more real than its customers? Or that he had been so caught up in the past, he hadn't properly registered his name, or that the one the waiter had used hadn't sounded like his without its last syllable? That he didn't know when, or if, it ever would.

Freddy was slowly growing used to the title *Inspector*, but, even after more than a year wearing it, *Schlüssel* still didn't feel right. He knew his hesitation wasn't rational: it had, after all, been his choice to shorten it. An obviously Jewish surname like Schlüsselberg might not have raised eyebrows when he had first joined the force, but that wasn't a chance Freddy was willing to take. Now, given the appointment of men as suspect as Brack, the shortened version was the only safe one if he wanted to forge a career. The change, however, had never felt like anything but a betrayal, of himself and of his family.

Freddy stared at the waiter, whose immaculately elegant appearance had turned him into a mannequin, and wondered about telling him the truth.

Sorry. I was thinking about my stolen family and my butchered name. Why don't you tell me what you did in the war and we'll take the rest of the conversation from there?

He would sound quite mad, which wasn't the best look for a detective. He gathered himself together instead and mumbled a 'I'm fine, thank you', which was enough to relax the waiter's stiff face for a moment.

'There is a boy at the door.' The man's expression tightened again. 'A scruffy individual, I have to say, who has no place coming in here. He insists, however, that he has business with you. Do I admit him?'

Given the sniffed stress on *admit*, the expected answer was clearly 'no' and the expected way of dealing with the problem was clearly for Freddy to go outside and keep the *scruffy individual* well away from the café's more sensitive clientele. Freddy, however, had very little time for snobbery of any kind. He knew where separating people out into 'them' and 'us' could lead. More than that, the waiter's pompous manner was the excuse he needed to offload some of the anger that was still caught in his throat. He kept his tone civil for the sake of the other customers; his words were anything but.

'What do you think? If he says he has business with me, then he has *police* business with me. Is his appearance important to that? Is police business something you have the authority to interfere with?'

Sweat broke out across the waiter's top lip and he took a step back. Freddy, however, was enjoying himself.

'I'll assume your answer is no, shall I? So maybe you could do what I need you to do and *admit* my visitor.'

The waiter coughed and spluttered and vanished.

A moment later, a familiar – and, it was fair to say, very scruffy – figure appeared and began weaving his way towards Freddy's table. It was Oli, one of the street kids the police forces across all four of Berlin's occupied sectors used as informants. Freddy had picked Oli out six months earlier as one of the brightest of the roaming bands of boys – and girls – who had seen things no child should and now kept him on a retainer that he hoped might at least keep Oli out of prison. His appearance at the café suggested something more interesting might be happening than the meeting Freddy was already running late for, so, ignoring the pursed mouths retreating from Oli's tattered coat and unkempt hair, Freddy waved him over and into a seat.

When he pushed his untouched rolls across the table, Oli fell on them. Freddy lit a cigarette as the boy hoovered up the last crumbs. He didn't bother to ask how Oli had known where to find him: Oli watched his patch of the city with as much care as any policeman and had no doubt learned Freddy's movements a long time ago.

'Who's started up trouble at this time in the morning? If it's soldiers causing havoc, you know I can't touch them.'

That soldiers were the ones potentially disturbing the peace was a reasonable assumption. There were bars around the Unter den Linden whose opening hours lingered on until morning, irrespective of curfews, and plenty of working girls with rooms above them whose hours never closed. Four different armies had their troops in the city now and – although their behaviour was tame compared to the terror the city had experienced eighteen months earlier during the ferocious last battles for its streets – those armies were full of young men who were far from home and novices when it came to drink. And all of them were under military, not civil, jurisdiction. That was a wrinkle in the law which drove Freddy mad, so, when Oli shook his head, he switched on his full attention.

'It's not soldiers. I'm not stupid – I wouldn't have wasted your time with that. If it was, I'd have taken it to the Russians: they pay a hefty fee to keep any business with their lot quiet. And it's not a disturbance, not like you mean. I don't rightly know what it is, except a girl paid me to find a policeman, and she paid Joey to guard that heap of old bricks opposite the Adlon.'

Oli picked up the milk jug and drained it dry, to the disgust of the fur-wrapped woman sitting nearest them. 'Maybe she's found one of those bombs that didn't explode, or some of the missing Nazi millions the Americans are obsessed with. Whatever it is, she had a fancy camera, and she wouldn't let us near.'

'Show me.'

Freddy pulled on his coat and threw a pile of notes on the table, slapping Oli's hand before he could snatch them.

The Adlon was a five-minute walk away; Freddy covered the distance in two, his blood pumping. A girl with a camera posting a guard outside Third Reich ruins was an unusual start to a dreary November Wednesday. It definitely deserved better than dawdling.

For all his haste, it proved a challenge to get into the building. The obstacle wasn't, initially, Joey the guard, but the frustrated rubble-women being held at bay by the scowling boy's folded arms. It took Freddy's warrant card and his signature on the workers' timesheets to clear them and then another coin to shift Joey, whose scarred cheeks had made him a far better choice than baby-faced Oli to play the menace.

Freddy climbed into the ruins, keeping the two boys firmly behind him. He barely looked at his surroundings. Freddy had no interest in the bomb-battered Nazi ministries beyond the hope that somebody would level them. As far as he was concerned, there was a stink clinging round the buildings that Berlin didn't need.

Half a dozen steps inside, however, and his nerve endings were tingling. There was a body stretched out on the ground. It wasn't the first body he had seen; it wasn't by a long stretch the worst body he had seen. But it was clearly a murder, and it was the first one of those post the war he had managed to arrive at alone.

'I haven't touched it.'

He hadn't noticed the girl standing on the other side of the corpse. The moment Freddy did, body or not, he couldn't understand how he'd missed her. The curve of her cheek and the bow of her lips was, quite simply, lovely. She was also extraordinarily scruffy, so much so that Freddy wondered for a moment if she might be Oli's elder sister. She had obviously tried to confine her mass of dark blonde hair into some kind of order, but whatever clips she had used had lost their battle against a barrage of thick curls. Her green-and-brown checked coat was covered with brick dust. Her face was smeared with the same grey, smudged there, or so Freddy assumed, when she had lifted and lowered the camera currently slung round her neck. He had never seen anyone who combined such striking looks with such apparent disregard for them.

'Him, I mean. I haven't touched him. I didn't want to do anything that might mess up your investigation.'

She had a lilt in her voice that momentarily made Freddy

forget where he was standing. At least until the chorus of snorts from the too observant boys pulled him back.

'Thank you. Yes, that was the right thing to do. You should never touch anything.'

He coughed and wished he could cuff the giggling Oli, who was clearly a moment away from an off-colour comment.

'You were the one who found it?' He shook his head. 'Who found him?'

'Yes. About half an hour ago. I was in here photographing the building. That's what I do – I'm a photographer.'

The girl stuck out her hand. Freddy was glad he was wearing gloves when he took it. He had a sudden image of himself stammering at the touch of her skin and then having to strangle the boys.

'Hanni Winter, from the Stein Studio.'

A photographer promised a good eye for detail. Freddy glanced from the girl to the body lying between them and his professional instincts kicked straight back in. He scanned it, taking in every strange aspect of the scene. Whatever had happened here, this wasn't a straightforward killing – this was something far darker. It was obvious when Hanni spoke that she thought the same.

'It's quite something, isn't it? Quite deliberate.'

It was a good choice of words. The man had been arranged – Freddy could think of no other way to describe the body's positioning – on his back. His upper clothing had been removed and was folded in a neat pile beside him. There was a sign looped round his neck and resting on his bare chest. And his left arm had been extended and angled so that the small black tattoo on the underside was clearly visible.

'Do you work with the Russians?'

Freddy dragged his attention back from the figures inked onto the loose skin and realised he hadn't introduced himself.

'No, I'm with the German police force based in Kreuzberg, in the American sector. Inspector Freddy Schlüssel. I should have said that first, I'm sorry.'

Hanni frowned. 'But I thought this area came under Soviet jurisdiction, or, if not them, the British. Shouldn't the boy I sent have fetched one of them?'

Freddy began walking slowly round the body, studying it, filing away what he saw while he answered.

'Probably. This part of Wilhelmstraβe is, strictly speaking, Russian territory, yes. But Oli here knows me, and he knows that I'm always in this part of Mitte on Wednesdays for a meeting with my counterparts in the Soviet and the British sectors. And that I reward him for this kind of information better than they do. It isn't quite by the book, I suppose, if you're a stickler for that sort of thing, but policing boundaries are blurred at the moment. I don't imagine that will last much longer.'

Freddy didn't imagine – he knew. The German police force was in a constant state of flux and had been since it had first limped back into life. The war's end had swept away most of Berlin's long-established institutions, including the forces of law and order. The police headquarters in Alexanderplatz – the feared and infamous Red Castle, where the rumours also had it that Brack had held sway – had been destroyed in the bombing raids. The police's reputation was also in tatters, torn apart by the collusion with the Nazis which had permeated every level.

In the first summer of the Allied occupation, law had been dispensed solely by the military. When German participation in that was, rather reluctantly, reallowed, the local officers who the Allies put on the streets were largely young and hopelessly inexperienced for the chaos they were faced with. They had no weapons and little authority beyond an armband and a set of cards with words such as *theft* and *murder* printed on them in a variety of languages. Their main remit was to wave these cards at the nearest soldier they could find if they were unfortunate enough to stumble over a crime. That – and the clumsy violence which the frustrated and poorly trained officers inevitably resorted to – wasn't a response which had won much respect.

By the time Freddy had reached the rank of inspector in July 1946 – at a speed far quicker than he would have reached it before 1939 – resources and training had begun to improve, the cards were gone and there was, once again, a properly active German police force. That, however, was understaffed and over-stretched, its officers buried beneath the pressures of the booming black market and the shortages which inspired both that and the gangs who were competing to control resources and to control the city. Crime rates were rising. Due, however, to the poor reputation of its earlier days, and the worse reputation of the men like Brack re-employed to plug the gaps at the higher levels, public trust in the men meant to solve those crimes was falling. Berlin's police forces continued, therefore, to rely on each other and to operate as if the city had not been carved up. Freddy and his colleagues knew that wouldn't last, that the other Allied powers were already pulling away from the Soviets. Until then, however, detectives like Freddy, who were eager to make their mark, operated on a 'first come, first served' basis and rushed to grab the most interesting cases, no matter which side of a division line they fell on.

And everything about this promises to be an interesting case.

Stepping away briefly from the body, Freddy sent Oli and Joey running to find a telephone and summon his division's murder van before anyone else got wind of what was happening, giving them enough coins to make the call and to ensure that they actually would. When he turned back, Hanni was crouched by the dead man's extended arm, her camera clicking. Freddy watched her for a moment, noting how thoughtfully she approached each shot. She had been at the scene the longest, she had observed it closely; he assumed she had already made some potentially useful deductions.

'Does any of what's been done here mean anything to you?'

Hanni looked up and lowered the camera.

'I think so. The sign, yes, definitely. I saw that wording a lot in 1945. It meant traitor then, or it did to the Nazis who hung it on the people they murdered. There were bodies wearing the same message all over Berlin in the last days of the war. Although using it on this man seems odd, because the tattoo on his arm…'

The hesitation was momentary, less than that, but Freddy still caught it.

'Well, it means he was in the SS. The letter is his blood group, the numbers would identify his body if his identification papers were lost.'

Hanni stopped again and began fiddling with the camera's shutter. Freddy could sense there was a story there which would account for her knowledge, but it wasn't – yet – the one he needed to assemble.

'There's something else as well, although I'm not sure what it is.' She pointed to the fingers curled close by her foot. 'He's holding a piece of paper.'

Freddy bent down and eased what was actually a rectangle of thin card out of the man's hand. It wasn't a simple task. The fingers were stiff and unyielding, which suggested a relatively recent time of death, although that was a detail for the pathologist to determine. Like the sign round the body's neck, the wording on this card was also printed in capitals without a flourish of handwriting to betray its author.

'What does it say?'

Hanni was leaning over his shoulder. Freddy was about to shield the piece of evidence from her, but he changed his mind and held it out so that she could read it along with him. She had already seen, and presumably recorded, most of the crime scene's details and she had, apparently, understand them as well as, if not better than, he had. He had been familiar with the tattoo; the message on the sign, however, was new to him. He was more than happy to hear whatever other insights she might have.

'It's his name, Luka Albrecht, and it's telling his life in the war.' Freddy paused, waiting a moment while Hanni scanned the neatly laid-out rows. 'His rank. His promotions and the places he served. His last address when he was serving, his wife.'

'He was supposed to be found. We are supposed to know all about him. It wasn't a random attack.'

Hanni sat back on her heels and stared at the body. Freddy carefully pocketed the card, aware of the shiver running round his neck. A precisely laid-out corpse, a deliberately chosen and elaborately identified victim. None of this, even in his limited experience of murder sites, felt like a commonplace crime.

'Did you photograph the area around him?'

Hanni nodded. 'There's some blood there near his head, and a few more drops scattered about the stones as you come in. And I don't know, but I think... well, it's your area of expertise not mine...'

She stopped. Freddy was certain she hadn't done that out of a lack of confidence in what she wanted to say; nothing about Hanni suggested a lack of confidence. For all her untidy appearance, Freddy was beginning to think that there was a deliberateness in Hanni which made her as watchful and as careful as him. He curbed his natural inclination to hurry her up and chose a friendlier prompt.

'Don't worry about overstepping if that's what's bothering you. I'm honestly interested in what you think.'

She regarded him briefly. Whatever she saw in him must have been reassuring.

'Okay, well it's dusty, so I thought there might be a footprint or two left behind. I looked and there isn't. But the pathway between here and the entrance, the normal way anyone would come in – especially if they were dragging or carrying a body, which the murderer could have been doing if the actual killing took place out there – is too tidy. I looked at the stones through a closer focus on the camera lens and there are fine lines, which, I don't know, but they could be some sort of brushstrokes.'

'He cleaned up. He wasn't in a hurry.' Freddy finally remembered his notebook, took it out and began scribbling. 'Tell me about the words on the sign again.'

Hanni was halfway through her explanation when the siren that signalled the arrival of the murder van screeched down the street. Freddy stood up and brushed the dust from his trousers and the hem of his coat. Hanni stood up and didn't.

'How long will it take you to develop the photographs you took?'

His tone was pointedly more distant.

Hanni glanced over at the group gathering on the pavement outside and matched it.

'Forty-eight hours at the most – quicker I hope. I can send them to your office when they're done if you like.'

And let me risk not seeing you again?

'No. It's fine. Give me the address and I'll come to the studio and collect them.'

If she noticed how overeager he sounded, she didn't react. As she handed him a business card and began repacking her camera bag, Freddy's assistant inspector Matz Laube appeared in the doorway, with the forensic team jostling at his elbow. Freddy was glad of their arrival. At least shouting at them to 'hold back your feet – there could be evidence on the ground there' stopped him staring like a lovesick schoolboy after Hanni as she slipped quietly away.

CHAPTER 6

23 DECEMBER 1946

Majdanek.

Gerhard had been expecting to see an officer's record sheet stamped with that particular location since he had picked up his first card. The immediate – and visceral – reaction the name provoked in him was, however, a surprise. The word had set his mind tumbling and his pulse racing and made him unable to focus on the counting strategies that normally never failed.

Focus on your body; calm that down first.

Gerhard willed himself to glance up. Nobody appeared to be looking at him. He placed the record card face down on his desk and began to take stock of himself. His pulse had reached a speed which was troubling. His palms were slippery and covered in a light film of sweat, a condition which he assumed would shortly be replicated, more obviously, on his face. When he swallowed, his throat was dry. Whatever else he did, he had to remove himself from the office before his colleagues spotted that he was suffering from any kind of distress, or *betraying weakness*, as his father would have called it. Something as remarkable as that would feed their need for gossip for weeks.

He checked the office clock. His break was due, which meant

that he could find a quieter spot and properly manage himself. He got up, keeping his movements controlled. There was a small and neglected courtyard at the rear of the building which would offer him some privacy. It would, admittedly, be snow covered and freezing, but that also meant the space was sure to be empty.

Gerhard wanted to run down the corridor to the back door, but he held a steady pace, resisting the urge to mop his brow until he was safely outside the building.

The courtyard was, as he knew it would be, deserted. It was also far too cold for his threadbare woollen jumper. That, however, was an acceptable discomfort and a better, less note-worthy, option than collecting his overcoat at break time – a time in the day when he never went anywhere but a solitary table in the canteen – would have been. If he could summon up his normal routines, he shouldn't need long.

Five minutes.

The number jumped into his head, and he seized on it. Five minutes was the length of time he had whittled his calming tech-niques down to as a child, when the voices were shouting and his father's fists wouldn't wait. Now it wasn't his father squaring up to him and making him shake but his memories of the war.

Which are good things, which are fuel.

He found a bench and brushed off the snowflakes.

Majdanek. It was his defining event, the massacre which had started him down the path he was currently following and, now that he was alone, he knew how to tackle the stresses it brought. He closed his eyes, turned his brain into a blackboard. Dates, statistics, numbers. Certainties, not a mess of emotions he couldn't see his way through. He turned his face up to the falling snow and let the figures come.

November the third and November the fourth 1943. Five o'clock in the morning until seven o'clock at night on the first day and a shorter time spent on the second. Three equal trenches dug in a field outside the Majdanek concentration camp on the outskirts of Lublin. Each trench approximately ninety-five metres long, two metres wide and one and a half metres deep, their capacity carefully balanced with the numbers destined to fill them and the ease of concealment once the task was complete. Execution squads organised into interchangeable units of between ten and twelve men; one bullet per prisoner set as each soldier's target. The Jewish prisoners marched out from the camp and into the field in groups of one hundred, each of which was then divided into groups of ten to walk into the trenches. The despatch process continuing until all three pits were filled up – 18,400 dead at Majdanek by the end of the day and then the execution squads transferred to the Poniatowa camp, fifty kilometres away, where a further 14,500 were eliminated over the course of the next morning.

Gerhard hadn't known the precise figures on the day itself of course – he had estimated them based on what he had witnessed and hadn't seen the exact statistics until Nuremberg – but their details matched his memories and were the quickest ones to recall.

Anger had surged through him as the numbers scrolled, making his pulse race again. This, however, was good anger, the type he could use. And now that he had run the figures, it was also controllable.

He switched off the mathematical side of his brain and got up, began making slow circuits of the small courtyard as his head cleared. Keeping a clear head was another thing he was good at. It was the skill he had tried to demonstrate at Majdanek, but nobody had appreciated it then.

The clearance of the Jewish prisoners from Majdanek and the surrounding camps had been wrongly carried out from the start. No one, however, had listened to him when he had tried to outline the key problems.

'No laws have been drafted which make the operation legal.'

'The numbers involved are too large to manage without some factor of error.'

'Soldiers should not be expected to carry out tasks of this nature.'

Three sensible arguments and each one had been ignored. The errors and the lack of discipline that blindness had led to had been shocking.

Gerhard had noted whips being used, and no soldier should ever use a whip. The men in the firing squads had not only been drunk, they had been openly drinking from bottles of schnapps, which they'd carried on clutching the whole time that they fired. That had made them sloppy and inaccurate. That had, in turn, meant extra bullets had been required to finish the botched job. Drunken soldiers had had to jump into the trenches and climb over piles of bodies to reach the ones that were still moving. No German soldier should have had to suffer an indignity like that. And the music blaring out over the loudspeakers hadn't drowned out the screaming the way it was intended to. The fact that the noise could be heard, not only in the immediate vicinity but five kilometres away in Lublin, was no doubt one of the reasons the details of the massacre had eventually come to light. The operation had been a mess, flawed from beginning to end.

All of that was bad enough, but what had shocked Gerhard even more was that no one else had followed his lead when he had refused to participate.

He stopped, drew a breath, let the snow-blanketed silence soothe him.

'You aren't sheep. German soldiers do not need to follow orders which aren't legally sound, which could be classed as demeaning. It is your right to refuse them.'

He had tried once again to be clear, but most of the enlisted men he had encountered had never bothered to read the military code they had signed up to. Gerhard had also tried to explain the finer points of that, but, unfortunately, the soldiers he had addressed had lacked his intellectual abilities and hadn't shared his understanding of the meaning of honour. Some of them had, in fact, turned rather nasty when he persisted.

Gerhard had pitied those men for their lack of learning, but he put no blame on them. The officers in charge, however, were a different matter entirely. They knew the code. They should have understood about the lack of a legal framework and the dangers of a breakdown in discipline. They should have been grateful that he had pointed their responsibilities out. It was a searing indictment of how far military ethics had fallen that none of them did. The transfer that had followed his refusal to pick up his gun – to the worst of the battlefields on the frontlines in Russia, and, inexplicably, without retaining his rank – wasn't his choice. Removing him from the camp-clearing project had wasted an opportunity for them all to do better.

But at least I can remedy some of those failings now.

A bell in a nearby church chimed the quarter-hour. Gerhard checked his pulse: it had slowed again, and his hands were dry and steady. He returned to his desk and picked up the record sheet. It was a good one. It contained all the name and address information on the SS officer that he needed, plus the specialised knowledge – transport and logistics this time – that could well have restarted this man's life, exactly as had happened to the chemist. Gerhard smoothed the paper out. There were so many records still to be sorted and yet this was the one he had been handed. That wasn't a coincidence, especially given its timing. His previous project had turned out very well, and he was physically and mentally ready now to tackle another.

Gerhard glanced across at his supervisor: the man was barely awake. He opened his desk drawer and took out a blank index card. He was ahead with his work, and no one was paying him the slightest attention, so there was no need to wait for his dinner break. Besides, he had funnelled his anger well today and had turned it into an energy he had no intention of wasting.

Gerhard picked up his pen, filled it slowly with ink and checked the nib to make sure nothing was clinging to it that would cause it to blot. It was vital not to ruin this first key stage.

Taking care to keep the pressure even, he began to copy the details from the record sheet onto the card in a series of rows filled with neatly printed capitals. It was such a joy to have a sense of pride and a sense of purpose again.

CHAPTER 7

16 JANUARY 1947

Hanni spread the photographs out across the top of a glass display cabinet filled with sample wedding and christening portraits. The contrast was a stark one; the images she had shot were badly out of place next to the smiles and the finery and the bright silver frames. They were also no easier to look at than they had been when she had pulled the wet sheets out of the fixing tray and pegged them out to dry.

The ones on the top of the pile were, to the unsuspecting eye at least, harmless enough. They were the ones her father would have picked out and smiled at. A view across Leitmeritz which took in the cathedral's elegant bell tower and the slopes of the legend-wrapped Říp Mountain. A sweeping shot of Theresienstadt's wide streets and squat square buildings dotted with snow the way Hanni had first seen them. A stage filled with a choir and then again with a gaggle of children dressed as fireflies performing at the Christmas concert which had been staged to welcome the Foss family to the town in 1943.

Hanni no longer, however, looked at those scenes in the same unquestioning way as she had when they were first presented to her. Now she looked at the eighteenth-century barracks which had once held Emperor Joseph II's soldiers and saw what had been hidden from her on her first visit: the fifty thousand people crammed into their overflowing rooms and living in squalor. Now she looked at Leitmeritz and saw only the work camp whose operations Reiner had also helped to organise, where slave workers died in the mines they had dug and were left there. And now she knew that behind the flower-garlanded stage...

Hanni picked another photograph up – a copy of the one which had cost the young guard his life and had taught her the need for caution – gripping the edge of the counter as the terrible evening swam back. The picture she was holding made a mockery of the firefly children and the smiling choirs. It shouldn't have done; this image should have been as joyous as the rest. Her plan that night had been to go backstage after the concert and congratulate the performers, to capture a few shots of them in their dressing rooms celebrating what had been a wonderful show. Except there weren't any dressing rooms. There was nothing behind the red curtains and the spotlights except darkness and a stench so rank Hanni had retched at her first taste of it.

Two turns in and she had been lost, caught up in a rabbit warren of narrow corridors and claustrophobically low ceilings, a step away from what looked and smelled like an open sewer. She hadn't been able to get a bearing.

She had blundered on, confused by the sudden shift from gold-framed chairs and warmth to mould and damp walls. Finally, as she was on the verge of crying out for help, she had heard a murmuring noise that suggested voices and caught sight of a dull chink of light that promised a low-burning fire. Another few steps had brought her to a half-open door and a spill of flickering yellow. She had pushed the splintery wood with an uneasy sense that she wasn't meant to see what was behind it but was unable to step back. She hadn't, however, got over the threshold.

The space in front of her had been cavernous and filthy, the fire barely alight. The room had been crammed with thin mattresses piled so closely together there wasn't a finger's breadth in between them. And on top of those were men and women who had passed from old to ancient. Whose faces turned towards her with stretched skin and empty eyes.

Somehow she hadn't screamed. Somehow she had managed to hold her hands steady enough to take a photograph, before a guard finally found her and hustled her back.

And my father told me that I had dreamed it all up. That I had seen shadows and sticks of wood piled up in an empty room and made a nightmare out of it.

She hadn't believed him then any more than she had believed him in 1935 when he had told her that the Nuremberg Race Laws, which had turned men like Ezra Stein into objects of hatred, were a 'great thing for Germany'. Or when he had told her two years later that the Party's girls' association, the Bund Deutscher Mädel, which he had forced her to join, would turn her into 'the right kind of German woman'. Hanni wasn't certain when she had first realised that Reiner was a liar, although Ezra, and her grandmother, had both helped her to get there, but Theresienstadt had been the final seal. Ezra's advice to look for the honest story and Alice's fury at Ezra's broken studio had become Hanni's rulebook for measuring the world. Once she started doing that, her past had become a disturbing place. And once her father's role in the SS had stopped being a remote thing played out at camps far away from his family and he had moved her and Talie with him to Theresienstadt…

I learned that he was far worse than a liar.

The photographs felt like daggers beneath her cold fingers. The studio no longer felt like the workplace that she loved; it felt empty and lonely. No one had come through the door since she had turned the sign to *Open*, and she doubted anyone would. It was too close to the expense of Christmas for there to be any customers, and Natan was away, which was the reason Hanni had been able to use the darkroom and finally develop some of the rolls of film she had brought out of the war. She had been desperate to do it, but she hadn't readied herself for what they would bring. The photographs were spilling memories she didn't want to relive in the daytime, memories it was hard enough to keep out of her dreams.

Think about something else then. Think about Natan.

That was difficult too, but it would be a breathing space while she steeled herself to properly look at the rest of the pictures. It was also what he had asked her to do the previous evening, before he left for a meeting in Hanover with one of the new clients he was courting.

Just consider it, Hanni, how good it could be between us, if you would let it. I don't need a definite answer, I don't need anything to change between us faster than you're ready for, but I do need to know that the possibility is there.

It hadn't been an unexpected request; it wasn't as if he had hidden his feelings. Hanni, however, had no idea what to do with his awkward declaration. From the minute she had realised how Natan felt about her, she had purposely held him away. Natan, however – or so he had said – could no longer do what Hanni quietly hoped that they would: muddle along with nothing overtly declared until he eventually lost heart and found someone else.

So he's left me with nowhere to go but away.

Hanni had known for months what Natan wanted, even if he had stammered and stumbled when it came to actually saying it. He wanted, quite simply, to be allowed to love her. And he wanted her to be an anchor for him, to give him a future. Part of Hanni wished that she could provide that for him, that he could provide it for her. Natan was a gentle and a kind man, a safe bet in an unsettled world. He longed as much as she did for the ties of a family to replace the one he had lost. None of that, however, mattered. Part of Hanni Winter would always be Hannelore Foss: the gulf that put between them was far wider than any longing for love could span.

Hanni realised that she had continued automatically separating the photographs into the ones focused on buildings and the ones focused on people. She slowed her fingers down, forced herself to look closely at them. In almost every shot, someone was holding on to someone else as if they couldn't bear to let go. That was all Natan wanted. Was it really so much to ask? To let a good man want her? To try to want him in return?

And what then? Live a lie for the rest of my life?

It couldn't be done, not on the level a marriage would need. The pretence that required would be wrong on every level, and the pain it would unleash if he ever found out the truth would destroy them both.

I accepted his generosity without counting the cost on him. I betrayed his kindness on the first day I burst into the studio.

She hadn't meant to do it. She had been so overjoyed to arrive at the studio when she ran from Reiner, and to find it intact when so much of Berlin had been broken, she had pushed the door open without preparing herself for the wrong outcome. She had assumed that the man bent over the counter was the one she wanted it to be.

When she had called out 'Ezra?' and the man had looked up, she had thought for a brief joyful moment that it was him. But then he had answered 'No, not Ezra; Natan, his son' and his face had shed thirty years. Before Hanni could react, however, and rethink how to explain why she had come, this new version of the old had rushed towards her with his face bathed in smiles. Hanni had barely managed to tumble out her chopped-up name and 'I knew Ezra when I was a child; he gave me my first camera' before Natan had clasped her hands in his. And then Natan's eyes had been shining and so many words had poured from his mouth, hers had disappeared. He was thrilled to have finally met someone who had known his beloved father – he couldn't stop saying it. Or referring to the 'lost' and the 'too few who survived' and it was clear that he thought – or was determined to think – that Hanni was someone very different than she was.

There was no space after that to nudge him back from the Hanni she had instantly become to the truth of Hannelore, or so she had told herself ever since. There was instead Ezra's kindness to her that was too precious to spoil and the story of a war that was too full of loss to add to it.

Natan did his best to recount his life briefly, but neither of them had made it through the telling dry-eyed. Ezra had managed to rebuild the studio after it had been vandalised in 1933, but not when it was smashed to pieces again during the anti-Jewish rampages five years later on Kristallnacht. And defending it had cost him his life. He had been sent to the concentration camp at Sachsenhausen, where he had died from some cause the two-line letter announcing it described as 'natural' when it had to be anything but. Natan had fled with the rest of his family then to France, only to lose his mother and sister there when the Nazis marched in. He had, somehow, survived, although he wouldn't talk about how. And the shop too had been saved, by the Aryan friends Natan had entrusted the keys and equipment to, who turned out to be the good Germans he'd believed them to be.

It was a hard story to lay out and a hard story to hear. Hanni couldn't add to it by swapping the image he had wrapped around her with reality. Instead, she became, over the months that followed, the girl Natan needed her to be – the survivor, his father's long-lost pupil, part of Ezra's legacy. He had given her a start in the career which she had longed for ever since she had worked her way through Ezra's instruction manual and taken her first fuzzy pictures. He had found her a room in the boarding house he shared with half a dozen equally as displaced souls. Hanni treasured his kindness that was so like his father's, and she had known all along she deserved none of it. And she hadn't encouraged him to love her, although she couldn't stop him acting that way. Not even when Freddy Schlüssel had arrived to collect the crime-scene photographs and Natan had bundled him in and out of the studio like an outraged parent confronting an unacceptable lover.

Except he wasn't unacceptable to me.

Hanni's hands paused in their sorting as her skin suddenly warmed. *If only Natan hadn't been here when Freddy came* popped into her head and her skin warmed even more. The shop was a small one; Freddy would have been forced to stand close to her. Without Natan hovering around them, with the blinds drawn and the fire flickering...

She shook away the thought of Freddy's mouth finding hers before the image ran away with her. Natan had been there, and he had been as hostile as a guard dog. Once that became clear, Freddy hadn't attempted to speak to her about anything beyond the pictures. Or contacted her since or come back. That did not mean, however, that Hanni hadn't thought about Freddy; she had thought about Freddy a lot.

There was an intensity about the inspector she had spotted in the ruins and again at the studio, an intensity which pulled her towards him even when it shouldn't. Hanni had watched him noting her hesitation at the tattoo on the body – which she had recognised because it was identical to the one Reiner had – and filing that hesitation away. He had scrutinised her as closely as he had scrutinised the corpse. There was a danger in being so carefully observed when she was so determined not to be, but there was also – when the man doing the observing was as attractive as the dark-haired and dark-eyed Freddy Schlüssel – something magnetic in it. Freddy was... Hanni cast around for a word that wouldn't make her feel like a giddy schoolgirl and settled on the one that had struck her when she first saw him: he was interesting. He had a way of looking at her as if he couldn't see anyone else. Hanni had liked that very much. And Natan very much hadn't.

Hanni began flicking through the photographs again. There were too many things she was still hiding from and wasn't proud of, and that couldn't last. The very least she could do was make Natan understand that there was no future for them.

Perhaps I should just show him this and let him ask how I came by it.

The photograph she was holding was the hardest of them all to look at. It was the only picture Hanni had taken of Jannick.

Another good man. My teacher.

Hanni sank down on the stool beside the cabinet, all thoughts of Natan forgotten, and stared at the thin face whose defiance and despair she had so poignantly captured. Jannick had opened her eyes to the world even more than Ezra had and now she had no idea where he was. She didn't, to her shame, even know his last name: she hadn't asked, she hadn't known when she met him that she would never meet him again. He had vanished as so many had vanished, and the debt she owed him had never been repaid. Without Jannick's guiding hand, Hanni would never have understood the truth of Theresienstadt.

'What in God's name are you doing? Do you think those poor souls are there for your entertainment?'

His first words to her had been delivered in a roar that had made Hanni jump back from the scenes whose horror had trapped her by a pane of filthy glass. He had thought, at first, that she was heartless. A nosy little Nazi girl, snapping pictures of the wretched for her own sadistic amusement. Hanni hadn't blamed him for that assumption, but she had hated that he held it. That was why she had stood her ground and she had forced him to listen to her; that was how she had, in part, if nowhere near completely, won him over.

That, however, came later. Hanni's first response to his sudden appearance around the side of the building, and his furious accusation, had been panic.

'I don't think that at all, I swear. I know what it looks like, me peering in and photographing them, but it's not for pleasure. It's so awful in there, I had to record it. This place... it's like nothing I've ever known, and it needs to be known; it needs explaining. Can you at least tell me what it is?'

He had answered her as if she was an idiot.

'It's hell, what else could it be? It's where the desperate are flung and abandoned.'

Hanni had lowered her camera then and stepped away from the grime-encrusted window.

'The desperate? If that's what they are, don't they need more help than this? It's terrible in there; it's inhuman. They're screaming, so why does no one come? And why don't they have any clothes? Why are they so filthy?'

Her voice had broken on a sob which had dampened a fraction of Jannick's fury.

'Because no one with access to the clothes or the blankets or the care that they need believes they deserve it. These are the barracks where the insane are kept. It's Theresienstadt's version of a mental hospital.'

The way he had spat the last word had made Hanni shiver. It had reminded her of the way Ezra Stein had said *Goebbels.*

'Why do you say it like that? As if "hospital" here couldn't possibly be true?'

Jannick had properly looked at her then, although his clenched fists hadn't untwisted.

'Are you honestly asking? Or is this a trick? Are you bait? Is your father about to appear and drag me off for a beating? Don't look surprised. We both know I recognised you as Foss's daughter. I was at the Christmas concert when you all first arrived here three months ago.'

He wasn't snarling anymore, but he was nowhere near friendly. Hanni had visions of him calling a guard or calling some of the other prisoners and teaching her the kind of lesson about prying she had always been afraid her father would deliver. Terrified at the thought of either of those outcomes, she had answered him honestly, in a rush of words she couldn't stop once they started.

'Then you must remember that I was dragged away from that because I was screaming. I thought I was going crazy. The things I saw that night, behind the stage, were terrible. They were nothing like the picture my father had painted of this place, or the show I'd just sat through. The dirt and the smell, and the state of the poor sick people I found there, were so different from the pretty costumes and the music. But when I told my father what I'd seen, and asked him what was honestly going on, he told me I'd imagined the dying; that I had dreamed it. My father is a liar – I know that. I don't know what else he is, not yet. And he doesn't know that I'm here today – God knows what he'll do if he finds out, which he well might. I persuaded the guard at the gate that he was expecting me. That wasn't true, but I had to do something, I had to come back, and it's taken me too long to do it. I know Theresienstadt isn't what it appears to be, and I want to know what it actually is – that's why I sneaked in here. So you can hate me for who my father is if you want to, or you can help me.'

Jannick had stared at her for so long after she ran out of breath and stopped talking, Hanni had been sure he was going to refuse – or take her to Reiner. When he didn't do either, she would have promised him anything he asked.

'Will you get the story out, if I tell it to you?'

'Yes, of course. That's why I brought my camera. I want to make sure that what's really happening here gets told.'

She had meant it; it didn't matter that she had no idea how to do it.

Jannick had recognised the first part at least and he had thawed.

'We stick to the backstreets, you don't talk to anyone and, if I suddenly disappear, you don't follow me. There's no guarantee that guard didn't go straight to your father, and if he did, I don't want to be the one who's found with you. I'll tell you the truth of this place because that matters, but I won't pay for doing that with my life. Do you understand?'

Hanni had agreed that she did; Jannick had given her the tour that she wanted. It was a far worse experience than the sights she had stumbled on for herself.

Jannick was one of the Jewish Council of Elders, the group the Germans had tasked with running Theresienstadt and keeping order among its inhabitants. Or as he more brutally put it: 'We do the Nazis' dirty work so they can pretend to be the humans in here.' He had peeled away the thin veneer of respectability that covered the town and exposed an underbelly that was inhuman and terrifying. He had spared Hanni nothing.

He had led her away from the wide avenues that bisected the place and into the rat runs its trapped citizens were forced to live out their days in. As he guided her, sticking to the walls and the shadows, he told her the public story of Theresienstadt. How it had been sold as a fantasy to the elderly Jewish people who had handed over their life savings to be a part of its promises. How it had been described as an elegant spa town with lakeside villas and a rich cultural life, as a far happier place than the hostile cities they currently survived in. He conjured up a city of gold from a fairy tale while they stood in the middle of a nightmare, and then he stopped talking.

He stayed silent while he showed her the filthy lice-infested attics the swindled old people starved to death in. And the fly-encrusted latrines in the central courtyard which were shared, publicly, every day by thousands, one of the many humiliations designed to strip away dignity. And the hospital block, which was clean and grass-fringed on the outside but rank and overcrowded and neglected on the inside. When Hanni had seen all that and he had watched her cry, Jannick began talking again.

He told her how easy it was to die in Theresienstadt: from typhoid and dysentery, from starvation and the biting cold. He told her what the Council suspected about where the trains which they – not the SS officers who simply handed down a quota to be filled – were made to select the passengers for were actually going. And he asked her why she thought that all the artists and the musicians and the 'important' Jews who the world might miss had been sent to such an isolated and impenetrable place, if it wasn't because the Party was determined that the world would not only stop missing them; it would forget that they had ever existed.

Hanni had followed him in a haze she had wished would grow

numb, trying to reconcile all she had been told about the town with the warped and evil truth of it. Theresienstadt being 'granted as a gift to the Jews' by a benevolent Führer was as much of an illusion as the 'spontaneous' celebrations she had watched from the Adlon in 1933. As the idea that Leitmeritz and the rest of Czechoslovakia had happily waved the German armies into their country in 1938. As the myth that the Party would let Europe's Jewish people live.

Jannick had showed Hanni the Party's skeleton that day and all the lies it was built from. Hanni had left with a camera full of misery and walked the four kilometres back to Leitmeritz through a heavy March rain she barely felt. She had stared at her father at dinner that evening through eyes forced so wide open, they ached with the strain of it. She had wanted to race straight back to Theresienstadt that night, to find Jannick and gather more evidence.

It didn't prove easy to make it back there alone, and it took longer than one night, but she did it. And she learned to snap pictures in seconds when Reiner took her to concerts and plays and to meet visiting delegations and wouldn't let her out of his sight. No matter how hard she looked, however, she never found another trace of Jannick.

Because he wasn't there. Because I put him in danger. I did to him what I did to the guard.

It was the first time Hanni had made the connection, and the horror of it almost felled her. There was no proof that Jannick had been sent to the trains, that he hadn't made it through to the end. Hanni tried to picture him safe, surrounded by a family, but she couldn't do it. All she could see was her father, watching from the sidelines, waiting to hurt anyone she approached. The photographs she had collected under Jannick's protection – which, if taking them had led to his death, once again meant her work had resulted in nothing but misery – blurred. Hanni let her tears pour unchecked. Not for herself – she had no sympathy left for herself – but for all the good men like Jannick who were gone.

I have to do better. I have to do more with these pictures than merely develop them. I have to find a way to make them count.

Hanni stared at Jannick's lined face. She put that picture down and picked up the one of the laughing children tumbling against each other at the end of their dance. There was another set of films still to be developed, including the last one she had taken in March 1945 which contained the image of Reiner pushing children onto a train. All of their stories needed to be heard.

When the bell over the door suddenly burst into life, she was convinced that the shape outlined in the grey wintry light was Natan. She wasn't ready to show him the truth yet. She might not want him to love her, but she wasn't brave enough to be hated, or to ruin a precious memory of his father showing kindness to a little girl, no matter that the way he had been allowed to shape the memory was false. She had no idea, yet, how she could explain who she had been and avoid turning into one of the monsters who had ruined Natan's life, but she was determined to find the right time and try.

She grabbed the photographs and slipped them into her camera bag, wiping her sleeve hastily over her face as she pushed the bag out of sight under the cabinet. Then she turned with a shaky smile, ready to blame chemical fumes or a particularly moving newspaper story for her tears.

But it wasn't Natan watching her. It was Freddy Schlüssel, staring at her across the studio as if he wanted to gather her into his arms and never let her go.

CHAPTER 8

It was obvious that she had been crying, and equally obvious that she didn't want him to know. Now that Hanni was in front of him again, Freddy could have kicked himself for staying away so long. He hadn't intended for that to happen. He had hoped that his first visit to the studio six weeks ago might lead to others, especially when he was met with Hanni's welcoming smile. And then her sour-faced boss had appeared and the temperature in the shop felt like it had plummeted.

Freddy hovered a couple of steps inside the doorway, scanning the studio for Hanni's prickly minder. There was no sign of him, but that didn't mean he wasn't lurking in the backroom, ready to pounce, hackles flaring, at the sound of Freddy's voice. The prospect of having to face the man's ridiculous hostility stopped Freddy doing what all his instincts were screaming at him to do – pulling Hanni into his arms and swearing vengeance on whoever it was who had made her cry so hard her face was swollen.

I should do it anyway and to hell with him.

That moved him closer, but wanting to hold her wasn't reason enough to actually do it. Not when he was meant to be at the studio with no other purpose than to request her professional help at a new crime scene. And not when he didn't know how matters between Hanni and Natan Stein actually stood.

After Stein had bundled him so abruptly out the last time, Freddy knew exactly what Hanni was to her boss. He didn't, however, know what Stein was to her. Or how to ask a question which was so littered with pitfalls. Freddy had never had a problem attracting women – or returning their interest. As to relationships, however... Anything beyond a night or two relied on letting someone close enough to see under his skin, and since his return to Berlin, Freddy's loss-battered heart hadn't been strong enough to endure anything as intimate as that.

I could try for her. I could take a risk for her.

The sudden realisation made him forget that he had come to the studio because he needed her help again and turned him dumb. Hanni, luckily, didn't seem to notice his confusion, perhaps because she was so caught up in her own.

Freddy gave himself a mental shake. He had told Matz he would be inside the studio for no more than the few moments it would hopefully take for Hanni to collect her camera and come with him. The last thing he needed was his assistant crashing in if he was any longer than that and too accurately summing up why he was taking so long. As far as Freddy was concerned, his private life was his private life and not a sideshow for Matz and the rest of the team to pick over. What he hadn't bargained with, however, was finding Hanni in such a state of distress. He coughed, because that was easier than trying to work out what to say, and then lost any hope of finding his words when Hanni's tear-streaked face broke into a smile.

'Inspector, what a surprise. I'm so glad to see you. Last time you came we barely had a chance to speak, and I had so many questions. Can you tell me how the investigation is going? Have you solved it? Have you caught the killer?'

Freddy – who had got stuck at *so glad to see you* – shook his head and did his best to untangle his tongue.

'I'm afraid not, no. We're trying, but it's proved to be a tough one. There were so few clues at the site that we've barely built up a picture of the person who did it.'

Hanni's smile shifted. 'I don't understand. What about the tattoo and the sign, and the card he was holding? Didn't they tell you anything that might help?'

Freddy stiffened – he couldn't help it. Her expression, and the disappointment baked into her questions, was too reminiscent of the way the deeply unimpressed chief inspector increasingly dealt with him. Brack was already questioning the wisdom of allowing a 'rookie' to lead the investigation into such an odd case. Six weeks in without a lead and Freddy knew he was hanging on by his fingertips. Not that he had any intention of letting Hanni know that. His answer, therefore, was more defensive than he wanted it to be.

'Obviously there was information at the scene, but none of it was about the killer. The things he left told us the victim's identity and that the man was an SS officer and that – if your reading of the sign round his neck was correct – whoever killed Luka Albrecht thought he was a traitor, although we don't know what that means. So, yes, there was no shortage of clues, but our murderer is hiding himself very carefully behind them.'

If his tone had stung the way he had intended, she didn't show it.

'I'm sorry. This is all new to me and I think you heard a criticism that honestly wasn't intended. It sounds like he's going to prove hard to catch even with all your experience. That must be very frustrating.'

Freddy wished he could take his gruff words back. Hanni wasn't weighing him up the way his boss was and hearing failure. She was genuinely interested. And far more impressed with Freddy's abilities than she ought to be. He forced his ruffled feathers back down, aware of how much her good opinion mattered to him, and how keen he was to hold on to it.

'Frustrating's the word. We don't have a single lead to go on and that puts the killer in charge, which I don't like one bit.

There's a story in the clues, I know that much, but I don't understand what it is that he's telling us, and I don't know how to
crack it.'

Hanni had obviously forgotten whatever it was that had upset
her earlier. She was watching him with an intensity that made
Freddy shiver.

'A story he's telling? Do you mean that he's talking to you?'
Her eyes brightened. 'That he's setting you a puzzle?'

Her enthusiasm made him want to stand taller.

'That's the right way to put it, yes. It's not unusual: all
murderers do it, although some communicate through their
crime scenes more consciously than others. Whatever newspapers say to frighten their readers, murders are very seldom
random things. It's more common to find that the killer and the
victim are linked in some way. The problem for us as detectives is
that sometimes the connection is easy to find, and sometimes
there are multiple layers piled over it.'

Freddy stopped. He was all too aware that not only was he
showing off, but most of what he was saying was theoretical. That
it had been gathered not from crime scenes he had presided at but
from men with far more experience of investigating them than
him. He had too much pride, however – and too great a need to
carry on impressing her – to let Hanni guess how little of what he
was saying he had personally put into practice. To his relief,
however, she appeared to have heard not the 'rookie' he was but
the expert he was striving to be.

'So what would an easy link look like? I mean, what would be
the simplest crime to solve? One where you catch the killer in the
act?'

Freddy finally relaxed enough to smile. When Hanni smiled
back, albeit briefly, his heart soared.

'That would be quite a scenario, although I think it's a rare one
and it would certainly be too risky to deliberately employ as a
strategy. An easy link? Okay, well I suppose that's one where
there's an obvious motive for person A killing person B: a

connection that points a direct finger from the body to the perpetrator.'

He could hear himself slipping into lecture mode, but she was listening to him so eagerly, he couldn't resist playing up to her.

'Let me give you an example. Say a Jewish man was murdered in the neighbourhood where Luka Albrecht lived – someone with an SS background like him would be the first potential suspect we would look at. Killing a Jewish man would be a logical extension of his beliefs, likely a continuation of what he did in the war. There would be a clear motive. Of course, knowing those bastards, that still wouldn't get us a conviction. There would be no guilt so there'd be no confession and he'd no doubt hide behind "I was only following orders" or something similar, like all the liars who got away with murder at Nuremberg.'

He stopped and pulled back from the anti-Nazi tirade he was about to launch into. Whether it was because of what he had said, or the disgust-filled way that he'd said it, Hanni had flinched, and her face had closed down exactly as it had when she saw the tattoo at the first crime scene. It was clear to him that Hanni, no doubt like everyone else in Berlin, was carrying a story of her own. What he couldn't tell was whether it was one she was ready to share. Or whether it was one he needed to know a lot more about before he involved her any further in the case.

'That's by the by. What I'm trying to say is that I've got a hunch that this investigation won't go straight from A to B. That it's multi-layered instead and it's not going to be easy to unpick.'

He was suddenly aware that time was passing, and how likely that meant Matz was about to burst in. That was an interruption he wasn't ready for, not if he wanted to find out what made Hanni Winter tick.

'Your photographs were so detailed, Fraulein Winter...'

She shook her head, so he switched to her first name and managed – just – not to trip over the intimacy.

'I can't tell you how valuable they were, Hanni. None of the other photographers we wheel in are anything as thorough as you. Looking at your shots was like standing in the middle of the crime scene again. I've got good people round me, but no one with eyes like yours and, with the way this case now appears to be going, I need that skill on my team.'

He paused, conscious that the next words out of his mouth could open her up or push her away. Hanni carried on watching him, her eyes still wary.

'The thing is, though, I'm worried that there's something in this that you're struggling with, beyond the fact of it being an unpleasant murder. Maybe something personal. When you saw the tattoo, and now when I was mouthing off about guilt and Nuremberg, your whole face changed. Am I right? Would getting more involved be difficult for you? I would understand if you didn't want to. None of this is pleasant.'

She didn't answer at once. She glanced down at the floor, her knuckles tightening.

Freddy followed her gaze: all he could see was the corner of what looked like her camera bag poking out of the side of the display cabinet. He didn't ask why she was looking at it. He had the sense that, if he pushed her too fast, she would shy away from him and retreat back into whatever secrets she was keeping. He did, therefore, what he didn't like to do, and he waited.

When she finally looked back up at him, her lips were drawn so tight he wondered if his probing had silenced her. Then she stretched her clenched fingers, tapped them lightly on the counter and nodded – to herself, or so it seemed.

'You're right: it's not pleasant – or easy. Nothing that needs doing ever is. And I know you saw me flinch, both times. I want to help you if that's what you need, I really do, but you're also right that there are things, if I'm honest, about this case that make it...' She hesitated and was clearly not happy with the word she eventually chose. 'Uncomfortable. No, that's not it. That make it what you said – personal. I have things in my own life I need to sort out and make right and the truth is...'

Whatever the truth was, it was lost in the crash of the door as Matz barged through it.

'Sorry, boss, but we've picked up a message on the radio to say that the British are sniffing around. I know we were promised the lead on this because of the last one, but if we don't get down there quickly…'

Freddy snapped on his most professional manner, as quickly as if he had been wearing it all along.

'Thank you. I was just about to explain the situation to Fraulein Winter.'

He turned to Hanni whose lips were firmly clamped shut again. 'As I should have said when I first came in, I would appreciate it if you could spare us your eye and your camera again. We've found another body.'

This one was lying in a newly cleared building on the corner of Fehrbelliner Platz in the British sector. Apart from the location – and that there were police officers rather than scruffy boys guarding it – the second crime scene was a duplicate of the first. There was the same positioning, with the dead man's left arm angled to reveal his blood group tattoo. There was the same neatly lettered sign hung around the victim's neck; the same identity-revealing card clutched in his hand. And the same lack of boot prints or fingerprints or any other evidence – apart from the messages left on the body – that the killer had ever been there at all.

Hanni crouched and snapped image after image while Freddy and Matz retrieved the card and questioned the white-faced civil servant whose morning journey to work had taken a rather macabre turn.

'He's done it again, hasn't he?'

Hanni stood up as Freddy came back towards her, scanning through his scribble-filled notebook.

It was clear from the staccato way that he spoke that his

answer was as much for himself as for her. 'It looks that way. We didn't release any details of the last one to the press, so it can't be a copycat. It's the same victim profile, the same method of display. The last time, the body was left in a building which was in the process of being cleared, this one was visible from the road, so both were easy to find. I think it would be safe for even the most cautious investigator to assume it's the same killer.'

Hanni glanced round the building. Like the one in Wilhelmstraße where the first body had been found, this one was a ruin, but it was in far better condition than the toppling ministry had been. The floors were clear of rubble; there was a row of scaffolding supporting the rear wall; some of the upper windows had been reglazed. It looked like a place with a refound purpose; it certainly didn't have the echoes that clung around the old government district.

'Do you think the site itself is significant? The victim is another ex-SS officer, but is this building also linked to the Third Reich?'

Matz, who had finished with the witness and joined them, shook his head.

'It's a good question, but no, we don't think so. There were the usual Nazi administration offices round here that you can find all over the city, but nothing major, which is presumably why this one's being refurbished. This whole area is a British administration hub now and we think this Nils Buchtel worked for them. I've sent an officer over to the British Command Centre to check, and to flesh out the details on the killer's calling card.'

'The first victim, Luka Albrecht, worked for the Allies too, for the Americans.' Freddy flipped back through his notebook until he found the right page. 'Here it is. Albrecht was in the SS, same as this guy was, but he was also a chemist by training, with a pretty dodgy record for consulting with IG Farben during the war. They were the company who produced Zyklon B, the gas that was used in the extermination chambers.'

He paused for a moment and his face tightened. Matz asked him if he was all right, but Freddy ignored the question.

'Albrecht must have been able to whitewash away that part of his record to get a research job with the Americans – or they whitewashed it for him. I wonder if Buchtel was in the same lucky boat with the Brits.'

Freddy stopped again, his breathing suddenly heavier.

Matz started to speak but thought better of it. Hanni, however, did not know Freddy well enough to notice the strain on his face which had silenced Matz.

'Both men worked for the Allies even though they were once in the SS?' Hanni frowned. 'Is that usual? I thought there had been a purge.'

Freddy pushed away his suspicions about what the Allies may or may not have been doing and looked properly at Hanni. She was concentrating too hard for the question to have been a casual one.

'There was, but it's not been as successful as the British and the Americans would like you to think. Have you heard the term *Persilschein?*'

Hanni nodded. 'It means a clean bill of health, doesn't it?'

Freddy glanced down at the file card he was still holding. 'Sort of. It can also mean what I meant when I said whitewashed. Suspected Nazis who have been "washed clean" because they had skills that were needed. Albrecht was a chemist who potentially worked on one of the war's worst weapons. Buchtel seems to have been something high up in transport logistics and that's a term that comes with multiple meanings given his background. *Persilschein* could fit them both very well.'

Why are her hands trembling?

Hanni started speaking again before Freddy could think of a way to ask.

'Do you think there could be some sort of a pattern here? Both the dead men have rebuilt their lives and been rewarded for their skills, not punished for how they might once have used them. Do you think that could be why they're dead? That maybe the killer is targeting ex-SS officers employed by the occupation armies who have never paid for their crimes?'

A vigilante? Cleaning up the men who the trials should have caught?

His heart was hammering. He couldn't work out whether it was with horror or with a twisted sense of delight that someone was finishing the job the forces of justice had failed at. He knew he couldn't say that out loud.

'It was only a thought.'

Freddy forced his swirling thoughts to settle. It was clear from Hanni's drawn face that it was far more than that.

I can't leap on this, not until I've worked out what it means, for me and for the investigation.

He bent down and began re-examining the body, resisting the impulse to either grab at or dismiss Hanni's theory. He needed a clear head to find his way through this second murder, not one that was racing.

'It's an interesting idea. It could be a possible motive. And working for the Allies might be a link, and we desperately need one of those.'

Stay focused, stay professional. Stick to procedure.

His heart rate calmed. Nobody seemed to think his voice was as strained as it sounded to him.

'And I think there could be another link here.' He pointed to the bloodstain surrounding the head, grateful to have found a clue that led to a more straightforward conclusion. 'The killing method looks to be the same as the one used on Albrecht: one or more heavy blows to the back of the skull. That doesn't necessarily need a lot of physical strength—'

'And this victim is slight in terms of his build and his height, like Albrecht was.'

Matz's face brightened as he picked up Freddy's train of thought. Freddy was happy to let him run with it.

'Neither of them would be difficult to overpower, especially if there was the element of surprise a blow from behind suggests.'

Matz began walking the length of the body as if he was measuring it. 'Which suggests that our killer doesn't need to be a big man either.'

For the first time, the murderer, or at least a hint of him, was there beside them, hovering next to the body. Freddy's shoulders began to unclench. Hanni, however, was looking, if anything, more tense.

'Not a big man, maybe, but a vengeful one.'

She had her camera out of its bag again. She raised it to her eye and peered through the lens straight at the dead man's face, but she didn't take a picture. It looked to Freddy as if she was using the metal body as some kind of a shield to regroup behind.

She's as thrown by the potential implications of this as I am, and I have no idea why.

'What are you thinking, Hanni?'

She turned slightly towards him, but she didn't lower the camera.

'What if he really is killing SS officers who escaped justice? What if he's mopping them up? How many potential targets would there be for someone on a crusade like that?'

And why on earth would we stop him?

Matz, thankfully, wasn't looking at him as that thought popped up. He was looking at Hanni, who was still grasping tight to the camera. Freddy couldn't look at either of them, not until he was certain his body was steady.

A crusade. Aimed at men like the ones who had murdered his family.

It's wrong. People can't take the law into their own hands. It's wrong.

He really wanted to believe that. He wasn't sure that he did. And he wasn't sure that Hanni did either. Unless he was hearing everyone else through his own confused filter, he was sure he had heard her voice lift on *crusade*. She wasn't Jewish like him – he knew next to nothing about her, but he was fairly certain of that – but he could have sworn he had heard hope in it.

'Inspector, what do you think? Is that a theory we should follow up on?'

Matz had finally noticed Freddy's silence. Freddy couldn't let him notice anything else. He stood up and answered in the most neutral tone he could manage.

'It's a possibility. Based on two murders, however, it's too early to say. We would need far more proof to make it our lead idea.'

Freddy didn't address the other thought Hanni had raised: that more proof could be coming. That a man who had killed two and left so little of himself could easily kill more, or that – if she was even partway right – the potential pool of victims was a deep one.

And an evil one, by anyone's measure.

He knew he was out of his depth, although he had no intention of showing that. He didn't want to deal with a man on a mission. With a killer whose victims – if Hanni was right – he would struggle to care about. What he had wanted to make his name with was a murderer who had a simple motive, who was bad in a proper old-fashioned, opposite-of-good way. What he seemed to have – a murderer with a limitless supply of targets and targets who, God help him for thinking it but he couldn't stop himself, might deserve their fates – wasn't what he, or the city, needed. It would be hard enough keeping a second murder away from the press. He wouldn't have a hope if there was a third, and the post-war atmosphere in Berlin was still too fragile to withstand a killer intending to dig up and then, all too literally, lay bare the past. That could polarise old wounds nobody wanted reopening.

Freddy closed his notebook, carefully avoiding eye contact with either Matz or Hanni. He couldn't let this get personal, and he couldn't afford, at the moment, to find out what was upsetting Hanni, not if either of those things were going to threaten the investigation. What he needed was a fast way to solve it. The British had only agreed to let him investigate this murder because of the close links with the first one. They had made it very clear – as had Brack, who hated to be under the spotlight – that they wanted a quick resolution or he could forget about keeping it.

'We'll follow the theory up, but first we need to get all the basics covered. We need to interview Buchtel's workmates and his wife, if she's still around, and find out what happened to him during and after the war beyond what's on the card. Matz, can you check into his job and get this place cleared while I follow up on the wife?'

Matz waved in the team waiting with evidence bags and a stretcher.

'If you're going to meet with Frau Buchtel, do you want me to pull in the Women's Division officer you used for Frau Albrecht's interview and request that she goes with you again?'

My husband was a good man, one of the best. Don't you dare tell me any different. Don't you dare tell me he was anything less than a hero.

The interview with Dora Albrecht had been an ordeal from start to finish. Freddy had loathed the woman from the moment she'd started howling about the 'great service to his country' Luka Albrecht had performed during the war and what 'a loss to the world' his death was. He suddenly wished that he had allocated the tasks out differently. The thought of meeting another woman as besotted with a man who Freddy could only see as a criminal was not a pleasant one. Especially if he had to take a female officer with him who he suspected had shared Frau Albrecht's political sympathies.

'Dear God, no.' He handed the record card over to the evidence team and stuffed his notebook back into his coat. 'She was hopeless. She was too full of tea and sympathy to get us anything useful.' He paused and then decided to follow his instincts. 'Hanni?'

It took her a moment to properly turn and lower her camera. When she did, it looked as if she wasn't inhabiting the same space as the two men. Freddy began to wonder if his instincts were wrong, if involving her any further really was a mistake. Unfortunately he needed a woman with an eye for what was hidden, so he ploughed on.

'Hanni, could you come with me to see the wife, if we determine there is one? I prefer to have a woman with me for this kind of interview and there's no one else I can trust.'

She was as pale as if all the colour had spilled out of her.

'You want me to go to her house? To visit a woman who married into the SS?'

Her voice was strained; her use of *married into* was strange. Freddy could feel himself starting to flounder. There was a chill nibbling at his neck. It was the same one he had felt when Hanni had looked at the tattoo at the first killing and then again when she had said *crusade*. The same chill that had crept round him when he realised that Buchtel was also an SS man and had likely borne as much Jewish blood on his hands when he was alive as Albrecht had.

It's too hard for her. It can't be too hard for both of us – that's too much to manage.

He started, clumsily, to backtrack. 'It was a silly idea. I'll call in someone else. I shouldn't have asked you.'

But Hanni shook her head. 'No, I want to do it. I want to know what this Buchtel was like. And if there's someone out there killing SS officers, I want to know why. I want to know where he might look next.'

This time, there was no mistaking the hope he thought he'd heard earlier.

What have you seen, Hanni? What have you been through? How close was your war to mine?

He let her walk away. It was neither the time nor the place to ask.

CHAPTER 9

16 JANUARY 1947

Hanni arrived at the Buchtel family home in Charlottenburg with her stomach in free fall. She had tried to convince herself that the butterfly-sick feeling was because she was nervous. She was about to meet the wife of an SS man; a woman who might – despite the war's end – have remained as committed to her husband and his beliefs as Freddy had said Frau Albrecht had been. She was also about to witness a woman hearing the worst kind of news. Nerves were, therefore, a reasonable excuse for the somersaults her stomach had flipped through on the car ride, but they weren't the real cause. Hanni knew perfectly well that she wasn't sick with nerves; she was sick with herself.

What if he has a list? What if my father's name is on it?

That had been her first thought when she'd realised that the murderer had struck again, that he had sought out the same kind of victim. That thought alone was bad enough. Her second – *please God that he is* – was surely unforgiveable. What kind of a daughter wished such a terrible fate on her father, no matter what his sins might be? Hanni hadn't been able to stop the hope that had crept into *What if he's mopping them up?* and *crusade*. She knew Freddy had heard it too. She had no idea what he had made of it

or where that unconscious slip had left their fledgling relationship – if they even had a fledgling relationship. The car journey
from Fehrbelliner Platz had been so uncomfortable, Hanni was
beginning to think she had dreamed that up.

Freddy had barely spoken after their car drove them away
from the site. He hadn't wanted to discuss her theory again
because it was 'too early to establish a pattern' and 'there was no
real substance in it.' Hanni didn't believe him. She had seen the
look that had flashed across his face when she had proposed the
idea, although she hadn't understood its mix of agreement and
shock. She had also seen the way he'd stared at her in the
moments before they left the crime scene. *I want to know where he
might look next* had unnerved him. He had heard secrets in that.

*Which he has too. Never mind me seeming on edge, he didn't know
whether to applaud or run from my idea, and he looked sick when he
mentioned Zyklon B and the camps.*

Hanni glanced across the worn leather seat. Freddy was
staring out at the streets, scowling at whatever it was he could see
there. Hanni wasn't sure what had caused the bad mood he had
clearly fallen into. What she did know was that the connection
she had thought was developing between them at the studio had
vanished – he had turned back into Inspector Schlüssel the
moment they had climbed into the car. She was also certain that
he would rather be anywhere else than heading to do an interview with Buchtel's wife.

The meeting with Frau Albrecht – from the brief recap he had
given her – sounded as if it had been very unpleasant. It had, in
his words, uncovered nothing but outrage and hysteria – especially when she had kept insisting that her husband was a 'war
hero'. Freddy had lost his patience at that and told her what no
grieving widow needed to hear: that Albrecht appeared to have
been attacked on his way to visit his mistress in her rooms on the
Unter den Linden.

It was obvious from his manner that he was about to carry
the echoes of that experience into the next one and that made

Hanni more nervous than she already was. Stepping into a house which could be full of unwanted echoes of her own past was going to be difficult enough. She did not want to do that with Freddy wound tight as a drum. As the car pulled up outside an elegant, detached villa, she decided, therefore, that someone had to break through the silence that had flared up between them.

Hanni shook her head as the driver turned to open the screen that divided him from his passengers and put a tentative hand on Freddy's arm, keeping her fingers deliberately on his sleeve and away from his skin. He still jumped at her touch. When he turned towards her, his eyes were unfocused. Then he blinked and looked at her and made Hanni gasp. His naked stare – which was almost too intense to be caught in – lasted barely a moment, but it wiped away any doubts that this was a purely working relationship.

'Help me out, Freddy. Tell me why you want me here. Isn't it against the rules, given that I'm not actually with the police?'

It took him a few seconds to answer – he had clearly been lost in thoughts that were miles away from the case.

'Maybe. Does it matter? Anyway, I've told Matz to put you on the books as a freelance photographer so you working with us is covered for this and for the crime scenes you've been to and for more assignments if you want them. It's good money, better I imagine than you can make at the studio. And I told you: I need your eye for detail.'

That she could earn another income was welcome news, but Freddy's response was a defensive and deflecting one, and it wasn't enough. Hanni kept her hand on his arm and pressed on.

'You said that about the crime scenes, and that made sense there. But not here, at the house. I assume you don't want photographs of Frau Buchtel, so what do you want me to do?'

She hesitated, and then decided that she had to speak honestly if either of them were going to get the outcome from the interview that they wanted. 'You've been distracted since we got in the car: it would help to know why. Have I done something to upset you?'

Freddy picked at his thumb and wouldn't look at her. 'No, it's not you. It's the case.'

He paused. Hanni could see he was weighing up exactly how much he was prepared to say. It was hard to stay quiet, not to push him on, but she bit her lip and she managed. Her silence, thankfully, loosened his tongue.

'I'm not as experienced at all this as I let you think. And I'm not good with this side of the job, dealing with the relatives, all the messy emotional bits. I'm happier with clues that don't talk back. I charge in apparently, or so I was told after the last session. And I'm "insensitive". I brought you because I was hoping you would balance that side of me out.'

It was flattering, but Hanni still wasn't convinced he was giving her the whole story. Freddy was a lot of things, but he wasn't insensitive. He hadn't charged in at the studio or at either of the crime sites when she was struggling to define her own discomfort. He hadn't missed the fact that on both those occasions she was battling with a mix of emotions – Hanni doubted Freddy missed very much at all – but he had watched and he had waited and he had treated her gently. He hadn't pushed her to reveal anything, which was why she had almost – and possibly foolishly given how little she actually knew him – told him who Hanni Winter really was. It had, however, been the right way to approach her, so she decided to follow the same careful line with him.

'Do you think that perhaps the problem wasn't with you last time but with Frau Albrecht? That there was something about her that made her a difficult subject to talk to?'

His face hardened so quickly, Hanni pulled her hand back.

'It wasn't *something*, it was everything.'

He was trembling. When he started to talk again, all his hesitation and weighing up of words was gone.

'She was loathsome. She was convinced her husband was a

paragon of virtue, an opinion the women's officer I took with me was far too eager to encourage. When I tried to probe into Albrecht's SS activities, she accused me of being "one of those fantasy spinners like the fools at Nuremberg". When I mentioned the mistress, that was simply more proof of what "a wicked liar" I was. She sickened me and I got cross. I told her some home truths about why the camps needed the services of a chemist and exactly what Zyklon B does to the human body. She went ballistic. She threw me out.'

He was still refusing to meet her eyes. Hanni wanted to hold his arm again, but the tight lines round his mouth held her away.

'I hated her, Hanni. I hated every inch of her, and I showed it, which was hardly professional – as my pompously self-righteous colleague went to great pains to report. And I'm afraid I'll hate Frau Buchtel too – especially if she also tells me her husband was a good man – and I'll make another mess, which won't help my confusion over the case or my standing with my superiors. That's what's been niggling me. I'm afraid I won't be able to speak to her in anything close to a professional manner. That's why I need you here, as an observer who might pick up details from her that I don't, and as a quieter, steadier head.' He suddenly looked back at her. 'You can be that, can't you? You were going to tell me something at the studio that you didn't get time to say and then you were a little strange back at Fehrbelliner Platz. If there's something going—'

'It was nothing. I'll be fine – you've nothing to worry about.'

It was an automatic answer designed to stop him. This wasn't the time for the questions she was desperate to ask him. About how he knew as much about Zyklon B as he seemed to. And what he meant by *confusion over the case*, which she instinctively knew did not mean the absence of clues. It was clear that Freddy was holding as much back as she was. It was also clear that he was wavering and close to rethinking his decision to bring her along. Stopping that impulse mattered far more than rooting through his vulnerabilities – or trying to distract him from rooting through hers.

Hanni got out of the car before he could say anything else. She had come to the Buchtel house with her heart in her mouth, not wanting to meet the wife any more than he did. She still had to be there. She needed to know who these men were and why the killer had chosen them. She could be as steady as Freddy wanted her to be if she found some answers to that.

In the end, Freddy got very little chance to speak at all. As soon as he broke the news of her husband's death, Frau Buchtel flew into hysterics. As soon as he explained that the cause of his death was murder, she flew into a rage. Freddy immediately gave up and sat back with a scowl. Hanni forced herself not to copy him, but to wrap her arms round the shaking woman instead and try to calm her to a point where she might be of some use.

Touching Sonja Buchtel was far harder than Hanni made it look. Being in the house was far harder than she made it look. From the moment Hanni had walked in, she had understood exactly what kind of a woman she was dealing with.

Nothing was overt. There were none of the swastikas or Party portraits that had hung in Hanni's home. That Hanni knew had hung in the Buchtel home before the symbols were banned and the men who lauded them were forced into the shadows. The signs of past – and unmistakeably present – affiliations were subtle ones, but they were everywhere for someone who knew how to look.

The fluted crystal vases in the hallway held silk sprigs of edelweiss. The chairs Hanni glimpsed in the dining room had oak leaves carved into their backs and an angular tapestry pattern on their cushions which was picked out in red, white and black. The photographs of snowy slopes and masked skiers which hung on the sitting-room walls had been taken at Obersalzberg, the mountaintop resort above Berchtesgaden in Bavaria which had been Hitler's beloved retreat.

Sonja Buchtel's house was Nazi-soaked – Hanni could feel it in the walls. She had, after all, lived in a similar one; she had, after all, skied on those same slopes. And no matter what was hidden or banned, Hanni knew that the woman weeping in her arms was perfectly at one with her home, that she was as committed an SS wife as Freddy said Dora Albrecht had been.

Hanni had, however, kept all that knowledge to herself. Even when Sonja insisted that her husband was a 'hero' who had been 'shamefully treated'.

'He was arrested under the Allies' Law of Automatic Arrest, which was the most ridiculous thing I've ever heard. How such pettiness could be enshrined into law is beyond me. Tens of thousands of decent German men and women, including my poor Nils, interred in camps in the most squalid conditions simply for fighting for their country and doing their duty. Interrogated as if they were felons and accused of crimes that were based on a pack of enemy lies. How could such a travesty have been allowed?'

'Because he deserved it and should never have been let out.'

Hanni flashed Freddy a look that shut him up – not that Sonja had heard him. She was too busy ranting about the insult to her husband and 'all the good men like him' and the way too many of the other wives had hung their heads and accepted it.

'But not me. I got him out. Look.'

She wrenched herself away from Hanni and ran over to a desk in the corner and grabbed a small silver box from the top.

'Here, read this. This is what proper wives do. They stand up for their husbands.'

The letter she thrust into Hanni's hand was a carbon copy of the one she had presumably sent to the commanding officer of the internment camp in Paderborn, Westphalia, where Nils Buchtel had been sent after the war. Hanni scanned its contents as quickly as she could. It made her feel sick.

My husband has lived his whole life bound by honour and the concept of duty. To his family, to his country; to me. Whatever burden was given to him to carry, he bore it with no thought for himself. You, however, have refused to see that man. You have alleged that he was present when murders were committed, that he participated in a massacre. Anyone who knows him would tell you what a slur that is. They would tell you that his detention is a mistake. Before the war, my husband was a civil servant in Berlin. He organised train routes, he helped to ensure the smooth running of the city he was born in and loves. He carried out similar operational tasks while serving – as all good Germans had to – during the difficult years of the war. Is that the type of man who murders? Who stands witness to massacres? Look to your own conscience, sir, and look properly at my husband. He is, and always has been, an honourable man. What higher praise can a wife offer than that?

'That did the trick, let me tell you. That got him properly recognised and rewarded. Look, this is who he is now.'

Sonja was back at the desk, digging among the piles of paper which spilled out of it. She returned to the sofa cradling a pile of business cards engraved with *Herr Nils Buchtel, Transport Advisor, British Control Commission for Germany, Fehrbelliner Platz, Berlin*, holding them out to Hanni and Freddy as if she was offering them treasure.

Hanni had managed to keep the letter away from Freddy, but she wasn't quick enough this time. Freddy grabbed and scanned one of the cards and cursed. Sonja immediately turned towards him, her face as furious as his. Hanni – realising she only had seconds before a fight broke out which would do no one any good at all – leaned quickly forward in an unsubtle attempt to keep the two of them apart.

'We have to go, Frau Buchtel, I'm sorry. Is there anyone I can call to come and sit with you?'

Hanni hoped that there wasn't: she had no desire to deal with anyone who could be friends with a woman like Sonja. She nodded to Freddy and began to gather up her bag, desperate to be gone, when another loud sob cut through her hurried goodbyes. Hanni looked up, praying that Sonja hadn't collapsed into more tears that might require soothing. The noise wasn't, however, Sonja's doing. This sob had come from a little girl – a child of no more than six or seven, with her blonde hair braided into long plaits and dressed in an old-fashioned smocked dress – who was standing in the doorway, clutching an obviously well-loved doll. She was shifting and staring wide-eyed at Sonja and clearly unsure of herself – presumably, Hanni assumed, because she was shy in front of strangers.

'Mama? Why are you crying? Has Papa still not come back?'

The child's voice rose and split once again into tears.

Sonja stiffened, but she didn't move. 'Why are you down here? Where is your nanny?'

The girl froze, her lip trembling.

Sonja turned to Hanni. 'I can't deal with her, not now. I shouldn't be expected to. Can you do something? Can you take her away?'

The person making the child nervous evidently wasn't Hanni or Freddy. Hanni forced herself to swallow and not to snap back a furious 'isn't it your job to take care of her', hoping that the woman's callous manner was shock speaking, not her normal reaction to seeing her child in distress. Sonja, however, continued to sit where she was and raised an eyebrow as if she was waiting for Hanni to jump to her bidding. It was a step too far for her already stretched self-control to manage.

'Dear God, how can you be so cold when your daughter is so upset? What is wrong with you?'

No longer interested in staying polite, Hanni scrambled to her feet, ready to scoop the girl up and deliver her to kinder arms. As she did so, however, she caught sight of Freddy. He wasn't rolling his eyes and cursing anymore. He was as colour-leached as the white-faced child. He had also got to his feet, but he was swaying, his body folded in on itself.

'Freddy, what's wrong? Are you ill?'

He didn't seem to hear her. He didn't seem to know that either she or Sonja were still in the room. He was staring at the girl as if his skin was on fire.

'Freddy, what is it? You're scaring me.'

He jerked round. He looked straight through Hanni and pitched himself towards the girl instead, moving with his hands outstretched as if his limbs didn't belong to him. The girl shrank back. He didn't notice. To Hanni's – and the child's – horror, he grabbed the girl by her shoulders, half-lifting her as if he was about to bundle her away. The doll fell to the floor; the little girl screamed and burst into loud, terrified tears. The noise finally broke Freddy out of his trance. He let go of her and leaped back, falling over himself to apologise.

'I'm sorry. I am so, so sorry.'

It didn't help. The girl's sobs grew louder. Sonja finally turned into a mother and launched herself at Freddy. Before she could reach him, however – and before Hanni could reach her – Freddy rushed past them all and was gone.

———

He couldn't breathe. There wasn't enough air in the street to fill him. Not that he could see the street he had plunged into. Freddy wasn't in Charlottenburg anymore. The Buchtels' leafy road had vanished, swallowed up by a far narrower one filled with closely packed peeling tenements and a column of soldiers who were minutes away from ruining his life.

Their little unit had survived things that would have broken families less tightly bound than theirs. The never-ending laws which narrowed their lives and gradually pushed them out of society. The loss of the bakery in November 1938 when the SA's thugs went on the rampage on Kristallnacht and smashed up Berlin's Jewish businesses. The shortages and restrictions the war had brought with it, including the rationing laws which put

Jewish families at the desperate end of the permanent queues. The seizure of their comfortable flat in 1941 and the forced move the same day to an insulting set of cramped and inadequate rooms in a tenement in Bachstraße which felt like a ghetto. There were so many blows, but of all the ones they had endured since the Nazis came to power, Freddy had been afraid that it was the move and its haste that would finally break his heavily pregnant mother's heart.

The relocation from Kreuzberg to Mitte came so quickly, a tearful Rosa had had to leave some of her most precious possessions behind, including the heavy silver cutlery set she had inherited from her grandmother and the inlaid mahogany sewing table she spent every evening at. More difficult to bear than that, however, was being snatched away from the people she had built her daily life round. When they arrived at the Mitte tenement, none of the other families who they had lived alongside for years had been relocated there. As for the rooms themselves, they were so damp that Leo's weak chest worsened in a day.

Freddy had looked at his mother's devastated face and had been ready to kick down the doors of the housing department until they understood what housing actually meant. He had not, however, had to face the beating or imprisonment, or worse, that protest would have led to. He had not reckoned with Rosa's determination to remain her family's backbone. After one bout of tears, she had wiped her face and reclaimed her smile. She had hung on to that, albeit grimly sometimes, even when Renny's birth made it impossible to find a space in the overcrowded flat for Freddy's lanky limbs. He was the one who volunteered to go, although he couldn't bear the thought of it. Rosa was the one who swung into action. She called on all the new connections she had forged, found him a lodging less than half an hour's walk away in Moabit and called his leaving 'an adventure', with a flourish that made doing it possible.

There had been other leavings besides Freddy's, and more permanent ones than his. Jakub and Rosa's elderly parents had also moved to new homes in 1941, relocated from Berlin along with hundreds of the city's older Jewish residents to the newly established spa town of Theresienstadt. Everyone in both families had expected complaints at such a faraway move, but the two couples professed themselves happy to go. War and the hatred of Jews which had soaked through Germany until it ran as wide as a river had aged them faster than their years. Once they received the details of the elegant property that Theresienstadt could offer, they had pooled their savings to purchase one of the town's lakeside villas and had left for their train declaring themselves glad to be done with 'Berlin's madness'. A postcard arrived from the town's reception committee confirming their arrival, which put Rosa's mind at rest and – although no one was blunt enough to say it – their departure had at least meant four fewer mouths to feed.

There had been leavings and loss and change, but the Schlüsselbergs kept going. Not that Rosa was made of steel. She had lost her temper quite spectacularly when Freddy – who had been forced out of the law office in 1940 and onto the production line of an armaments factory together with Jakub and Leo – got himself so badly beaten by the guards at his work that he couldn't walk for a week. His defence – that he had been standing up for a workmate who had been wrongly accused of tampering with shell cases – did nothing to calm her. Rosa was angry that he wouldn't learn to keep his mouth shut. And she was angrier still when she discovered – because she discovered everything – that Freddy was acting as a courier for a resistance group printing false identity papers. There were days, Freddy knew, when he filled his mother with fear. But their little unit muddled through and, together, they survived.

By the end of February 1943, Freddy – despite the yellow stars they all had to wear and the increasingly bitter grip of persecution, despite everything he now knew about the packed trains emptying the Jewish population out of Berlin, and despite the fact that there had never been another postcard from Theresienstadt

– had convinced himself that his family would be the one which would make it through to better days. It was a fool's dream he would never forgive himself for indulging.

The end, when it came, came quickly. The warning, when it came, came too late. *They're clearing the factories of the last of us: don't go in, spread the word, warn your families.* Freddy was still in his tiny frozen room when the cry went up, shaking with a fever that had stuck him in a pool of sweat to his bed. The sharp knock and the shouted message got him upright and into his clothes, frantically trying to work out what he could do. He had no doubt that the clearance squads would come looking for him when they discovered he wasn't at the factory where he was meant to be. That, however, wasn't his main concern. Freddy was certain he could look after himself, but he didn't have the same confidence about his family. Or any confidence that he could help all of them escape.

When the knock had roused him, his watch had said it was long past seven o'clock. Jakub and Leo would have set out before six to walk the two hours it took to get to the factory in Treptow. He couldn't get to them; he had to hope someone else would and not allow himself to be buried by the fear that nobody would. What he could do, however, and what he had to do, was get to his mother and Renny, who – through Rosa's job running a work-place creche – could also be part of the sweep-up. That got him down the dark corridor and onto the stairs, although his clothes were drenched within half a dozen steps and his body was burning.

When he staggered outside, the street was unnaturally quiet. The bakery was closed, the newspaper kiosk was shuttered. There were no yellow-starred labourers huddling their thin bodies into thinner coats as they stumbled to work. There was no sign of the brave runners who had delivered the morning's impossible news.

Freddy refused to be frightened by any of that. He pushed himself along Kirchstraße towards the river and Rosa. He had forgotten his scarf in his haste, and the cold bit at his face and neck, turning his fevered body into a swamp. He ignored that; he ignored his aching muscles. He moved steadily on, crossing the black water without stopping, hugging hard to the edge of the bridge. He turned onto Altonaer Straße, focusing on his feet, focusing on the few moments which was all he needed to stay upright.

He was so caught up in his own body that, when he first heard the noise, he didn't understand it. It was a harsh grating rasp, like a dry cough. It wasn't him and there was no one else around to make it.

The rasp came again, deeper and louder. Freddy stopped, shaking his head to clear the fog running round it. And then it came a third time and he understood, and his blood froze. It wasn't a cough. It was a bark, rising up from the direction of Rosa's street. A street where there wasn't a dog or a cat or a pet of any kind left.

Freddy refused to think. He began to run. He flung himself down the deserted pavement, flung himself round the corner into the narrower confines of Bachstraße. The barking grew louder, undercut now he was closer by shouts that cracked whip-sharp through the morning's weak light.

It was soldiers, of course, as he had known that it would be. Lined up along the length of the street, their grey uniforms solidified into a wall that separated Freddy from Rosa. The sight of them made him want to howl. If he had had the strength, he would have yelled so loudly the dogs would have turned on him; he would have hurled himself against the soldiers' rigid backs and kicked his way through. His legs, however, could barely manage one more step and his lungs were bursting. He stopped, bent over, gulped in great mouthfuls of air that stung like ice. And then, as his breath eased to ragged gasps, he straightened, and he saw her.

Rosa had emerged onto the building's high steps, with a sleep-heavy Renny pressed into her shoulder. She didn't look at the soldiers. She ignored the snarling dogs straining against their leashes. She carried herself as if it were any normal day. Freddy had never seen her look so beautiful. Or so far from his help.

They were being deported – Freddy knew that. They were caught inside that catch-all word which meant a dawn train and no goodbye – which meant disappeared. His beloved mother and his adored baby sister, going God knows where without him.

Freddy choked back the yell that was threatening to swallow him. He couldn't stop what was happening – one shout and all he would meet was a bullet. He couldn't, however, let them go alone. He stepped forward, strangely calm, ready to slip into the line, ready to go with his family wherever that led. And then Rosa switched her gaze from Renny's blonde hair, and she saw him.

Her head barely moved, her lips barely flickered, but every inch of her screamed 'no!' The hand she cupped over Renny's head shouted it. The look she gave him – which could only have lasted seconds but went on for a lifetime – shouted it. Freddy fell back against the wall, pinned into the shadows by her pain. He couldn't move, because Rosa wouldn't allow him to move.

The lines formed up; the soldiers surrounded their prisoners. Rosa turned her back and settled Renny more securely. Another order to march cracked through the air and pierced Freddy's skin. And Rosa walked, silently and unstoppably, away.

———

It took Hanni an age to calm Sonja down to the point where she wouldn't make a complaint and to settle the terrified child with her nanny. By the time she emerged onto the street, there was no sign of Freddy. His despair had been a terrible thing to watch. His anguish, when he snapped out of whatever spell he was under, had been filled with echoes of Talie.

What if he's vanished like she did? What if I never find him?

Hanni knew that was crazy. Berlin wasn't a city full of strangers caught up at war anymore. Freddy was known to far more people than just her; someone would find him even if she couldn't.

The logic in that knowledge did nothing to calm her. She slipped past the waiting police car – a refitted relic of the war which had seen better days – without speaking to the driver. He was too buried in his newspaper to notice Hanni coming out of the house, and she had to assume that he wouldn't be reading as calmly if he had seen the state Freddy was in.

She ran up and down the pavement, scanning the street. Its houses continued to sit quietly behind their immaculate lawns. There was no one around; there were no curtains twitching. Hanni wondered about knocking on some of the polished front doors, but the thought of trying to explain that she was looking for a potentially deranged police officer stopped her. The only safe thing she could think of to do was to try to put a call out for Matz on the unreliable car radio, in the hope that he would know Freddy's home address and some of his usual hangouts.

As she turned to run back and do that, however, she caught sight of him – or the edge of him – crouching by a high garden wall, clinging to it as if his bones had crumbled.

'Freddy?'

His eyes were vacant. His face was as pinched and sunken as Talie's had turned when she was in the grip of a night-time – or a daytime – terror.

'Freddy, can you hear me?'

Hanni kneeled down beside him and took his hands in hers. They were freezing. She wanted to kiss them, to kiss him and breathe him back into life. She knew from experience with her mother, however, that the state he was in needed delicate handling. She began to warm his hands instead, stroking them as gently as if she was handling an injured animal. His fingers gradually stopped trembling, and his shallow breathing started to ease.

'Can you stand?'

He didn't answer, but he let Hanni help him straighten up until he was leaning on the wall and not hugging it.

'I thought it was Renny.'

His voice was a wisp, cracked and raw at the edges. Hanni kept a gentle hold on his hands and picked her words carefully, all too aware that a barrage of questions could lose him again.

'Who, Freddy? Who did you think was Renny?'

When he looked at her, so much pain flooded his face, it was all Hanni could do not to cry out.

'The little girl. In the house. I thought she was my baby sister Renny.'

Now it was her who lost him, as her head spun and took her back to another lost little sister and a misery that could too easily drown her. It was only when he repeated the child's name that Hanni snapped back. This wasn't her sorrow, it was his, and the danger it had brought wasn't over. His voice was flat. Hanni knew that whatever trick of the mind had gripped him had gone. She also knew that his release from the memory didn't mean he was safe again, and that the hollowness in the way he said *Renny* told its own story. Hanni chose her next words as carefully as she had chosen her last ones, trying to balance the need to bring him back into the world without tipping him once more out of it.

'I didn't know you had a sister. Is she here with you, in Berlin?'

Freddy shook his head. His words dropped so slowly, Hanni could almost hear the weight of them fall.

'No. Not in Berlin. I don't where she is. I don't know what happened to her.'

Hanni opened her mouth ready to soothe him with 'I know the agony of that loss; I've felt that too' and then he continued and she realised that she knew nothing.

'But I can guess. The Nazis took her when she was only two. I haven't seen her in four years. I haven't seen any of them in four years.'

The Nazis.

Hanni could feel her throat closing. A shiver ran through her.

All she had wanted to do when she came out of the house was to help heal whatever agony Freddy was suffering, but how could she, if she was tied up in the cause of it?

She tried to slip her hands away from his – not with any thought of abandoning him but because she was convinced he would feel the stain of the guilt branding her and that could only hurt him more – but he held on to her harder the second she tried.

'I am so sorry, Freddy. So very sorry. More than you will ever know.'

His eyes filled with tears that tore at her heart. Hanni tried to swallow, but her mouth was too dry.

His voice hardened, and so did the grip on her fingers. He kept on talking as if he hadn't heard her.

'She was a little girl, but they didn't see that – they saw a *Jew*. They saw a *problem*, a threat to their beloved Reich. They saw the same in my mother, and my father, and my brother too. Not a family, not people, but vermin. Something to be disposed of. They all disappeared, all of them taken out of their lives and out of mine for no other reason except that we were Jewish and Jewish meant wrong.'

Vermin. It was Reiner's word.

His hold on her was so tight, Hanni could feel her finger bones grinding. She couldn't speak. There were no soft platitudes suitable for this. Not that he seemed to want her to talk. Once he began again, his words tumbled out in a torrent.

'I lost them all on the same day in February 1943. I couldn't get to my father and my brother. I watched my sister and my mother marched away and I couldn't do anything to stop that either. I tried to go with them; I wanted to. I had this crazy idea that me being with them would keep them safe, but she wouldn't let me. My mother wouldn't let me. And that's the thing, Hanni: I stayed alive when I shouldn't have done. That's not right. Me being here when they're all gone isn't right. And neither is this, having to go into that woman's house, or into Dora Albrecht's.

Having to speak politely to them when I know that they would cheer if it was me who was dead. Having to pretend to be sorry that someone with more courage than me is killing their husbands. How am I supposed to do that, Hanni? How am I supposed to be sorry for them? How am I supposed to care?'

His eyes were burning. Hanni finally understood the depths of his hatred towards Frau Albrecht and Frau Buchtel, and everything they stood for. She could also see that his mind was racing, that it wouldn't be long before he tried to make a connection between his confused feelings towards the killer and what he had glimpsed of hers.

Which, God help us, surely aren't that different, even if the reason is. Do either of us actually want him to stop?

She couldn't share that thought; she couldn't have this conversation. How could she? How would he get past the impossibility of 'my father was in the SS' that she would have to tell him, that she had almost – as unthinkable as it was now – revealed at the studio? Freddy was Jewish – he couldn't take the weight of her life any more than Natan could. And she couldn't invent a story for him that would make her a better woman than she was. All she could do, until she came up with a way of making her own life right, was remind him who he was now.

'You have to, Freddy. It's your job. Which you are good at, a fact you will remember soon enough. But you're not in any fit state to do that now, so let's concentrate on sorting you out first and worry about the rest of it later.'

She managed to loosen her hands from his, took his elbow instead and began steering him towards the car.

'I'll tell the driver you've been taken ill and need to go home. It might not hurt for you to be on your own for a while, to take some time to rid yourself of these awful wives and knock the case back into a manageable state.'

To her relief, he followed her lead and climbed into the back of the car without arguing.

'What about you? Don't you need a ride somewhere?'

Hanni shook her head. She didn't want to leave him but there was too much danger to be had in staying by his side. One more desperate revelation from him, one plea for help, and she would break and spill all she was. She couldn't begin to imagine the pain and the hatred that would follow that collapse. 'No, it's fine. I'm going to stay around here for a while and photograph some of the houses. We're planning an exhibition about local architecture at the studio.'

She was babbling. If Freddy had looked at her properly, he would have seen her distress and chased after the cause, if only to forget about his. Freddy, however, was barely with her anymore. His head had fallen back; his eyes were closing. Hanni guessed he would barely make it through his front door before the kind of deep sleep gripped him that Talie always fell into when she had had too close a brush with her ghosts. He didn't even manage a goodbye.

Hanni stood alone on the pavement, waiting until the car disappeared out of sight. Then she began to walk along the leafy streets as blindly as Freddy had run down them. Freddy was Jewish. His family had been taken and no doubt murdered, the same as Natan's had been. And the cause of all that agony, of all the blood whose stain still spilled across every block of Berlin, was men devoted to the same evil cause as her father. Hanni didn't know how any of them were meant to make their peace with that.

I shouldn't be around him.

That was the logical outcome of this. If Freddy knew about Reiner, he would hate her the same as he hated Dora Albrecht and Sonja Buchtel, and she would deserve it. That Hanni hated Reiner too, that she wouldn't care if he was the killer's next victim, that she wanted him to be, wouldn't matter. So she shouldn't be around Freddy, and she shouldn't add to his burden.

Which would be simpler to do if I didn't think I could have loved him. If I didn't think, perhaps, he could have loved me too.

Within seconds of that realisation hitting her, Hanni was the one on her knees clutching the wall. It made no difference. Whatever Hanni had seen in Freddy's face at the studio, whatever bond she was sure had begun to build between them, it would wither the moment Hanni Winter became Hannelore Foss.

Which I would have to do.

She had already dismissed a relationship with Natan because she couldn't base it on a lie; it would be unforgiveable, impossible, to spin that lie around Freddy.

So I won't.

Hanni stood up and wiped her eyes. She had to stop hiding from what had to be done for the sake of an easy life. She hadn't earned that yet. So she had to find a way to deal with her father that wouldn't bring harm to anyone else. And she had to disentangle herself from Natan and from the studio. She didn't have a solution to the first problem yet, but the second was easier, and Freddy had, albeit unknowingly, given her the route to achieving it: using her photography skills to help investigate crime scenes. It was work Hanni already sensed she was good at, it was fascinating and whatever it paid would help her to financially find her own feet.

Except achieving all that will take a courage you don't have.

The voice that said that wasn't hers, it was Reiner's, with the same sneer in it that had shot through it when he had thrown *how hard it must be to be you* at her on the platform at Theresienstadt. Hanni couldn't listen to that voice. She couldn't carry on being the girl who took the safest way out. What she could do was what she had to: make difficult choices, even if that meant keeping her relationship with Freddy at a safely professional distance.

Until I make things right and then I don't have to keep him away from me anymore.

She pushed that thought away. There were no guarantees Freddy would ever make peace with her past even if she did what she had promised herself she would do in 1945 and brought Reiner to justice. And she couldn't make Freddy her only reason for doing that. That promise belonged to Jannick and Ezra and the men in the mines and all the lost souls sent on the trains out of Theresienstadt.

Hanni picked up her bag and set off down the road again, her heart bruised but still holding, more worried about Freddy than she was about herself. Doing her best to ignore the voice in her head that was all too familiar, that wouldn't stop whispering *coward.*

CHAPTER 10

23–30 JANUARY 1947

'We have a nickname for your father in here – we call him *The Ringmaster*. Do you want to know why? Because no one is more skilled than Reiner Foss at putting on a show, and he's really quite the artist with a whip.'

Freddy's revelations about the fate of his family – and Hanni's realisation that she could no longer delay dealing with her own – had brought Reiner crashing back. Everything Hanni had seen or suspected, everything she had overheard and had been told about her father reared back, with all its ugliness intact. The information that the town had given him a nickname – and had chosen one that was so chillingly fitting – had come from Jannick. He had shared it, and made horrible sense of it, on the day that he had led Hanni through the back alleys of Theresienstadt in March 1944.

'Taking you to any part of Theresienstadt is a risk, but I'll show you what I can. What you'll see, however, is only a fraction of the whole story, and what you won't see is worse.'

'What do you mean?'

Nothing could have prepared her for the answer Jannick gave.

'That the town has two parts. There's where we are now, which is where, for want of a better word, all the people who've been despatched here "live", and then, outside the walls, there's the part that we call the Little Fortress. That's a hellhole, a maze of underground punishment cells surrounded by a moat that stinks to the heavens. Very few people come out of there, and the ones that do are damaged beyond repair. I can't take you to it, although it would tell you a lot that you need to know, especially about your father. He has his hands in both sides. In this part, he's all about his "embellishments". So far, he's put in a bank when none of us have any money and a café that's a façade. It presumably makes sense to him, but none of us know what they mean. The Little Fortress, however, is different. Everyone understands what it is he does in that place: he's its star performer. Rumour has it that when he puts his mind to it in there, he can take the skin off a man's back in three strokes.'

Hanni had stopped in her tracks and been violently sick when Jannick told her that, which had finally stopped him talking. He hadn't said anything else about Reiner, but the image of her father with a whip in his hand had never left her since. Whenever she pictured him raising its leather fall above some blood-soaked body, he was smiling. His smile haunted her as much as the whip. The way he could switch it on and off, how charming it was, and how hollow.

The Red Cross delegation who had visited the town a few months later in June 1944 to check that the Germans were 'dealing kindly' with the Jews who lived in it hadn't, however, seen the Reiner she saw. They had applauded the bank and the café and all the *embellishments*, which it turned out had been built for their benefit. They hadn't looked beyond the fresh paint or their guide's smile: all they had seen was the show. The delegation had left Theresienstadt happy and impressed and without any of the fears for its Jewish population which had prompted their visit, exactly as they were meant to do. So Reiner the Ringmaster was a perfect description. The man in control, the man conducting the rhythm of everyone's lives.

Which he – or the fear of him – is still doing.

Hanni had shut herself away from the world for almost a week after the visit to Sonja Buchtel, determined to make Reiner's voice stop. She hadn't contacted Freddy, although she was desperate to. She hadn't contacted Natan, beyond telling him she was too sick to come into work. Both men needed honesty from her, and she couldn't offer that until she had dealt honestly with her father. She had, therefore, constructed a plan.

One quick phone call to Matz had established that she was, as Freddy had promised, now officially retained as a freelance photographer by the Kreuzberg police. The rate for that, while not a fortune, was higher than anything Natan could offer and would still give her the time for other commissions. Step one, financial independence from the Stein Studio – and perhaps a step closer to owning one of her own – was therefore in place.

Next, she focused on step two: making herself a new home away from the lodging house which Natan had found for her. She found that in a quiet block in Blücherstraße, a short walk away across the canal. The room was pleasant and, more importantly, it came with a space in the basement the landlady said she could turn into a darkroom. It was also close enough to the friends she had found, and hoped to keep, to make leaving everything that had spelled security for the last eighteen months a little more bearable.

It was the third step which mattered most, however, which would allow her to pay her debt to Natan and tell him the truth, and free her to be properly herself with Freddy. The third step in the plan was Reiner.

The 'why' behind that step was simple. Denouncing him was an atonement, a restitution. Something she could offer both Natan and Freddy to prove, or so she hoped, that she might be flawed, and she might not have been as brave as she should have been, but she wasn't the beast that her father was. She had no idea if that offering would work. It didn't matter. The 'why' therefore was simple. It was the 'how' that had kept her awake long into the night. Her first thought had been to involve Oli. According to

Freddy, the boy had a way into all the city's nooks and crannies and no fear of going digging in them. That, however, was the problem: Oli boasted that he owed loyalty to no one, but, if he was anyone's, he was Freddy's. Oli, therefore, wasn't an option.

Step three was full of pitfalls. It had also faltered too often before. In the end, Hanni decided that the only thing she could do if her nerve wasn't going to fail again was to stop trying to work out every stage of it and jump in. She went back, therefore, to the last spot where she had seen her father: to Lietzenseeufer and the British who now ran the area. She retraced her steps from the station at Sophie-Charlotte-Platz, trying not to let its echoes bury her. Trying to convince herself that this wouldn't be a repeat of her failed attempt to denounce Reiner to the Russians.

The Americans and the British, or so it seemed from the newspaper reports, were more approachable when it came to uncovering war criminals. Although the main Nuremberg Trials were over, they hadn't abandoned their efforts to bring other Nazis to justice. Proceedings had begun against a number of doctors charged with carrying out brutal medical experiments in the camps, including Dachau, and, once that trial was done, the promise was that Auschwitz would be next. Natan had no more faith in those than he had respect for the first set of verdicts at Nuremberg, but Hanni had refused to be cynical and give up. If she didn't believe in the process of justice, what was the alternative?

Finding a way to slip Reiner's name to the killer?

That thought hadn't left her, although she did her best to keep it at arm's-length. Murder was her father's way of doing things, not hers. She had set off for Lietzenseeufer, therefore, determined to believe that honesty would bring rewards. She had blocked out the niggling voice that was still whispering *coward* in her head.

I am finally doing the right thing. I am standing up; I am being brave.

So surely her plan had to work?

. . .

Reiner wasn't there.

Hanni stood on a corner, watching the house as he had once done, wishing she had learned the lesson from when she went looking for Ezra, so certain he would be at the studio simply because she wanted him to be. There was life at the villa – it wasn't closed up or empty – but there was no trace of Reiner in it. Instead of her father, a steady stream of uniformed men and women hurried in and out, or dawdled in the front garden, hunched over their carefully cupped cigarettes.

Hanni had no idea how to approach them. If the house had still been a family home, then she could have knocked on the door, posed as a photographer with an interest in the local area and ferreted out what the occupants knew of its history. Walking up to a building full of soldiers, however, and asking questions about a missing Nazi felt ridiculously clumsy. Hanni had never had any dealings with the British authorities; beyond the first days crawling out of the war, she had had no close dealings with the Allied powers at all. She had no way of gauging how sensitive the British were to inquisitive strangers. And she couldn't shake the feeling that Reiner would appear out of the building the moment she stepped into the spotlight and pounce on her first.

I can't alert anyone I don't know that I'm looking for him. And I can't hand him over if I don't know where he is.

What she needed was information. The corner, however, was no place to linger while she worked out how to get that. The January cold was biting; her feet and fingers were numb. Hanni's hand strayed to her camera bag. If it had been summer, she would have wandered over to the park by the lake, hung round the beer garden and got out her Leica. A photographer always made people curious and willing to talk. Unfortunately, the wind blowing across the grey water was a vicious one and the park was ice-edged and deserted.

But my instinct to find an accommodating group is the right one. I just need to find a comfier setting to do it in.

Having something definite to do warmed Hanni into action.

She rubbed her fingers back to life and began to explore Masure-nallee – the thoroughfare connecting Lietzenseeufer with the main British military hub twenty minutes' walk away at Reich-skanzlerplatz – searching for a café that looked like it would attract the ranks not the officers.

The one she eventually went into wasn't exactly comfy: it was a small and overheated space, tightly packed with limply covered tables and indelibly perfumed with the scent of burned coffee. It was, however, according to the owner, the favourite place for the local secretaries to avoid their bosses and fill up on gossip. By the time the lunch crowd arrived, Hanni had persuaded the owner to brush up the photography skills he claimed he had when she told him her profession and was showing him how to take wide-angled shots. That activity – as she had hoped it would – immediately made her the centre of attention. Ten minutes of rather chaotic posing later, and Hanni was one of the crowd, sat at a table surrounded by sticky plates and ashtrays and all the chatter she needed.

'I didn't expect you to speak the language so fluently.'

Hanni's flattery was genuine. Her schoolgirl English had been no match for the British girls who had quickly, and noisily, swarmed round her. It had been quite a relief when they had switched as one into an oddly overenunciated German rather than letting her carry on floundering.

'Being able to talk to the locals, and read their testimonies, is a condition of entry to the service here, darling, for secretaries at our level anyway. And most of us learned it years ago because we have a family connection to Germany, a detail which didn't make the war any easier.'

The speaker – whose copper hair Hanni wished she could capture in all its colourful glory – paused and lit another cigarette. When she looked up again, Hanni caught a sadness in the girl's eyes she had never expected to encounter on the winning side.

'Anyway, that's all old news now and no use crying over it. If you're doing a feature on women working in the military, you should probably come and see where we do it.'

This was it, her way in.

Hanni tried to keep her smile and her tone casual.

'That would be very helpful – it would be great to get some pictures in an office. I don't suppose any of you work at the lemon-painted villa down the road, do you? It would make such a good backdrop. I used to know the family who lived there, a little anyway, a long time ago before the war. I was pleased to see it hadn't been damaged.'

'We do.' A brunette at the next table stuck out her hand, introduced herself as Megs and nodded to the three girls sitting with her. 'We all work there. You're right, it is very lovely, although, to be honest, if you're talking about damage, we've probably dinged it up a bit inside. Did you say you knew the family? Does that mean you know Emil Foss?'

Emil? Hanni wracked her brains, but she couldn't think of even the remotest relative with that name. She needed, however, to keep the conversation going, so she agreed that she did.

Megs whistled. 'That's quite some story, isn't it?'

All the tables had quietened. Hanni tried to shrug as if she was interested but not overly so; her shoulders, however, had stiffened. There had never been an Emil Foss in the past. If there was one now, she could think of only one man it could be: Reiner, reinventing himself with an arrogance that was breath-taking.

'I'm not sure that I do know it, or not all of it.'

Megs sat back, crossed her ankles and let her audience settle.

'Okay, well let's pop aside for a moment the fact that most of the women in the office would throw their hats at the dashing Herr Emil if they had half a chance and quiz you about him later. Does the "not all of it" include the brother?'

Hanni shook her head, trying not to focus on *dashing*, her skin prickling at *brother* and unsure how to respond to either. Luckily, Megs was more than happy to rattle on uninterrupted.

'Reiner Foss, the older one. Apparently he was quite the evil

Nazi. He ran a labour camp somewhere in Bohemia and he was involved with the abuses at Theresienstadt – the town that was meant to be a paradise for the old but turned out to be a processing centre for the ovens. Reiner Foss is on everyone's chase list now. And poor Emil knew nothing. He was in Switzerland during the war – he'd been there for years apparently and couldn't uproot his life to return to Germany when it broke out. Well, I'm sure you can imagine the shock when he did make it back and discovered his whole family had turned into ardent SS supporters. That's why he gave the villa over to us to use as offices – when he found out the truth, he didn't want to be tainted by it.'

Nothing felt solid anymore. Not her body, not the chair, not the table. Hanni blinked to stop Megs' face blurring.

'Goodness, that's terrible. I didn't know. And did you say the whole family were involved?'

Megs leaned forward, her blue eyes sparkling. 'That's what makes it even more of a scandal. The wife was your standard SS-issue one by all accounts, so no surprises there, but, according to what Emil uncovered, the daughter was as big of a monster as Daddy. Apparently she was a photographer and was talented enough for Goebbels to spot her. Emil was devastated when he discovered that – who wouldn't be? He left behind a cute little niece and came back to discover that she'd turned into one of that old goat's protégées.' Megs gave a shudder that her audience copied. 'I mean, that's horrible enough. But even worse – or so the story goes – she used to like to go into Theresienstadt and take pictures of the prisoners getting tortured. How awful is that?'

Hanni sat perfectly still. One move and she would start shaking; one word and she would be sick.

Megs tapped the ash off her cigarette and began gathering up her belongings.

'Anyway, she's as big a catch as he is, probably more so. There's hardly been any women charged with war crimes, although there were plenty involved. The authorities would make such an example out of her if they could.'

Hanni swallowed. She couldn't trust her voice not to crack, but she had to say something.

'How did Emil find out, about his brother and the daughter's activities, I mean?'

Megs shrugged. 'Does it matter? Probably from some of the survivors, or maybe from SS prisoners trying to barter information for freedom, or through the Red Cross. He's very reluctant to talk about it now the whole thing is out there, which is hardly surprising.'

He's very reluctant to talk, but he's made sure everyone knows his version. Is there a better way to turn lies into truth?

The lunch hour was ending – the café was emptying. Megs began collecting up the scattered contents of her purse; the copper-haired girl Hanni had spoken to first began pulling on her coat. She turned back to Hanni as she headed for the door.

'Do you want to come with us? You said your name was Hanni, didn't you? Hanni Winter? I can do the paperwork to get you into the villa if you like.'

The villa was the last place Hanni wanted to be. She managed, however, to look disappointed.

'That would have been great, but I'm out of time now today. Maybe I could come back tomorrow?'

The girl handed over a card with an office phone number on it and left, with Megs following close behind her.

'Is he still around? Emil, I mean?'

The strain of asking, the strain of hoping that the answer would be *no* drained all the life from her voice.

Megs stopped in the doorway. Her stare was suddenly far more scrutinising than Hanni wanted it to be.

'You sound like you'd rather he wasn't, which would make you unique around here. But, yes, he's very much around and very much in demand. With the background he has in education, and his clean war record, we were lucky to keep him with us and away from the Americans. He works at the Control Commission at Fehrbelliner Platz now, setting up schools. I'm sure Caro – the redhead – could get you a phone number for him there if you want it.' Megs paused and the frown which had been hovering over her face since Hanni had asked how Emil knew about the daughter finally took root. 'Forgive me, but it rather sounded like it's him you're actually after, not us military women.'

'No, not at all.'

It wasn't easy with everything that she'd heard, but Hanni forced some energy back into her voice.

'It was what you said, about this being "some story". You were right, but I do the photographs not the words. I might pass it on, that's all.'

The calls to 'hurry it up' from the girls waiting on the pavement pulled Megs away without any more questions. Hanni didn't follow them. She never wanted to see any of them again. They thought that her father was dashing, they felt sorry for him having to live under the shadow of such a terrible family.

I need to focus on my future and that will take a little reinventing.

The memory made her shiver far more than the draughts blowing in through the open doorway. Reiner had done more than a little reinventing: he had created a whole new character for himself and walked right back wearing it into a position of power. More than that, he had completely whitewashed himself and blackened her.

And I gave him the ammunition to do it.

What would Megs say if she knew that 'she was talented enough for Goebbels to spot her' was true? What would she say if she knew Hanni had let Goebbels take her under his wing? Hanni's stomach heaved. She knew how badly her defence – 'I was seventeen, I only wanted to take photographs and I wanted my father to be proud of me' – would fall. She had known it was wrong when she did it; she wasn't going to pretend anything different now. The prize had been a place to perfect her photography skills at Berlin's

Technische Hochschule; the price had been accepting Goebbels as her patron. He had seen her work at a competition run by the Bund Deutscher Mädel at which – after seven years of photography lessons paid for by her grandmother – Hanni had shone. It didn't matter that she never saw Goebbels again after that day. Or that she had never been allowed to work as a professional in the field that she loved – 'good German girls from good Party families', as her father explained to her more than once, didn't pursue careers with their cameras; they took family snaps. Mentioning that Hitler's favourite photographer – Leni Riefenstahl – was female had almost got all Hanni's equipment destroyed.

It also didn't matter that she had never taken photographs of torture or of anything else in Theresienstadt for her own pleasure. She hadn't yet made those images public or used them in the way that she wanted to – to denounce her father and the horrors he had presided over. Fear of what had happened to the young guard and Jannick had made her too cautious yet to do that. What mattered was that there was a kernel of truth in the story, and Reiner had fed that and sown it out in the world.

He's gone on the attack. If I step forward, it's not him who becomes the sacrifice, it's me.

Who would believe her story now – that there had never been an Emil, that there had only ever been Reiner – when wicked Hannelore and her evil father offered a better tale? When there was enough substance in his portrayal of her to twist and make it convincing. Hanni couldn't pretend that wasn't frightening, that it didn't make her want to run.

She sat in the café until the afternoon's light was gone. Trying to make herself braver. Trying to work out a new plan. Trying to persuade herself that the truth always came out and that she, not her father, would be believed if she stepped forward. That the photographs she had taken would be seen as proof of his wrong-doing if she showed them, not of hers.

I still have to do what I set out to do. He hasn't gone quietly away.

He's up to something or why go to all the effort he's made to turn himself into someone new?

Never mind her promise to Jannick to get Theresienstadt's story out, or her promise to herself to make redress for all the wrongs she had lived beside, or to tell the truth to Natan and Freddy. They all mattered as much as they ever did, but it was 'education' that wouldn't stop pricking. Reiner's change of identity to keep himself alive was one that she could follow, but why pretend an interest in education? He had no background in that, so why choose it? The thought of his malign influence extending over schools, infiltrating what was taught to young children and shaping their impressionable minds, was a terrifying one.

Fear for myself can't be the winner here.

It was a brave thought; she really wanted to follow it. But Reiner was no longer a distant bogeyman. He had climbed out of his past with the same mix of ferocity and charm that had given him the upper hand then and he had edged closer to her than she had imagined: he worked in the building where Buchtel had worked.

He will know I've come looking for him. I've crossed back into his life and he will sense me there.

She couldn't shake the feeling. Or the certainty creeping in the chill round her neck that he would, one day very soon, come looking for her.

'So, this is where you ran to.'

It was Reiner, and it wasn't. He had kept the longer hair and the beard he had been sporting when he came back to Berlin, although that was closely trimmed now. He had gained a little weight, enough to soften his features, not coarsen him. His dark grey coat was well cut, his white collar was spotless. Hanni could understand *dashing*.

'Back to the old Jew photographer. I should have guessed you'd come here when you weren't at the house, rather than starting up on your own. You never were blessed with much courage.'

And it was Reiner again, the whip still in his voice if not in his hand.

Hanni put down the receipts she had been sorting when he came into the studio before her shaking fingers made them rustle and stayed silent as Reiner continued. In a strange kind of way, it was a relief that the waiting for him to find her was done.

'Ezra Stein. Is he still here? That would be quite a feat of survival. Does he still think that I'm a "self-satisfied bastard" like he did at the Adlon? Don't frown – I heard him cursing me on the way out. Well, he paid for that little bon mot, or this place did.'

The thugs who follow Adolf Hitler.

Grandma Alice had said that with such fury when she had looked at the wreck of the studio and Hanni had asked her who was to blame. Hanni doubted that she had suspected Reiner of having a hand in it, despite the episode on the balcony. She was glad of that: she missed her grandmother terribly, but it was a blessing that she had missed the worst of what her son had become.

He's been hurting the people I care about since I was ten years old and he will never stop, unless I stop him first.

Hanni gripped the counter and refused to let the images of the dripping paint and the broken glass engulf her. She hadn't reacted when Reiner had walked into the studio – although her heart had nearly exploded – and she was not going to react now.

'Herr Stein is dead. His son runs things here.'

Her flat tone simply made Reiner smile.

'His son? Well, isn't he the lucky one, inheriting the empire? And does he know about you, this son? Or did *Hanni Winter* rise like a phoenix untouched by the past?'

The mocking tone: she had remembered his smile but forgotten that. Now it made her bones ache. She stayed behind the counter, watching him pick up and put down the studio's small set of display photographs as if they were crawling with lice. She doubted it mattered what she said next – whatever he had planned for her was already planned – but she wasn't going to go down meekly.

'What do you want Natan to know about me, *Emil*? That I managed to escape from a brute and restart my life, or the lies that you've been spinning about the innocent brother and his murdering family?'

Her words bounced off him as if his overcoat was steel-plated.

'I don't care. I assume that you haven't told him a thing, or at least nothing honest, or you wouldn't be working here. And I doubt that you want him to know my version in case he marches you straight off to the Allies. Do you want to test that? Shall I call for him?'

He was treating her like prey, as if tormenting her was a pleasure. Hanni refused to let him see how much that frightened her.

'He's not here.'

But he would be, and soon, and Reiner couldn't be allowed to play with him too. Hanni wanted her father gone so badly she could have thrown him through the door. But there were, however, questions she needed to ask, about what Reiner had done, and about what he was intending to do next, even if she couldn't afford to linger over them.

'How did you do it? How did you convince everyone that you were Emil?'

Reiner smiled again. Hanni knew that he had been waiting for her to ask and was looking forward to telling her.

'Very easily. You know what it was like here in 1945: so many people displaced with no papers, so many lives lost with no records. Anyone with a brain could be anyone they wanted to be, and there was no one to contradict the identity I chose. The neighbours who knew us had packed up and gone. I paid the right amount of people to come forward and "remember" Emil. I replayed our revised family history with the right amount of hesitation and slathered every "difficult discovery" in regret. Who wouldn't believe such a heartfelt, horror-filled story? The only potential flaw in the web, of course, was you, so I added in a few more details and there you were, dealt with. It was all ticking smoothly along, and then up you pop, snapping your pictures and pretending you weren't actually looking for me. Why did you bother, Hannelore. Can I guess? Has your conscience been biting again? Did you plan to denounce me?'

His smirk as much as his words told her there was no point in lying. Not that she had any desire – or time – to do so.

'Yes.'

His face hardened back into Reiner's, which helped her swallow the fear and focus on the memories.

'It's what you deserve. You should have been put on trial long ago. For the mines at Leitmeritz. For all those who rotted to death in Theresienstadt or were packed onto trains and reduced to ashes at Auschwitz and Dachau and Treblinka. I've seen the numbers now, or the first guess at them. There were thousands at the work camp – they're still digging up the bodies. And tens of thousands dead in the town or shipped from there to the gas chambers. Your signature must be on the papers; survivors must know you. You deserve to pay for all of it.'

It was the longest, most hate-filled speech she had ever made to him. It was a waste of breath.

Reiner sighed. 'Oh Hannelore, are we really doing this again? You flinging allegations around really is a bit rich. Maybe my memory has failed me, so do correct me if I'm wrong, but wasn't your life then rather a good one? I don't remember you complaining when you were all safely tucked up in Bohemia away from the shortages and the bombing raids decimating Berlin. And again forgive me if I'm mistaken, but didn't you photograph Theresienstadt? Didn't you attend concerts and plays there? And didn't you know all about my job, or wasn't that what you and that dreadful little Jannick man spent your time talking about?'

He waved a hand as Hanni opened her mouth to fight back. 'Spare me your indignation. I know all about you and I know all about him. And as for my signature and survivors. Where is that?

Where are they? What can you prove of any of it? Where is my name on the testimonies, or on the indictment lists? Which camps list me as their commandant?'

He paused but what could she say? *You were too clever to step out onto the main stage. You made sure that everyone who could put you there is gone.*

'There will be something – there is always something. I have…' She stopped. Reiner's face was unreadable.

'What do you have, Hannelore? Photographs? So what. That was Reiner. I am Emil. All that photographs prove is that you were there to take them.'

She stared at him, her mind racing, unable to find a rebuttal to fling back.

Reiner brushed off his leather gloves. 'Good girl, now you are with me. You brought this unfortunate meeting on yourself, you know, with your snooping. I have no interest in you, as long as you have no interest in me. I told you that a long time ago. What I do have, however, is contacts – which you must have guessed since I knew all about your little trip to the café. There are a lot of people in Berlin who live on the edge of the law, who are desperate to earn a little cash. I collect them, and I pay them well to keep me well informed. I have a very nice life now, Hannelore, and I don't mind if you have one too. I don't want to stir the past up, but I could, and I could very easily make sure that you don't have a future. So, be warned. Leave me alone and I'll return the courtesy. Come after me and it won't be me staring at a prison cell and a noose.'

She knew that he meant it. What he had said was terrifying, but there was no malice in his voice. Reiner had spoken with the certainty that he would do as he promised, and that she would do as she was told. And he hadn't finished with her yet.

'And if you don't have a care for your own safety, have a care for the people around you. I don't know who is key in your life, but I will. I imagine this Natan matters; I imagine there are others. Remember the guard, Hannelore. Remember Jannick and dear old Ezra. I can make people disappear with very little effort – you of all people should know that.'

And he meant that too. Hanni held on tight to the cabinet as the world threatened to buckle beneath her. There would be Natan and then there would be Freddy and God knows who else and, if he came for her, he would come for her last.

Everyone I love will become his hostage.

'I hate you.'

It was heartfelt and it was pointless.

Reiner shrugged. 'I don't care.'

There was nothing left for her to say. Reiner was halfway out of the door before she suddenly remembered that there was.

'Why education? Why did you tell the British that you had a background in that?'

The smile he bestowed on her wasn't hollow anymore.

'Hearts and minds, Hannelore, hearts and minds. Once you have those, the cause might be sidelined for a little while, but it is never ever lost.'

CHAPTER 11

2 FEBRUARY 1947

He had let his feelings get the better of him and that, as he had long ago learned, was his family's biggest sin.

'Control yourself, Gerhard. Men in this family do not cry. They do not show weakness. They learn the value of self-discipline and self-respect. Your brother understood that – why can't you?'

For years, Gerhard had been unable to offer his father an answer to that question which didn't lead to a beating or a locked room. For years, he had been, in his father's words, 'too soft to be a proper man'. That was a cruelty which his mother had echoed, which had wormed its way through him until he began to believe that 'soft' and 'useless' was all that he was.

In the end, it was the numbers, which nobody cared he was good at, that had saved him. Multiplying, dividing. Counting them up, counting them down. Using their rhythm to calm the tears that nobody listened to; using the balance they brought as a shield against the world. Once Gerhard had learned his counting tricks, he was able to thicken his skin against the pain of never being good enough, of never being his dead brother. He was able to keep his father's hands, if not his tongue, off him. He had held himself steady for years like that, except today he had failed and now he was paying.

He lurched along Teutonenstraße, his body on fire. The feeling frightened him. He knew there was no logical reason for it – the day wasn't warm, he wasn't overdressed. He knew the sensations gripping him weren't rational ones, but he hadn't been able to find rational since he had beaten up his mother.

The violence that had erupted and thrown him out of line had been her fault, he knew that. She had goaded him; she had pushed him. He had warned her not to do it, but she hadn't listened.

When has she ever listened?

He shook his head, but it wouldn't clear. It was too full of her. His whole body was too full of her. There was more blood pumping through his veins than they could comfortably hold. There was a pulse throbbing at the side of his eye, and a band tightening round his forehead. He could hear his breath coming in great spluttering gasps. The sound was disgusting, like an animal.

I should have been better prepared for her.

He had grown complacent; he hadn't picked up the warning signs. Gerhard's meetings with his mother had followed the same pattern since he had been discharged from the army and he had assumed that they always would. One hour of politeness, one Sunday a month. No affection on either side, no interest. Gerhard went to the family home whose every memory he hated in order to establish whether or not his mother was still alive. She requested his presence to prove to the neighbours that she was a good mother.

It was always the same routine, outside and in. He knocked. She let him stand on the doorstep for a full three minutes to make sure that the women she never allowed over the threshold saw that he was there. She let him inside without a word. He sat on an armchair; she looked down on him from the sofa. They shared one pot of tea; they each ate one slice of seed cake whose sawdust texture was as constant as the rest. Information about nothing that mattered was exchanged until Gerhard left. Nothing had disturbed the meeting's dry misery before.

Until today. Today, his mother had dragged out her dusty photograph albums and pushed the afternoon from the polite tone he could manage to the personal one he couldn't. That was when he should have left, when he realised that she wasn't going to stick to the rules. Instead, he had broken over twenty-five years of hard-won lessons and he had lost his self-control.

There was sweat on his upper lip; there was sweat running into his eyes. His body felt as if it was loosening, breaking down. Gerhard tried to fight back. He began running his numbers the way he had tried to when she had started baiting him. The index cards he had filed on Friday and their breakdown across the different army ranks. The records that were still uncounted, figures which ran into six and seven places, which he could normally split into the women's and the men's totals without missing a beat. He still couldn't grab hold of anything. His head was the same jumble it had been half an hour ago, disconnected digits flying in and out. The muddle was frightening.

He had spotted the red leather binders spread out across the dining-room table the moment he walked into the stuffy room, but he had been too slow to make sense of them. By the time that he did, his mother had unleashed an unexpected wave of tears that stuck him to the faded carpet like glue. Then she had wheedled and sniffed and droned on about anniversaries and her fear of forgetting them, and somehow he had been sitting where he always sat, staring at faces he had no wish to see.

His father first, in his cavalry uniform. His mother's favourite snap of him. Chin up, shoulders back; the Iron Cross he had won for bravery in the first war stuck front and centre on his chest. The proud soldier in his element, setting the standard for his sons to follow.

His sister Minnie next, resplendent in a white frilly dress and elaborately bouncing curls. The family beauty bound one day to make a great marriage.

And then his elder brother Stefan, the golden son, a miniature copy of his father in his cadet uniform. The two of them captured on film at seven and nine and destined to never get any older. Barely remembered by Gerhard beyond vague shapes and the fleeting warmth of small hands holding his. Both of them dead in the influenza epidemic of 1919 when he was six. Both of them 'angels' enshrined forever in the bitterness of 'and everything you are not'.

If his mother had only stayed with that refrain perhaps they could both have got through the hour. It wasn't as if it was a new complaint: Gerhard might prize his numerical skills, but he had lost count long ago of the times he had heard it, repeated by both his parents as a prelude to a punishment for the crime – as far as he could understand it – of being alive when his brother and sister weren't. It was, however, 'darling Stefan's' birthday – a fact that Gerhard had totally overlooked, and why wouldn't he, given that it was nearly thirty years since Stefan had actually been around to celebrate it – and that had loosened his mother's nasty old tongue.

'He wouldn't have made such an utter shambles of things' had been her opening gambit. Closely followed by 'he would have been a hero, not an embarrassment' and 'he was so like your father: the two of them both understood the meaning of honour, a concept that appears to have utterly passed you by'.

Honour.

That was the word which had brought the red mist down. Which had left him struggling for breath. Not that his mother had noticed his distress. Not that she had ever noticed anything about him at all, not when there were ghosts to mourn who she loved far better than she loved the living.

Gerhard had managed to keep hold of his temper. And he had warned her, he had given her the chance not to set them on the wrong road. He had said 'Mother don't' perfectly clearly. She had carried on anyway.

'Your father's family, and mine, have always dedicated their lives to the military. We have offered a tradition of service to our country that ran on in an unbroken line.'

A tradition of service. Once upon a time, when Gerhard had been a very small boy, those words had thrilled him. They had been a sign that his favourite stories were about to begin. The ones where his father recounted his adventures – and those of Gerhard's grandfathers before him – in the Imperial Army. Those stories had been wonderful things. Each one had been filled with magical words he hadn't understood but had fallen in love with, like *brotherhood,* and with descriptions of *oaths* that were taken by *the righteous and the dutiful,* by soldiers whose only aim in life was to follow the rules of the military code they had sworn to live and die by, to *help and defend and heal.* The German Army his father had believed in was filled with saints. Gerhard had sat on the rug beside Stefan with his mouth open in awe, while visions of white-clad crusaders whirled past his mesmerised eyes. Both brothers had known exactly what the future held, and they were ready – no, eager – to embrace all the glory that future would bring.

Except that future had never arrived.

The influenza had killed Stefan and left Gerhard with hearing issues and a tendency to weakness in muscles that never quite made the change from skinny to thick. The stories had stopped. *We have always dedicated our lives to the military* wasn't followed by tales of quests and sacrifice anymore. *Unbroken line* no longer had a space after it for Gerhard's name. It led instead into 'until you' and beatings laced through with 'this will end when you learn to live an honourable life'.

Gerhard had stopped being a son when his brother died. He had become a disappointment; he had become the 'wrong one'. Nothing he did was right. Everything he achieved was pointless. Sons of military families joined the military. Sons of military families didn't waste their days in classrooms. Being the first of the Bayers to win a place to read law at the great Humboldt University wasn't an honour.

Honour.

Back she had come to that word, again and again. She kept flinging it, even though Gerhard had told her that he understood it far more than she ever would and had warned her a second and a third time to stop. On and on she had gone. University wasn't an honour. Losing the commission he had finally managed to secure in 1943 when the army 'ran out of real men' was the very opposite of an honour. She had picked up steam and she wouldn't stop.

So Gerhard had hit her. Hard. And it had felt so good to see her finally look at him with fear and not with disgust that he had hit her again. With his fist this time and harder. With enough blows to put her on the floor, to split her stupid mouth open and leave it bleeding. To render her finally silent.

He had left the house when that was done, expecting to feel better about his victory, but he hadn't. After so many tightly controlled years, the unstoppable rush of emotion his actions had unleashed was too much.

He was still seesawing between disgust at what he had done and elation that he had finally done it when somebody shouted and a car swerved so close to him that its tyres squealed. Gerhard stumbled to a stop. He hadn't noticed the end of the pavement; he hadn't noticed the road. There were people staring at him, nudging each other. The shock of exposure sobered him. It was clear that his emotions were spiralling. It was equally clear that he could not be near people until his edges were once more tightly in place.

Gerhard crossed carefully over to the quieter side of the road, away from the watchers, found a handkerchief and wiped his face. He clenched and unclenched his fingers and gave his tight shoulders a shake. He had intended to do as he always did after a visit to his mother: to walk back to his neat room in Glocken-straβe and read; to drink one small beer in a pub first to wash away the taste of her. This was not, however, a normal day and it could not, therefore, follow normal routines. His usual route would be busy with Sunday-afternoon strollers, the pub would be filled with Sunday-afternoon idlers. He could not afford to encounter any of those in his current raw state. What he needed to do was regroup. To find a place of peace before he had to deal with the streets.

He put his handkerchief away and looked around him. His blind wanderings had taken him to the fringes of Schlactensee and the edges of Grunewald's far-stretching forest. The lake would be too lively: it was chilly near the water, but there were enough early-spring flowers and hints of the sun to tempt out the walkers. The forest, however, would be colder and less likely to attract crowds. The forest would welcome him; it would offer him somewhere to sit and take stock.

Gerhard slipped inside the dark shade of the trees and felt his chest loosen. Five minutes. If he was in the right place, all he would need was five minutes to pull back the day.

It was beautifully silent. There was so little light, he could have been in a cave. He moved further in, letting his fevered mind settle into the solitude. And then – in a burst so sweet he could taste it – the numbers came back. His body stopped burning. His heart eased. Another few cycles up and down the records and his mind was his own again.

Gerhard stopped walking and leaned against a tree's solid bulk, letting the churn of feelings that had gripped him form into the cold and contained anger he was far more comfortable with. The anger he knew how to ride and how to release.

Now that he was safe inside the forest, the afternoon's events took on the logic they had been missing. Gerhard could see his explosion for what it was: a natural progression from the cruelties that had led up to it. His mother had failed to protect him as a child, and she had taunted him as a man. She had refused to accept that the stance he had taken during the war had followed directly from the lessons his father had taught him. That he had been behaving as he had always been told to do – as a Bayer, putting the honour of the army and its military codes above everything. All that she had heard was that he wasn't an officer anymore. All that she had heard was disgrace.

Because she is ignorant, and she is vicious, and now she is dealt with.

Gerhard's whole body lightened. He didn't need to fight the rage she had stirred up in him; he could use it. He could put it to work. He imagined telling her 'it was you who inspired me' and almost smiled. As if he would give her credit for anything.

He checked his watch – exactly five minutes had been all that was needed. There was a great deal of comfort in that. He straightened up and dusted himself off and picked a path that would take him out of the forest. One beer, he would allow himself that. He deserved to have that. And he didn't need to worry about watchers anymore now that he was steady.

He emerged out of the trees ready to continue his walk home, doubling back on himself around the lakeshore to take a quicker route and crossing a small patch of parkland where couples and family groups were wandering. No one took any notice of him; he didn't expect anyone to.

He walked on, imagining the taste of the hops, thinking about the book waiting for him in his room; the plans he would start making tomorrow. He was so lost in thought, he almost bumped into a noisy mix of generations whose jumble of ages and speeds was cluttering the path. They bowed, smiled apologies without looking at him, moved on.

Gerhard, however, stopped. There was something familiar about the tall man bringing up the rear. As the man bent to speak to the woman whose arm he was holding, Gerhard finally slotted him into place. He had been in the internment camp near Hanover where Gerhard had been so unjustly sent in 1945. The camp where every German who was held there – no matter whether they had served out the war in the SS or in the Gestapo or were rank-and-file soldiers or bemused civil servants – had been branded as Nazi mass murderers and treated without any pretence of respect.

Gerhard stared after the man who was busy trying to settle an argument between two clearly tired, snappy little boys. Wittke, that was his name. Konrad Wittke. Gerhard had recognised Berlin in the man's voice when they met in the camp and he had tried, more than once, to get him involved in the petitions and protests Gerhard had regularly organised, convinced that the legal wording he had wrapped them in would set them all free. It was a surprise to see Wittke strolling in the park; Gerhard had never encountered anyone else from the past who he recognised. It was such a surprise, in fact, that Gerhard did what he never did, and he called out.

'Konrad Wittke, how good to see you! You made it back to Berlin in one piece then!'

His voice sounded too loud, too familiar. And the words were barely out of his mouth before Gerhard suddenly remembered the man properly. How rude Wittke had been to all his overtures and offers of friendship. How he had dismissed the petitions as 'pointless'. How unimpressed he had been with Gerhard's legal expertise when Gerhard had been forced to admit that he hadn't actually taken his final qualifying examination because of the start of the war. How, in fact, Wittke had made fun of him.

'Having a doctorate is hardly the same as being an actual doctor now, is it?' That was it. A sneering putdown made in front of a cliquey group of officers who had found the insult hilarious. It was the last time they had spoken. It was also the last time Gerhard had seen Wittke in the camp, although Gerhard himself had been stuck there for months. And now Gerhard, his self-control still more fragile than he thought it was, had shouted out across the park like a common street trader and Wittke was staring at him in that same frosty way again. Worse, he was turning his back, shooing the boys on, steering the woman away.

Gerhard watched him go, his face burning again, and let a new wave of anger come. Konrad Wittke had been in the camp one day and gone the next. Another of the chosen ones, no doubt, walking to freedom, while men like Gerhard, honest men without connections, were left to rot. Nobody caring that Konrad Wittke had been a leading light in the SS medical ranks. Nobody caring that – if his boasts could be believed – he had been the experimenting sort, with a penchant for hurting, not healing, his patients and a disgrace therefore to his uniform.

Perhaps they knew. Perhaps how he acquired his expertise didn't matter.

Konrad Wittke was the very definition of dishonourable. He should have walked out of the war and into disgrace, but what did his insults to the spirit of the army matter when weighed against skills that the Allies could use? Nothing, to anyone apparently.

Certainly nothing to my mother who would have heard his rank and his title and treated him like a god.

Well, it mattered to Gerhard.

He sat down on a secluded bench and pushed the park's babble away. He let his rage warm through his blood the right way. This was a good thing. It had been a few weeks since he had completed his last task, now here was the perfect opportunity presenting itself precisely at the moment when he was ready to pick up his work again. He didn't even need to wait for a card to come to him. This time he knew exactly which one to go hunting for.

CHAPTER 12

21 FEBRUARY 1947

How did I not realise that I'd taken this one?

Hanni lifted the print out of the fixing tray with her rubber tongs, rinsed the chemicals away and put it to dry with the other images left over from the last roll she had shot at Fehrbelliner Platz.

She hadn't posed the picture or waited for the right moment to capture him. She must have taken it automatically when she was hiding behind her lens and wrestling with her conscience. Freddy was kneeling beside Nils Buchtel's body, but he wasn't looking at it, he was looking up at her. His eyes were slightly narrowed, and his face was full of questions.

He looks so young, and he looks like he doesn't trust anything at all.

Hanni stared at the image, scrutinising its details the way she had never had the chance to scrutinise Freddy's face when the two of them were together. She knew so little about him, including his age. When they had first met, she had placed him somewhere in his late twenties, a few years older than her, although when he had seen the little Buchtel girl he had looked triple that. She had also noticed on that first day how attractive he was, an attribute which the camera – as it always did when it caught a subject who was photogenic – had elevated. The angle of the picture played up his high cheekbones and his slim nose, and gave his sweep of dark hair a movie star's sheen. Look deeper, however, and there was a thinness cut into his face that Hanni wasn't convinced was purely the result of poor post-war rations.

He doesn't look like a man who's found peace.

Before Freddy's collapse, Hanni would have dismissed that thought as a fanciful one. The photograph had, after all, been taken at a crime scene: anyone kneeling next to a murdered body would be uncomfortable, policeman or not. He had also, Hanni knew, been concerned that day about her reaction to the killer's motives, which could account for the wariness in his eyes. Take a closer look, however, and there were other shadows hovering which she now knew came from a deeper place. One where he had watched his mother and his sister marched forever away from him, lost behind a wall of soldiers and snapping dogs.

And what else?

Freddy had survived the war, despite being Jewish, despite – she suspected – having lived for some time in hiding and, for some time, God knows where.

What else have you seen? And how can I ask?

She couldn't imagine how to begin. She already knew how badly such a conversation could end: with the same 'I hate you' that Natan had hit her with and splintered Hanni's heart.

'I mean it. You're not someone my father would have been proud of; you are one of the tribe who killed him. You are a liar of the very worst kind.'

Natan had spat his fury out with a bitterness that had turned his face vicious, and then he had burst into agonised tears. Hanni still didn't know which of those states had been worse. He hadn't let her help him through either.

I should have warned him what was coming, not blindsided him so badly.

'I have something I want to tell you, Natan. Something that you deserve to hear, that I've been keeping to myself for far too long.'

It had been a stupid opening. It had allowed hope to flare in his eyes.

And then I destroyed him.

The smell of the chemicals filling the trays stopped being Hanni's favourite perfume and stung at her eyes instead. The basement's lack of light stopped being her quiet sanctuary and turned into a darkness that was smothering. Hanni put Freddy's picture down. She couldn't see it anymore. All she could see was Natan and the terrible pain she had caused him.

Once Reiner had discovered the studio, Hanni knew that – whatever her father had said about leaving her alone unless she tangled with him again – her time to tell Natan the truth was fast running out. It had still taken her longer than it should to pluck up the courage to do it. She had finally sat him down one night when the shop was empty and the streets were dark, hoping against hope that her revelations wouldn't lead to disaster.

'My past is not what you think it is, and that is nobody's fault but mine.'

Once she had finally started, her only goal was to be fair to him. She had refused to weigh him down with expectations of forgiveness. She had told her story – including the first meeting with Ezra and the terrible discoveries at Theresienstadt – without sparing any of its details. She had stayed calm, although that had been hard. She hadn't cried or begged the way that she wanted to. She had accepted her guilt. She had explained as concisely as she could who her father was and how deeply she loathed him for it. She had told Natan how much she wanted Reiner to pay for his crimes, about the threats he had made that had stopped her denouncing him and what those threats meant for everyone she crossed paths with.

'None of this was done with malice or to deliberately deceive you. I regret very much that it has.'

She had told him that at the start and again at the end. And she had told him – she had sworn to him – that she was a coward and that she was a fool, but that she had never been, and never would be, her father.

Natan had listened to it all in complete silence. Natan, however, hadn't heard the honesty that she had hoped that he would. Natan had heard coldness. He had heard calculating. He had heard a Nazi justifying her warped re-entry into the world.

'You are one of them. It's in your blood. If it wasn't, you would have gone to the authorities whatever the cost and taken your punishment along with him. That would be justice. That's what I deserve. That's what my family deserves, not a monster and a murderer still walking around in the world because you were afraid of being found out.'

His verdict on her had been right and it had been wrong, and she hadn't argued with any of it. And it had been followed by everything Hanni had dreaded from the moment she had opened her mouth.

'Get out. I hate you, more than I've got words for. I never want to see you again. The thought that I could ever have loved you makes me feel physically sick.'

He had meant it – his grey face and reddened eyes had told Hanni that as much as his words had – but he had still stumbled over *loved*. That was when she had, foolishly, reached out to him. When she had convinced herself that he would be able to feel in her touch that she wasn't the enemy, even if that was all he could hear and see.

The moment her fingers landed on his wrist, however, he had slapped her away. The slap wasn't hard, but his hand had caught her cheek in the confusion and the shock of that had made her cry out. Natan had wept again when he realised that he had struck her, and he had stared at his palm as if it revolted him. He hadn't, however, apologised and he had refused to listen to anything else she tried to say.

That confrontation had taken place over a week ago. Hanni had left the studio at once. She had returned to their shared lodging house and collected her things, leaving him a note with her new address that she assumed he wouldn't read. Hanni knew that she would never see Natan again. And she now knew as a fact what she had told herself in Charlottenburg but hadn't truly believed: that Freddy could never know who Hanni Winter really was. That some agonies ran too deep and that, if she told him even a part of it, he would loathe her too – he would look at her and see a black uniform and a backdrop of hatred exactly as Natan had. That there could be nothing therefore between her and Freddy Schlüssel but secrets. It was a fact, but it was hard to look into the dark eyes she had captured so beautifully in the photograph and accept it.

'Fraulein Winter?'

The knock was, as always, a hesitant one. Hanni had shown her new landlady the stages involved in developing photographs the day she had set up the darkroom and had taken a picture of the nervous woman to illustrate how everything worked. Frau Greber, however, continued to treat the whole process as if it were magical and approached the basement, if she had to, as if goblins had taken up residence there.

'Fraulein Winter, can you hear me? There is a police officer at the door. Apparently you work with them and I am not to be worried by that.'

Every sensible thought flew out of Hanni's head at the prospect that the unexpected visitor might be Freddy. She wriggled behind the light-deadening blanket pinned over the door and hurried up the stairs after her landlady, buttoning up the coat she always wore when she worked in the freezing darkroom. She didn't, however, make it as far as her visitor.

'My dear girl, you need to sort out your hair, and your face. Even if you don't care what you look like, I cannot let you leave my house in such a dishevelled state.'

Before Hanni could protest, Frau Greber had swept her into the house's cosily cramped kitchen and set her in front of a mirror with a hairbrush and strict instructions to 'wipe off the smuts and use some of this'. The 'this' was a lipstick, a jaunty red that was far removed from the pale pink that Hanni wore when she thought to wear any at all. It was quite a revelation how much the shade brightened her face.

When she was finally pronounced satisfactory and was released and Matz saw her – because it was Matz waiting, not Freddy, which Hanni belatedly realised was by far the best thing – it took him a moment to stop staring and collect himself.

'I went to the studio, but the guy in charge said you don't work there anymore. He seemed upset and he wasn't exactly friendly. He took some persuading to hand over your new address.'

Hanni said nothing. She hadn't told anyone that she was leaving the studio or her lodgings in her haste to be gone and she had no idea what, if anything, Natan had said about her. Whether it was good or bad, she had no intention of commenting on it. To her relief, Matz clearly had more pressing matters on his mind than interrogating the ins and outs of her life. He glanced at the camera bag she had thrown over her shoulder.

'Good, you're ready to go. The boss needs your help.'

Hanni felt the air thicken around her.

'Another one?'

Matz nodded, his face grim. 'Another one.'

———

He didn't overlook her this time the way he had at Wilhelmstraβe. He couldn't look anywhere else but at Hanni from the moment she stepped out of the car and into his sight. And he also couldn't speak.

The last time she saw me I was outside my skin.

Freddy didn't know how he was supposed to behave towards her after she had witnessed his collapse; he was dreading how she might behave towards him. The years dealing alone with loss, the months he had spent in hiding during the war and the hell that had come after that had taught him how dangerous vulnerability could be. Hanni, however, had seen him like nobody else had: stripped raw, caught up by ghosts, on the edge of a despair that came knocking too often and terrified him. How was he meant to be Inspector Schlüssel again now that she had seen that?

How am I meant to be the Freddy I want her to see now that she has seen that?

Hanni's face was a blank and his was frozen. It was a relief, therefore, when she took charge and made no reference to their last meeting or where she had been in the days in between. When her first words turned him into no more than a colleague. It was a relief – and a crushing disappointment.

'Good morning, Inspector. Is the body in here?'

She didn't even offer him a handshake.

What if my behaviour at the Buchtels' revolted her?

He couldn't believe that was true: Hanni had shown him nothing but compassion when he collapsed. Once the doubt took hold, however, it stuck fast. It also didn't help that she looked so groomed. Her curls were neatly pinned back, her face was elegantly made up with colours far more sophisticated than he had ever seen her wear. It was as if an older, more poised woman was standing in front of Hanni. When he didn't answer her first question because he was still trying to catch up with who they now were to each other, she asked him another. Her level of politeness was numbing.

'Is it the same style of crime scene, Inspector? Is it the same type of victim?'

Hanni was waiting, and Matz was staring. Freddy forced himself out of his trance. He had deliberately asked Matz not to tell Hanni any of the details of the crime during the car journey so that she could see the site with fresh eyes. He coughed and snapped on a tone that was as professional as hers. The case, at least, was safer ground.

'In essence it is, yes.'

He stepped aside and ushered her into the building where the latest victim lay. The small house – which was an annex to the main Oskar-Helene-Heim hospital and stood a little apart from the main complex – was in the throes of being refurbished and was littered with pieces of wood and half-full paint cans.

'Take your time. Tell me what you see.'

Hanni was already beside the body, her camera raised. She walked round the man – who was lying, as the others had been, with his torso bared and one arm outstretched – bent down to him, then straightened up and checked her surroundings.

'It's the same as the last two, and it's different. The body is visible from the doorway again, so he was intended to be found, but look at the clothes: they haven't been piled neatly, they've been thrown and there are rips in the front of the shirt. The killer didn't undress this victim – he stripped him.'

Freddy's pulse quickened as she continued picking up the details that he, but not Matz, had already noted.

'He was in the SS like the others were – I can see the tattoo, and the sign round his neck has the same traitor message as before. I assume there was also a note in his hand?'

'There was, yes.'

Freddy held it out between his gloved fingers for Hanni to read. As he expected that she would, she looked at it first through her lens. For the first time since she had arrived, her voice quickened.

'There are errors here, exactly the same as the ones he's made on the sign. The letters aren't evenly drawn, some have been pressed into the card harder than others, the thickness varies and there is a small blot beside *Doctor*.' She glanced back at the body. 'Did the victim work here, do we know yet?'

Freddy nodded, absurdly pleased by her use of *we*.

'One of the workmen who found the body identified him. The hospital is a small one, more research- than patient-based, and most of the staff have taken an interest in the refurbishment that's been started in this section. I've had a chance to speak to some of his colleagues and, according to them, Doctor Wittke was well respected by everyone who works here.'

'But not by the killer. I imagine he has a very different story about the doctor to tell.'

Hanni continued to walk around the body, photographing every inch of it, and then she suddenly dropped to her knees. Freddy assumed that she had noticed that the pool of dried blood around Wittke's head was wider than those at the previous sites, which suggested that a far greater ferocity had been used in the killing. Hanni, however, was looking further to the left.

'Have you seen this?' She lowered the camera and pointed to one of the areas of the floor where a tin of paint had been spilled. 'It looks, on the surface, like a collection of paint splatters similar to the others that are scattered everywhere, but there are whirls in these ones which could be a boot or a shoe print. They are faint, but they are definitely there.'

Freddy leaped to her side. She was right. His eye hadn't caught the slight patterning, but the focus on the lens had. It could be a workman's tread – Freddy knew they would have to rule that possibility out – he refused, however, to believe it. He had been waiting for a clue through three months of no leads. As far as he was concerned, this was him, the murderer, finally physically there. Freddy would have pried out the flagstone if he could. Instead, he made a chalk mark around the paint and straightened up.

'You're right about all of it. I knew you would spot what I'd seen: that the site is the same as the others and it's different too. The killer didn't, as you pointed out, tidy up as carefully as he normally does or remove the clothing as carefully, or write the note and the sign as precisely as he's always done before. If this was a public place, I would blame those factors on him not having the time to do things properly, because he was – or he feared he would be – disturbed. But the annex is secluded – no one comes here after dark. And this time, the murder site is where the victim works. That might not mean anything, or it could mean that – even more than with the others – Wittke's job, and any connection through it to the Allies, or to Wittke himself, really matters in whatever narrative our murderer is telling. I think there could be a breakthrough here if we look hard enough.'

He had spoken with hope in his voice for the first time in weeks and Hanni had heard it. When she looked up at him, Freddy knew that all her instincts matched his.

'What can you feel here, Hanni? What is all this telling you?'

She didn't hesitate. 'Anger. I can feel anger.'

It was exactly what he wanted to hear. Anger. Freddy had felt it the moment he had seen the force contained in the letters. It was there in the tiny ink blots marring the note and the sign. It was also there in the hole torn through the neck of Wittke's shirt. And now it was present in the boot print stamped next to the body. This killing was personal in a way that the other two weren't, Freddy would have staked his career on it.

Hanni was still watching him. The detached gaze she had been wearing since she arrived had finally gone; she looked like herself again. Maybe she had been horrified by the way he had fallen apart at Frau Buchtel's home, maybe she hadn't. Maybe they would never be able to discuss it. At that moment, Freddy didn't care. The case was what mattered, and she was by his side on that. There was another body, which meant there could be another wife. If Freddy had to face another woman as devoted to the SS as she had been to her husband, he couldn't do that without Hanni.

'Hanni.'

Her eyes were wary, her manner when she turned towards him was uncertain. Freddy tried to phrase his request as if the answer didn't matter to him half as much as it did.

'If Wittke was married, I'll need to do another interview. Will you come with me to that?'

She didn't say anything, but she nodded and that was enough.

————

The crime scene had been different, and so was Ottilie Wittke. Unlike Dora Albrecht and Sonja Buchtel, she was perfectly calm about her husband's death when they told her what had happened, and she was brutally honest about what kind of a man Konrad Wittke had been.

There was no anxious maid hovering when they knocked on the door as there had been at the Buchtel home. Ottilie opened it herself and led them into a house which, to Hanni's relief, carried no taints of the past in its decor or its furnishings. It was instead a homely place, full of the tangle of toys and books that suggested that the children who lived here were loved ones. Ottilie saw Hanni glance at the building blocks scattered over the rug and managed a smile. It turned her briefly into a much younger woman than the one who had looked at their faces and instantly assumed bad news.

'I have twin boys. They are five years old, and they spend twelve hours a day running and twelve hours a day sleeping. They are quite the team, although, I think for the moment, I am winning. Not that my husband would agree. He thinks the boys lack discipline and need a much firmer hand than mine.' She glanced through the window and into the garden, where two curly-haired little boys were loudly kicking a football. 'Which I don't suppose matters anymore now, does it?' She turned back to Hanni and Freddy. 'He is dead, isn't he – that's why you're here? He didn't come home last night, and he always comes home, and when I telephoned his office this morning, nobody would speak to me.'

Freddy made no attempt to soften the blow. 'He is, yes. It was me who requested that nobody spoke to you – it's our standard procedure.'

Hanni glared at him and was about to launch into a mouthful of platitudes to fill the space his brusque answer had left, but Ottilie stopped her.

'Please don't. Was it an accident?'

Freddy shook his head.

Ottilie gripped the arm of the sofa. Hanni half rose to go to her side, but Ottilie waved her back down.

'I am fine. My husband was a terrible man, Inspector. There, I have said it, and I am sorry if that shocks you, but it is the truth. All the people who will now flock to pay their condolences and list his wonderful qualities haven't a clue who he really was. If they did...' She glanced at the boys again, but they were happily playing. 'They deserve the same fate.'

It wasn't a challenge; she didn't sound defiant or angry. She sounded utterly empty.

Hanni glanced at Freddy, waiting for his steer. He was sitting forward, the distant manner he had brought in with him totally gone.

'Why would you say that, Frau Wittke? I have to be honest – it isn't the reaction I was expecting from you.'

She's no Sonja Buchtel and he's not going to fall apart here.

Hanni let her shoulders drop. Freddy was a different man in this room than he had been in the last, which was a relief. They hadn't spoken about anything other than the facts of the case on the short car ride from the hospital to the Wittkes' home in Terrassenstraße. That had been a relief too. Hanni had only agreed to go with Freddy because she was worried sick about how he would get through the interview. She hadn't told him that. From the silence he fell into once there was nothing professional left to be said, she assumed he had no more desire than she did to stray again across personal lines. Or that he too was worried about what was coming, the way he had sounded when he asked her to go with him.

Hanni had walked up to the polished front door with her nerves ticking, steeling herself against the word or the image that would tip Freddy into the past, determined to keep a firm hand on whatever way the conversation unfolded. She could see now that wouldn't be needed. Ottilie Wittke wasn't a loyal SS wife determined to paint her husband as a hero. Her clipped tone and clenched hands as she continued told the same story as her words: she had hated him.

'No, I don't suppose that it is.' Ottilie glanced at Hanni. 'I presume you expected tears and hysterics or there wouldn't be two of you here. But I am tired, Inspector. Being married to a man like Konrad demanded a lot of pretence and mourning him would need more than I have left. I am done with it.'

She reached for the packet of cigarettes on the coffee table and began picking at the thin paper covering its top. 'I don't suppose you know, do you, that my husband served in the SS during the war?'

Freddy nodded. 'Actually yes, that has come to light.'

Her eyes widened. She pulled out a cigarette and didn't seem to know what to do with it. 'Already? Well, to borrow your words, Inspector, that wasn't the reaction I expected. I thought Konrad had made sure that part of his life was well hidden.'

She paused, her fingers tapping the cigarette against the tabletop as if she was making connections. 'I don't suppose that had anything to do with why he was killed?'

She nodded to herself when Freddy didn't reply. 'I'll take that as a yes, shall I? If it did, that is fitting. It was, after all, who my husband really was.'

She stopped again and looked across at a sideboard where a wedding photograph sat in a solid silver frame. Hanni followed her gaze. The picture was a standard shot of a bridal couple, but it wasn't a comfortable one. Konrad Wittke dominated the frame, resplendent in his black SS uniform. Ottilie, who was covered in old and heavy-looking lace and half-hidden by a tumbling bouquet, stood next to his crooked elbow, attempting a smile which made her look lost. To Hanni's experienced eyes, that and the stiffly held space between the couple told the relationship's story far more than the wedding-day trappings.

Ottilie saw Hanni looking at it and, for the first time since Freddy and Hanni arrived, her face lost its composure.

'I can't remember being that girl anymore. I was so young – twelve years younger than Konrad. I hardly knew him. But there was a war coming and an inheritance that needed sons to protect it, so my family arranged things with his, the way families like

ours did then, and we were married. I had such silly dreams of
what marriage would be like, a head stuffed full of romantic
nonsense, but Konrad was—' She lit her cigarette and cut the
sentence short. 'Anyway, then he was gone and there were the
babies to care for and I don't think I ever wondered for a moment
what his war was like, beyond hoping of course that he would
survive it.'

The way she said *of course* suggested that wasn't a feeling that
had lasted. Hanni caught Freddy's eye and saw that he had heard
the same thing. Neither of them, by tacit agreement, interrupted
her. Hanni had the feeling that it had been a long time since
Ottilie had spoken to anyone about what her life had been like
since her wedding.

'When he came home…' She took a deep drag on the cigarette.
'Let's just say that it wasn't easy. Divorce, however, was not an
option. As Konrad so carefully explained when I was stupid
enough to suggest that separate lives might be better for both of
us, "divorce implies failure, and the Wittke family does not trade
in failure". He did tell me that I could go if I wanted to, that he
didn't care enough to keep me. But he also made it very clear that,
if I did, I would be leaving without the children. And that he
would make sure that they would never remember me. So that
wasn't an option either.' Her voice trailed away; her face turned
bleak.

'What went wrong, Frau Wittke? Why did you want to divorce
your husband?'

Freddy's voice was low and warm, full of the gentleness
Ottilie's life was so obviously lacking.

'Because he was a monster.'

Hanni had to stifle a gasp at her choice of the word and where
it might be leading to, but Freddy didn't falter.

'Can you explain what you mean by that?'

Ottilie looked straight at him, and then the words began
pouring out as if he had pulled at a loose thread.

'He called himself a doctor. He wasn't, not by the time he was in the SS anyway. Doctors care for their patients; they want to help people. My husband tortured his and he killed. He took the most vulnerable people he could, and he treated them as if they were rats in his own private laboratory. He wasn't the only one, but you probably know that. Have you read any of the reports from the Doctors' Trial? The one that's happening now in Nuremberg?'

And there it was, the past flooding back into the room. Hanni instinctively moved a fraction closer to Freddy, waiting to grab hold of him at the first sign of distress.

'Yes, I have. Does it have some connection with your husband?'

If he was struggling with the direction the conversation was taking, he didn't show it. He sounded, and looked, perfectly calm. Ottilie, however, had torn most of the cigarette packet to pieces.

'My husband was one of those men. He should have been on trial there beside them.'

She jumped up and ran over to the sideboard, began pulling at the drawers. 'Here, I have proof.' She was holding out a soft-backed leather book with the tips of her fingers. 'This is his. A record of all his crimes. I found it and I confronted him with it, and he didn't care. He didn't even try to get rid of it. Why would he? He's proud of what he did, and he knew I wouldn't use what I had found and risk losing the boys. He thinks, or he thought, that he was invincible.' Her voice was rising.

Freddy held out his hand. 'What is it, Frau Wittke? Let me see.'

She dropped it onto the table in front of him.

'It's his research log, from Dachau. The work he's most proud of. All of those animals had a speciality and my husband's was the study of hypothermia – exposing prisoners to inhuman temperatures and then boiling them back to life. Sending them to the ovens if they survived his experiments. It's all in there.'

She sank down on to the sofa, her body gone suddenly limp, as Freddy picked up the book and turned it over and over in his hands.

'You don't have to read it here – you could take it back to the station. Or I could go through it first, see how bad it is.' Hanni kept her voice to a whisper, although Ottilie was now staring through the window at the boys as if neither she nor Freddy were there.

Freddy shook his head. 'She's talking and this might unlock more, so it has to be here. I'll be all right, if we do it together.'

He didn't look at her when he said *we*; he didn't need to. Hanni slipped her hand through his arm as he opened the first page.

The opening pages were set out like a diary, with the entries beginning in 1942 and running on for almost a year. The contrast between what had been done and the factual way the events were described was chilling.

Dachau Concentration Camp, October 1942
Human Hypothermia Study, Month Three
Six subjects immersed in tank of ice water. Three anesthetised, three conscious. Three naked, three dressed in clothing of various weights, including one in fighter-pilot uniform.
Subjects removed after three hours and placed in rewarming baths of various temperatures, including one set to boiling.
No survivors.

Dachau Concentration Camp, December 1942
Human Hypothermia Study, Month Five
Eight subjects tied naked to posts on parade ground, external temperatures monitored and averaging minus six degrees centigrade. Time spent outside varying from thirty minutes to six hours. Screaming suggested high levels of pain experienced as bodies froze.
All living subjects rewarmed. Those kept outside for the shortest time noted as having the highest chance of survival.
All surviving subjects sent to selections.

All the dated sections followed the same pattern. Hanni and Freddy read the first few and then Freddy flicked through to the back pages. Those were stuffed with tables and graphs and photographs supporting the written entries and with appendices comparing body weights to immersion times. It was a complete and diligently kept catalogue of nine months of experiments using forced freezing which had been carried out to test the capacity of the human body. All sanctioned, according to the log, by Reichsführer-SS Heinrich Himmler and implemented by Wittke.

The work he's most proud of.

Hanni swallowed hard as Freddy opened an envelope which had been tucked into the flap in the book's back cover. That contained a set of reports from the Doctor's Trial. Hanni skimmed through them, wondering if Wittke had been comparing his own work against the horrors laid out in the newspaper columns. Wondering how Freddy could still be holding the papers without shaking.

The reports carried no details, but the briefly sketched charges were enough to cast a darkness over the room. Experiments on twins; bone and muscle transplants; attempts to replicate and study head injuries; injections of contagious diseases; experiments that exposed prisoners to mustard gas and to drinking seawater and to phosphorous burns and deprived them of oxygen. Not a single procedure carried out under anaesthetic, and the victims who died or were maimed running past counting. The defence offered in every case was the same: that these experiments were not part of a programme of persecution or murder, but research carried out in the name of medical science. Hanni sped through those until she got to the names. Some of the sixteen men arraigned had been based at Dachau, but there was no mention anywhere of Konrad Wittke.

He was like my father – he knew better than to leave his name on the page.

The room had slipped into an eerie quiet, the only sounds the rustling pages and the soft thud of the ball from outside. It was quiet and yet so full of ghosts, the air was thick with them.

Freddy closed the book and let his fingers rest on top of it. Hanni looked at him, expecting to see anger or hatred or fear. Instead, his face was empty, his eyes were blank.

He's walking there with them.

Hanni could sense him moving through the diary entries, trying to put faces to the broken bodies, trying to imagine endings that no one ever should.

'Freddy.' She squeezed his arm, but he didn't come back. 'Freddy, maybe we should go. Maybe we should do this another day.' She squeezed his arm again and this time he shuddered and gasped and his face became one closer to his own.

'No. I'm all right. I can do this.'

He put the book onto the table and turned his attention back onto Ottilie.

'If this is his and if everything in it is true – which I have no reason to doubt – how was your husband able to hide it? How did he step out of Dachau and into a highly paid research post with the Americans?'

Freddy's voice wasn't cold, but the warmth he had flooded through it earlier to get Ottilie to talk was gone.

She sat up straighter. Her face was a study in misery.

'I don't know. With help I imagine, or with daring, or luck. Perhaps because his skills mattered more than where he acquired them. Perhaps because of people like me.'

Now Freddy's voice found a bite. 'What do you mean, Frau Wittke, people like you?'

It took her a moment to answer, but her voice was crystal clear when she did.

'People who knew and did nothing. People like me, who didn't act. I confronted my husband, Inspector. When that made no difference, I didn't do anything else.'

Ottilie was sitting perfectly still now, her hands folded in her lap, every part of her focused on the story she needed to tell. One Hanni knew would be full of echoes of her own and a torture for Freddy.

'Not a day goes by when I don't wish I'd done everything differently or the timescale had played out another way. If I had found the book when Konrad was interned and I had had the time to work out a plan for myself and the children, then he might have been one of those put on trial in the first round of prosecutions at Nuremberg. If I had taken the information straight to the Allied authorities rather than confronting him, he could be standing in the dock now at the Doctors' Trial. If I had had more courage and had gone to the hospital which funds his work and told them who he had been, perhaps they would have done what I didn't and filed the report. It's a lot of "coulds" and a lot of "ifs". It's a lot of regret to carry.'

'So why didn't you do any of those things?'

Freddy's tone had a sting in it that made Hanni shrink, that she didn't ever want to hear turned her way.

Ottilie also heard it, and the blame they all knew it carried. Her body stiffened.

'How many excuses do you want? Because, when it comes to his work, I suspect that, on some level, they already knew. Because I can stand the loss of him but not the loss of my boys. And because I am no one. Who would have believed me if I had tried to expose him in the way that I threatened, that he laughed at? I have no power, no family, no friends with connections the way that he has. He would have had me committed, Inspector – he promised as much – and who would keep my children safe from him then?'

'I am so sorry.'

Ottilie's self-control finally crumbled. She started to cry silently, with her head turned away from the window so that the boys wouldn't see. Her distress made no impression on Freddy; he had already turned round to look at Hanni.

'What are you sorry for? She's right: if she had acted sooner, or better, Wittke might have got the punishment he deserved.'

Hanni blinked furiously. She could hardly explain how close her life felt to Ottilie's, or the shame that came with that. 'Does it matter now what she did or didn't do? He's been punished anyway.'

'She's right.'

Ottilie's voice cut through the room before Freddy could start the argument he was clearly looking for.

'Konrad is dead. That might not be as good as a courtroom, but it's some kind of justice. Can't you leave it there? Can't you stop this investigation? My husband was soaked with sin to his core. If someone has chosen to wipe that from the world, then I for one don't want you to catch him.'

Freddy flinched and his face fell. When he turned towards Ottilie, Hanni thought, for the briefest moment, he was going to answer her with 'and neither do I'. Then he gathered himself up and the moment was lost.

'That is not your choice. A man has died, and it is my job to find out the reason. Which is why I am here, Frau Wittke. Which is what I need your help with.'

He has no sympathy for her. She is not as bad as the others perhaps, but to him she is still the wife of a Nazi.

Hanni couldn't look at him – she was afraid she would see contempt in his face and imagine that it was for her. Luckily, his switch to a clinically professional manner instantly calmed Ottilie.

'Forgive me.' She wiped her face with a handkerchief untucked from her sleeve and then refolded her hands. 'You have a job to do, and I am wasting your time with histrionics. What is it you want to know?'

The room resettled itself into a workplace. Freddy got out his notebook and began running through the standard list of questions designed to establish changes in routine or behaviour. Ottilie shook her head at each enquiry. The doctor was, apparently, a man who stuck to his schedules and nothing about that had varied in the days before his death. Just as Freddy was putting the book away, however, she frowned.

'There is something. I can't see that it's relevant, but you asked about anything that was different. We had a visitor about a week ago, or I did – Konrad was at work. A man came from the local planning department to ask if we might have any objection to proposals for a new children's playground which is apparently going to be built on the corner of the street. I said no we didn't – it's wasteland at the moment and a bit of an eyesore. I thought nothing more of it until yesterday when I mentioned the plans to Frau Drachmann next door and she, and Frau Wexler on the other side, knew nothing about them. Perhaps he simply hasn't got as far as them yet, but it does seem a little odd now that I think about it that he only came here.'

Hanni's neck prickled at the same time as Freddy reopened his notebook.

'Can you describe this man?'

Ottilie looked at the armchair opposite her as if she was trying to picture the man who had sat in it. It didn't, however, appear to help her powers of recall.

'No, not at all, which is also odd now that I think about that too. He was ordinary. Perhaps that was the main thing about him, how very ordinary he was. I can't recall a single feature or anything beyond his build and his height except that it was non-descript. You don't think his visit has something to do with Konrad's death, do you? Konrad never even saw him.'

Freddy's eyes were gleaming as he handed over his business card. 'I don't know, but we will check into it. And if there is anything at all that you remember about him, no matter how small it seems, please call me at the station at once.'

He stopped as the door opened and the frost-nipped children clattered back in.

'I have to tell them. And Konrad's mother too.' Ottilie got heavily to her feet and looked across at the boys, who were squabbling over a toy car. 'The boys loved him very much; they will be heartbroken. Perhaps his mother will find some comfort in that.'

She led them to the door. Freddy shook her hand, but Hanni

couldn't touch it: the burden of shared guilt felt strong enough to be visible.

As they walked down the path towards their waiting car, however, Hanni forced herself to turn. Ottilie was standing with her back to them, squaring her shoulders, bending down to the boys, about to crack their world in two. No matter how wrong a man Konrad Wittke had been, the sight of that was heartbreaking. She coughed to hide a sob, faltered and didn't pull away when Freddy unexpectedly took her arm.

'Are you all right?' He let out his breath in a long sigh. 'None of that went how I thought it would. I certainly didn't expect her to hate him so much.'

Hanni looked up at him. Now that they were out of the house again, his face was white and slack. He had been holding himself under even tighter control than she had realised.

'Neither did I. She was raw with it. And that book... It's one thing to read about the brutality at Dachau in the newspapers, but to see it documented in someone's handwriting like that. To touch it...'

Freddy's grip on her elbow tightened. 'Maybe if everyone saw the horror that way, that real, something more would be done. Or maybe not. People left the cinemas when they showed the films from the Nuremberg Trials. Apparently, we're a nation with weaker stomachs for torture these days.'

Hanni climbed into the car without answering. They had both seen far worse than a book, but she couldn't say that, and it was far too late to say what she wanted to: that she was desperately sorry about his family, that she was grateful that he had trusted her enough to tell her about his loss. The time to do that had long since slipped away. She tried instead to bring the conversation round to the case and calmer waters.

'What did you make of the visitor? Do you think it's important?'

Freddy wasn't listening – he was still caught up in Ottilie Wittke. 'Do you think that there are others like her?' He saw the driver look up and closed the partition between the front seat and the back before he continued. 'Wives who have come out of the war hating their husbands, mothers who now hate their sons. Who wouldn't care if someone killed them – who would be glad because they saw the killing as punishment? Do you think that they would mean it? Do you think that is possible?'

Hanni's heart lodged in her throat.

This could be my chance. If I can convince him that it is more than possible, that I feel it too, maybe he won't look so badly on me when the time comes to tell him.

She wanted to blurt out 'yes and they need our forgiveness and maybe our help'. Instead, she skirted slowly round the answer, trying to bring it as close to herself as she dared.

'I think it is possible to feel like that, yes. I know we are meant to love our families unconditionally, but is it always so simple? Ottilie definitely meant what she said, and I doubt that she's alone in that. My grandmother...' She hesitated, and only managed to carry on because Freddy wasn't looking at her. 'She stopped loving my father, her son, because of who he became. And even if she hadn't – stopped loving him, I mean – is it fair to assume that she shared his beliefs? That people in her position, and Ottilie's position, share in the guilt of the things that those who are close to them do?'

She waited for him to pick up on 'grandmother' and 'father', but he didn't. From his frown, she guessed that he was thinking more about his question than her answer.

'Maybe not.'

Hanni's stomach flipped. It was only two words, but those two words implied doubt; they could imply hope. And then his face hardened.

'No, that's rubbish and I'm not going to pretend I believe it. There's no "maybe". There are people who do dreadful things and there are those who stand by and let them and there's no differ-ence between the two as far as I'm concerned. Those who know the truth have a responsibility to do the right thing: to denounce the criminal, not to bury their secrets. If they don't do that – if they don't allow punishment to be a possibility – then it's simple: they share in the guilt.'

The hope slipped away under Freddy's rigid view of the world. Hanni, however, managed somehow to keep her voice level.

'But what if they are afraid, Freddy? I understand why you would think the way that you do, given everything that you've been through, but what if they've been threatened like Ottilie was? What if going public brings danger or means that they lose everything?'

The sneer in his voice cut through her. 'You saw her house and her clothes. Ottilie Wittke might hate her husband, but she lives inside his wealth exactly the same way as Dora Albrecht and Sonja Buchtel live in theirs, and she chose to stay there even when she knew that he was a murderer, when she had proof that would force anyone she told to believe her. Proof she didn't use until today when she knew he was safely dead. They are all the same, no matter what moral high ground this one thinks she stands on. They put themselves first. None of those men have been touched by their actions, none of them have suffered. None of their wives have either, Frau Wittke included. What do people like them know about losing everything? And why shouldn't they pay for the pain they have caused?'

It would have been easier to stop pushing him, but she couldn't.

'But you heard her: he threatened to take her children away. That would be the exact definition of losing everything for her. And you heard what else she said: *I don't want you to catch him.* She meant that, I know she did. She doesn't want to get justice for her husband through a trial of his killer – she thinks justice has been done; she said as much. And I bet if we told her what we think is happening, that our man is targeting murderers and torturers whose crimes have been washed away, who have been rewarded not punished for their past lives, she would want more of them dead.'

Freddy's temper finally cracked. 'Good. So she should. And you know what, maybe she's right. Maybe "some kind of justice" is better than them getting away with their new lives. Maybe it is enough.'

For a moment, Hanni wasn't sure she had heard him correctly. She waited for him to remember that he was a policeman and correct himself. He didn't.

Tell him you agree. Tell him you'd give the killer your father's name if you could.

His face was too tight, his war was too visible. This was about his feelings, his confusion, not hers.

'Maybe that's true, Freddy, for people like Ottilie. But where does that leave you as the police officer charged with solving the case?' She took a deep breath, but there was no turning back from the question. 'Do you really want to bring the killer in or do you want him to carry on?'

He turned away from her and stared out of the window, but not before Hanni had seen the shadow that darkened his face.

'I don't know. I really don't know.'

Neither of them spoke another word beyond 'goodbye' until the journey back to Kreuzberg and Hanni's lodgings was done.

CHAPTER 13

'How the hell did this reach the newspapers?'

Hanni flinched as the door to Freddy's office slammed open and a copy of the *Berliner Zeitung* flew through the air and landed with a thud on his desk.

'Was this your doing? Are you selling off your story to the highest bidder?'

It took Hanni a moment to register that the thick-necked man taking up too much of the room was spitting his questions at her. Before she could snap a 'don't be ridiculous' back at him, however, Freddy jumped in.

'Really, Chief Inspector?'

His stress on the title was clearly a warning. Hanni – who had never met Chief Inspector Brack before but had heard nothing good from Freddy about him – bit her retort reluctantly back and let Freddy continue.

'Don't you think it's rather unfair to blame Fraulein Winter, given that there isn't actually a photograph of anyone next to the article?'

His tone was just on the right side of polite. It didn't stop Brack squaring up.

'Fine, but it'd better not be her doing. It's bad enough that you've pulled your girlfriend onto the team without running the appropriate checks. God help you if she turns out to be in bed with the press as well as with you.'

Hanni caught Freddy's warning look in time to stop her from protesting. She waited for Freddy to correct Brack's crude assumption instead. When he didn't, and when he didn't interrupt the chief inspector's continuing tirade either, Hanni could only assume that contradicting the man would have been pointless or would add fuel to Brack's fire. Brack – who turned his venom off her only to turn it onto Freddy – was clearly the kind of bully who liked to make everything personal.

'So, if it wasn't her, do I assume it's your fault that this got printed? Haven't you learned how to lock down a crime scene yet?'

Freddy picked up the newspaper and scanned it. Hanni could see from the muscle twitching next to his mouth that he wasn't reading the report at all, that he was buying time to calm himself down instead. When he did answer, his voice was steady, but his knuckles stayed white.

'This isn't worth worrying about. So the workmen who found Wittke talked. That was inevitable, but they've said nothing of note. They haven't given his name. There are no details about the state the body was found in, beyond "there were indications that the victim had been a member of the SS". There's no mention of the other murders, because they didn't know about them.'

Freddy put the paper down as if it didn't merit any more of his attention. 'This site was more public than the last two, more people were aware of what had happened, so the press were obviously going to come sniffing. I asked the workmen not to leak anything of significance to the case and, to their credit, they haven't. Short of beating them up or bribing them – which I'm pretty sure aren't witness-handling techniques recommended by the police manual – that was the best I could do to contain things.'

'*The best I could do.*' Brack snatched the newspaper off the desk and flung it into the wastepaper bin. 'That about sums you up, doesn't it? Never quite good enough. God knows how this case fell into your hands, Schlüssel. I swear I'm a hair's breadth from taking it away from you; if we weren't so overstretched, I would. If anything else leaks out, or if there are any more bodies, I promise you I will. I've given you the extra men you've been badgering me for, so get this solved and get it done fast. I don't need some vigilante killer stirring up trouble, and I don't need the superintendent or the press crawling all over me, have you got that?'

Freddy managed a stiff-faced nod and Brack stormed out.

Hanni finally exhaled. 'Wow. He's a charmer.'

Freddy slammed his fist against his desk and watched the paperclips dance.

'He's probably worried that one of his buddies will be next on the hit list, or that he will be, which wouldn't be an outcome I'd get upset about.'

Hanni frowned. 'Wait a minute, are you saying that your boss was in the SS?'

'No, not exactly.' Freddy began picking over the mess his blow had made of his paperwork. 'Or not officially anyway. I doubt you'd ever find a trace of him, but he's no innocent either. There are rumours about Brack, and about some of the other higher-ups who served in the police during the war and have been let back in since – about the depth of their past allegiances. Brack was stationed at the Red Fort in the war, the police headquarters in Alexanderplatz which the Nazis infiltrated from the bottom to the top. At the very least, he must have turned a blind eye to all the Gestapo-sanctioned horrors that went on in the cells there, and he doesn't strike me as a man much given to turning a blind eye to anything.'

'In other words, he's another one who got rewarded, not punished, for what went before.'

Hanni's mouth had turned sour. She picked up the glass of water Freddy had poured her when she first arrived and took a sip. So Brack and some of his peers potentially still harboured National Socialist sympathies: given what she now knew about how well her father – and the killer's victims – had covered their tracks and prospered, that hardly surprised her. What she couldn't square, however, was Freddy's involvement with men like Brack or the type of division he ran.

There hadn't been any need for Hanni to come into the police station at Friesenstraße before. Now that she was finally in it, she wasn't sorry about that. She was already struggling to see where Freddy fitted in with the rougher men who had eyed her up and down and made deliberately audible comments when she walked past them. She had tried to remind herself that the whole force couldn't be made up of brute stereotypes – Matz wasn't one of those any more than Freddy was – and then Brack had burst in and she had changed her mind back again. What an intelligent and sensitive man like Freddy, whose history should have given him a horror of authority, was doing working for a thug like the chief inspector was beyond her. Which was why she decided to ask him.

'Is this what you always wanted to be, Freddy: a police officer?'

He stopped fiddling with the scattered paperclips and shook his head. 'No, not at all. I imagine my mother would be very surprised to find me sitting in here. She certainly wouldn't have been impressed that I'm working for a man with Brack's reputation. She would have utterly loathed him.'

He's mentioned his family and it hasn't upset him. Maybe this is my chance to learn more.

It wasn't an easy thing to do. Matters were so delicate between them that Hanni wasn't sure how to ask him anything beyond case-related matters at all. Apart from the car ride back from Terrassenstraße which had ended in a deeply uncomfortable silence, they had barely been alone. They hadn't spoken about what had happened at the Buchtel interview, or at the Wittke one. And Hanni – despite the tentative steps she had taken to introduce her family into the question of guilt – was still too raw from the confrontation with Natan to want to blunder unprepared into another one.

Except now it was Freddy who had brought his family into the room and Hanni couldn't let that go, not if there was a chance of learning anything more about what he had been through. She tidied up the last few paperclips while she worked out how to phrase all the questions she had without closing him down or opening herself back up.

Which pouncing too eagerly on 'mother' could do.

Freddy's attention had wandered away from his desk and, Hanni presumed from the unfocused look on his face, away from the present. She put the last paperclip in the tray and did her best to sound casual. 'Why did you join up?'

It took a moment for Freddy to answer, and he carried on staring into the distance while he did so.

'That's a good question. I suppose because, in 1945, it was an opportunity and there weren't many of them around, especially for someone like me, with no family and still ill from—' He stopped.

He had begun his reply without thinking too deeply about it. Now Hanni could see him weighing up his words, deliberating what to tell her and what not to. He didn't turn back to the desk or to her. Hanni began to wonder if that was less because he was caught up in memories and rather because it was easier to come up with an answer she might settle for if he wasn't watching her reactions. When he started to talk again, his voice was more guarded.

'I joined because it mattered to me that justice was done. Which perhaps sounds a little ironic in light of current events. Anyway, the law and how people interpret and bend it to what they want it to be had always been an interest of mine and – as odd as it might sound given everything that happened in it – the war hadn't knocked that interest out of me. I was very lost in 1945. Not just because of what happened to my family but because I didn't have any understanding of who I was anymore. It might not make much sense, but I thought I should start working that out by trying to be German again, the way I had always been before the Nazis told me that I wasn't. I didn't know how to do that except by being part of something that was looking to the country's future, which the new police force promised it would do.'

He stopped. Hanni could almost see the name *Brack* running through his head.

'Anyway, even if *new* didn't play out as well as it should have done, I definitely needed to believe that a better world could come out of the one Hitler had ruined and I had an idea, based on God knows what, that I could play a part in building whatever that would be. So, when an opportunity came up to make myself useful, I took it.'

He stopped again and didn't resume until Hanni – who could sense that he wasn't planning to carry on if he could help it – pushed him.

'What opportunity was that?'

He shrugged. 'Nothing startling, just one of those accidents of fate. Not long after I got back to Berlin in 1945, a soldier was picked up for the murder of a German civilian. That wouldn't have mattered in April or May when the city was still in chaos, but this was July, and it did. I happened to be around when the soldier was caught and I had language skills, so I helped out. I had an idea that the new German police should carry language cards around with them so they could liaise better with the Allied troops who were doing the real policing. Things snowballed from there. Also, there weren't men like Brack around then, so joining up seemed like a more reasonable idea than it might do now.'

I happened to be around... things snowballed from there.

Hanni had been right about his deliberating. It had been a longer explanation than she had expected, and it all sounded perfectly plausible – she assumed that, in essence, it was, including his idealism. He was also, however – or so she suspected – presenting her with an edited version of his life, filled

more with holes than with facts. And that version gave her almost
no more detail about his circumstances than she already had. She
had no idea where he had come back to Berlin from. She could
place him briefly in February 1943 and place him briefly in the
summer of 1945. Anything more than that was still a mist. Two
brief moments were, however, a starting point into his life that
she was willing to work with.

'If not a policeman then what did you originally want to be?'

She kept her tone light and kept a firm hold on her expectations.

Freddy still didn't look at her, but he responded more personally than she'd thought he might.

'A lawyer, from as early as I can remember wanting to be
anything. You should have seen me in those days – I had such
plans, and I was so certain I could achieve them, the way only a
teenager does. And I wasn't going to be the money-grabbing type
of lawyer; I was going to stand up for the working man. I was
going to be a "pillar of justice". He smiled suddenly and shook his
head. 'I was such an idealist then, it's hard to remember how that
felt. And it didn't stop there. I was going to be a judge and change
society for the better.'

'So why didn't you do it?'

As soon as the words were out of her mouth, Hanni could
have bitten her tongue off. His sharing, and his smile, had made
her forget his reality. And her stupid question made Freddy
remember it. Now he swivelled all his attention back onto her,
and Hanni desperately wished that he hadn't.

'What? Are you seriously asking me that? Do you think the
answer might be: because I'm Jewish?' His eyes had hardened so
much, they were unreadable.

'Freddy, I—'

It was pointless trying to interrupt him. She had tapped not
into his memories of the hopeful boy he once was, but into the
anger the destruction of that boy had left in its place. She wasn't
even sure whether he was talking specifically to her anymore or

railing instead at everyone whose life and whose war had been different to his.

'Do I honestly have to spell out what being Jewish meant then? Is that all it takes? Two years without Hitler and his henchmen reminding everyone how foul we were and all that gets wiped away? Well, lucky for you if that's the case. I wish I could ditch the scars so easily. Unfortunately, in 1935 when I was sixteen, the Nazis brought in their race laws and they made boys like me – not men like Konrad Wittke, whatever his wife now chooses to call him – into monsters. That label was hard to shake off, and it ruined my plans. I'm sure with a bit of imagination you can try to understand that. Monsters, you see, don't get to study in schools or universities. Monsters don't get to take exams and hold their heads up in the world. Monsters get chased with flaming torches instead, and then they get killed.'

His bitter sarcasm burned through her. Hanni knew he was seconds away from 'what is wrong with you – what kind of a person are you that you even need to ask?' and remembering 'grandmother' and 'who my father became'.

'I'm sorry, I truly am. I wasn't thinking.'

His curled lip dismissed her apology.

I am not going to lose someone else. I can't. I don't have enough people in my life to waste.

'What did it feel like?'

Hanni didn't think about the question – she blurted it out.

Freddy's frown changed from anger into confusion. 'What do you mean, how did what feel?'

Hanni was conscious that she only had one chance to make things even partly right, so she forced herself to meet his eyes, although she was still so ashamed of herself it was hard not to squirm. She had to find an explanation for her question that he wouldn't retreat from. And she needed to learn. Hanni had been shown one face of the Party in 1933 and she had witnessed another ten years later at Theresienstadt. The years in between were filled with too many blanks, too many moments when she walked around her life blinkered by her father and her privileged position to the truth of what edged and underpinned it. That had shamed her when she finally woke up in 1943. Now she knew the details of the numbers and the brutality, but there were still gaps in her knowledge and there was no end to the shame.

The policies her father had applauded when Hitler came into power, and had glorified ever since, had ruined people's lives while hers had continued to run comfortably on. She had been brought face to face with the end result of the persecutions in Theresienstadt's attics and trains. She had little idea, however, what daily life under the weight of them had meant for the people the Party had excluded from its definition of human, and she needed to remedy that. The new life she wanted couldn't be based solely on denouncing Reiner: that would be a hollow thing if she didn't fully acknowledge what being his daughter had meant. And somehow, she had to put all that into an answer that would let Freddy talk.

'To be cut out of your life, Freddy, and out of society, the way that you were. To be banned. To be treated as *other*. What did that feel like?'

His reaction was immediate. His body slumped; his face sagged. He didn't seem to know what to do with his hands. When he finally spoke, all the fight had run out of him.

'No one has ever asked me that. I'm not sure I know how to answer.'

Hanni didn't want to push him or to guide him – she needed this to be his story in his own words – so all she said, as gently as she could, was 'Try.'

The simplicity of the word unlocked him. His words poured out in a voice that sounded surprised to hear them let loose.

'Unreal in the first days. As if the laws that transformed everyday citizens into alien beings were about someone who wasn't me. I wasn't a fool – I saw it unfold. I could hardly escape the propaganda that flooded the streets and my school. I saw the same things in there that you must have seen in your own classroom: the charts explaining how being Jewish worked and all the levels laid out in them. I saw that you could be Jewish in different degrees, depending on your parents and your grandparents, and God knows how many generations back, and that, whatever the category they slotted you into, it was bad. None of it matched anything I'd been taught about my religion at the synagogue or at home.

'And I saw the pictures too. All the hooked noses and the clawed hands, and the scary bearded men running off with shrieking blonde virgins. None of them looked like anyone Jewish I'd ever met. It all seemed like the stuff of sick fairy tales. Even when they closed the schools and the universities to us, I didn't take it as seriously as I should have done. I was sixteen – I thought I was invincible. I figured that the good people would see sense, or that there would be a way around the bans. Or that my mother would find a loophole, the way that she always did: with a smile on her face, and an answer for every problem I threw at her.'

He stopped, gulped and sniffed. His distress at the memory of her was printed in the red rims round his eyes. It was unbearable to watch. Hanni wanted to throw her arms around him and tell him some nonsense about his mother 'being in a happier place now' that would have insulted them both. She sat on her hands instead, and bit her lip, and gave Freddy the space to find his tongue again.

'And then even the *good people* turned against us and the laws got tighter, and it finally dawned on me that the bans and the hatred and the indifference to that hatred was real. That they were nothing my mother could change. Then I got angry, so angry it consumed me. I kicked my way through God knows how many street fights, pitching my fists against boys in Hitler Youth uniforms who were as angry as me, and frightening the life out of my mother. It made no difference. Our lives shrank and shrank. Not just physically – we lost our flat and our business, which was bad enough – but in the way that we were allowed to be in the world. That got smaller and crueller. We had no value. Everyone was a threat. No one could be trusted. In the end, after they were all taken, I became invisible, for as long as I could be. And then... then, I became what I'd been told for years that I was: something far less than human.'

He was in a camp. He was a prisoner.

Hanni could feel the starved bodies pressing. She could smell the sickly-sweet stench of the attics. She grabbed for her water and spilled most of it. Freddy didn't appear to notice.

'You asked me how it felt. Like a death that never properly came. Like disappearing bit by bit. Like fear had replaced my bones.'

Images of Theresienstadt filled up her head. Stretched skin and vacant eyes. Children who were as old and as hopeless as the adults trying to hide the horror of the world from them. Jannick telling her all the ways he could die. Her father with a whip in his hand and a mocking smile on his face. Hanni could imagine, but she didn't know what it was like to have lived the war that Freddy had lived. She had, however, seen far too many of the horrors that had been inflicted, albeit from the other side. She knew that the scars branded in the places where they had both – so differently – been never truly left.

'As if it would never end? As if some days it still hasn't?'

This time when he turned to her, his eyes were as full of tears as hers. Hanni jumped to her feet, desperate to hold him, not caring what came next as long as he allowed her to absorb some of his pain. As she moved towards him, however, there was a knock neither of them fully registered and the office door swung open.

'Boss, I've got the—'

Matz stopped. Hanni sat hastily down; Freddy rubbed at his eyes. It was too late, however, to reset the room.

'I'm sorry. I'll come back. Whatever it is, you don't have to tell me.'

Matz's embarrassment was painful. Freddy managed, somehow, to find him an explanation that saved everyone's faces.

'It's nothing. A difficult anniversary – you know what they're like. Can you give us a minute – grab us some coffee? We'll meet you in the incident room in five.'

Matz barrelled back through the door without having to be asked twice.

Freddy began to gather up his papers. 'He won't ask what just happened. He knows I won't answer.'

There was nothing else to say: they both knew that the moment had passed. Hanni picked up her camera bag and the envelope of crime-scene photographs she had spent the weekend developing and had been about to show Freddy before Brack stormed in.

'Thank you.'

He didn't reply.

Hanni, however, wasn't about to let him get defensive again and dismiss her.

'I mean it, Freddy. I know I was stupid and clumsy, and that sharing what you've shared with me – today and before – wasn't easy. So thank you.'

'You won't tell anyone, will you?' His naked face was back. 'No one here even knows that I'm Jewish. I shortened my name when I joined the force. I didn't want to do that, but I needed to feel safe. That's all I want, Hanni, to feel safe, and I don't know if that will ever happen.'

Unless you help me hung unsaid in the air. Hanni couldn't acknowledge that, she couldn't answer that, not in the light of what he had told her. She had stupidly thought that Freddy had less to forgive her for than Natan had, but there wasn't a scale to measure this. And Freddy hadn't only suffered the indescribable misery of losing his whole family at the hands of men like her father, he had also been inside one of the hellholes those men had built and had run.

If he knew, he would never look at me like this again. As if I mattered.

Freddy was staring at her, his face heavy with want. It was obvious that he needed far more from her. That the 'of course' which she gave him fell short of the care-filled words that he needed. That the brief nod she followed her answer with as she opened the door – a nod which signalled her switch from being his confidante to his colleague – wasn't any kind of comfort at all. Hanni, however, had nothing more she dared give.

———

Matz had set the incident room out ready with two rows of chairs and a corkboard that was a web of maps and photographs linked together with lengths of red string. Freddy nodded to the assembled group, most of whom weren't known to him, and dropped into the central seat at the front which had been left vacant in recognition of his rank. He let Matz continue to hand out the folders his assistant had painstakingly assembled and stared at the strands running across the board, pinning people to places and times. He was grateful to have something to focus on that wasn't Hanni. It was hard enough that she was in the same room; he couldn't bear to actually look at her. Not after he had stripped himself bare again.

And she pushed me away.

Freddy knew that wasn't strictly fair. Hanni had been completely his in the office. He had seen the tears brimming as full in her eyes as they had filled up his own. He had heard the compassion in her voice when she had realised that his nightmare was still a living thing. For one glorious longed-for moment – until Matz had blundered in – Freddy had thought she was going to fling her arms around him and make him feel whole. And then the Hanni who had read the depths of the need in him, who – he was certain – was about to answer it, had vanished again behind her professional mask. It had been a deliberate rejection – far more so than the distance she had kept from him after the Buchtel interview – and it hurt beyond words.

Maybe it was me. Maybe it was my anger when she asked why I hadn't become a lawyer. Maybe the depth of it frightened her off.

Freddy would have felt better about that – and more ready to apologise for his outburst – if he hadn't also felt that his anger had been justified. What else did the ridiculous question she had asked deserve except a furious response? And didn't Hanni asking it in the first place mean that the compassion he thought he had felt in her couldn't possibly be real, that it was nothing but his own desperate longing layered onto her? And didn't it also mean that Hanni had lived through a very different war from his, that she had lived a very different life?

One I know nothing about because she doesn't want me to.

Part of Freddy wasn't surprised by that. He had no illusions about life in post-war Berlin. He knew that it was a construct, that peace required a communal pretence in which – apart from offering up a few carefully selected sacrificial lambs – the past was no longer where anyone wanted to look. Everyone who could had made a sparkling new start. Everyone had deeply buried secrets or, if they didn't, they lived too closely next to someone who had. He was proof of that. The killer and his victims were proof of that. And so was Hanni. Freddy knew that there was a shadow clouding her story she didn't want him to see. She had dropped a hint about it in the car, although he hadn't been properly listening, and now he couldn't piece it together. When he had been hiding from her too, he could live with whatever secrets she needed to keep. But now? With so many layers stripped from him and so many still clinging around her? He couldn't stand it. Hanni's past was keeping him away from her, and he didn't want to be kept away from her.

Which means she has to tell me, or I have to ask and go digging when she pushes me away again.

'Sir? Do you want me to run through the reports?'

Matz was frowning and fiddling with his pen; the junior

detectives were shuffling. Freddy shook himself quickly back into the room. It was obvious from the coughing that he wasn't creating a positive impression – if Brack had come in and caught him daydreaming, he would have already lost control of the case. He tapped his nose with his fingers as if he had been busy making connections and nodded.

'Of course. What have you got for us?'

Matz cleared his throat and straightened his tie. He was clearly enjoying commanding the room, which Freddy didn't object to. One of the reasons he had put Matz on his team was that they both shared the same drive to put their stamp on the world.

'Well, we were right to reinterview the other two wives, which Ortmann and I' – he waved a hand at a tall man in the back row – 'did over the weekend. Both of them had been paid visits in the week before their husbands' deaths which followed the same lines as the one made to Frau Wittke. A man they didn't know, claiming to be from local government, turning up unannounced with a cover story about a local issue. Frau Albrecht's caller said he was carrying out a survey into road-crossing blackspots. Frau Buchtel's was canvassing opinions on whether the area would benefit from a public swimming pool. None of the other neighbours in either street were visited. Both women described the man they spoke to as unremarkable and ordinary.'

'It's the final check. He's making sure he's got the right target. I think—'

Hanni ground to a halt as a mumbled 'why is she in here doing our jobs?' cut across what she was starting to say. This time, however, unlike with Brack, Freddy did intervene. He got slowly to his feet and stared from one sullen face to the next until the room was graveyard silent.

'Let's address this right now, shall we? You want to know why Fraulein Winter is here? For a start, because I asked her to be, which should be enough for you. Also because she is our crime-scene photographer and that makes her part of our team. And I invited her to do that because she has an eye for detail most of you will take years to develop.'

He stopped and looked round the room, making eye contact with each one of his listeners. 'Fraulein Winter is a professional and she is our colleague. She deserves – and she will get – our respect. I won't be explaining any of that again, but if some of you find it too difficult a concept to manage, be my guest and step down from the case. Does anyone want to do that?'

There was a lot of head shaking and mutters of 'no, boss; sorry, boss' which Freddy allowed to continue until he was ready for it to stop. He had expected resistance to bringing in a young woman rather than the grizzled campaigners the department usually used, and he wasn't prepared to put up with it. If they had to believe he was tricky, so be it.

'Good.'

For the first time since they had entered the room, Freddy managed to look at Hanni, who had taken a seat on the end of the back row.

'Could you elaborate on what you wanted to say, Fraulein Winter?'

She waited until all the men turned to face her. If their rudeness had upset her, it didn't show. It gave Freddy a jolt to remember her grace.

'The killer knows his victims – we can see that on the cards he leaves. He clearly has access to information about them, but he doesn't rely solely on that: he's more thorough. That's what I meant about a final check. I think he makes these visits to reinforce what he has read: to see if their houses hold clues to their pasts, or to see what their wives will divulge. He wants to know more about his victims than a set of statistics, no matter how important those are. He wants to make sure that what he is doing – and when I say this, I mean in his eyes, not mine – is right.'

The word *right* sent a ripple round the room. Freddy avoided her eyes and didn't respond to it. He nodded to Matz to carry on with the briefing instead.

'I think Fraulein Winter is correct: he wants to learn as much as he can about the people he kills.' Matz shuffled through the papers on the table in front of him. 'All the men who died had routines. Albrecht always met with his mistress on a Tuesday, which was the night he was killed. Buchtel always had a meeting that finished at 5.45 on a Wednesday. Wittke had a dinner with colleagues on a Thursday – in other words, they all always did the same thing on the night our killer chose to go after them. I think he studied their habits and followed them.'

That was safer ground. Freddy walked over to the board, acknowledging Matz and Hanni's work with a nod.

'That's good. He gives himself planning and checking time, that's interesting.' He scanned the dates pinned under the men's photographs. 'And that could explain the gaps between the killings: approximately eight weeks between two and three, and five between one and two. He takes time to get ready for them. Perhaps he also takes time to recover from them. We can presume, therefore, that if he sticks to what seems to be his pattern – and if Christmas and the altered work routines that go with that affected the first timeline – we should be expecting another murder to take place around late March or, more likely, early April.' He paused as the atmosphere in the room tightened. 'In other words, we have a deadline. And, despite all the work Assistant Inspector Laube and Fraulein Winter and I have been doing, we are, unfortunately, still hunting for a phantom. Which is why we have expanded the team.'

No one was muttering now. Everyone was focused on Freddy. He deliberately dropped his voice so the men leaned forward, their faces wrinkled with concentration.

'We know a lot about the individual victims, but there is little to connect them beyond their SS membership and their deaths. Their profiles are in your files, so study them. You will see from those that they weren't in the same units, or in the same post-war internment camps. Our main challenge is that we know a lot about them and almost nothing about the killer, other than the hints he leaves with the bodies. From those, he appears to be methodical and precise, although the last kill had some anomalies and may have had a more personal slant. He appears to be targeting ex-SS officers who now work for the Allies, and he has access to detailed information about them. He isn't confining himself to any specific area or sector of Berlin, and he takes time to get to know his victims. According to the wives' statements, he is unremarkable, easy to overlook, but he is also confident – he walks into the victims' homes; he kills near pavements or where people are working.'

He stopped, scanned the room, made sure every eye was on him.

'We have no reason to believe that he will stop at three – quite the opposite in fact. And that's it: beyond those few strands, he is invisible. If anyone, therefore, has anything else they want to throw into the mix, I would be very happy to hear it.'

There was a pause as the detectives digested what Freddy had said and then a hand rose in the front row. Freddy gestured to the officer to speak.

'What if he's Jewish? Wouldn't that be a reason for this type of vendetta, if that's what it is? Perhaps he was in a camp and the men he killed were based there.'

Freddy deliberately did not look at Hanni.

'That's good thinking. Being Jewish is not an unreasonable assumption to make and it's one Laube and I have been considering. I don't, however, think that a concentration camp is the key – only Wittke seems to have been based at one and it's highly unlikely that anyone who came into contact with him at Dachau would have survived. Someone who suffered at SS hands, however, and is now seeking vengeance, that makes sense.'

He stopped and swallowed and hoped that nobody had heard the crack in his voice. 'But it's also – if we do assume the murderer is Jewish and we proceed that way – a nightmare to try to investigate. One breath of this in the synagogues – that the police are looking for an SS killer among their community – and I suspect that they will, understandably, close ranks.'

The officer who had spoken nodded. 'That's fair enough, but if we were to go down the route of a Jewish man, at least it's not going to be a big number of potential suspects to deal with.'

He backtracked as a low whistle circled the room and Freddy looked daggers at him. 'I'm sorry, I didn't mean it to come out like that. It's a lead though, isn't it, and worth exploring? If a direct approach could trigger alarm bells, which I understand that it could, why don't I have a look at the 1945 census? See if I can come up with an overall number of men of the right working age and religion who might fit. It would be a start.'

Freddy thought for a moment about throwing him out of the room. The idea, however, was a good one, so he swallowed his anger as best as he could.

'Fine, look at the census, but that's all you do. And as for the rest of you, for God's sake, tread more carefully than he did and don't discuss what you're doing with anyone – it's essential that nothing about this investigation leaves this room. I don't want to see one hint in a newspaper about crusades or SS killers or police persecution of Berlin's Jewish population. And I don't want to hear any more comments like the one this idiot just made or the next person who makes them will lose their badge.'

He looked round the room, wondering how many of the men in it had sympathies which ran closer to Brack's than to his own.

'I mean that. If any of you has an axe to grind, something left over from your own war that will cloud your judgement, it's got no place in here and it's another reason you need to stand down.'

He stopped, conscious that his voice was rising, remembering all too clearly Hanni's question in the car on the way back from the Wittke interview and his inability to answer it. He was also conscious that the tension in the room was building again, and not in a good way. Freddy didn't mind being thought of as a difficult boss, but he needed allies, not a team who thought he didn't trust them. He forced his grim expression into something softer.

'Okay, well, that's one solid avenue to explore, which is more than we had yesterday. As for the rest... You have a copy of the pathology report in your packs. The cause of death is the same in all three cases: one or more sharp blows to the back of the head with a brick, presumably one taken from the killing site, although none of those have been found.'

He turned to Matz. 'Do we have any word on the footprint yet?'

Matz shook his head. 'Not yet, although I'm expecting it soon. What we do have, though, is some information on the materials the killer used for the record card and the sign. It's rudimentary, obviously, but there are patterns, especially now that we have the messages from the last one which were messier.'

He looked down at his notebook. 'According to the lab, it's very likely that the signs left with the bodies were written with a refill-able fountain pen rather than the dip pen which is most commonly used in German offices. There was also a bluer tint in the black ink than is commonly used by businesses here, and as for the card he used, well...' Matz gestured to the flimsy sheets that filled the information packs. 'The quality was streets ahead of anything we have access to, even in the chief inspector's office. I know this is speculative, like everything else to do with this case, but I'm begin-ning to wonder, given the supplies he has access to, if our man maybe works not for a German company, but for the Allies.'

Freddy didn't know whether to applaud Matz's deduction or groan at it. A German working in an Allied office potentially narrowed what was currently an unwieldy pool of suspects, espe-cially if the man was Jewish and had, more importantly, noted his religion on his application form. Which was a detail that Freddy couldn't count on, given that he, for one, hadn't done that. If the murderer wasn't a German national, however, but American or British or French, the whole case could get mired in a mess of legal complications that could conceivably take the whole thing out of his hands.

'Perhaps he works in one of the intelligence units. That could account for the information he has on his victims.'

It was a good thought. Freddy was about to ask the officer who had suggested it to investigate that strand further when another hand went up. It was Ortmann, the officer who had visited Frau Albrecht.

'The intelligence services will have some information on SS officers, but isn't that likely to be more limited, and more protected, than all the stuff our guy seems to know? We could try them, if they'll co-operate, but there's somewhere else in the American sector I think we should be looking – a document centre where all the Party membership and SS records that were recovered at the end of the war were sent in 1945.'

Freddy frowned – he had never heard of the place. 'How do you know about that?'

Ortmann shrugged. 'It's not a secret; it's just not talked about very much. I knew a guy who drove one of the collection trucks when the facility was set up and apparently there were sack loads of documents brought in. So I was wondering, what if that's where our man works? Can you imagine how much information he would have at his fingertips?'

The hair on Freddy's arms snapped to attention. This time, he couldn't resist a glance at Hanni: she was perched on the edge of her chair, her eyes fixed on Ortmann.

'Whereabouts is it, do you know?'

Ortmann nodded. 'Yes, it's in Zehlendorf, on the edges of Grunewald. My family live there, so I know the area. The building itself is on Wasserkäfersteig.' He paused. 'Which, now that I think of it, is only about half an hour's walk from where the third body was found.'

Freddy instinctively knew that wasn't a coincidence, but he had to play it out as if it was.

'And that body was a long way from the first, which was nowhere close to the second. And Zehlendorf, and therefore,

Wasserkäfersteig, is a long way out of the city, which is where the first two killings took place.'

'But that's the thing, it's not.' Ortmann was quivering with an excitement that had begun to spread around the room. 'Everyone thinks it is because the lakes and the woods make the area feel like the countryside, but it's actually a transport hub with loads of connections into the city. The Document Centre is close to the stations at Krumme Lanke and Sundgauer Straβe: there are trains and buses from there which would take you to Wilhelmstraβe and Fehrbelliner Platz in thirty to forty minutes.'

'So our man could work there and could also have easy access to all the crime scenes. And if he's Jewish and his employer knows that, surely he'd be easy to find on their books.'

Freddy could understand why Matz was grinning so widely and the other men were starting to follow him, but someone had to hold on to the room.

'Maybe. It's a theory. Okay, I'll agree it's another promising lead. We'll get someone down there to do some sniffing around. But we need to remember that this is also another potential minefield: whoever goes to the Centre needs to tread as lightly with the Americans as we would if we went to the synagogues.'

He thought for a moment. It was one thing for the German police authorities to co-operate across the sectors, but liaising with the Allied authorities themselves was a very different matter.

'We'll have to use a cover, maybe that somebody's been leaking information, and we'll have to see if we can get a look at their staff records, which I don't imagine for a moment will be easy. What we can't do is alert anyone to the possibility that they've got a killer on their staff who's using their files like a chocolate box to select their next victim.'

He did his best to sound calm, but having lines of enquiry and something to do rather than sitting round waiting to find the next body had galvanised both him and the rest of the team. Everyone was up, eager to get their roles fixed and get on with the job.

When the door opened and a secretary appeared holding a

note marked Forensics, Freddy was halfway through sorting out and allocating the tasks. He grabbed it eagerly from her, assuming it was the footprint analysis and ready for that to support the conclusion the whole team had now come to.

It took him less than two minutes to read the results and watch his investigation crash into a wall.

'Hold it. All of you, stop.'

He waved the note in the air until he had everyone's attention.

'We need to rethink this. He's not Jewish, not if this is accurate: he can't be. The print in the paint splashes came from a Wehrmacht-issue army boot.'

From their frowns, no one but him seemed to know what that meant.

'Think about it. Jewish men weren't allowed to serve. And no Jewish man would have a pair of Wehrmacht army boots unless he bought them on the black market, which, trust me, anyone Jewish would have to be barefoot and blistered and desperate to do. So there's no point in going through the census or bothering the synagogues. I think we have to assume, instead, that our man definitely isn't Jewish and that either he bought these boots after the war or – and I can't help but think this is more likely because boots are the one thing most people hang on to if they have them – he could have been a soldier.'

He stopped and waited a moment for the news to sink in.

'If that's true, that could be half the city. And it would mean that he's not killing the enemy.'

Hanni's face was no longer shuttered – it was as puzzled as all the others staring back at him.

Freddy shook his head, suddenly feeling far wearier than he could let the room see. 'Not the enemy, no. If we've got this right, he's killing his own.'

CHAPTER 14

28 FEBRUARY 1947

'This is incredible. To be honest, until a few days ago, I didn't even know that this place existed, never mind the scale of it.'

Hanni followed Freddy's gaze along the maze of corridors. Every inch of their walls was lined with shelving which stretched from floor to ceiling and was packed with binders or boxes or, in the case of the lower levels, sacks still waiting to be opened. *Incredible* was an understatement. The number of records was impossible to imagine; the weight of them was unthinkable. Hanni found herself listening for creaks, picturing the shelves shifting, the papers shivering and starting to fall, and had to fight off a shudder.

Freddy was still talking, saying something about the outside of the building hardly preparing visitors for what they would find when they came in. He was right about that too: there was a marked disconnect between the Centre's neatly compact exterior and its cavernous insides.

That HQ771, as the small signboard designated the area, was a military compound was obvious: the barbed-wire fences and floodlights and the armed sentries who patrolled its perimeters made that abundantly clear. Blink those away, however, and the street was no different from the dozens of identical suburban cul-de-sacs they had driven past, and the whitewashed Alpine-style villas which made up the compound could have been home to any number of middle-class German families. The interior, however, was more reminiscent of a set of giant mine-workings. A few steps past a suite of offices and the complex extended deep underground, culminating in a huge central sorting hall that was reached via a labyrinth of corridors formed of thick concrete walls and thick blast-proof doors. The fluorescent tubes they were lit with had turned all their faces a sickly pale green.

'It really is something, isn't it?' Captain Cooper – the duty officer who had insisted on giving Hanni and Freddy a 'grand tour' – grinned. 'It's even more astonishing when you consider that this place was once one of the Nazis' major intelligence hubs. Göring ran it as a listening post for his spies. It was riddled with wires when we first took it over, and yet now it's filled with Nazi records and it's where we investigate them. Here, look.'

He led them round another corner and waved at a set of shelves which were double Hanni's height. 'This section here is where we keep the big boys. That's Göring's file up there, and next to that are Himmler's and Mengele's. And down that corridor to the left is a whole chamber devoted to Goebbels and his propaganda division. We've netted ourselves a complete who's who of the Nazi Party and we've barely scratched the surface of it yet. There's over ten million records here – can you believe it? And all of them were only saved because the owner of the paper mill where they were sent to didn't have the coal to do the job he was ordered to do and pulp them. It's incredible all right.'

'Or it's a disgrace.'

Freddy's skin had suddenly turned sicklier than the lights should have made it. Hanni nudged his elbow to get him to stop before he launched into one of the rants she could sense was brewing despite his earlier pretence of enthusiasm.

He ignored her, however, as he had been ignoring her the whole way from the police station to Zehlendorf. 'Over ten million? And how many Nazis have been punished for their war crimes to date? Not even a hundred – in fact less than twenty. Forgive me if I'm not as impressed by all this as you'd like me to be.'

Captain Cooper's grin disappeared. Hanni could tell from his tight mouth that he was starting to question why he had let them in, not that Freddy had noticed. He was too busy winding himself up and had clearly forgotten that they needed Cooper's co-operation far more than he needed them criticising his work. Hanni couldn't allow him the luxury of threatening their access. They couldn't risk being asked to leave – they were nowhere near close to achieving what they had come to the Centre to do. She glanced over at him, wondering if a grimace or a cough might be enough to remind him why they were there, but Freddy was staring at the shelves as if he was about to set fire to them. Hanni decided, therefore, to win Cooper back by playing a card that Freddy would never reach for. She knew that she had no right to do it, that Freddy would be furious with her and see her intervention as a betrayal.

But he's furious with me anyway, or he's acting like it, and I cannot be thrown out of here.

She crossed her fingers behind her back in an act of superstition that she knew was childish but still did anyway and deliberately avoided looking at Freddy.

'Captain Cooper, this is very awkward. You have been so welcoming and so generous with your time – I know that the last thing we would want is to appear ungrateful. I would never normally speak up like this and I know the inspector won't thank me for doing it, he is such a private man. But the thing is, Inspector Schlüssel isn't being intentionally rude, no matter what it sounds like. He is Jewish, you see, and he lost his whole family to the camps. To be here, surrounded by these men – even when they are reduced to no more than pieces of paper – it isn't an easy thing for him.'

Her explanation sounded heartfelt because it was. The minute she began talking, she could feel Freddy's discomfort at where they were standing, even if she hadn't fully appreciated the impact it would have on him before.

She turned to him and mouthed, 'I'm sorry.'

His face was rigid, and he didn't react.

The captain, however, was instantly all handshakes and contrition and 'you should have told me; no: I should have spoken better'.

At that, Freddy, to Hanni's relief, found him an apology and a smile in return, although the look he sent her was a clenched one. That wasn't pleasant, but she could manage it. Relations between her and Freddy were so strained that one more misstep hardly mattered. She had shifted to her professional face at the station because she had to, but she knew she had hurt him badly in doing that. She also knew that he had hoped his honesty would propel her into his arms. It wasn't an unfair assumption: if Matz hadn't arrived, his arms were where she would have been. But she had snapped herself back and he had dealt with his confusion at that by moving so far from professional, he was barely civil. Hanni hated the distance between them, but its resolution was still out of her control, and staying in the building – and gathering the information that she needed – wasn't.

Given Freddy's hostile mood, Hanni had expected to be left behind when he had decided to visit Wasserkäfersteig. He had, however, requested that she – or to be more accurate her camera – accompany him. His instructions as they got into the car had been both curt and oblique: 'Take all the photographs you can and then distract our guide when I tell you to.' Hanni still didn't know what he meant by that, and now that they had arrived, acting as a distraction wasn't her priority.

Hanni – like Freddy – had had an instinctive sense that the Document Centre was where their killer would be the moment Ortmann had mentioned it. Seeing the wealth of information about SS members that was available, and hearing that the facility employed a number of German nationals among their filing clerks, had only deepened that feeling. That was a good enough reason for making their visit as smooth as it could be, but Hanni also had reasons of her own. She had come not only because she wanted to stay closely involved in the investigation, but because she wanted to know exactly how the killer worked. How the names got to him; how names could be got to him. She hadn't allowed herself to follow where that knowledge might lead, but neither had she had any intention of leaving without it.

She stuck close to the captain therefore as he led them back upstairs, giving Freddy time to resettle himself and asking inoffensive questions about his team's working arrangements. That softened Cooper up enough to get her access to the ground-floor offices where the bulk of the filing clerks worked, where she might be able to gain a better understanding of their processes. Even though these were deserted, however – because Freddy had deliberately chosen to schedule their visit outside working hours so as not to alert any of the workers – Cooper would not leave her alone in them. To her dismay, there were no record cards lying on any of the tables – there wasn't as much as a pen. All Hanni could deduce was that the offices were functional rather than comfortable: she spent five minutes snapping the grey walls and the spartan desks which lacked any personal mementos and learned absolutely nothing from them. She followed Freddy and Cooper to his office, trying frantically to work out how to sneak back to the offices and take a look in the filing cabinets lining their walls and coming up with nothing.

'You'll have to make do with black coffee, I'm afraid: we're always out of milk by this time of the day. The cookies, however, are great.'

Cooper's twanging approach to the German language had altered *Kekse* – the word for biscuits – into something far more American than the plate of *vanillekipferl* he offered them. Hanni accepted a cup and a biscuit, which she immediately picked into crumbs.

'That was quite a number you gave us earlier, for all the

records you hold here. You must have a staff of hundreds to process them.'

Freddy had decided to be charming again, which relaxed Cooper.

The captain helped himself to another biscuit and smiled. 'I wish. We've got around sixty clerks working in shifts at the moment, and a handful of supervisors, and that's it. They keep promising us more bodies, but...' He shrugged, and Freddy mirrored him.

'What a nightmare, and I thought we were short-staffed.'

Hanni sipped at her coffee as Freddy and the captain swapped stories about being overworked and under-resourced, although the first taste had told her that the drink was stewed and bitter. The conversation too was beginning to grate on her. Freddy was going far too slowly round the houses and Hanni wished that he would get to the point. He had warned her that he was going to keep the conversation general for as long as he could, in order to build up trust between himself and the captain. He had also been clear that he would be the one asking the questions. It was still hard not to jump in and hurry him. They had been at the Document Centre for almost an hour, and they had, so far, learned nothing of value to the case, or to her. She, however, had no choice but to sit in silence as Freddy meandered or risk never accompanying him anywhere again.

'At least I don't have ten million crimes on my desk to sort out. How long is organising all the records going to take?'

The captain laughed and replied in the same chummy tone. 'Years at the rate we're going, probably decades. We've pulled out the main culprits, as you've seen, but, other than that, we've barely sorted through to the end of the Bs and that's just finding never mind filing them.'

Which accounts for Albrecht and Buchtel, but means the killer will never get to F, not unless I push him there.

The first thought spinning through her head stopped Hanni from catching the second one before it leaped out of her mouth.

'But that's no good. If that's true, then how was it possible for him to get up to Wittke?'

'Hanni, what the hell?'

Cooper sat back and stared at them both. Hanni couldn't tell from his closed face whether it had been her outburst or Freddy's that had stripped away his friendly manner. Not that it mattered. Captain Cooper wasn't their *chum* anymore; he was a soldier. And, as his next words made clear, he had been that all along.

'Okay. Can we stop the pretence now? Don't you think it's time to tell me what you're actually doing here?'

He waved a dismissive hand as Freddy's expression turned rather too dramatically to shocked.

'Don't, Inspector, please. This has all been very pleasant, but don't think I fell for it. I know what you said on the telephone. That you were having "neighbourhood issues" with trouble-makers you suspect of having SS backgrounds. That you want us to work together to identify those who, as you put it, might be an "ongoing threat to the peace". Well, that's all very laudable, but I didn't believe you when you rang, and I don't believe you now.'

He opened his desk drawer and pulled out a newspaper. 'And I've read this. I know about the body found less than two miles from here, the one that bore "indications that the victim was a member of the SS".'

He paused and gave Freddy a chance to correct him or to step up and explain himself. Freddy, however, waited in silence, his face impassive. And Hanni, for once, didn't dare speak.

Cooper sighed. 'Fine, if that's how you want to play it. Well, why don't I get everything out on the table instead? I know – because our intelligence services know, which means so do the Brits and the Soviets – that there have been two more bodies found with these *indications*. Policemen talk to each other, Inspector, but the right ones also talk to us – as does your network of street kids. With the earnings some of them receive from all the sides they're in bed with, they could probably finance this place. Anyway, that's by the by. What's interesting here is you turning up, "fascinated" by the "incredible" work we're doing. I don't do coincidences and I don't imagine you do either, so I'll ask you again: what is really going on? Are you going to tell me or shall I hazard a guess? Is one of our clerks picking off Nazis?'

'I'm not certain.' Freddy tapped his fingers briefly together, as if he was counting the pros and cons of an honest response, and then he served his ball and sat back. 'But I think it's a distinct possibility, yes.'

Cooper swore profusely under his breath. 'Dear God, I was hoping you would tell me I was imagining things. This isn't good – it isn't good at all.' He stared at the newspaper again and then he locked his eyes onto Freddy's. 'That's it now, no more stalling: tell me what you know, or what you suspect at any rate.'

Hanni watched the captain's face move through a palette of colours as Freddy ran through the facts of the case. By the time he had finished, Cooper was sweating.

'This needs solving before it gets any worse.' He ignored Freddy's snorted 'you think'. 'The division of the city has always been shaky at best and the Russians are already pushing against it: they'd have us all out of Berlin if they could and make the whole city part of Soviet-run Germany. Have you any idea what a public relations disaster it would be if it got out that an American-run documents facility was implicated in a string of murders? At best it would look as if we let our staff run amok; at worst it could look like... well, collusion is how the anti-American sections of Berlin's press will spin it, no matter how ridiculous that is.' He shook his head. 'There's already been three, and you think there'll be more? At what point were you planning to tell me any of this?'

Freddy shrugged. 'I wasn't – or not today. To be honest, what I was intending to do was to have a look at your staff records while Hanni dragged you away for a photograph and see what I could piece together from those. It wasn't the greatest plan, I'll grant you, but I thought that, if you got wind of our suspicions at this stage, you'd close ranks against our investigation – precisely because, as you say, this is, in so many ways, a disaster.'

Cooper stared at the floodlights, whose silver arc looked far more menacing now that it was dark.

'You're not wrong with that conclusion. Closing ranks is exactly what I should do. But if me playing hardball leads to more murders, then none of us will come out of this well.'

He paused and came to a conclusion that clearly sat heavily on him. 'Whatever assistance I do give you, however, it goes by my rules. Is that understood?'

Cooper waited for something more reassuring than Freddy's bland 'of course'. When it didn't come, he continued anyway.

'Fine. Well, we have both American and German personnel working here with access to the information that you think is being used. I can't give you access to the American staff records – that would get me court-martialled. There could, however, be a way around with the German ones. You need to understand something though and I mean you have to take this seriously: I'm only going to get involved if you promise to keep the Centre's name out of any subsequent arrest and any trial. I don't care how you do that, but if it turns out that your man is operating out of here, that fact can never come to light.'

'I can do that.'

Hanni knew Freddy couldn't guarantee that at all, and she knew he didn't care about promising it, not if it got him the result that he needed. She held her breath as Cooper fiddled with his pen.

'All right then, this is how it will go. First of all, nothing leaves the premises. There would be questions raised if I sent personnel files to a German police station and the sentries here are authorised to carry out random searches, on everyone regardless of rank. What I can do, however, is look through the German personnel records and see if there is anyone who flags up as someone worth looking at, or if there is anyone I can elim-inate – we have a couple of workers who walk with a stick, for example. That should help me whittle the numbers down into something useful. I will send you some notes, which won't be in my name. I will answer some questions, if you put them discreetly. Now I need your help. I know what you've told me about the profile you've built up of the killer, which is little enough: is there anything else you can think of that might help me?'

Freddy sighed. 'I wish I could give you a template to scour the records with. I don't know how much detail your employees are required to go into when they apply for a position here, although, hopefully, they will have completed a *Fragebogen* and told something close to the truth on that. What we need more than anything is a link to the victims. I suggest you look for anyone with past connections to IG Farben, which is where one of them worked. Or anyone who was in a post-war internment camp in Westphalia, or Hanover or at Bad Nenndorf, which are the three where our dead SS officers were held. Or Dachau, which is unlikely. Beyond that, we're grasping at straws. We know – or rather we suspect – that he was a soldier, but any German male who was between seventeen and sixty during the war could tick that box.'

'And send photographs if you can.'

Hanni was relieved that Freddy didn't try to stop her when she spoke, although she would have made her point even if he had got angry with her again. He had said all along that he wanted her because of her eye for detail, and this was her kind of detail.

She leaned forward and made sure Cooper's attention was focused on her. 'Our man has been described as ordinary, remarkably so. A photograph would eliminate any distinctive features and act as another screening method. And given what we've noted at the crime scenes, maybe you could also look for someone whose work is efficient and neat, who makes a virtue of that.'

She warmed to her theme as Freddy remained silent. 'And this is just a hunch, but there seems to be an air of confidence about the killer and perhaps a sense of righteousness – as if he's on a crusade. So maybe someone who holds themselves separate, or who acts as if he has a chip on his shoulder. Someone who might feel superior to the work that he does here.'

'Dear God. The chip on the shoulder probably describes half the men we employ. Most of them held jobs with far more status than they can claim now, and some have struggled to accept that. As for a crusade...' Cooper exhaled. 'That is a frightening thought given the unlimited pool of people we've got here for him to pick from. But that's helpful, so thank you. Leave it with me. I'll work on it now, get you something by Monday morning. It won't do any of us any good to delay.'

He showed them out in an uncomfortable silence, which continued as Hanni and Freddy got back into the car.

'I'm sorry.' Hanni left her apology until they were well away from the patrols and the wire. 'I shouldn't have told him personal information about you, and I shouldn't have blurted Wittke's name out like that.'

She had been hoping for some softening and at least a renewed professional connection, but Freddy didn't respond in any way that she wanted.

'No, you shouldn't have done either. Thankfully, however, your intervention and your... impulsiveness actually got us where we needed to be. Don't do it again though, Hanni. You're good at what you do, and I want you on the team, but I won't keep you if you become a liability.'

A liability? She stared at Freddy's averted face, her cheeks smarting.

'Seriously? That's hardly—'

'Can you drop Fraulein Winter at her lodgings first please? And then take me back to the station.'

Hanni's mouth fell open as Freddy leaned forward to tap on the driver's partition and totally ignored her protest. And then, with a conversation-stopping 'now, if you don't mind, I've got work to do', he buried himself in his papers.

CHAPTER 15

'Our contact has sent us five names who he considers our most likely candidates if the killer actually does work out of Wasserkäfersteig. That's not a given, but it's the line of investigation that Brack is happiest for us to follow, rather than alerting all the Allied intelligence units.'

Freddy didn't bother to tell his team that the Allies already knew as much as they did and that Brack had already been warned by the Americans that they weren't going to leave the case in his hands unless there was 'some substantial progress'. They didn't need to feel under the kind of pressure to solve or face losing the case that could lead to wrong-headed decisions. He spread Cooper's notes across the desk and kept his tone optimistic.

'This list has been compiled based on all the information we've gleaned from the crime scenes and the visits to the victims' homes. It also takes into account the physical profile that would make it feasible to move a body even a short distance from a pavement into a building. That eliminated a lot of people – it seems that more of the Centre's male clerks have physical injuries left from the war than I realised. As well as the names, we have also been sent these.' Freddy waved at the board behind him, which was now adorned with a new set of photographs. 'Fraulein Winter, do you have any thoughts on them?'

Hanni stepped forward, feeling uncomfortably as if her skills were on trial. She wished that he had taken a moment to show her the pictures privately first, but Freddy was still avoiding any close contact with her. She focused on the photographs instead of him, conscious of the detectives waiting eagerly behind her, pushing Freddy out of her mind.

Captain Cooper had certainly been listening: all the faces she was looking at could certainly be described as ordinary. She peered closer and scrutinised them one by one, looking for the faint impression of scars, or noses with bumps or chins that protruded or doubled. There was nothing noteworthy. Two of the men, however, were looking more directly into the camera than the others. And both of them were bland enough to be forgettable. Hanni cut the room away and stared into the men's eyes, trying to determine what, if anything, the camera had captured.

'These two.' She pointed at the two photographs which had most caught her eye and read out their captions. 'Elias Lehner and Gerhard Bayer. There's a directness in their gaze which suggests, perhaps, more confidence than the other three. They aren't looking to the side – they're looking right into the lens.' She looked closer again. 'And there's a tension round their mouths which could mean they're uncomfortable or irritated.'

Or they just don't like having their photographs taken.

She waited for someone to say it, but nobody did. The junior officers were all waiting for Freddy to pull up the names from Cooper's notes. When he did – and when he looked over at Hanni – it was the first time she had seen respect on his face in days.

'That's an interesting call, thank you. Those are also the two names that our source put stars against. Both of them are high-achieving workers, and both make sure the bosses know that, but neither of them, apparently, are particularly well liked. Bayer is described as a "cold fish" and Lehner has a temper. Somebody once suggested – as a joke supposedly – that he'd only taken the job to find and destroy his own SS record and his reaction was extreme enough to merit a warning.'

He looked down at the papers again. 'There are also a couple of other notes next to Bayer. One mentions some hearing loss, but he's apparently an excellent lip-reader so that offsets any difficulties there. The other says that his immediate boss describes him as a "know-it-all". I know we have five names to look at, but I would suggest that either of these men could particularly fit the loner, chip-on-the-shoulder-but-confident type we're looking for.'

'Do either of them – or any of the others – have links with the victims?'

Freddy thumbed through the sheets Cooper had sent him before he answered Matz's question.

'Lehner was at the Westphalia internment camp where Buchtel was held, although the overlap is uncertain. We can, however, put Bayer at Hanover at the same time as Wittke. The other three failed to enter that information on their *Fragebogen* forms, although it was requested at the time.'

Matz shook his head. 'And, as usual, I bet nobody followed that up.'

'That isn't necessarily a problem. It could be more significant that both Lehner and Bayer completed their questionnaires correctly. That could suggest that they don't like gaps, that they're efficient. That they have a respect for, or an interest in, information being correct.' Hanni leaned into the pictures again. 'Whoever wrote the notes and the signs left with the bodies shows those characteristics.'

This time, Freddy almost smiled at her. 'She's right. So Bayer and Lehner go to the top of the list of people we want to know more about.'

The room instantly began to hum. Matz was the first to his feet.

'Brilliant. Shall we pull all five of them in for questioning or interview those two first?'

Everyone, including Hanni, stared at Freddy, waiting for him to issue the orders which would ignite the investigation. He fiddled with his notes. He did not, however, answer.

Why is he stalling?

And then Hanni remembered what she had asked Freddy after Wittke's murder – 'Do you really want to bring the killer in?' – and the shadows that had darkened his face.

He still doesn't know the answer.

Matz's frown had been picked up by everyone else.

They can't catch any hint that he's hesitating, not when they can feel the killer in their sights. Someone will go to Brack and complain.

'Inspector, sir: do you have a different plan?'

The look he gave her was hardly bursting with gratitude, but he picked up her cue.

'I do, Fraulein, yes.'

Freddy glared round the room, as if it was the men who were at fault, not him, which simply underlined to Hanni how conflicted he was.

'And that plan doesn't involve charging in and firing up the press, never mind the Americans.'

Hanni could see him assembling his argument as he went, but the others didn't know him as personally as she did, and they couldn't. They read confidence not conflict in his deliberations, and they settled as Freddy continued.

'Think about it: our source hasn't alerted anyone else at the facility that we're looking at their staff. If we burst into the Document Centre and arrest five, or even two, of their workers in one swoop, someone will be straight on the phone and selling the story. Or, and this is more likely, American military security will ramp up and we won't get our suspects out of the building.

'Our source was rattled when we told him what we suspected and – if he's right about what the intelligence services already know – I'd say the wider American military command is on edge about this case. They are worried that, if the killer does turn out to work for them, they'll be attacked by the press for having no control over their employees. I don't need them getting spooked and blocking us, or us picking up the wrong man and the guilty party escaping, so...' He paused and then his voice finally grew as confident as his audience needed. 'We're going to come at this sideways. We're going to gather information about the named men – including where they were when the murders took place – but not from them. We're going to do it via their families.'

'I'm sorry, sir, but what do you mean?'

Matz's question, thankfully, sounded confused but not chal- lenging. Hanni knew that if Freddy could convince Matz that he had thought his plan through, or that he at least wasn't making it up on the spot the way she was all too aware that he was doing, the other men would take their lead from his more popular assistant.

To her relief, Freddy didn't bridle at the interruption, which meant that he also knew who his best ally was.

'It sounds a little left field, I know. But I want the officers who carry out the questioning to talk not to the suspects but to the parents who they all seem – if these notes are up to date – to still have.'

He looked away from Matz to include the rest of the men. 'We need to soften them up, so we tell Mum and Dad that it's a missing person's enquiry. That somehow the press has got hold of their son's name as the one the police are worried about and we have come to reassure them that's not the case before the wrong story breaks. It's a simple enough deception. Lay it on thick, as if the papers will suggest our man isn't missing but dead.'

'Will they really buy that?'

Matz grimaced at Ortmann before Freddy had to. 'They will if we tell it well enough, and then they'll be so relieved that their boy's not disappeared – or worse – they'll be desperate to sing his praises and spill everything we need to know about him.' He turned back to Freddy, his face eager. 'That's the idea, isn't it, sir? Build up a set of profiles and gather proof regarding locations and motives so that we only need to bring in the front runners?'

Freddy's face finally relaxed as Matz shaped his hesitations into a solid story that the room would accept. 'Thank you. I couldn't have put it better myself. Take them into your confidence, offer plenty of sympathy and one of you will catch our killer. Are we agreed?'

Hanni watched the men move from the sidelines into the palm of Freddy's hand. It was hard not to applaud as he pulled them all in.

'Excellent. Right then, let's get this done. Matz, you take Lehner and decide on the allocation of the other three and I'll visit' – he glanced down at his notes – 'Bayer's mother.' He smiled again and clapped his hands. 'Let's get moving – let's narrow down our suspects!'

It took ten minutes to clear the room, ten minutes which Freddy spent buzzing from officer to officer, giving pep talks, patting backs and keeping his distance from Hanni, whose name hadn't been mentioned in connection with any of the allocated tasks, not even the basic office ones. She knew she had no right to demand to accompany him, or anyone else, but that didn't stop her wanting to. Or wanting to know why he seemed so reluctant to follow what she had guessed – from the frowns that had initially greeted his plan – was standard police procedure.

The moment the room emptied, she rounded on him. 'What was that about, not bringing the suspects in straight away like everyone expected you would? You know Cooper would help you do it discreetly, so what is it? Are you still on the fence about stopping the killer?'

'Are you?'

She hadn't expected that challenge and didn't know how Freddy had come so close to digging up her doubts, although she knew he was watching her and trying to join up the few clues she had let slip. While she was trying to work out an answer, however, his shoulders sagged and the bluster disappeared.

'I shouldn't have said that – I'm sorry. I'm struggling; I won't pretend that I'm not. And if you're struggling for the same

reasons as me, which I think you are – that it's hard to feel any
sympathy for the victims he chooses – then I don't blame you. I
know your background isn't the same as mine, that you're not
Jewish, but how could any decent person not feel at least a little
bit glad that men like Wittke and Buchtel have faced "some kind
of justice"?'

He paused. He didn't, however, seem to be looking for an
answer, and Hanni was too frozen by the fact that he had just
unwittingly offered her a lifeline to explain her own hesitations
to try to think of one. She gave a nod instead and he continued.

'But I also know what I have to do, Hanni, and I do want to do
it, I promise. I can hardly leave a murderer running unchecked
around the city. It was being at the Centre, seeing all those
records. Knowing how many of the men identified in them are
still out there, untouched, probably untouchable. I couldn't help
but feel that—' He stopped.

Hanni blinked away the tears that had suddenly come pressing. For the first time since the case began, she was able to
honestly share in his feelings. 'Getting rid of a few more of them
wouldn't be such a bad plan?'

He nodded. He looked suddenly old. 'Does that make me a
monster?'

And there it was again: that word with all its poisoned
meanings.

Part of Hanni wanted to keep responding with the same
honesty he kept showing her. To admit that she had looked at the
thousands of files at the Document Centre with as much revul-
sion as he had. That unlike him, however, she hadn't wanted to
destroy the mass of information they contained: what she had
longed for was time alone to comb through them. To find *F*. To
find her father and manoeuvre his record onto a desk where, with
a bit of luck, it would find the right clerk.

It was the right moment – Freddy's exhausted face told her
that. It would never, however – or not until she had dealt one way
or another with Reiner – be the right story. She could share with

Freddy that she was as conflicted and ambivalent about solving the case as he was but not why. She could, however, offer him some comfort. She could tell him what she truly believed.

Hanni looked into his tired eyes, shook her head and gave him the smile that he had been waiting for. 'No, Freddy. Not a monster, never that. What it makes you is human.'

'Can you take the lead with her? I've told everyone to tread lightly and now I don't think that I can. I'm too wrapped up in the mess of it.'

Freddy had asked Hanni to go with him to visit Bayer's mother the moment she had assured him that the confusion which had dogged him throughout the whole case was justified. And, somewhere between the incident room and Teutonenstraβe where Frau Bayer lived, he had stopped acting as if he disliked her. Hanni wasn't entirely sure why. Perhaps because she had been kind. Perhaps because they hadn't made the journey from Kreuzberg by car, forced into the false intimacy of a back seat which had already played host to too many awkward conversations and too many worse silences. Freddy had decided, instead, to see if the journey from the city to the suburbs was as quick by public transport as Ortmann had said it was.

They had taken the train from Moritzplatz to Nikolassee and walked the short rest of the way through leafy streets and a gentle spring sunshine which had warmed them both. It had been a quick and straightforward trip and Hanni hadn't had any desire to spoil it by picking over past hostilities. Despite that, Freddy's lighter mood collapsed as soon as they arrived at Frau Bayer's home. He stared at the villa, whose exterior and garden were neatly kept and identical to every other house in the street, and grimaced.

'Look at this place, so spick and span and yet I can't shake the feeling that nothing good is going to come out of us being here. Do you feel it? That everything we've encountered so far with this case has been rotten underneath? Or can you tell me that I'm being overimaginative?'

She couldn't do that. Rotten underneath seemed to sum up not just the case but most of life in post-war Berlin.

And too much before that.

Hanni kept those thoughts to herself. Freddy was already on edge; she had no desire to turn the coming interview into another minefield. She gave a non-comital shrug instead and knocked, noticing the neighbours' curtains twitch as she did so.

It took two knocks for the door to inch open; when it did, Hanni could barely see through it.

'Frau Bayer? I'm sorry to disturb you. My name is Fraulein Hanni Winter; I am with the Kreuzberg police. And this is my colleague, Inspector Freddy Schlüssel. Could we have a quick word with you?' She smiled as warmly as she could, although she could barely make out the features she was aiming the smile at. 'Maybe inside, away from an audience?'

The door finally opened wide enough for them to properly see the thin woman standing behind it. She was elegantly dressed in a pale blue wool suit and a short string of pearls, but her face was mottled with the yellow and purple stains left by fading bruises, and her right eyelid was winged with black.

'What is this about?'

Frau Bayer's manner was as imperious as if her face was beautifully made-up, not battered.

She looks like a victim, but she won't thank us for treating her like one.

Hanni switched from the sympathetic tone she had been about to use and into her most professional one. 'Your son, Frau Bayer: we would like to have a talk with you about Gerhard.'

There it was – the momentary flinch that named Frau Bayer's attacker. There was, however, no other reaction to Hanni's request. Frau Bayer stood aside and waved them both through a dark hallway into an overstuffed room whose decor Hanni doubted had been touched since the turn of the century. Everything that could be covered was decked in embroidered cloths dripping in lace. Every wall bristled with bearded men tightly bound into military uniforms. Every surface was crowded with ornately framed photographs of stiffly posed and fussily dressed children. It felt like a museum of long-lost days and, despite the daylight still attempting to push through the thick curtains, it was oppressive.

'Is that him?' Hanni pointed at a picture of a little boy dressed up as a miniature soldier.

Frau Bayer's response was a snort which pulled Freddy onto the edge of his spindly seat. 'Gerhard? Dear God, no. That is my eldest boy, Stefan. He was destined for a great career in the army, like all the men in my family. He died, however, when he was nine years old. It was a terrible loss for us all.'

The way she stressed *all* told Hanni that Frau Bayer perceived the tragedy of her son's death as rippling out far wider than family.

'I'm very sorry to hear that.'

She looked back at the endless photographs again, trying in vain to see a face in the dozen images that wasn't so clearly Stefan's.

'So which of these then is Gerhard?'

Frau Bayer blinked as if she had never considered the possibility that her other son might be present. 'None of them.'

Hanni waited. When no explanation was forthcoming, she began to unravel the story of the missing person and the muddled identity which she and Freddy had practised. She was barely halfway through it when Frau Bayer stopped her.

'Are you telling me that my son is dead?'

The question was so bluntly put, all Hanni could answer was 'no'.

'Then what has he done?'

'Why would you assume that he's done anything?'

Hanni was genuinely taken aback that a mother would come

to that conclusion before any other, or before expressing any relief that her child was alive.

Frau Bayer, however, chose to hear mock surprise and to be insulted.

'Do not take me for a fool, young lady.' She glanced at Freddy, who still hadn't spoken. 'Police inspectors do not travel from the city, and they don't bring a "sympathetic female", which is what I assume you are, because of a newspaper mix-up. Not when they could telephone or send round a local man. So, let me ask you again: what has Gerhard done?'

There was no emotion, no concern beyond her irritation that Hanni was somehow trying to trick her. The woman could have been enquiring about a stranger.

There is no love here. If we told her our suspicions, she would offer him up on a platter.

Hanni, however, had learned her lesson at the Document Centre so instead of blurting out 'possibly murdered three men', she batted the question back.

'You seem certain that he could have done something. What do you think he might be capable of?'

Frau Bayer raised an eyebrow as if the question was ridiculous and gestured to her face. 'How should I answer that? Gerhard was the one responsible for this, but I rather thought you might have deduced that if he is somehow a person of interest to you. What is a man who can beat his own mother capable of? Anything, I imagine. I can certainly tell you what Gerhard is *not* capable of doing and that is making me proud, but you have no doubt realised that from the lack of the photographs you were looking for. My son has never been the man that he should have been, Fraulein Winter – I can also tell you that. And now, it seems, if he can raise a hand to me and you are interested in him, he has become even less.'

'Why aren't you proud of your son?'

Frau Bayer turned to Freddy and answered him in the same disdainful tone. 'Why would I be? Perhaps in your family, *son* entitles you to special privileges. Our family is not one of those. We have standards: Gerhard never met them. And we held a special place in this country: we were an army family through and through, Inspector, an honour which comes with responsibilities and expectations. Or at least we were, until Gerhard.'

'An "army family" no matter who commanded that army?'

Hanni shook her head as discreetly as she could at Freddy before he could start an argument which would close down any confidences. Frau Bayer, however, continued as if she hadn't heard him.

'Gerhard was expected to follow in his father's, and his grand-fathers', footsteps and make a career in the military. He, however, never made the grade his elder brother would have exceeded. And when Gerhard was finally admitted – because the army had been forced to reduce its entry requirements, not because he had suddenly bloomed into a man who deserved a place in it – he squandered his opportunity. He was an officer, and then he wasn't. How does that happen?'

She tutted as Hanni started to attempt an answer. 'That was a rhetorical question: it doesn't. If you ask him, however, he will tell you that it happened because he is an "honourable" man. That he refused to follow an order because it would have been "dishon-ourable" to obey it. That is a ridiculous answer. What is a soldier there for except to obey orders?'

'Do you know the details of what he refused to do, Frau Bayer?'

Freddy had kept his voice neutral, despite the cruelty in hers. When she answered him, however, her voice dripped with scorn.

'No, Inspector, I do not. Nor do I want to: the word "refuse" was enough for me. My son finally managed to become an army officer and he was stripped of his rank. Now he is a filing clerk. What details do I need to know but that?'

It was clear from her pursed mouth that she had no wish to talk about him anymore. It was also clear that there was nothing in this house for Gerhard Bayer but disgust; Hanni suspected that there had never been. For the first time, she let her gaze linger on the marks which covered most of the right side of the old woman's face. For all her poise – and the apparently limitless depths of her coldness towards him – it must have been terrifying to have been hurt so badly by her own child.

'When do you expect to see Gerhard again?'

The steady gaze dropped.

'He visits once a month, for appearance's sake. The next time he comes, I will not be answering the door. Let him make what he wishes of that.'

Frau Bayer's face switched from combative to lost with a speed that took Hanni by surprise. She glanced round the room, at the dead children who were glorified and the spaces where the live child was missing, and knew that the change did not mean that the woman was softening.

There was nothing further in this house that they needed to hear or to see. Gerhard Bayer had been high on their suspect list when they arrived: based on his mother's testimony, and her face, Hanni guessed that Freddy would now have moved him into top place. She needed to get out, away from the darkness that she feared had settled here so long ago it was part of the fabric. She nodded to Freddy, who got to his feet.

Frau Bayer didn't lead them to the front door or acknowledge their goodbyes. She remained motionless in her chair, as frozen in time as the room. Neither of them pretended that they would be returning; both of them were glad to be outside in fresher air.

Hanni was the first to break their stunned silence.

'That was horrible – and heartbreaking. Whatever Gerhard Bayer has done, or not done, can you imagine being so loathed by your own mother, and for so long?'

And then she stopped. She realised that she was fighting back an unexpected rush of tears. That a sudden memory of Talie, who had never stopped loving her elder daughter even after her heart had been broken by the death of another, had rushed back too hard to push it away again.

'Some people don't deserve children. Some people just aren't good enough. And the ones that were…'

Freddy was instantly at her side, with his hand on her elbow as her words ran out.

'What happened to your mother, Hanni? You never speak about her, or any of your family at all.'

His voice was so soft, so full of care for her. The relief of finally having something personal she could share with him was more welcome than she knew how to say. It was impossible, therefore, not to open herself up – at least a little.

'She disappeared, in a bombing raid in the last days of the war. She used to wander you see, even when the streets were so dangerous, and I couldn't stop her from doing it. I had a little sister, like you did. And she died and my mother never got over it. Her heart cracked. But I loved her through all of it and I know she loved me…'

And then the words were too much and the tears overtook her, and there was nothing after that except Freddy's arms and a kiss whose completeness melted the past.

CHAPTER 16

4–8 MARCH 1947

Hanni had pulled away from his embrace. No, that wasn't true. She had pushed Freddy away from her – torn between the fear that she would lose herself in his arms and the longing to do exactly that – and the shock of her rejection had blown up an argument neither of them could find a way back from.

She 'blew hot and cold beyond anything bearable'. He 'had no idea what a mistake getting involved with her would be'. Both of those facts were true, and neither could be resolved on a rain-spotted pavement in Zehlendorf. In the end, Hanni had stormed away and forbidden Freddy to follow, forcing herself not to look back to see if he tried.

She spent the whole night awake. When she stumbled down with no appetite to breakfast the next morning, there was a message – but no caller's name – to say that she wasn't needed at the station for the rest of the week. Freddy was travelling to Hanover to follow up on Bayer, Matz was travelling to West-phalia to follow up on Lehner and the murder team wasn't due to convene again until Saturday. It was a pause in her involvement with the case that Hanni didn't want, but it was one that she needed. It would keep her away from any more emotional disasters, and it would give her the time that she needed to finally sort out her life.

Whatever she had pretended, to him and to herself – and whatever reality dictated their relationship should be – Hanni wanted more than a working involvement with Freddy. She had known the truth of that for long enough, but the kiss had forced her to face it. Wanting, however, was still a long way from having. And having didn't even begin to be possible until she did what she had spent too long avoiding and dealt conclusively with Reiner.

She had to denounce him – there were no excuses left and there were too many promises still unfulfilled. She would do it and she would take the proof of it to Freddy, and she would do that in the knowledge that it might not be enough. That he still might hate her couldn't matter. Over the course of a long and sleepless night with the imprint of his lips still traced on her own, Hanni had come to an inescapable conclusion: there was more pain to be had in hiding from her past than in trying to secure a better future.

It was that conclusion that had kept her out of the darkroom, which was her usual bolthole when the station or her private commissions didn't need her. That had taken her early on Tuesday morning to Fehrbelliner Platz instead and into a café where she could shelter from the leaden grey skies and the spotting rain and wait for a glimpse of her father. From the moment she entered it, however, she couldn't settle.

At first, she fiddled with a newspaper and then picked up, turned over and put down a book. She couldn't concentrate. The sleepless night had stirred up far more than just her longing for Freddy. Memories of her own which she had long ago buried were now resurfacing, mixed up with the ones that he had shared with her. Their images had been flashing through her dreams since Reiner had returned, growing stronger since she had witnessed Freddy's collapse and read Konrad Wittke's evil-soaked diary.

A little girl being marched away behind a pack of snarling

dogs. Freddy redrawn as a pyjama-clad skeleton in a prison camp. And one that was stronger than the rest, a sight that she hadn't imagined but had witnessed, whose details had flooded back vivid and visceral and refused to let go. A row of barracks and, behind them, a row of... Hanni wanted to say men, but the word wouldn't fit.

Hanni ordered another coffee she wouldn't drink and stared across the horseshoe-shaped sweep of the square. It didn't take much imagination to replace its smooth flagstones with gravel. To swap the wooden poles still in place from the early morning's now cleared-away market stalls for a set of far crueller contraptions. To be in the summer of 1940, not the spring of 1947.

'No wandering, Hannelore. And no photographs.'

Reiner's instructions washed over her, although she smiled and agreed to them. She might be seventeen with all the expectations of behaviour that almost adulthood brought with it, but she was still at heart the ten-year-old girl at the Adlon looking for an opportunity to slip away from the grown-ups.

Not that she had come to the reception with any plans to slip away from it: she hadn't expected there to be anything interesting enough to risk her father's anger if she tried. Hannelore had assumed that this party – which had taken her to the Sachsenhausen Concentration Camp on the outskirts of Berlin and its commandant's elegant villa there – would follow the pattern these events usually clung to. Dull drinks in an overly polished drawing room, followed by a dull lunch, followed by dull speeches that were endlessly the same. Three hours of increasingly weary smiles and agreeing that 'yes, it was a shame that her mother was too ill to attend' and thanking the leering men who declared her to be 'a delightful stand-in'. Playing hostess in place of Talie was the price Hannelore endured in exchange for being allowed to continue with her photography course and it was a role that she normally daydreamed her way through. Today, however, had turned out to be different. Camp Commandant Loritz – who was eager to show off the improvements to his 'facilities' that Reiner's department had financed – had forgone the speeches and offered his guests a tour instead.

Hannelore had left the villa at a trot, eager to finally see one of the camps her father was obsessed with, and to get some answers to the fears that filled her about them. It soon transpired, however, that the tour was to be a cursory and tightly controlled event. Despite the fact that the camp was apparently close to capacity, there wasn't a soul other than the guards to be seen. She guessed that the prisoners had been confined away from curious eyes inside the long lines of low-slung barracks. Their absence did not make the prison any less brutal. Even in June, the wind that swept through its wide spaces had a sharp bite, and it was impossible not to notice the machine gun and the gallows looming over the opposite sides of the parade ground.

Hannelore quickly realised that she didn't need to find a prisoner to question to know that Sachsenhausen – which Loritz had referred to as the model all the other concentration camps Hitler had ordered were based on – was a bleak and soulless place. The strips of soil edging the stony grounds were bare; the barracks were tightly shuttered and blank. Nothing about the place suggested an interest in life.

Loritz whirled the party from block to block, waxing lyrical about the camp's latest medical acquisitions, letting them peep through a high wall across to the adjoining brick factory where most of the invisible prisoners were employed. Hannelore kept to the edges of the group, her hands feeling heavy and useless without the camera that she couldn't find a safe moment to slip out of her bag. Despite her misgivings, she still wanted to get a proper look at one of the barracks, if only to get a sense of how many men it might contain and the conditions that they were held in.

Finally – as Loritz launched into yet another lecture about the improvements he hoped to make to the factory complex – she found her moment. She edged carefully away and around the side of the nearest building. The blinds were tightly drawn across the narrow windows and she couldn't see in, so she kept moving forward to the next, her eyes searching for a chink. A dozen steps more, however, and she wished that she hadn't gone searching at all.

A gap had opened up between the blocks, leading onto a wider space, a smaller version of the main parade ground. Hannelore walked towards it, although every tingling nerve end was telling her to walk away from the curious grouping she had spotted at the far end. *Be careful what you wish for* wouldn't leave her head. She had wanted to see a prisoner. Now she could see three of them and she didn't want to see any of them at all. If it hadn't been for the slight twitch from a dangling foot, Hannelore would have assumed that what she was walking towards was a sculpture, not a group of still living human beings.

The men whose limbs formed triangles against the gnarled wooden posts were waxen and bloodless. Their wrists had been fixed above and behind them and bound tight with cords of rope thicker than their arms. Their shoulders were twisted, their neck muscles strained; their bodies were pushed forward at an impossible angle. The lines etched on their faces ran deeper than pain.

She instinctively reached for her camera – the torture needed a more permanent witness than her horrified stare, and she needed a shield to separate her from it. She didn't, however, have a chance to take even one frame.

'So here you are, where you shouldn't be. Why are you staring at them, Hannelore? They are criminals – they are being punished. They don't deserve your attention.'

Hannelore jerked away from Reiner's deliberately bored tone. 'What can they possibly have done to deserve such an agony? Who treats other people like this?'

'What does it matter what they have done, and why would you refer to them as people?'

Reiner's hand shot out and gripped onto her shoulder. 'I told you not to wander. Don't blame me if you disobey and then don't like what you see. And now we are going to go back and re-join the Commander, who, luckily, is still boring the rest of his listeners to sleep and won't have noticed your absence. Don't make a fuss about this, Hannelore – don't discuss it. You are, after all, a good National Socialist girl, aren't you? The daughter of an SS officer and part of the clan. You support the Party's policies? That's certainly what your sponsor Goebbels believes, and your lecturers, and that is all this is: the Party's policies in action. Girls like you don't question those, or what happens to Jews; girls like you aren't squeamish. Not if they want to keep their privileges and their college places anyway.'

He kept a tight hold on her for the rest of the tour, although anyone looking at his arm looped through hers would have seen only affection. And when Hannelore tackled him the next day about the justification for such a violent punishment, he walked away and ignored her.

And set up a pattern which I blindly followed and now we both need to atone for.

Hanni wasn't sorry that Sachsenhausen had come back to haunt her: the memory of its horrors – the thought that Freddy could have endured even a fraction of them – had strengthened her resolve.

She pushed away her cold coffee and asked for her bill. It was lunchtime and a steady flow of people had begun to pour out of the offices of the British Control Commission, no doubt some of whom would be heading into her café. Hanni had no desire to fall into even the most casual conversation and repeat her experience at Masurenallee – she was convinced one of the secretaries she had met there had been the one to betray her. She also had no wish to ever speak directly to Reiner again. What she wanted was a quiet corner and one sight of him, to prove to herself that he was still employed at the Commission, that he was still living his *very nice life*. And then what she wanted was to take that nice life away.

It took another twenty minutes of waiting, pressed into the shelter of a doorway, before he finally appeared. When he did, Hanni could have spit. If the bouncy-haired girl hanging on his arm was anything to go by, Reiner's life wasn't merely nice, it was overflowing.

As Hanni watched, the girl tipped her creamy face up to Reiner's; Reiner bent his dark head over hers. When they kissed, Hanni had to bite down on a snarl. Her father had not only rebuilt his professional life, he had conjured up a new and obviously equally successful personal one. He looked happy and Hanni couldn't bear it. The last thing Reiner Foss deserved to enjoy was happiness.

And he won't enjoy it for long, not if I get this next move right. He'll be paying for his sins then, not profiting from them.

She curled into the doorway's hiding place until her pulse calmed and watched the laughing couple walk away. She wanted to storm after Reiner and tear at his eyes. She wanted to storm into the Commission and scream out all his transgressions. She wasn't, however, going to do either of those things. Hanni had a far better plan than that, a properly considered one, which was the only way, she now knew, to deal with Reiner. There wouldn't be another guard or another Jannick. The only person she was going to put in danger was herself and, if her plan worked, she would hardly be in danger at all.

The approach she had decided on was a simple one. She might not have managed the moment alone in the Document Centre which she had needed to find Reiner's files, but nobody ever supervised her at the police station. Hanni had already located the telephone number of the British Intelligence Section, and she had located the right name to ask the switchboard to connect her to. All she had to do now was make an appointment and gather up her evidence, of which she had plenty. So she could wait and she could let Reiner enjoy his last girlfriend and his last lunch: he had, after all, no idea what was coming.

The plan might have been a simple one, but she hadn't thought it through as carefully as she had convinced herself that she had. She hadn't thought about the pitfalls beyond not involving anyone else. She had measured the danger to herself in terms of the time it would take to put her idea in motion and not the one that she actually faced: her name.

Hanni Winter – now that Reiner knew who Hanni Winter was – carried all the same risks when she used it as Hannelore Foss would have done. To make her plan work, what Hanni had needed was to be a third girl, for a day or two at least. By the time she had realised that mistake, however, and cursed her stupidity, the damage was done.

Everything had begun so well. The officer Hanni had spoken to – a man whose plummy tones could have made him Megs' brother – was not only the right one to speak to, he had been very accommodating: he had given her an appointment to meet with him the next afternoon. To secure that, however, Hanni had had to outline the nature of her business. That had made her uncomfortable, but she had worked her way through it. Then, however, he had insisted that she reveal the surname of the man whose war record she wanted to talk about, so that 'we can access our own files and be ready for you'.

Although the explanation, and the officer's manner, had seemed reasonable, it had been hard, almost impossible, for Hanni to shake off her father's threat about his web of informers – she had spent most of the call listening for suspicious breathing or clicks on the line. In the end, Hanni had only complied with the conditions because she couldn't think of a reason to refuse which wouldn't forfeit the meeting. And saying 'Reiner Foss' had flustered her so badly, she hadn't given herself the second she needed to think when the charming officer asked her to identify herself.

Announcing herself as Hanni Winter rather than using an alias was a slip that threatened to drop Hanni into a spiral in which she regretted ever making the call. To pull herself out of that, and to force herself to go through with the next steps, she had therefore forced herself to focus on all the reasons she had to be positive.

Firstly, she had finally begun the process she had been edging round for too long, which was in itself an achievement. Secondly, Schlüterstraße – where the British Intelligence Services were based – was physically separate enough from the Commission offices where Reiner worked and far enough from the girls at Lietzenseeufer for her to hope that Reiner's network of connections wouldn't cover it. More importantly, there would be less than twenty-four hours between her placing the call and the actual meeting which would bring Reiner's charmed life to an end, and it had taken Reiner a day or so longer than that to track her down the last time. What she had done, therefore, was a risk, but it was, Hanni decided, a manageable one. It had to put Reiner in more danger than her.

She had spent the rest of the night refusing to worry. She had focused instead on writing up her notes and collecting together her photographs – including the one of him pushing the children onto the train which she put at the top of the pile – into a dossier that pulled her father apart. Rereading that and staring at the terrified faces she had captured at Theresienstadt had made the risk not only manageable but worthwhile.

It was shortly after noon on Wednesday when Hanni arrived at Hallesches Tor station with more than an hour to spare before her appointment. She hadn't slept. The photographs had stayed with her through the long night, as had a fear she couldn't quite quell that Reiner would be the one to act first. That he would sense that she was coming. That he would hit out not at her but at

Natan or – and this was the real fear that had twisted her stomach long past dawn – at Freddy.

I don't know who is key in your life, but I will.

Reiner's threats were never idle ones.

And I won't let them stop me, not now when I'm so close.

She walked up the wooden stairs, holding tight to her bag, convincing herself that time would stay on her side. That she could, and that she would, beat him.

The platform when she reached it was busy, but not uncomfortably so. According to the announcements there was less than five minutes to wait for the train that would take her to the Uhlandstraße subway stop on the Kurfürstendamm and the short walk to her meeting.

And once it's done, then I can go to Freddy.

She clamped down on the thought as soon as it surfaced. What she needed to do once the meeting was over was to lie low and keep away from anyone who mattered to her until Reiner's arrest was safely in hand. That – the gap between her presenting her evidence and the authorities acting on it – was the danger point. That was where Reiner could stretch out his tendrils and find her.

And I can't think about that or I won't get onto the train.

She was trying to distract herself with the thought of Reiner safely in a cell when the train was announced as approaching and the waiting passengers, with Hanni at the front of them, shuffled closer to the platform's edge. She was also distracted by the strap of her bag, which was digging into her shoulder. Hanni had borrowed the elegant leather handbag from Frau Greber – she had nothing herself that was smart enough to create the competent impression she wanted to make – and its metal frame and buckled strap was far more uncomfortable than the canvas camera bag which she was used to carrying. As she fiddled with it, the tracks buzzed and the train rumbled closer. A few seconds later, it appeared at the far end of the platform, slowing as it approached the station.

Hanni moved to the spot where the doors would open and put

up a hand to hold back her hair as a gust of rain-speckled wind descended. As she did so, there was a surge from the overeager passengers behind her which threatened to knock her off balance. The track was suddenly far closer than it should have been and the drop down to it was dizzying. Hanni turned, or tried to, ready to remonstrate with whoever it was whose arm was pressed tight against her elbow – to point out that Hallesches Tor was so near the start of the line that no one needed to jostle their way into the carriages. The man standing behind her was tall and wide and too close for her to find his face. That didn't stop her starting to protest at his rudeness. Before she got more than a few words into her complaint, however, there was a sharp and very definite tug at her bag.

'Hey, what are you doing? Get off!'

Her voice sailed away into the clatter of the oncoming train. Hanni twisted again, trying to keep her balance, trying see the pickpocket who still had his hand curled round her bag. She couldn't see anything but the thickset man's tweed-covered chest.

'I said, get—'

She didn't have a chance to get the last words out. The shove was short and sharp and precise, straight into the middle of her back. She barely had a second to register the blow, however, before she was staggering, feeling her feet dancing away from her and knowing she was powerless to change the course they were set on.

The fall – because that was what the tumbling dance had quickly turned into – was so fast it swallowed up her reactions. The platform surged up, the train surged forward. As the momentum carried her impossibly on, all Hanni could see were the tracks yawning and ready. She hurtled towards them as a scream rang around her – Hanni didn't think it was her making the terrible noise, but her body had passed out of her control, and she had no way of knowing.

And then her body snapped agonisingly back. A pain tore through her shoulder. A worse one smashed through her cheek.

And then there was an agony which consumed her whole upper body. And then there was nothing at all.

'Hanni! What on earth has happened to you?'

Freddy would have leaped towards her if Hanni hadn't instinctively taken a step back and put her hand out to block him.

'It's nothing. It's not as bad as it looks.'

Neither of those statements were true. The pain in her reset shoulder and bruised ribs was battling and beating the painkillers the hospital had pumped her with, and her bruised and torn cheekbone felt as brittle as glass. Freddy, however, did not need to hear that. Or to hear the truth about what had caused the state she was in.

'I slipped on the stairs going down to my darkroom, but I'm fine.'

Neither of those statements were true either, but it was the best she could do to keep his panic at arm's-length. She had only just managed to rein in her own.

'He pushed you on purpose, I'd swear on it. It was a miracle that I saw what was happening and grabbed you in time. Whoever it was, they got your bag.'

Hanni had come back to a pain-shrouded consciousness surrounded by gasps of relief and a garbled explanation that she was too stunned to follow. She could barely comprehend that she was lying in one piece on the edge of the platform not ripped apart on the tracks, never mind that the shove in her back hadn't been accidental.

'We've called an ambulance and the police, but we couldn't stop him, or get a good look at him. I'm so sorry.'

Her kind-hearted rescuer – whose name had got lost somewhere in the haze of sirens and morphine – had insisted on accompanying Hanni to the hospital and providing a statement, which was, in the end, no more use than the empty one that she later offered. All Hanni had seen was a broad expanse of dark-cloth-covered chest, so that was all that she said; it wasn't, however, all that she knew.

The medical staff and the police wanted her to believe that she had been the victim of a madman, of a random attack and that she had been terribly unlucky and was perfectly safe now, so she agreed that was true. She knew that it wasn't; she knew that she would never be safe again. There was no point in upsetting anyone, however, by admitting that. Her bag was gone and so was her evidence, and she had no doubt at all who was responsible. If she had been unsure, the proof was waiting for her when she returned home from the hospital.

Frau Greber had met her at the door clutching a newly delivered bouquet of red roses whose long stems were intertwined with silk sprigs of edelweiss. When Hanni read the card which accompanied them – which her landlady assumed must have come from that 'nice young policeman' – she at least knew where the battlelines stood, even if no one else ever could.

With best wishes for your recovery after your unfortunate accident and hopes that, in the future, you will take greater care. And with heartfelt thanks for the photographs.

There was no name – there didn't need to be. Hanni doubted Reiner would care that she had the negatives, that she could make other copies. Not now that he had so physically demonstrated their cost.

It wasn't the cellar steps that did this; it was my father. I tried to go after him because he's a Nazi and he tried to have me killed because he'll do anything to protect himself and his new life. And if I don't stop, then neither will he.

Hanni dropped her eyes away from Freddy's horrified gaze. It was the truth, but she couldn't say it. Before he could throw out a net to catch Reiner in – as Hanni knew he would – she would be dragged under a car, or beneath the wheels of a bus, or thrown into a canal with her throat cut.

Or maybe he'll wait and let me watch him kill Freddy first.

It didn't matter whether it was the British officer who had tipped Reiner off, or the switchboard girl, or the secretary who filled in the daily diary – someone had warned Reiner that Hanni was coming. Someone had told him where she lived and where she would be.

Hanni had held the bouquet Frau Greber had thought was delightful and seen only its thorns. She had been a fool to underestimate her father. She should have learned long ago that he was too clever to outwit without the kind of watertight plan hers had never quite been. That, when he said he had contacts, he had meant a carefully cultivated network of informers, not a handful of street kids who would turn against him for a pocketful of coins as quickly as they would work on his behalf. She should also have learned long ago that Reiner Foss was a survivor and that there was no obstacle to his safety that he wouldn't destroy. Well, she had learned that lesson now.

Hanni groped her way to a chair, ignoring Freddy's heartfelt 'should you even be here?' Where else was she going to be? Where else but in the middle of a murder investigation could she learn the cunning she would need if she was ever going to bring Reiner to his knees? And she was going to bring Reiner somehow to his knees – she had never been more certain of that.

She managed a smile and a 'I need the distraction', even though the effort of moving her face and speaking made her feel sick. Given that the briefing should already have started and that Brack had already stomped past the room's open door twice, that was enough to get Freddy's attention away from her and back onto his waiting men.

Hanni sank back in her chair, trying to clamp down on the daggers shooting through her ribs. When Freddy started speaking, however, she instantly forgot the pain: in the time since the whole team had last come together, the investigation had finally picked up its pace.

Frau Bayer might not have been fooled by the missing person

story, but the other families had lapped it up. They had all given their sons unprompted alibis for two or more of the killings. The three lesser suspects had been discounted and Lehner too was out of the frame. There had been no overlap between him and Buchtel at Westphalia, and he hadn't been in the city for either his or the Wittke murder. Bayer, however, was a different proposition. As soon as Freddy said Bayer's name, his voice warmed up.

'He wasn't just at Hanover at the same time as Konrad Wittke – they were known to each other there and, according to the officer who ran the camp then, the relationship between the two men was a difficult one. Bayer, it seems, spent most of his time trying to impress Wittke, and Wittke spent most of his doing his best to belittle Bayer.'

Freddy picked up and studied his notes, not – or so Hanni assumed from the way he barely glanced at them – because he needed to, but because he wanted to create a pause for that image of mutual hostility to sink in.

'Bayer was no more popular at Hanover than he is at the Document Centre, and for broadly the same reasons. He was described as a "nuisance" and a "busybody". He was also at the camp for considerably longer than Wittke and most of the other men he came in with, who all possessed skills which got them out of confinement quicker. He complained a lot about that too.'

Hanni could sense the excitement rising as Bayer's profile began to form itself around the one they were looking for. Freddy caught it too, but he immediately held up his hand and clamped down on it.

'It sounds promising, I know, but we're not there yet. Wittke and Bayer didn't get on, and we've already said that there were aspects of the Wittke murder that made it, more than the previous two, feel personal. That, however, is all that we've got: two men at odds and one of them who, possibly, felt humiliated by the encounter. Beyond that, there isn't a connection between Bayer and Wittke and there is nothing, so far, to link Bayer with any of the other victims.'

He fanned through his notes again as the room, reluctantly, resettled. It wasn't an easy balance to navigate between firing his team up and making sure they didn't run forward without all the details, but Hanni could see that he was determined to hold it. Once they were quiet again, he allowed himself to sound a little more positive.

'We do know that Bayer's family background is a troubled one, which might be relevant, and that there is the possibility of recent violence from him towards his mother, which is not to be overlooked in assessing his character. That was a useful interview, and Matz and I have taken what was gleaned there and we've pieced together what we can of Bayer's war record. Again, there are no obvious connections with the victims, but it's fair to say there are oddities in his background. We already knew that Bayer had struggled when he was young to get into the army, although there was a lot of family pressure on him to join up. When he was finally admitted, it was in February 1943, after the German defeat at Stalingrad and the huge losses there meant that his less than perfect physique and his hearing issues no longer went against him. I think we can assume that getting into the army would have been a huge thing for him and, initially, he seems to have done well. He graduated from the Armoured Troops School at Munster, and he was good enough to go from there into the Fifth Panzer Division.'

He paused to acknowledge the whistle that went round the room.

'Exactly: he did better than well; he joined an elite tank division. That took him to Poland and a promotion to captain.'

Hanni leaned gingerly forward, not sure that she understood the implications of what Freddy had said. 'So he was an officer, which corroborates Frau Bayer's testimony, but does that mean he was in the SS?'

Freddy tried but couldn't quite look at her battered face.

'That didn't necessarily apply in all divisions, no, but in the Fifth it did, so yes. The Fifth was largely made up of men from the Waffen SS right from the start of the war and they stuck as much as they could to that tradition. From what I can make out, Bayer wasn't in the SS when he joined them, but he was conscripted into the organisation shortly after that. And that is one of the oddities I alluded to. We thought it was strange enough that a soldier would kill soldiers, but why would an SS man kill his fellow officers? There was supposed to be a clan system and an honour code that bound them.

'And that brings me onto the next peculiarity – which is something his mother also referred to – by November 1943, Bayer wasn't an officer anymore. We have a record of him being assigned to one of the *Einsatzgruppen* killing units which were deployed to Majdanek at the start of that month, and then he disappears. He next resurfaces in Ukraine, where he is injured and, when he arrives back in Berlin in June 1944, he's invalided out as an ordinary soldier, not as an officer. Like I said, there are oddities.'

Hanni was still a few paces behind Freddy's narrative, stuck on a name that was horribly familiar from the Nuremberg Trials. Her mind raced back through the theory about the killer being Jewish that had been discounted but might still, in part, carry some weight.

'Did you say he was at Majdanek?'

She turned briefly to the rest of the team, keen that they could follow where she was tentatively going.

'If you don't know, that was the massacre where over 40,000 Jewish prisoners were murdered in a day and piled up like rubbish in the burial trenches they had been forced to dig for themselves.'

The room grew still as she directed her words back to Freddy.

'Do you think Majdanek, or massacres like it, could be the reason he's doing it?'

Freddy was watching her now, but she couldn't read his expression. 'What do you mean?'

This time, she held his gaze and wouldn't let him look away from her bruises.

'We thought at first that the killer was killing, and was selecting the men he selected, because he was Jewish and had suffered because of it. We now know that's almost certainly not the case, but what if taking revenge for Jewish prisoners who were murdered is still the reason for his crimes? What if he was sickened by Majdanek? It was particularly horrific, even by SS standards. From the reports I've read, most of the soldiers had to be drunk to go through with what they were ordered to do. If our man was conscripted into the SS, maybe he didn't sign up to their code or share their beliefs. Maybe he's killing SS officers precisely because he wasn't like them and because he hated what they did?'

Freddy's eyes were saucer wide. 'So what you're saying is that he's choosing his victims because of what they did to the Jews? That, whatever his background, his motives for the murders are good ones?'

He shouldn't have said that last bit out loud.

Freddy realised his mistake at the same time as Hanni. He tried to pull himself back as Matz and some of the other officers frowned, but it was obvious to Hanni at least that he had meant it.

'That obviously makes no difference. A murderer is still a murderer, whatever the reason he comes up with for killing. So…'
He hesitated and stared round the room. All the waiting officers were now on the edge of their seats.

He's brought them to a tipping point. If he backs down now, if he doesn't want to go after Bayer now, they'll lose all their confidence in him.

Freddy picked up his notes and put them down again and then, to Hanni's relief, came to the same conclusion.

'So we bring Bayer in.'

The tension exploded in a cheer and nobody but her noticed that Freddy's acknowledging smile was a shaky one. He let the noise run on for a few seconds and then he held up his hand again.

'Okay, let's take a breath here. I know this feels like a victory, but it's also a gamble. Everything we have remains an assumption. Bayer could have alibis we haven't uncovered yet and he could also be innocent, so we tread very carefully. I am not ordering an arrest.'

He waited for the groan which greeted that statement to peter out. 'I'm not risking it. Two officers will collect him from his rooms on Monday morning on the pretext that we need him to help with enquiries about a security breach at the Centre. Once he is on his way here, two further officers will make a fingertip search of his lodging. I could be wrong, but nothing in the killer's patterns to date suggests that he's eager to confess and give up doing what he's doing, so we need irrefutable evidence that ties Bayer to one or more of the murder sites or all this falls apart. As for the interview itself...' He paused and looked over at Hanni. 'I will do that with Matz, and Fraulein Winter, who was also present at the interview with Bayer's mother, will observe.'

Hanni – who hadn't expected Freddy to involve her at all given the way they had parted outside Frau Bayer's house – didn't dare react in case he changed his mind. He hadn't asked whether she was willing to be in the room and nothing in her deliberately still manner could have suggested to him how eager she was to be there. She waited for someone to mutter at the choice, but no one did.

Freddy continued to hand out responsibilities and didn't address her directly until she got up with the rest to leave.

'Fraulein Winter, a moment.'

The last of the team left as he called for her and Freddy's tone immediately switched to one brimming over with concern.

'I asked you to be present when we interview Bayer because, like I said, you had your eyes on his mother and now I need your eyes on him, to help me join up the family dots. I don't think I should have said it though without speaking to you first, especially given the state you're in. What's going on? I know the houses where you live, Hanni: the basements are rarely more than ten steps down, and the stairwells are narrow enough to catch yourself if you trip. How could you have taken such a bad fall there?'

Her story hadn't fooled him. That didn't matter – that was another day's problem. She shrugged the one shoulder that she could easily move.

'I was distracted. I get clumsy when my mind is on my work.'

His twisted mouth told her that he didn't believe that explanation any more than he had believed the first one, but pushing her further would mean calling her a liar and Hanni knew that was a word Freddy would never willingly use about her. All that mattered to her was staying on the case and being in the room, face to face with a killer whose blood was as cold as her father's. A killer who, if she was clever enough, might be able to do to Reiner what she hadn't managed. Who might be able to destroy him. She couldn't let Freddy see any trace of that any more than she could tell him the truth about why she was wearing a sling. So she waited, until he sighed.

'Fine. Then rest tomorrow and be here on Monday by eight. Hanni...' He paused and then his words came out in a rush. 'You know you can tell me anything, don't you?'

He wanted to hear 'yes', so yes was what she said.

CHAPTER 17

9 MARCH 1947

Something had changed. There had been a subtle shift in the Centre's normally stagnant air.

Gerhard had noticed the first signs on the previous Tuesday when the haphazard security checks had turned suddenly more focused. Every bag was opened as the workforce left; everyone's pockets were patted – no one was waved through with a bored nod. Some people were taken aside. One light-fingered colleague with a penchant for helping himself to fountain pens and writing pads had been relieved of his duties. The whisper doing the rounds was that there had been a 'security breach', although no one seemed to know what was meant by that cover-all term. Gerhard did not ask any of the gossipers to try to explain it.

He had continued to keep himself to himself and to keep to his normal routines, even when the guards, and then his boss, changed theirs. His boss had started getting up from his desk rather than lounging at it. He had begun to prowl the room two or three times an hour, dripping his vinegary odour as he went, leaning over shoulders, querying work rates and quizzing the hapless clerk caught in his spotlight about the batches of cards spread over their desk. Gerhard's colleagues jumped and twitched under the snuffling intrusions. Gerhard didn't. Gerhard refused to allow himself to be disturbed by his boss or by the changed atmosphere. He did not, however, like it. And he wasn't a fool: he had a very good idea what 'security breach' meant.

Gerhard had combed the newspapers very carefully since the completion of his first 'clearance', as he liked to think of the killings. The police, it seemed, had done a very good job of keeping his work under wraps. It was only after the Wittke episode that the first report had appeared, and even then the details were sketchy, giving the impression that Wittke's was the first death and making only vague allusions to his one-time role in the SS. Gerhard hadn't been concerned at the lack of reporting, detailed or otherwise, about the earlier cases. As far as he was concerned, he was performing a service that did not require public recognition: his personal sense of pride at another wrong righted was reward enough. He had not been pleased, however, that it was the Wittke killing which had attracted attention – he wasn't proud of the way he had tackled it. He had made the death personal, which had made him unforgivably sloppy. He had let himself down.

As for the increased checks and supervision, Gerhard had not been concerned about those either because none of what was being done impacted on him. There was nothing untoward in his work for his boss to notice. There was nothing a search of his bag or body would uncover. He had no need to carry anything physical away from the Centre: he had taken all the materials that he needed in the days after the shambles at Nuremberg had set him on his course. He had enough completed cards and stores of blank ones and enough ink sequestered away in a nook of his landlady's garden shed to furnish his requirements for years. And he had all the facts that he needed to fill up the empty cards safely stored in his head, although he was always happy to acquire more.

So Gerhard had not been concerned – even if 'security breach' was code for the police sniffing round the Document Centre and starting to stick together the story he had left them about SS officers who had been rewarded not punished for the dishonour they had brought on their uniforms. He was certain that they couldn't be looking for him. He hadn't left a trail that led anywhere.

And then he had paid his monthly Sunday visit to his mother, and his mother, just as she had always done, had stripped his confidence away.

Something had changed at his mother's house too, although Gerhard didn't realise it at first. He had followed the same routines as he always did. He arrived at noon on the Sunday which fell exactly one month from his last visit. He knocked and he waited the mandatory three minutes she insisted on. That, however, was when the day had changed. His mother did not open the door.

Gerhard had been forced to knock again. That was an irritating development – it had left him feeling exposed. For a moment, he had contemplated walking away, but that would have been as uncomfortable a change in his habits as standing ignored on the doorstep was proving to be. He knew that she would not have forgotten their appointment. He knew that she was somewhere in the house – not only was she expecting him, she rarely ventured outside anymore beyond the most necessary trips. For all the neighbours' nosiness, his mother was no more blessed with friends than he was. He had assumed, therefore, that she was trying to make some heavy-handed point linked to his last visit by ignoring him, and that made him cross.

Gerhard had no knowledge of what his mother did with her days – and he had no interest in asking – but he knew what she was meant to be doing on that particular Sunday, and it wasn't making a fool out of him. He had given her one more minute to appear and to apologise. When she didn't, he took out the key she had no idea that he had copied, and he let himself in. He did not call out.

One step into the hallway and he could sense her. Her coat was hanging on its peg. Her perfume filled the air – the over-sweet cloying scent she had always worn that smelled of flowers gone past their peak. The house might be silent, but she was very much there.

Gerhard had sighed. He had thought that she'd learned her lesson about showing him a proper level of respect on his last visit. He was not a man for games – or for repeating himself.

He had crossed the hall and entered the stuffy sitting room and, finally, there she was, cowering in the corner of the ancient green sofa as if it was a wolf approaching her sorry old bones, not her only living child. When he scanned the room, there was no tray of tea waiting, no plate of dried-up seed cake. It was clear that she was going to waste his time with some kind of melodrama he was not in the mood for.

'Why didn't you answer when I knocked?'

'Why haven't they taken you in?'

They both spoke at once. For a moment, Gerhard could not follow what she had said. He was too surprised that she would speak across him, that she hadn't, in fact, learned her lesson at all and wasn't immediately apologising for her behaviour. When her words finally did register, however, a tremor he wasn't quick enough to hide ran through him. She had noticed that: some of the whipped-dog look went out of her eyes. Gerhard decided in that instant not to sit down. He had stepped closer to her instead, so that she had to crane up to properly look at him.

'Who is *they*, Mother? Who do you mean? And where is *in*?'

She had looked unnerved, but not unnerved enough: there was a curl to her lip that suggested some remaining defiance.

Gerhard had stepped closer again, until his knees were an inch away from her bony legs, and he had slowly curled and uncurled his right hand until he had her full attention. Then the words had poured out of her. According to the garbled rush, the police had called at the house on Monday, just before the mood in the Document Centre had changed. Asking questions about him, primed with a story about a missing person that was patently false.

Gerhard hadn't reacted. He had let her finish. He had flexed his right hand again when she did, and then his left.

'And what did you tell them about me?'

He had to give it to her: even when she was cornered and pinned against the cushions with no hope of escape, she still tried to fight back. Her voice was the same as it had always been when she dealt with him: all flint and disappointment.

'That you have never brought anything but shame on your family. That you are the kind of man who could attack his own mother. That you claim to be honourable when you have no conception of what that word means.'

And there it was again: his lack of honour, the insult that she knew made his insides wince, that she knew would rile him. His jaw had clenched as she peered up at him, her face rodent thin in the shadows, her voice needle sharp.

'What have you done this time, Gerhard? Why are the police interested in you?'

He had leaned down and was pleased when she shrank back. It was time to show her who was really in charge. He would have smiled, but that felt too theatrical. There was no need for gestures anyway: the truth would do very well.

'I have killed three people. And I have got away with it. And I plan to kill an awful lot more.'

Then the fear had flooded in. Gerhard had watched without moving as her mind tried to navigate the new landscape he had tossed her into, as the horror came, first at what he had admitted, and then at what that admitting surely meant was coming for her. That was the moment when he had decided to smile.

'Good, you understand.'

It had been odd to do it face to face, with the victim aware of what was happening. He hadn't killed like that since he was fighting tooth and nail for his own life on the battlefields of Ukraine. It wasn't something Gerhard took pleasure in, but, as he told himself on the walk home, sometimes needs must.

He had waited another handful of seconds, until the exact moment at which her eyes widened and her mouth fell open ready to beg. And then he had picked up a pillow, and he had pressed. It didn't take long – there was barely enough movement from beneath the soft cloth to call it a struggle.

When Gerhard was sure that she was done with, he uncovered her face, closed her eyes and tidied up her smudged lipstick. Then he had carried her upstairs and placed her in the centre of her neatly made bed. Someone, someday, would find her.

He hadn't lingered after that. His mother's stale bedroom was nowhere he wanted to be.

When he came back downstairs again, however, he took a few moments to look round the cluttered sitting room. It was full, as it always was, of his brother and sister. There was nothing of him in it; there were no happy childhood memories of cosy nights and maternal cuddles to call up. And there was nothing he wanted to take away, apart from the certain knowledge that he never had to come back.

Gerhard had left by the front door as openly as he had entered – he would undoubtedly have been seen arriving, so there was no point in pretending that he had never been there. He didn't hurry. He walked at his usual pace down the garden path, and he stopped at the pub for his usual drink and to make his next set of plans.

The task he had started on did not need to change. His lodgings and, unfortunately, his workplace did. The police, it seemed, had got him in their sights after all. Gerhard wasn't overly concerned by that – he doubted their interest would come to much. He presumed that anyone asking questions at the Centre would have been alerted to his lack of popularity. If they had looked into his background, they might have found him in the same camp as Wittke. None of that was proof. They had no proof of his involvement in anything at all, apart perhaps from the earlier assault on his mother, and that, if they dug into it, could easily be turned into a story of self-defence that had got out of hand. Plenty of old people became confused as they got older, and violent no doubt when they thought the man in their house was a burglar not a son simply trying to do his best.

So Gerhard wasn't concerned that he was about to be identified and linked to the killings. He did not, however, wish to be
disturbed from the task he was still busy with by some clumsy
police inspector getting in his way. So he had to slip off their
radar.

Gerhard might doubt that the police had enough information
to talk to him any time soon, but neither was he about to take any
chances – his work was too important for that. He decided, therefore, to hand in his notice the following morning and to cite a
family emergency for not working any notice period that his boss
might demand. After that, he would find another quiet room,
with another disinterested landlady. And as soon as he was settled
– and, most importantly, safe – he would step up his programme.
His processes were quicker; he no longer needed the long gaps
between the clearings that he had when he had started.

Gerhard smiled to himself as he swallowed the last few drops
of his beer. A little more speed would not be a bad thing: he had,
after all, a very long list still to work through.

CHAPTER 18

10 MARCH 1947

Freddy slammed into the back seat of the car and grunted at the driver to head straight back to the station. The morning had begun well: according to the officers who had been sent to collect him, Bayer had complied with their request to accompany them 'in order to assist with an ongoing enquiry' without any argument. The search of his room – which Freddy had decided at the last minute to supervise – had, however, been a deeply frustrating experience.

Bayer's landlady – who had made it clear from the start that she was no fan of the police, particularly when they were escorting away one of her lodgers – had bridled when Freddy had suggested that Herr Bayer might not be quite what he seemed, hearing a slur against her 'very respectable establishment' that he hadn't intended to make. According to her tight-lipped testimony, Bayer was a man of 'neat habits and reasonable hours', a model of what a lodger should be. With her back firmly up, she had refused to offer a single personal detail about him, and she had tested Freddy's patience to its limits when she had proved reluctant to open his room.

When she finally did, his first thought was that she had been through the place and emptied it. It was the barest place Freddy had ever been in. Its overly tidy surfaces and lack of anything that might make it homely did not, however, suggest to him – as it apparently did to the landlady – that Bayer was 'private and modest'. It suggested that the man was secretive, or that he had the kind of closed personality it would be hard to crack.

The only items laid out on the dressing table were a shaving kit and a hairbrush which could have been army issue. There wasn't a picture on the walls beyond a sermon stitched into a sampler that Freddy assumed was the landlady's attempt at deco-ration. There also wasn't a family photograph anywhere, not that Freddy was surprised at that omission after the visit to Bayer's mother. The books lining the cheap bookcase comprised a couple of battered law texts and the standard set of fiction works any German with an aspiration to being a connoisseur of the classics would collect: Goethe, Fontane, Thomas Mann. Freddy was no great reader, but even he had a handful of modern paperbacks that kept pace with the times, including *For Whom the Bell Tolls*, the novel the whole city was apparently obsessed with, although he had only read that to stop Matz telling him that he should. There was nothing in Bayer's choices, however, to suggest that his tastes had progressed beyond his schoolmasters' choices.

Beyond the books, there wasn't a sign of any hobbies or inter-ests, or any items that could tie Bayer to the crime scenes. There were a couple of sharpened pencils but no pen of any description, and the only paper had been a rough-quality notebook of the type available in every street corner kiosk, and that had been blank. His clothes similarly gave nothing away. The white shirts, drab brown jumpers and dark trousers could have been bought in bulk. And none of them on inspection revealed as much as a speck of blood.

After half an hour's fruitless searching, Freddy had begun to think that the ordinariness of the room was intended, that no one could in reality be so devoid of a life. He was glad that he hadn't wasted Hanni's time by bringing her – there hadn't been anything in it worth wasting film on.

Hanni. Freddy drummed his fingers against the worn leather seat. She was another frustration and, worse, she was one who, even more so than Bayer, he didn't have a clue how to get through to. The sight of her on Saturday morning had almost stopped his heart. And so had the way she dismissed him. A fall down the cellar steps: did she genuinely think he was that stupid? It had been obvious that she was lying – she had been as uncomfortable with her explanation as she had been with her injuries – although Freddy wished that he could believe her, rather than facing the alternative, which was what he had spent the last twenty-four hours shrinking from. He was certain that her bruises and her torn shoulder had been caused deliberately, and that thought had made him sick every time he considered it.

Freddy's first impulse when he saw her sling and the state of her face had been the same as the one he had fought off when he caught her crying in the Stein Studio: to wrap her up tight in his arms and never let go. Forgetting all about the fight they had fallen into the last time he had held her, he had leaped towards her, not caring that he was surrounded by the rest of his equally horrified team. Hanni, however, had stepped back and spurned him with a blocking hand, so that impulse had been hopeless.

His second, therefore, had been to go after Natan Stein. Freddy had never believed Hanni's story that her split from the studio and its owner had been a mutual parting. He had assumed that tale had been told to spare the man's embarrassment after she had, presumably, turned down his attentions. He had seen the way Stein had looked at her; he knew Stein would never have willingly let Hanni walk out of his life.

The more time Freddy had spent probing at it – and he couldn't stop probing at it – the more likely it became in his head that Natan Stein was her attacker. By the time he had finished organising Monday's pick-up and interrogation, Freddy had worked himself into a state in which he could picture a gigantic and furious Stein attacking a defenceless and cowering Hanni as if it was running in widescreen and technicolour. He had stormed out of the station and into the nearest pub, planning to sink a couple of whiskies and then to go and teach the studio owner a lesson to match the one Stein had inflicted on Hanni until reason – in the shape of Matz – intervened.

'You've worked yourself up way too far. Stein's not a bad man and he's too crazy about Hanni to hurt her, I'd lay money on it. When I went looking for her at the studio that time, after she quit working there, he was sad – not angry – that she had gone. I think she broke his heart; I'm certain he would never take revenge on her for that. And I did some looking into him when you brought Hanni onto the team. Trust me, that man's war was a dreadful thing. He's been through enough pain of his own to go wilfully inflicting the same on anyone else.'

That – and Matz's refusal to let him anywhere near another drink – had sobered Freddy up. It had not, however, stopped him picking over the worry that was Hanni's battered face. Stein might not be his man, but somebody was.

With that in mind, Freddy hadn't gone straight to his office when he returned to the station on Sunday morning to finish reviewing Bayer's files – he had taken a detour instead to the uniformed section to see if anything had been reported about an 'accident' that he could link to Hanni. It had taken him the best part of the morning to process the shock of what he had discovered there.

Getting to the truth hadn't taken long – the unusual nature of the episode at Halleyches Tor meant it was fresh in everyone's minds, and the desk sergeant, who wasn't used to being drilled by a white-faced inspector, had fallen over himself to be helpful. He had blustered about as Freddy's expression grew stiffer, insisting that everything that could be done to investigate 'the unfortunate event' had been done. That the lack of corroborating statements meant that the only reasonable conclusion was that the incident had been no more malicious in intent than a pickpocketing attempt which had gone badly wrong. Freddy by then, however, had read the notes and seen the witness report's starkly recorded *deliberate attack* and Freddy knew different.

Hanni had been assaulted in what looked like – according to the man who had saved her life – an attempt to kill her. And Hanni had lied to him about that. Freddy didn't know how to make sense of either of those things.

He did know, however, that they fitted with – and made more disturbing – the secrets he had always been aware she came wrapped in. Someone had tried to, at best, seriously hurt her, and surely her silence meant that she was determined to protect that someone. Freddy had seen that kind of behaviour before in other cases, and the word that had fitted the attacker in every one of those had been *husband*. The more Freddy had thought about it, and he had thought about it for hours, the more he grew convinced that *husband* was where the truth of Hanni's reticence with him lay. That she had been married or that she still was – in some way she was trying to hide from.

As with his suspicions over Natan, the more Freddy brooded on it, the more his conclusion made sense to him. An entanglement like that would explain why Hanni had pushed him away, when Freddy knew – as the kiss had proved – that she felt the attraction between them as strongly as he did. There was a husband lurking, a potentially very dangerous and jealous husband, and Hanni didn't want Freddy knowing it. He was aware that was her choice. He had also seen enough women damaged at the hands of violent men to know that the fear could be paralysing or could result in a badly misplaced sense of loyalty. Whatever the reason for it, however, he could not pretend that her silence didn't hurt. It suggested a lack of trust in him that he hadn't shown to her. It suggested that she was not only secretive but that she had learned to be a very good liar.

And I cannot let any of that distract me now.

The car had arrived at the station, which was buzzing. As quiet as he had tried to keep it, news that the prime suspect in the SS case had been brought in had leaked through the building. He avoided eye contact as he walked through the knots of gossipers trying to pretend they were busy. Matz had been instructed to keep Bayer waiting alone in a room with no explanation of why he was there beyond the vague 'helping with enquiries'. In Freddy's experience, that tended to rattle even the most confident subject, and rattling Bayer was exactly what Freddy needed to do.

This case was the biggest one his division had handled; this case could make or break his career. All his team would be watching him; Brack would be watching him. Freddy couldn't afford to be distracted or to make a single mistake in the interview. He also couldn't afford to show any of the ambivalence about the killer's mission that he was still grappling with, particularly if it was true that Bayer's motives had something to do with avenging the massacres of Freddy's own people. He had an uneasy sense that Bayer might be very good at spotting, and twisting, weakness.

He went to his office and closed the door. He needed a few minutes alone to push away personal conflicts and to push himself into being the man the coming interview would require. Hanni would be in the room to do her job. He would be in the room to do his job. Their relationship, or lack of it, was no longer important. For the next however many hours that it took to break him, the only person in the station who mattered was Bayer.

Ordinary might describe Gerhard Bayer's features and manner – they were as anonymous as everyone had said they were – but Freddy knew within minutes of meeting him that Bayer was anything but an ordinary man. He had the most watchful eyes Freddy had ever seen, and he was as skilled at saying nothing as he was at being nothing. *He is very much the one in charge* could have been as easily applied to the interview room as it had been to the crime scenes.

Almost an hour had passed since he and Matz and Hanni had entered the small office and introduced themselves and Freddy felt no closer to getting a handle on who Bayer really was than he had been when he had searched the man's featureless room. It wasn't that Bayer was being impolite or obstructive. He was, in many ways, a model of co-operation – Freddy could understand why his landlady had chosen a similar phrase to describe him.

He had answered all the basic questions – about his family background and his living situation and his job. He hadn't once shown hesitation or wavered from the facts they already knew. His responses had been as neat and tidy as he was, and that was where Freddy was beginning to become unstuck. Bayer hadn't offered one word beyond what was asked of him, no matter how open-ended Freddy, or Matz, worded their questions. When Matz had asked him – following the interview script he and Freddy had agreed – whether he knew why he had been brought to the station, Bayer had simply said 'no'. And when no explanation had been forthcoming from Freddy, Bayer hadn't requested that one should. He didn't ask and he didn't speculate; he didn't show any emotion at all.

This isn't important to him. He's tolerating us, but it's a sideshow.

That was an unsettling thought and not a helpful one, not when the stakes were as high as the ones Freddy was facing. Brack had been very clear that he expected Freddy to deliver – 'one way or another' – an arrest and then a conviction, preferably with a confession thrown in too. He had also been very clear what he would do to Freddy if he failed.

The longer the interview went on, however, the further away that positive outcome seemed. And Bayer, or so Freddy was becoming more and more convinced, was aware of that. He decided, therefore, that it was time to rip off the gloves and give the man a taste of where the investigation was heading.

He opened one of the buff-coloured envelopes stacked in front of him and took out three photographs. Keeping his eyes firmly on Bayer's impassive face, he slid them across the desk.

'Do you recognise any of these men?'

The photographs had been selected from the ones Hanni had

taken at the killing sites and they were calculated to shock. They had been cropped to show only the victims' faces – Freddy wanted to keep the handwritten signs and the presentation of the bodies to himself for now – but it was obvious from the pallor and the slack faces, never mind the closed eyes, that all three men were dead.

Bayer didn't pick them up, but he didn't flinch from them either. He took his time. He considered each one. And he didn't ask why he had been instructed to look at them.

'This one is familiar.' He pointed to the picture of Wittke. 'If I am correct, we were interred together at a camp near Hanover in the summer of 1945. When he was alive – which I am assuming from this image he is now not – I believe he was a doctor. His name, as I recall, was Konrad Wittke.'

It was the longest speech Bayer had made, and it was delivered in the same light and uninvolved tone as he had used when he'd confirmed that he worked at the Document Centre.

Freddy left the photographs lying on the table, although Bayer had stopped looking at them.

'Do you remember anything about him?'

'Beyond his profession?'

Bayer glanced at Wittke's image again, although Freddy was sure that he didn't need to, that he had already collected everything that he wanted from it.

'I don't believe that I do, no, other than him having fought in the war, the same as everyone else in the camp.'

He sat back and regarded Freddy again with the same level gaze he had worn all along. 'If you have made enquiries among the other inmates or the guards, then I assume that you already know that Wittke and I were not on friendly terms.'

Freddy wanted to believe that Bayer had just offered him something personal, a chink in his armour that Freddy could probe. Unfortunately, he – and Bayer – knew better.

He's putting me on notice that he understands what is happening here. That he knows we've been digging into him, and that he's not in the slightest bit disturbed by that.

He had to ask the question anyway. 'Was there a reason for that hostility?'

Anyone else would have offered a smile or a shrug: a self-deprecating gesture to suggest that 'whatever the problem was, it wasn't with me'. Bayer, however, remained expressionless as he corrected Freddy's choice of words.

'Hostility is a stronger description than I would use. The reason for our distance was a professional one. Wittke was a student of medicine; I was a student of law. The doctor did not believe that those disciplines should be placed on the same level.'

It wasn't much – there was no rancour in Bayer's tone – but it was, finally, an opening into a more personal level of discussion and Freddy jumped on it. He opened another folder and deliberately took his time flicking through the typed sheets it contained.

'Your law career, yes. I was coming to that. Our records show that you entered the Humboldt in 1936 to begin studying for your doctorate. That is quite an achievement. It was something that I had hoped to do myself at one time.'

He smiled at Bayer and received the blank look in response to the attempted connection that he expected he would.

'My family would have been delighted if I had succeeded and incredibly proud of me.' He paused and made sure Bayer was looking straight at him. 'I understand from your mother, however, that your family was not proud of you at all. That, in fact, university, even the Humboldt, and your choice of the law as a career, was a disappointment to them. That any future which didn't lead to the army would only ever be a disappointment to them.'

And there it was: the split-second reaction which proved that Bayer wasn't quite as without emotion as he wanted them to think. The signs were slight – a blink, a tightening at the corner of his mouth. They were almost undetectable, but they were there.

And, with a little careful cultivation, this will be what helps me crack him.

Freddy pushed the file towards Matz and let him switch the conversation back to a run-through of Bayer's academic career. There was anger there, buried deep – Freddy could sense it. It was simply a matter of finding the right key to unlock it: he knew from his own experience that one always existed.

He glanced over at Hanni while Bayer's attention was still on Matz. She had seemed distracted since she had entered the room and kept fiddling with the folder of papers on her knee, although she hadn't once opened it. She nodded, however, when he looked at her and he assumed that she had seen the signs too.

Freddy's head came up – the chase suddenly felt like a more equal thing. He waited for Matz to finish, and then he picked up the challenge from where he had left it.

'You got there in the end though, didn't you? Into the army, I mean. You finally managed to secure the only career your family thought was a suitable one. I hope that made your mother happier.'

Bayer didn't respond; again, Freddy hadn't expected him to.

'And your war record is very impressive, Herr Bayer. Straight into the Fifth Panzer Division; promoted to officer almost as soon as you joined; a heroic rescue of an injured comrade while under partisan attack in Poland. I would have expected a man who could overcome some physical deficiencies and make a start like that to leap through the ranks. But that isn't what happened to you, is it?'

Freddy stopped and leafed through his notes, letting the pause ride. Bayer didn't move, but his body suddenly looked stiffer, as if he was holding it in place.

'We arrive next at November 1943, at Majdanek, which is not, admittedly, a destination I would choose to come to, but anyway, there you are and then where do you go? What happens to your stellar career after that?'

Anyone not looking closely enough would have still called

Bayer's demeanour impassive, but Freddy now knew the tells. The blink, the tightening; not once now but twice. When Freddy let the pause stretch, this time Bayer filled it.

'You have my file, Inspector. Everything is in there. I transferred to the Eastern Front, to Ukraine. I was wounded while fighting – an injury to my shoulder which has now healed but was damaging enough when it happened to make me unfit for service. I was, as a consequence, invalided out of my unit and sent home to Berlin.'

It was the right story, but it wasn't the complete one. He had left a gap that – for a man as deliberate as Bayer – felt like a glaring one. Freddy patted the folder and tried not to look too eager.

'But that's not *everything*, is it? In November 1943, you were an officer. By the time you arrived back here, you were not. That is, as you say, all in your file, although you didn't mention it. Your mother, however, did. Your mother was very vocal about the opportunity you *squandered*.'

And then Freddy – although he didn't realise it at the time and because he was riding on the hope of a success that he could suddenly taste – made a mistake. Instead of remembering about finding the keys to Bayer's anger and giving the man a moment to react, or needling him with the other damning comments his mother had made, Freddy decided to tell the story of Bayer's fall from grace himself. Unfortunately, the emotions he embroidered the story with weren't Bayer's but his own.

'I think that the problem, Herr Bayer, was Majdanek. We know from your record that you were there. We all know what that name means. I think that what was asked of you there – the sheer scale of the massacre and the horrific treatment of the Jewish prisoners who were murdered by the SS killing squads – revolted you. How could it not? How could any decent man not be sickened by the level of the slaughter that was carried out there? I think that your sympathies were not with your fellow officers that day, but with the tens of thousands of innocents who

died. Perhaps your sympathies had been with them for a long
time: you were, after all, conscripted into the SS – you didn't
voluntarily join it. Perhaps you never shared their ideals, particularly when it came to the slaughter of the Jews. And I believe that
is where your sympathies – and the outrage, the need for justice
that nightmare led to – still lie.'

He stopped abruptly as Matz shifted in the seat next to him.
He realised that he had been speaking too fast and too loud, and
that he had been about to not only accuse Bayer of the murders
but to give him a reason for carrying them out. And he also
realised that Bayer's face had lost its stillness. His puzzled frown
made him look older – it gave him the air of a teacher observing a
pupil whose work had wandered wildly off track.

'That is an interesting conclusion, Inspector, and goodness
knows where it is heading. But I am at a loss to know how you
have arrived at it, or, indeed, why you would. Putting aside where
you were leading the conversation to for a moment, nothing in
the notes you have collected on me could suggest that I have any
connection with, or harbour such deep feelings for, Jews. Why
would you believe that was true? I was a member of the SS, as you
are clearly aware. It doesn't matter whether I was conscripted or
a volunteer: I swore an oath to uphold their codes and beliefs, and
oaths matter very much to me, as they should to all soldiers. Do
you honestly believe that those two positions, being in the SS and
wanting to protect Jews, are compatible?'

Sweat collected around Freddy's collar as Bayer finished. The
only thing he could think was: *I have done everything wrong.* He
had got lost in Majdanek and forgotten himself – and forgotten
Bayer. He had layered his own feelings across the killer's and
handed him control of the room. Reality crashed in and set Freddy's mind racing. If he attempted to charge the man now, even the
ever-loyal Matz would be forced to ask, 'Where is the motive,
never mind the evidence?'

Freddy pretended to consult his notes and nodded to Matz to
go back to establishing the details of Bayer's post-war intern-

ment, deliberately ignoring his assistant's worried stare. He couldn't look at Hanni. He stared at his files, his head spinning, until he realised that Matz had run out of ways to pad out his questions and had stopped talking. A silence gripped the room that Freddy knew he found far more unnerving than Bayer did.

Before he could find a way to take hold of it, however, Bayer sat back and folded his hands. He looked like a man who was finished with having his time wasted.

'Might I ask you, Inspector, why I am here? You have probed my life, and you have shown me photographs of three dead men, one of whom I have confirmed was known to me, and you have hinted at "something that someone with sympathies" would do. Perhaps this would be a good moment to inform you that I am already aware, from the recent newspaper report, that Dr Wittke has been murdered. And that I am also aware that there are concerns at my place of work about a possible security breach. Are those two things related? And do you have some indication that I am involved with one of them – or with both?' He glanced back at the photographs that were still on the table. 'Or with whatever may have happened to these other two men?'

His tone was as mild as if they were discussing the pleasant spring weather, but there was no mistaking the challenge. Freddy met it by not answering him directly.

'We are speaking to a number of your colleagues about their work at the Centre and about their whereabouts on three key dates, which I would now like to verify with you.'

Bayer's tone didn't change. 'That is interesting, but it is not what I asked. Am I a suspect for some crime, Inspector? If I am, perhaps it is time to consider questions of evidence – and a solicitor. If not, I do have, as you are obviously aware, a job waiting, and I think it is time I got back to it. I will, of course, make a note of the dates that interest you and check my diary against them.'

They both knew that there was no diary. What there was, however, were law texts and petitions drafted in the internment camp covered in legal jargon and, more importantly, no concrete grounds on which to hold him: Freddy assumed that would be the next point Bayer made.

Freddy shuffled his files and felt like a fool. He couldn't say 'yes, you are a suspect', and he couldn't say 'no, you are not', and he couldn't bear the thought of letting Bayer leave. He was as certain as he could be of anything that Bayer was the killer, and there wasn't a thing he could do to prove it. Hell would freeze over before this cold fish confessed.

Part of Freddy – the part he was trying not to listen to – wondered if he shouldn't be happier about that. Bayer was killing men who Freddy hated with every ounce of his being. If he walked away today, no doubt he would try to kill many more and would most probably succeed. Did it matter that Bayer had no love for Jews? That his motive wasn't the 'pure' one that Freddy had wanted it to be? Did the motive even matter when weighed against the deed? Freddy's thoughts were spinning too fast to hold on to a clear one.

Have I done this on purpose? Have I messed up the interview so I can release him and sign another death warrant? Or can I stop it now? Can I cross a different line and do what Brack would do: force him to confess what I know he has done?

Bayer was waiting politely; Matz was staring at the floor. When Freddy looked over at Hanni, she was knotting her fingers and biting her lip.

'Inspector? Could you at least give me some idea of what you are planning to do?'

He was so damn polite, Freddy longed to knock his teeth down his throat. That was when he realised that he hadn't stirred Bayer's anger, but he had stirred up his own and it was a hair's breadth away from breaking. If he let that happen, if he let his fists do the talking, the line from decent man to thug would be crossed and he would be the one who bore the cost of that shift, not Bayer.

Freddy stood up. He couldn't bear to be near the man for another minute. There was only one path out of this he could decently take. Whatever came after that, or so he convinced himself, was out of his hands.

'Take Herr Bayer to the waiting room.'

He knew that would be a temporary step. That he couldn't hold him. That Bayer would be out of the building within the next hour and Brack would be screaming for Freddy's badge. There was nothing he could do to stop any of that.

I need Hanni's advice. I need her help to find the right way through this. She's the only one who could understand the mess that I've made.

Hanni, however, had already run from the room. He went out into the corridor, following in Bayer's footsteps, and there she was, already halfway down it, on her knees outside the closed door of the room Bayer had been placed in. She was surrounded by folders and loose sheets of paper which – given the way she was scrabbling around them – Freddy presumed she had dropped.

'Here. Let me help you.'

But she was already on her feet, throwing him a look he could only describe as haunted, and then she was gone, leaving Freddy alone in the corridor with no one to turn to and no idea what to do.

CHAPTER 19

14–20 MARCH 1947

The killer had broken his pattern and struck again, and left the murder team with a body weeks before the predicted date. The mood at the crime scene was grim: everyone knew their allotted roles; nobody wanted to discuss them. Hanni prowled round the body, snapping frame after frame, recording all the details of the sign and the message and the tattoo that she had recorded before. Refusing to explain why her first words when she saw the latest victim were 'oh thank God'.

Matz visited the victim's place of work – the British Military Government Headquarters at Reichskanzlerplatz, a five-minute walk from where the dead man had been found – carrying the card which had been neatly tucked into his stiff hand.

Freddy interviewed another adoring, furious wife whose unswerving belief in her husband's goodness made his skin crawl. Hanni had suggested she should go with him to that, but he had barely acknowledged her offer. The site was combed for clues and the body was tidied up and despatched.

By the time the team arrived back at the station, they were tired and demoralised and valiantly trying to bolster each other up. And then Brack had burst in and pulled the ground away from beneath them.

'Get out, the lot of you.'

He cleared the incident room with a furious snarl, sending everyone running, with the exception of Freddy, Matz and Hanni, who he ordered to remain standing as if they were naughty children. When the door finally closed and he rounded on the three of them, his face was purple, and his fury flew straight at Freddy.

'By rights I should have let them stay. I should have ripped you apart in front of your team and made the fool out of you that you've made out of me. You should be thanking me for my decency.'

Please God don't take issue with that word and don't answer him back.

Hanni bored her eyes into Freddy's averted face as if she could will him into silence. Freddy, however, made no attempt to say anything. His body was crumpled, his attention wandering. Brack sensed how hopeless he felt at the same time as Hanni did, and his barrel chest expanded.

'Feel free to correct me if I'm the one in the wrong here, but didn't I warn you not to do this? When you stood in my office bleating about the lack of evidence and the lack of a motive with one breath, and then telling me Bayer was still your main suspect with the next, didn't I warn you not to let him go? Didn't I tell you to find a way to get a confession out of him?' He drew his breath up in a snort. 'But no. Not you. Something that simple was apparently beyond you – or beneath you, more like.'

'Even if I had tried it your way, it wouldn't have worked.'

Hanni winced at the defeat running through Freddy's voice. Brack latched on to it.

'What do you mean? Why don't you admit the truth: that you weren't man enough to do it?'

Freddy's shoulders were too slumped to shrug.

'No. That's an easy thing to say, but it's not true. I mean that beating a confession out of him, the way that you wanted me to, wouldn't have got us anywhere. Bayer has reserves in him that we've barely scratched. Anger maybe – or righteousness. I don't know what propels him, but whatever it is, I know that a beating wouldn't have cracked a way through it.'

Hanni stepped instinctively back as Brack's anger exploded, even though all she wanted to do was to step forward and shield Freddy.

'You *know*? Are you serious? No, *Inspector*, what you know is nothing. Shall I tell you what *I* know instead? What about the fact that you've danced around this investigation since day one, and you've danced around Bayer? And, thanks to that, we've now got four bodies and – according to the superintendent, who's just given me the bollocking he should have given you – headlines hitting the newspapers tomorrow screaming about a string of unsolved murders of supposedly respectable men who may once have been in the SS and an incompetent police force who can't catch the lunatic responsible. Oh, and let's not forget, a suspect who – from where I'm standing – you've let walk out of here with a free pass to carry on killing. How will that little lot do for starters?'

Freddy finally looked up and met Brack's furious gaze.

'That's not what I did. I let him go because there was nothing else I could do. I didn't want this result any more than you did.'

Brack brushed his protest away. 'Really? You see, I'm struggling with that even more than with the rest, so let's examine it a little, shall we? You keep telling me you know about Bayer and what makes him tick, but here's the thing: now I know the same about you. I've been doing some digging of my own and what I've learned is that I should have trusted my instincts and not listened to the idiots who think you're some sort of star in the making.'

Brack's voice dropped to a far more dangerous level than his earlier shouting. 'You should never have been put in charge of this case, should you? And why is that? Because you never had any intention of securing a conviction. Why would you? Why would a Jew want to save SS men who killed so many of his own kind?'

The room froze. Matz stared at Hanni with his mouth open

and his eyes wide, but there was nothing she could say or do that would help.

When Freddy finally found his voice again, it was as thin as a whisper.

'That's not fair. I have done my job. I have never let anything personal get in the way.'

He doesn't sound as if he believes that any more than Brack does.

That lack of conviction – or, more accurately, the over-conviction that had come before it – was also where the interview with Bayer had gone wrong, although Hanni hadn't been able to help Freddy there either. She had been too distracted by her own plans to hear what he was saying and then, when she did snap awake, it was too late. Freddy had got so carried away with his own beliefs, he had stopped giving Bayer the space to incriminate himself. He had lost sight of Bayer and then he had lost confidence in himself, and Bayer had seen it. Hanni had watched Freddy lose control of the interview – which she knew he despised himself for doing – but, unlike Brack, she knew it hadn't been deliberate.

And if I tried to explain any of that, Brack would think I was as useless, and as dangerous to the case, as he thinks Freddy is – which is even more true now than it was before – and Freddy wouldn't thank me for trying.

Brack was still staring at Freddy as if he wanted to punch him.

'I don't believe you. I think you look at the four dead men and you see revenge, and you look at Bayer and you see a champion. I'm done with it. I knew you didn't have the mettle for this, and now you've proved it and it's all too clear why. You're on his side. And you're off the case.'

Hanni started to protest, but Brack snapped at her to 'shut up or get out as well' and turned back to Freddy, whose face had collapsed.

'You're lucky I don't have you transferred – or thrown off the force. I would if I could, but I don't trust your type. Who's to say you won't go screaming about *persecution* and making the high-

ups twitchy? Go back to your office. Find yourself a nice little
robbery to solve and let the policemen, not the pretenders, do the
police work.'

Hanni had seen Freddy flinch at *your type*, but there was no
reaction left in him beyond that. He didn't answer back, he didn't
so much as glance at Hanni or Matz. He walked away instead,
looking so defeated it was all Hanni could do not to fly at Brack
and berate him for being such a heartless bully. Not that Brack
gave either her or Matz a chance to speak. He turned his fury on
them the second that Freddy slunk through the door.

'Don't think that I've any more liking for you two than I have
for him. I'm keeping you on because this mess of a case – and
whoever I pick to run it – needs continuity and you, God help
me, are the best chance of that I've got. Don't just stand there –
get this sorted. Laube, collect up all the case files; Winter, collect
up your photographs; both of you be ready to brief me in an hour.
Don't muck me about and don't miss anything out, no matter
how it reflects on your old boss. And hear the stress on that, both
of you: Schlüssel is your *old* boss.' He stopped and glared at Hanni.
'He is no longer part of this investigation, so you don't go running
to him to test theories, or to ask advice, or to share another
second of this investigation. I'm not asking for your loyalty here;
I'm demanding it. Do you understand me?'

Hanni nodded blank-faced, the way she used to nod at her
father.

Brack stormed out. Matz sank down on a chair. His face was
as white as Freddy's had been.

'What was all that about? I know he's frustrated with the case,
we all are, but why was he so vicious and why did he say that
Freddy is Jewish as if that was a crime and accuse him of sabo-
taging the investigation on purpose?'

Hanni sat down opposite him. There was no point in keeping
Freddy's secrets anymore. And there was too much to explain and
too little time to do it in, so she kept Freddy's story simple.

'Brack said Freddy is Jewish because he is. His real name is

Schlüsselberg, but he changed it when he joined the police. He lost his whole family in the war, in the extermination camps, which is why Brack accused him of wanting the killer to keep on killing. Freddy has good reason to hate anyone who was in the SS.'

Matz no longer looked boyish, and all his usual eagerness was gone. 'I don't understand. Why did he change his name? Why didn't he say who he was from the start? The war is done – what could being Jewish nowadays possibly matter?'

His innocence made her want to cry. She couldn't imagine how his kinder view of the world could survive the job he had chosen.

'I wish that it didn't. But you saw the way Brack looked at him; you heard the way he said *your type*. Who says that if they don't think that *your type* means *other*? There's still hatred and prejudice, Matz. In the force, in Berlin, probably everywhere, and Freddy didn't want to confront that when he joined up. He's seen and he's suffered enough, more than I know the half of. And he didn't want revenge either – you believe that, don't you? He's not on the same side as the killer. Brack is using any excuse he can to get rid of Freddy because he loathes who he is. But Freddy did not send Bayer back out there to kill.'

That was me.

For a strange, disconnected moment, Hanni thought she had said that out loud.

'A free pass to carry on killing.' Brack was right when he had said that, but he had aimed the attack at the wrong head. She glanced at Matz, who was sitting in silence, his face as white as it had been when she began talking.

'You do believe me, don't you?'

He nodded and found her a smile that told her all she needed to know: once Matz was loyal, he stayed loyal. He got up and left the room without speaking. It took Hanni far longer, however, to gather herself together. She couldn't let Freddy go under. She couldn't let herself go under and, unless this case was solved quickly, she would.

I shouldn't have done it.

She hadn't been able to shake the thought since the fourth body had turned up. When she had shoved the piece of paper with Reiner's name on it under Bayer's door, together with the photograph of her father and the train, it had seemed like the perfect solution. She couldn't get to her father, but Bayer could. He had no conscience. He wasn't going to stop killing. And then he had struck again, and her conscience had kicked horribly in.

I have ordered a murder. I am my father's daughter after all.

That was the thought that had led to 'oh thank God' at the last crime scene and had her dreading the next one. Bayer killing Reiner was certainly a solution, but Hanni knew now that – no matter how much she had tried to persuade herself differently – it wasn't the right one. It would wipe him at least physically from her life, but it would be a selfish act – it wouldn't bring her father's story to the world, and it wouldn't bring justice for his victims. It would be another burying of the past, and that was the last thing she wanted. So she couldn't let Freddy go under, and Brack could demand whatever loyalty he wanted, but that didn't mean she had to deliver it.

Hanni collected the photographs Matz would need for the briefing she wasn't planning to attend, left those on the desk and picked up her camera bag. She had no intention of speaking to the chief inspector again today. She had films to develop and a good man who needed reminding how good he was. She went down the now deserted corridor determined not to leave the building until she had spoken to Freddy and reassured herself that he wasn't as beaten as Brack had intended him to be. That somehow he could win the case back. When she reached his office, however, the blinds were pulled down and the door was locked, and nobody answered even when she stopped knocking and called out.

. . .

Freddy had disappeared from the office and – according to Matz who had tried to contact him – he wasn't returning any calls. More worryingly, Bayer too had gone to ground. He had vanished from the Document Centre and from his lodgings and left no forwarding address.

The team's new boss – a hatchet-faced man who delivered a lecture on 'proper practice' by way of a greeting and barely shared his name with them – rolled his eyes when they told him that their only suspect was missing. He marched off to Frau Bayer's home in Teutonenstraβe, convinced, despite what Hanni told him about their relationship, that Bayer would have taken refuge with his mother and anticipating a speedy arrest.

He came back looking sickened and far less spiky. Frau Bayer might have been found dead in her bed, but she was lying in it fully dressed and nothing about that felt right. An autopsy had been ordered, but nobody expected the cause of death to be natural. Which meant that they now had another body to add to the count, and one they could finally link directly to their suspect. No one, however, was celebrating. Not without a single lead pointing to Bayer's whereabouts and no way of predicting his new, and potentially accelerated, timetable.

The team gathered, as instructed, at eight o'clock on Tuesday morning and began, as instructed, to pore over every scrap of information about the murders that they had already scoured through. Messages requesting help were sent out to the American and the British intelligence services. Envelopes of money were sent out to the street kids. Nobody expected to see a result, not when Bayer had already proved himself so adept at hiding his tracks. The mood in the incident room was worse than it had been at the last crime scene, and the only person with any hope of lifting it was Hanni.

What I have is contacts and I pay them well to keep me well informed.

Her father's boast which had been intended to frighten her could now be the route to solving the case, if she could push him into using those contacts for and not against her. If anyone in Berlin could find Bayer, it had to be Reiner. It was one thing to know that, however, and a very different one to act on it. The thought of seeking Reiner out herself after what he had tried to do to her at Hallesches Tor was an impossible one. Except Freddy's door was still locked and the team was at breaking point, and impossible was a luxury that Hanni couldn't afford.

This time, Hanni did not telephone anyone to arrange an appointment. She slipped away from the silent office and headed straight for Fehrbelliner Platz, where she sat in a chilly hallway and waited while her heart danced a polka in her chest.

'Herr Foss will see you now.'

It was the creamy-faced girl who she had last seen hanging from Reiner's arm; she was a lot younger on closer inspection than Hanni wanted her to be.

Hanni got up and followed the girl's impossibly tiny waist down a corridor lined with closed doors and paintings of identically suited grey-haired men.

'Here we are, he said to go straight in. Can I get you a tea – or a coffee?'

Hanni shook her head, knowing she wouldn't be able to balance a cup, and let the girl open the door before she simpered away.

The office she stepped into was huge and shiny. Polished mirrors and gilt picture frames bounced back the light from a window whose wide expanse of glass felt like an insult to the still eyeless buildings visible through it. Hanni assumed that the dazzling effect was a deliberate one and forced herself not to blink.

Reiner was sitting behind a heavy-legged desk which would have dwarfed Freddy's cramped cubbyhole. He didn't get up.

'Hannelore, what a surprise. I have to confess you were the last person I expected to see today, or at all. Have you fully recovered from your accident?'

The chair set opposite him was bulky and difficult to pull out, but Hanni wasn't going to stand in front of him like a penitent. Neither was she going to acknowledge his question. She sat down and folded her hands in her lap so that she could keep a tight hold on them. She knew what she was going to say. She knew how much danger it put her in. She wasn't going to waste time on pleasantries.

'I need your help.'

'Well now, you really have taken the wind out of my sails.'

Reiner raised his eyebrows and rubbed his hands and widened his eyes in a way that Hanni knew was deliberately theatrical. She could sense his mind working, imagining the fun he was about to have with her. She refused to rise to that either.

'I am working with the police, helping them to solve a murder case.'

She bit her lip as Reiner burst out laughing and let him have his moment. Then she continued.

'The suspect has disappeared, and he is very good at that, better than we are at finding him. I hoped that your contacts might help me to track him down.'

Reiner sat back and plucked a cigarette from the engraved silver box on his desk. He took his time over lighting it, and he didn't stop grinning.

'So many questions. Where do I start? What about a little background perhaps, before I refuse you? Who has this man been killing that makes him matter so much?'

This was her moment, the one she had been practising for since she had decided to swallow her fear and approach him. She had rehearsed the tone and the words, and she knew she had only one chance of delivering it.

'A very carefully targeted group of men. Ex-SS officers who have walked away from their past crimes untouched and who now work in high-paying jobs for the Allies.'

And now it was Hanni's turn to sit back, although there was nothing in the atmosphere her words had created that could tempt her to match Reiner's wide grin. Reiner stubbed his cigarette out. Despite the control he managed to maintain over his features, his hand was unmistakeably trembling.

'Is this some kind of a joke?'

The tremble was also there in his voice. It steadied the nerves Hanni had been carefully hiding. She continued in the same measured way she had used to describe the killer's targets, without any pauses Reiner could step into and trip her.

'No, not at all.' There was a newspaper discarded in the wastepaper bin – she gestured to it as she spoke. 'You must have seen the headlines. Four bodies, all "supposedly respectable family men with dark pasts", all hit on the back of the head and left in "unusual circumstances" in derelict buildings. The police without a clue who is doing it. That, however, is not the whole story.

'What the papers didn't say – because our superintendent threatened to raid them out of business if they did – was that the "unusual circumstances" means that all the victims had been laid out so that the SS tattoos under their arms were visible. That the killer had taken his time to get to know them: that he left messages on their bodies with details which were taken from their SS files and provided the facts for some of their worst war crimes. And that the police do know who did it – they just can't prove it yet or find him.'

She had all his attention now and his smirk – and his colour – was gone.

'That's quite a story, and you are clearly enjoying telling it. But it doesn't change the questions I've been puzzling at since you turned up: why did you come to me? And why on earth do you think I would do anything to help you find him?'

For all his stiffly held posture, Reiner's mocking edge had gone, and he had slipped into bluster. Hanni waited long enough for the realisation to start creeping over his face before she replied.

'Because he isn't on a random killing spree; he's on a crusade and he's speeding up. We think he has potentially hundreds of targets in his sights, all of them ex-SS, all of them targets who he has already identified and researched and is ready to take. So, if you don't help, it will take us far longer to catch him, which means that far more of those men will die. Who knows, perhaps, please God, you are already one of the ones he has in his sights.'

She stopped. She wasn't ready to tell him the truth of that – not yet. She was hoping – naïvely she knew – that the first threat would be enough and that she wouldn't have to reveal how far she had gone to be rid of him.

'You little bitch.'

The insult glanced off her. He was afraid – she could smell it on him.

Good. Let him feel it. Let him understand what it's like to be on the wrong end of the whip.

Silence filled the room, heavy and thick. It would have been so easy to fill it – with promises that he would never see or hear from her again if he did this one thing; with threats that she would go to the police and reveal his role in the attack on her if he didn't. Hanni did neither; she had long ago learned the value of quiet. She sat and she watched him while he pulled out another cigarette and fumbled with a match and swore.

'So what? Even if I believed you about this killer – and it sounds far-fetched – why should I worry? I have money – money pays for protection. Let him kill off the idiots who are too stupid to cover their tracks – that is never going to include me.'

And there he was, back again: the smiling Reiner who thought she was a coward and easily controlled. The smug Reiner who thought the world was his to direct. Danger or no danger, Hanni knew she could no longer live under the shadow of that.

'Which might be true, except I have already given your name to him, in a way that cannot link you to me. He will find you, and you will die. Or you will help me catch him and you will stay alive.'

There was no smile now. Hanni knew he believed her. She was too calm, too matter-of-fact to be making it up. She had copied the cold tone he had perfected, the one that he used when he didn't care what happened to his victims, and it had worked. His response was immediate.

'Give me his details. If he's in Berlin, my people will find him.'

And he, and then I, will be dead once you do.

Hanni refolded her damp hands and delivered the second part of her message.

'And then you will give his location to me. If you don't, if I don't hear back from you by the end of the week, or if I suspect something has happened to him, then I will take this conversation to the police and tell them that you have murdered Gerhard Bayer, and why you did it, and every other secret you have been keeping. And if anything happens to me in the meantime, there is a letter explaining exactly who Emil Foss is and everything Reiner Foss has done. And the photographs which prove it.'

There wasn't any such letter – not yet – but Reiner's sharply caught breath told her that he believed there was and that would do. He was beaten. Hanni knew, however, that there was still danger in that. She gave him Bayer's name and waited while he wrote it down. And then, as she got up to leave, desperate to be away from him now that the task was done, his parting shot lashed out and stopped her.

'It won't work. He'll never love you. Not if he finds out who you are, which he will, no matter how clever you think you've been.'

Ice collected in her spine. 'I don't know what you mean.'

Reiner laughed and the ice trickled through her.

'Yes, you do. Your inspector, Hannelore. Your Jew. Come on, think about it: if I knew enough about your life to be able to find you on a train platform, don't you think that I would have some idea of the company you keep?'

Now the balance had shifted back again and Hanni was the one feeling sick.

'You never consider all of the angles, do you, daughter dear? I didn't, admittedly, expect you to be working so hand in glove with him, but if that's what it takes to get his attention, who am I to argue?'

Every time she thought she was a step ahead of him, he sped past her again. His smirk was back, and she wanted to scream. And he was still talking.

'That is who you are doing this for, isn't it, your inspector? What's his name? Schlüssel, that's it, which is presumably a hacked-up version of the one he was born with. I assume he is the officer who has been "relieved of his duties", as the paper so tactfully put it. A Jew and a failure. Oh, Hannelore: could you have set your sights any lower?'

He was still laughing when she slammed out of the room. *A Jew and a failure.* It might as well have been Brack speaking.

That thought brought Hanni to an abrupt halt halfway down the panelled corridor. Her blood was pounding too fast through her veins, and it wasn't only the strain of dealing with Reiner again that had fired it. She rested her head on the wall as a terrible sadness engulfed her. How would Freddy's war ever be over when the shadows of it stretched out so long?

We had no value. Everyone was a threat. His words crashed back, describing his life as it had been in the past, as it was still lived in his head in the present. What was the threat she lived under from her father – a threat that would disappear, physically at least, if she stopped scratching at it – compared to a life sentence of doubt and fear and looking over his shoulder like that?

He can't be made to fail, not by men like Brack and Reiner who have already stripped so much from him. I won't let it happen.

Hanni went back to the station and put her head down over the photography summary she had been asked to produce, wondering if Reiner would call her bluff and strike out at her again. Powerless to stop him if he did.

The day passed, and then the next, with a pace as slow as spilled treacle, but she stayed alive through them. And then, on

Thursday afternoon, as the team stared at folders they could no longer see and silently loathed their new boss, the note appeared on her desk. Hanni picked it up and put it into her bag next to the slip of paper onto which she had copied Freddy's address.

It was a short walk from the police station to Freddy's lodging house on Methfesselstraße on the eastern edge of Viktoriapark. Hanni spent it running through what she wanted to say to him and arrived without a single word clear in her head. The house was a more elegant one than she had expected, built of red sandstone and draped in green vines. The landlady who led her to a prettily decorated sitting room to wait was far younger than hers. And Freddy, when he appeared, was too far from himself. His skin was grey and bristly with stubble, and his hair was badly in need of a brush. Hanni waited for a smile, but it didn't come.

'What are you doing here?'

It was clear from his defeated tone that a gentle approach wouldn't work, that he needed a kick not cajoling. Hanni stood up and skewered him with a sharp frown.

'Working, like you ought to be. You need to sort yourself out.' She held out the note. 'I've found him.'

CHAPTER 20

20–26 MARCH 1947

Unlike him, Hanni hadn't given up. She had gone out and found Bayer while Freddy had hidden in his room and picked at his wounds. He was furious with himself, but it was easier to be furious with Hanni.

'I'm not sharing this with Brack.'

That was his first response, when it should have been 'thank you' or 'how on earth did you do it?' He sounded like a toddler snatching at a teddy bear. He was grateful Hanni had enough kindness left in her not to point that out.

'I don't expect you to, and I don't intend to either: Brack doesn't know that I've tracked Bayer down and I'm not going to tell him. I brought the information straight to you because it's you who needs to finish this.'

She had never looked lovelier, or more determined, or more thoroughly fed up with him. Freddy sank down on the plumply cushioned sofa and ran his hands through the bird's nest which had replaced his hair. He might be utterly sick of himself, but he couldn't bear it if Hanni felt the same way.

'I'm sorry. I should be thanking you, not trying to pick a fight.'

Her face softened. 'Then why are you?'

Open up – talk to her. She's always listened before.

It hurt to say the words out loud.

'Because this failure has knocked the stuffing out of me. Because I've been useless since Brack threw me off the case, since he questioned everything I am and turned me into *your type*. Hearing that was like watching the clock get reset.'

She didn't sit down next to him the way that he desperately wanted her to, but she was nodding and she wasn't angry with him, and that would do.

'I know. It was awful to watch, so God knows how it felt to be on the end of it. Brack really showed his colours, and they are as dirty as you said they were. But he didn't speak for the team, I promise. Everyone's upset that you're gone and nobody wanted you replaced – especially Matz, who hasn't repeated a word of the personal stuff Brack said to you. He was as sickened by all that as I was. And no one – or not on our team anyway – thought you should have tried to beat a confession out of Bayer. Except the new boss – he would definitely do that, which is presumably why Brack chose him.'

She finally sat down, although on the chair opposite, not beside him. 'He's old school too, in the worst way, and he's not to be trusted. So you have to solve this case, Freddy. You have to be the one who comes up with the plan that will finally catch Bayer.'

She hesitated and then she asked him the question he knew had to be asked.

'I know Brack hit a nerve and I know you've been struggling, but you do want to stop Bayer, don't you?'

I have to be honest with her. She has to know every inch of me, whether she ever lets me get as close to her in return or not.

Freddy sat up straighter and chose his words carefully.

'No, Hanni, I don't. Not even now that I know that I got his motives all wrong and that, whatever his reason for killing, it's got nothing to do with revenging "my kind", as Brack would call them. No, what I want is for him to keep killing until every last one of the bastards who treated my people like a plague is dead. I want him to carry on until every SS member is wiped from the earth the way we almost were.'

He paused. Hanni was as still as if his words had solidified her. 'That's the truth. But I won't let him do it. I can't or my soul goes too. So I don't want to catch Bayer, but I will. I don't have any other choice.'

Hanni let out her breath and the colour came back into her cheeks. Then she smiled and he knew that she understood him in a way that nobody had since his mother.

'I'm right, aren't I?'

She nodded. 'About the damage it would do to you if you colluded in this mission the killer is on? Yes, completely. It would destroy you in the end. As for the rest... I know it's hard. That what Bayer's doing could seem like a good deed not a crime. It isn't and I'm glad you can see it, although God knows I'm not the one to judge if you can't – I've spent more of this investigation than even you know in the same conflicted place. But I don't want you to be the one who is broken, Freddy, and I've been scared that you might be. You're a better man than that. Which is something that Brack, not just you, needs to know.'

His chest loosened for the first time in days.

'What about you, Hanni? You could get yourself in serious trouble over this. There'll be questions asked about where I got this information about Bayer's whereabouts from. You've put yourself in Brack's firing line.'

'I won't be in that if we catch him – nobody will.'

Her excitement was rising and brightening her eyes. Freddy could feel his bubbling up to meet it. He couldn't look away from her as she went on.

'And so what if he gets angry? I hate being at the station anyway: everyone is twisting themselves in knots and driving themselves mad trying to find clues in evidence we all know doesn't contain any. If you're not there...' She coughed and collected herself. 'The team need this solving as much as you do.

And, when you do, no one will care how you found out where Bayer was, and no one will connect the source of that with me.'

Freddy wasn't so certain of that and, as much as he didn't want her to retreat from him, he had to know, for his own peace of mind, how she had come by the address.

'Brack will care, and he will dig very deep if he thinks anyone withheld information from him. Will you tell me where you got it? In case you, or your source, need protecting?'

She didn't even pause to consider her answer.

'No, and please don't ask me again. I don't need protecting; I need you to use it.'

Hanni had put herself at risk getting Bayer's new location – that was obvious in the way her face had tightened when he said *protecting* and in the way she was still concealing so much.

Freddy stared at the note: the style of the writing was as featureless as the one Bayer had used. There were barely three lines on the paper and yet there was so much contained in them.

Getting it has been a danger to her, but it's a lifeline to me.

What Freddy hadn't told Hanni was that he had learned a frightening lesson since Brack had torn into him and sent him stumbling out of the station. Sitting alone in his room, picking over the case and the confusion of feelings it had led to, Freddy had learned that he was – for all his professional veneer – a mess. That, without the sense of purpose and the place in the world being a 'star in the making' detective brought with it, he was in free fall. And that anger and loss – and the fear he had always refused to acknowledge, that the past with all its persecution and hatred was only a heartbeat away from becoming the present again – had formed a deadly cocktail which would drown him unless he could find a way to face it and fight back.

Because it's you who needs to finish this.

Hanni understood him. She knew that he had to catch Bayer to prove to himself and to the world that he could leave the war – and the fears it had bred in him – behind. Hanni understood him and she cared. Giving him Bayer's address was evidence of that;

everything she had said since she had arrived was evidence of that.

It's more than caring – it has to be.

He knew it was love he could see in her eyes, but he didn't dare name the feeling, not to her or to himself, not with all the secrets that were currently keeping them apart.

And that can't be what matters, not now. She's here to save my career, I can't make her responsible for the rest of me.

Freddy forced himself to focus on the note. Hanni was waiting for a plan, not some outpouring of feelings he knew she would shrink from. And she was waiting for him to do as she said and sort himself out. He had seen himself in the mirror that morning: he looked like a man who had given up on life, and that wouldn't do. She had put her trust in him, and she deserved better.

He got up. 'You did the right thing, bringing me this. I've been wasting time and that's done with.'

Relief flooded her face as he began working his way round a plan.

'Bayer learns his victims, so I'm going to take a leaf out of his book and learn him, even if that means stalking every inch of his days until he picks up the next brick. I've no idea how long that will take, and I don't care. I'm going to catch him, and I'm going to see that justice is done. And then Brack can throw whatever insults he likes at me about siding with murderers because I will have proved him wrong. Are you in this with me?'

'Always.'

She answered without any hesitation and with a smile that made him feel like the world might be in his grasp again. He had to leave the room before he forgot all his good intentions and kissed her.

———

Being off the murder team meant that Freddy had no easy access to a police car or a driver. What he did have, however, was an accommodating landlady happy to put her slightly battered black Volkswagen at his disposal and a love of speed behind the wheel, which put Hanni uncomfortably in mind of her grandmother.

Bayer had moved himself into an anonymous building on Johann-Georg-Straße in Halensee, a small corner of Wilmersdorf about twenty minutes' drive from Freddy's lodgings. It wasn't until they spread their road map over the dashboard that Freddy and Hanni realised why he had chosen that particular district. Bayer's new home sat on the edge of the triangle formed by the American command posts clustered around Clayallee and the British control centres which were spread between Fehrbelliner and Reichskanzlerplatz. The lodging house was also – as Bayer's room in Zehlendorf had been – situated in the middle of an excellent transport hub, served by two train stations and a network of buses. Bayer had, as Freddy put it, stuck himself at the centre of another sticky web.

It was too late on the Thursday night for them to do anything more than drive to Bayer's street and locate his building. That in itself felt like a victory. On the Friday, however – when Hanni had assumed they would begin a more thorough day-long surveillance – Freddy decided to return to the station, and he sent her off to one of the newspaper offices which now gave her regular commissions. His rationale was that they both needed to give the impression of a return to routine, so that he could later claim that Bayer's whereabouts had been discovered while they were going about their normal business. Hanni could see as many flaws as degrees of logic in that. It was, however, a relief to be in an office that was buzzing and lively, where the boss was delighted to see her and filled her day up with work.

By the time Hanni arrived at Methfesselstraße, later than she meant to on the Friday evening, she was more energised than she had been in weeks. Four hours cooped up in the cramped confines of the Volkswagen, however, watching for a man who wouldn't come, soon put paid to that.

For the first hour they were both on too high alert to do

anything but stare across the road at the squat building's doorway and will Bayer to walk out of it. For the second, as their nerves kicked in, they fiddled with the radio and talked across each other and didn't listen to anything the other one said. By ten o' clock, they were both tired and prickly, and Freddy was frustrated and looking for an argument again.

'We left it too late. He's either done his research or he's still out there and we've missed what we needed. Why did you keep me waiting? What were you doing that was more important than this?'

When she didn't answer – because pointing out that he was the one who had sent her to the newspaper would have started the row he was after – Freddy decided instead to start crossing lines Hanni didn't want him going anywhere near.

'Does the person who gave you this' – he waved a hand at the deserted street – 'have anything to do with the one who tried to push you under a train?'

Hanni presumed the directness of the question was intended to catch her off guard. It didn't. She suspected that he would have done his own investigation into what had happened, and she had been waiting for a grilling since the day he had cried out at her bruises.

'That was an accident. And I didn't tell you about it because I didn't want a fuss.'

Freddy made a noise that was part way between a snort and a laugh and obviously intended to provoke her.

'So you made up a story instead. And it wasn't an "accident", not according to the man who saved your life. He was convinced that the push was a deliberate one – he said so in his witness statement.'

Hanni glanced across at him. His clenched hands were as combative as his tone. It wouldn't help either of them if she let this turn into a fight. A row in such close quarters would be too volatile, as could the reconciliation that might follow.

Hanni had no illusions about why Freddy was trying to

provoke her. He could pretend as much as he liked, but it had been clear from the moment she had appeared at his lodgings that he would do anything to rip away the walls they had both hidden behind. She couldn't let that happen, not given what Reiner was capable of. The warning of a letter that would expose him might offer her some protection, but it offered none to Freddy.

Who he would hurt if he thought it would hurt me and would not think twice about it. Which means that I have to do the thinking for both of us.

Reiner had always been the barrier between them and now the damage he could cause was real and it was close. She couldn't allow that to touch Freddy, and nor could she react to his rising temper.

'He made a mistake. The platform was busy, the passengers surged forward and a pickpocket took advantage. My bag being stolen was deliberate, yes, but none of the rest of it was.'

The heat from his anger spread through the car.

'I don't believe that and neither do you. So I want an honest answer to what I think is really going on here: are you married?'

This time he caught her as exactly off guard as he had intended to.

Hanni whirled round, wrong-footed, to face him. 'What? Why would you ask me that?'

His answer was so certain she knew he had been brewing it for far longer than the few hours they had been sat there.

'Because it's the only possible fit. You were attacked and you're keeping secrets about that, as well as the rest of your past, and you're protecting someone. In my experience, that's what a wife does when she's afraid of a dangerous husband.'

It was absurd, and it was perfect. A husband lurking in her background and not quite finished with would keep him away and keep him safe.

And break his heart – and mine.

Now she was the one torn between what was right and what was wanted, and without any choice about what had to be done.

He had given her the means to bury once and for all what had been growing between them, a feeling that she knew was love and didn't dare name. If she agreed to the madness of *husband*, all the tentative moves towards each other, all the panicked steps back, would be finished with. There would be a kind of peace in that.

She opened her mouth to say 'yes, that is it' but she couldn't do it. She couldn't completely slam the door.

'I can't talk about it, Freddy, and if you care about me at all, you won't ask me again. One day it will be finished, I swear it, and I will be free. When that happens, you will be the first one I tell.'

She knew it was cruel as she said it, that it offered him – and her – a sliver of hope that she had no right to dangle.

There was a moment of silence and then he rounded on her.

'You can't give me that and nothing else, Hanni. You can't. It sounds like a promise, and I don't know if it is.'

I should have said yes, there's a husband and I won't ever be free. That would have killed the hope in his eyes.

It was too late for that, but she had to draw boundaries somewhere.

'I have your back, Freddy. I'll always be your friend, if you want me to be. But we catch Bayer, and we do whatever else follows, as colleagues. If you want a guarantee…' She stopped herself. 'If you want more than that, I have to go now – I have to get out of the car.'

If he had looked at her, he would have seen the tears about to spill. If he had reached out and touched her, the boundaries would have broken. He didn't do either. He looked at his hands, he looked at his feet; he looked anywhere but at her.

'If that's what you want, then that is what we will be. Colleagues, friends if you like, although I don't know what that means with you and me. But I won't push you again, about anything, not until you tell me that I can.'

He was holding himself together and as far away from her as she was holding herself from him. They fell into a silence that was many miles from comfortable and focused all their broken thoughts on the building.

Bayer still never came.

'Bayer targets his victims near where they work, so the weekend won't need both of us. I'll do the watch alone today and on Sunday. If anything changes, I'll call.'

Freddy left that message with Frau Greber early on Saturday. He didn't telephone again until Monday morning and he turned that conversation into a report before Hanni had time to engage with it.

'He left the house for an hour on both days. A short walk, lunch and then home. Not much to go on, but at least we know that he's there. Tonight, I hope, things will change, so we should be in place by four o'clock. We should go separately from the station and meet in the café on the corner of his street and Joachim-Friedrich-Straße; you can see his building's entrance from there.'

He rang off as soon as he was done.

He had become exactly who Hanni had asked him to be. It was Inspector Schlüssel not Freddy who had telephoned; it was Inspector Schlüssel who she met in the café. A polite, professional and distant man who sat opposite her as if his seat at the table had been set behind a screen. The warm café was crowded and lively; their loneliness inside it made Hanni want to weep. She mirrored his detachment instead.

'Whatever mode of transport he uses, we split up. You take a seat as close behind him as you can, I will take one in the front. When he walks, we take opposite sides of the pavement, and you stay on the same side as him. I'm hoping that he won't so easily remember your face as mine, but we can't rely on that, not with his capacity for detail. At least it's cold enough for us to hide beneath hats and scarves.'

Hanni had brought those and had scraped her hair off her face and into a tight bun. She still felt uneasy – she had a feeling that once seen was never forgotten in Bayer's book. She also couldn't shake off the feeling that he would connect her somehow with the note and the photograph thrust under his door. None of that, however, could be said and, once the details of the plan were in place, it seemed that neither could anything else. They sat in silence instead, staring at their cooling cups of tea and waiting, surrounded by chatter and deaf to it all.

'He's on the move. There.'

Hanni jumped up a second behind Freddy, giddy as adrenaline pumped through her.

'He checked the street – did you see?'

Hanni nodded. The pause had been a short one and Bayer's head was down now, but he had definitely searched for watching eyes before he fully emerged. She pushed her way to the door as a couple converged on their seats.

'He's not carrying anything. That could mean it won't be tonight.'

'Or that he's got everything that he needs in his pockets.'

Freddy opened the door as they spoke over each other and let Hanni go through first. Luckily, the lights at the crossing point were in her favour and she was able to get a safe distance behind Bayer before he turned into the bustle of the Kurfürstendamm.

He moved steadily, weaving his way in and out of the waves of pedestrians without catching as much as the sleeve of a coat. Hanni hurried after him, resisting the urge to look round for Freddy, hoping that Bayer was heading for a bus stop rather than the faster-moving subway system.

Her hopes were rewarded. Bayer joined a queue, checking his watch as he waited, and again as the bus came into view. Hanni followed him and took a seat at the back, breathing a sigh of relief when Freddy took his place at the front only seconds before the bus pulled away. Bayer checked his watch at every stop – it was the only time he looked up and around him. It was clear to Hanni that he was timing the journey.

As the bus approached Masurenallee, it was also clear where he was heading: Reichskanzlerplatz – the scene of his most recent crime.

He's killing where he knows. Maybe he's stalking more than one victim at a time now he's speeding up his timetable.

Hanni followed Bayer off the bus without glancing at Freddy. The last body had been found in Thüringerallee, close to a tennis club used by the British officers stationed in the square and the civilians who worked with them. Bayer did not, however, turn that way but began skirting around to the west, following the roundabout which cut the square off from the wide streets leading into it.

Hanni followed him more slowly than she had done on the Kurfürstendamm. Unlike the busy shopping street, this wasn't the easiest area in which to find cover while she was moving, although she could see its attraction for Bayer. Great swathes of the concrete-slab buildings were still being renovated and weren't fully occupied, and empty and derelict spaces stretched out between them. The potential killing sites were endless.

Hanni crossed from building to building, trying not to be dwarfed by the square's echoes. It was a half-finished, still war-damaged and unattractive place now, but it hadn't always been so desolate, and it had associations she would have been happier to forget. Although everyone had, by tacit agreement, reverted to the area's original name, Reichskanzlerplatz was still officially called by the name it had been given during the Third Reich: Adolf-Hitler-Platz. And, although its fountain was now empty, Hanni could remember the days when that had been full and edged all round with swastikas, and the square had been a hive of shops and cafés filled with black-uniformed SS men, not with British soldiers.

She could also remember what the area was meant to become. In 1938 – according to her father, who had been obsessed with the plans for the new city of Germania which Hitler had intended to transform Berlin into – Adolf-Hitler-Platz had been designated as the new capital's power hub, the site of a people's Great Hall, with a dome bigger than anything to be found in Paris or Rome. It was hard to see the cranes and the scaffolding and not shudder.

A lorry rumbled past her and Hanni snapped back from the past in a panic. In the few minutes she had let her mind wander, she had lost sight of Bayer. She quickened her pace but still couldn't see any sign of him.

'Excuse me, Fraulein. Do you have the time please?'

She had been so busy peering down side streets, she had almost crashed into Freddy.

'Take a breath – you are acting too nervous. Look at your watch and smile.'

She did as he hissed and accepted the cigarette that he offered her.

'He's down there, in Pommernallee. Don't look – you won't see him, but he could be watching us. He's ducked into that group of buildings that are being renovated, just past the corner.'

Hanni leaned forward and cupped her hands round his lighter.

'Could you see what he's doing in there?'

'No. He could be hiding, but I don't think he's realised he's being followed; he didn't look around. I think it's the kill site, which means he's either waiting to strike, or he's preparing himself in some way for when he will. Walk down the street past it and wait at the bottom. I'll stay at this end. Find a spot where you can see but not be seen. If he leaves and retraces his steps, I'll come and find you. And if anything does happen, I'm closer – I'll get there first.'

'And what do I do?'

But Freddy had already moved away, which meant Hanni was forced to do the same. She was horribly aware that they didn't have a plan and it was a disturbing thing to walk past the half-derelict building. To know that Bayer was only the width of a wall away, that he could be watching her, remembering her face from the interview. That he might have grown curious once he found Reiner's name pushed under the door and dug into her past.

She strode past the scaffolding with her head down, as if she was negotiating the rubble scattered over the pavement, trying not to imagine any of the pieces of brick she stepped over being used as a weapon. There was a spill of yellow light a block ahead, outlining two aproned figures. Hanni headed for that, dropping the cigarette Freddy had given her and rummaging with shaking fingers in her bag for another. If Bayer was watching, hopefully he would assume that she was a harmless pedestrian on her way to the restaurant, and if anyone understood the rhythms of the street which he might be trying to tap into, the waiters would.

She slowed her pace and forced her face into a smile as she approached the two men.

'Do either of you have a match? The wind blew my last one out.'

Both of them produced their matchbooks with a flourish that would have made Hanni laugh on any other night.

She peered through the restaurant window. It was cosy and small and almost empty.

'A quiet night?'

The younger of the two smiled and waved her hand away as she tried to return his matches.

'Mondays always are, which means there's a table free if you want one.'

Hanni relaxed into the familiarity of the exchange and returned his smile as brightly.

'Another night perhaps – it looks inviting. Is there a good time to come?'

She laughed as he responded with a rundown of when he was working and when he was free and available to dance attendance on her.

'Fridays are the liveliest, but any night is good, except maybe Tuesdays. I'm not sure you'd like all the attention you'd get if you came in then.'

Hanni glanced up the street to make sure that Freddy wasn't on his way down it. She doubted the waiter would be quite so chatty if he thought there was a boyfriend in tow.

'What's wrong with Tuesdays?'

He made a face his co-worker clearly didn't appreciate.

'The place gets filled up with big shots from the British commission and it's all brandy and cigars and boasting. It's the same every week, and it's no pleasure to be serving them.'

'And they pay big tips we all need, so maybe you shouldn't be making rude comments about them to strangers.'

The older man's rebuke gave Hanni the opportunity to slip away. She stood at the bottom of the street waiting for Freddy, the cold nipping at her face and her fingers forgotten.

It's the same every week. They had him.

This time, Freddy came up with a plan, but it was too flimsy for Hanni to put any faith in it.

What would be the easiest crime to solve? Catching the killer in the act?

She had been hopelessly naïve when she had asked that, and Freddy had rightly dismissed the possibility of such a potentially dangerous strategy actually working. Now, however, catching Bayer in the act was exactly the course he intended to follow, and she was the one trying – without any luck – to persuade him out of it.

'What if we were to get the names of the regular attendees at the dinner and warn them? We could explain that we will be in place ready to stop anyone getting seriously hurt and get them to co-operate.'

He hadn't even taken a moment to consider it.

'And what if that's thirty people? There isn't time to check if any of them has recently had an odd visitor or to check up on their war records. And what about the night itself? We couldn't watch them all, and they wouldn't believe us if we said that we could. And then they wouldn't go to the restaurant. Would you, if you knew there was even a chance of getting killed when you left?'

Her second line of argument had been to bring in Matz, to give them three chances of catching Bayer or cutting off his escape route, not two. Freddy hadn't considered that possibility either.

'Matz is a rules man – he does everything by the book. He'd tell Brack or the new boss what we were planning because he would see that as the right thing to do. Then we would have a street full of police cars and no attempted murder to solve. You have to understand that Bayer is still the one in charge here. If we're right that this is where he's planning to strike next, he has watched the man he is after, he knows what time he leaves the restaurant and – presumably – the fact that he always does that alone. He knows his crime scene as intimately as he knows his victim. We have to catch him in the act, and we only have one chance to do it. If we spook him, he'll go deeper underground. Will you be able to find him a second time if he does?'

This time it had been her who didn't need to think about her answer.

'No.'

'Then we do it my way.'

Hanni had stopped arguing at that point. Freddy was right that they had only one chance. Nothing, not even a dozen dead bodies and Freddy's sacking, would get her to stand cap in hand in front of Reiner again. Besides, she had fired her best shot, in this round at least. Freddy's plan, therefore – as flimsy as it was – stood.

They met at the same time on Tuesday, but they did not follow Bayer: instead, they got into position in Pommernallee before he did, tucking themselves into separate dark corners in sight of where Bayer had hidden himself on Monday night.

Bayer appeared, as they expected him to, a shade after a quarter to six, when the street was at its quietest, and slipped through a gap in the renovations. His movements were as quick and silent as they had been before, but this time he was carrying a rucksack, which made Hanni's heart thud as she imagined the card and the note waiting inside it.

A few moments after he moved into place, the street grew busy again. Men in military great coats and businesslike over-coats wandered past Hanni's hiding place singly and in small groups, heading for the warm lights of the restaurant. She perched on a pile of rubble and wished she could join them. Despite the layers she had wrapped herself in, the cold was numbing. Worse than that, both the waiting and the silence which had settled back around her were too heavy. There was a man a few hundred yards away who was destined to die and didn't know it. Who they had talked about saving but didn't know if they could.

Who could be my father.

It hadn't occurred to her until that moment that the man Bayer was targeting could be Reiner. He didn't work at the offices nearby. He did, however, work for the British; he could, therefore, be one of the diners.

What if we can't stop Bayer in time? What if I am about to watch my father die?

The thought pulled her to her feet; it made her feel sick. And it made her realise yet again how poorly thought out Freddy's plan was.

'At what point do we move? When Bayer first emerges out of the building, or when he raises the brick, or when he delivers his first blow?'

Hanni had heard the split seconds between the actions as she had asked the question. Freddy's 'before he kills' hadn't stretched those out. Now that the reality of having to try to save a life inside those tiny gaps was staring at her, Hanni had never felt so alert – or so certain of failure. It took all her self-control not to run over to the restaurant and see if Reiner was there, to prevent a death she couldn't bear to have on her hands. The only thing that held her in place was the certainty that Freddy would never forgive her if she did.

The minutes ticked by and melted into hours. Hanni ran what was coming over and over in her head until she forced herself to see the steps working and tried not to leap up at every slightest speck of noise.

Eventually, at eight o'clock, the restaurant doors opened, and she was instantly wide awake. A man who was shorter than Reiner appeared and walked unsteadily away in the wrong direction. She slumped down again. When it opened the second time, twenty minutes later, the direction the laughing diners went in was the right one, but there were three of them and all of them were heavily built.

She calmed herself by taking out her camera, which she had brought in the hope that there would be an arrest or – if everything fell as badly as she feared it might – a crime scene with evidence she needed to capture. She couldn't risk taking any photographs from her hiding place – the flash in the darkness would act as a warning flare – but it helped to imagine the shots she might take if she could. The contrast between the brightly lit restaurant and the sightless office buildings where the night hung so thick it seemed solid. The eerie emptiness of the street. The outline of a man waiting to kill.

She conjured up scenes until the young waiter came out and lit a cigarette. And then, at eight thirty, the door swung open again and Hanni knew that this unremarkable and gently swaying diner – who was to her relief, no matter how callous thinking that felt, not her father but a stranger – was him, was the target. The man exiting the restaurant's fug and pulling his scarf tight against the sudden rush of cold was a little below average height and slightly built. He was also distracted, checking his watch, patting at his pockets – paying no attention to his surroundings at all.

Shout out and warn him chimed through Hanni's head. Closely followed by *it's better to let Bayer disappear than let another man die.*

The urge to act on the voice pulling at her, rather than Freddy's plan, was overwhelming, but she couldn't give into it. She had promised not to give herself away until there was a brick and the threat of a blow.

Instead of shouting, therefore, she got herself ready. She uncurled and got to her feet; she crept as close to the pavement as she dared. She comforted herself with the thought that Freddy was closer, that he could see what she could see, and he could get there, as he had promised, first. As the man wandered down the street whistling off key, she convinced herself that the plan would work.

She edged out further, pressed flat to the wall, ready to run as the man reached Bayer's building, as he closed in on the gap Bayer had slipped into; as he walked two, three steps past.

The speed of what came next was faster than it should have been, faster than either she or Freddy could have expected. That was what Hanni told Brack anyway.

It wasn't strictly true. There was a second between Bayer appearing and the brick falling when time stood still. When Hanni could see the scene unfolding as it would in a photograph, captured at that moment when the murder was at the same time both a certainty and something that hadn't yet happened. She stood transfixed by the raised arm, by the victim's utter oblivion. By the absence of Freddy. And then the frame moved on and the next scene flashed by. The brick smashed down, the man fell, onto his knees and then onto his face, crumpled instantly, as if the strings had been cut on a puppet. There was a pause, a second of silence, and then the sound of stone hitting skull and bones hitting concrete rushed through the air towards her.

'Freddy! In God's name, where are you?'

Her shout lifted Bayer's head and turned his searching eyes towards her. That movement pulled Hanni off the ground. She sprinted towards the stooped figure, yelling, ducking as the brick came hurtling now towards her.

Bayer moved as quickly as she did, fast and low, leaping over the motionless body. And that was the moment when Freddy finally materialised out of the shadows and ran with all the speed he had promised. Not at the same time as Bayer aimed the brick towards his unsuspecting victim, which was what Hanni told Brack when he questioned her later and made sure Freddy repeated, but at the moment which came after, when the damage was already done.

Freddy had been fast when he moved. He had caught Bayer almost at the same instant as the brick did its work. Hanni was at least able to be honest about that, even if some of the rest of the recounting was, by necessity, blurred. There were two stories that could be told about that night: the truth of what happened and the truth Hanni decided she could tell Brack. The two versions were close, but they were not the same: put them side by side and their timings faltered. Freddy had definitely stopped Bayer: he had flung him to the ground and wrenched his arms back with a force that would have held a far bigger man. Hanni was very confident when she described that. What Freddy had said next had, however, proved more problematic.

'Check his vital signs, then go to the restaurant and call for an ambulance.'

Hanni wasn't sure who Freddy had said that for, at the time or at any point after the attack happened. She had already been kneeling next to the body feeling for the man's pulse when Freddy had called to her to check it.

She repeated his instruction anyway when Brack interviewed her. She chose to use it as proof that their intervention had come in time, that they both believed that the blow was a glancing one no one could have thought would be fatal. It hadn't in reality been glancing at all. When Hanni had groped for the victim's wrist, she hadn't expected to find any sign of life. She had known before she looked that the blow to the man's head had splintered the bone, because she had seen the true force of it.

She said none of that.

What she told Brack was the hope that she had heard in Freddy's voice when he followed his instruction with, 'Is he alive?' His concern then hadn't sound forced, or like play-acting – there was too much anguish in it. Hanni hadn't known – and hadn't wanted to ask or believe – if Freddy's delaying had been deliberate. It was clear, however, as he kneeled with his knee in Bayer's back, that he had suddenly realised what the lost seconds had cost. It had been clear too in the groan that ran through him when she shook her head and said no.

Brack didn't need to know about Freddy's shock and remorse. It was bad enough that Bayer had sensed them. The side of Bayer's head had been pressed into the pavement, but his eyes had stayed open. He had smiled when Freddy had frozen at 'no'. He had smiled when he heard Freddy groan. He had made sure that Hanni had seen him. Hanni would never forget that. Bayer's delight at Freddy's pain had settled on her skin like a brand. She didn't tell Brack any of that either.

———

Bayer wasn't delighted, however, by the time he was placed in the murder van. This time, they saw the anger he had hidden from them at his previous interview. He burned with it. And so did Brack, who wanted to blame Freddy for another dead body, not praise him for finally catching the killer. He banned Hanni from the interviewing room and didn't seem to notice how grateful she was. He would have banned Freddy too, except Bayer refused to speak to anyone but Freddy and retreated into reciting numbers in an endless list when anyone else tried to approach him.

'He doesn't call all the shots, whatever he thinks. And he doesn't get to be interviewed by you on your own, which is apparently what he demanded. You caught him in the act – he was carrying the note and the sign in his rucksack. That's enough to convict him, so I don't care if he talks or he doesn't, but apparently the lawyers do, so we'll give him his moment. Laube, however, will be in there with you the whole time and he will write down every-thing that's said, or I'll have you both up on charges. And when this is done, you'll have more questions to answer than Bayer, believe me. Too much about this arrest stinks as far as I'm concerned, no matter who else might be singing your praises.'

Brack's threats were bluster – both he and Freddy knew that. The station was buzzing with Bayer's arrest and Freddy's bravery in catching him; the superintendent was talking about medals. Brack could shout all he liked when it was just the two of them, but Freddy was a hero now and heroes were never investigated. Freddy, however, didn't feel comfortable with that word – he knew he hadn't earned it. When he sat down opposite Bayer, he felt more like a man on trial.

'Why did you do it?'

Bayer's answer to Freddy's first question had made Matz fumble and drop his pen.

'For the same reason you and your very interesting assistant didn't try to stop me in time, Inspector. Because the man I killed didn't deserve to live. None of them did.'

Freddy swallowed hard and tried not to hear his career dying in the pages of Matz's notebook. He knew that Bayer was the one this time trying to forge a connection. Hanni had told him, reluctantly, what he hadn't seen when he wrestled Bayer to the pave-ment, what had made her cry out although she wouldn't explain why. That Bayer had smiled.

When Freddy had asked what Hanni thought he meant by that, she had stumbled over her answer: 'Maybe he knew we could have got to him quicker, that he thinks the delay makes us complicit.'

Even if Hanni had mistaken the reason for Bayer's smile – and Freddy didn't think Hanni had mistaken anything from the start to the end of the case, although she should have said *you* not *we* – Bayer's answer suggested she was close. A sense of complicity clanged through *for the same reason*. And Freddy couldn't let it stand. He had frozen, yes, but he hadn't meant to; he was as certain as he could be of that.

'But I have stopped you, Herr Bayer. Your crusade, if that's what it was, is finished.'

They both knew it was a question, even if it wasn't phrased that way. Freddy also knew what he wanted to hear in the answer.

Tell me that I was right, that I wrong-footed you last time, but I didn't make a mistake. Tell me that, yes, you were on a mission to take revenge for the lost. Absolve me from the death I could have prevented.

It was as if Bayer could read his mind.

'A crusade is an interesting word, Inspector. It is how you couched my work at our last meeting, when you described it as stemming from my "outrage" and my "need for justice". I will accept your description, but not – as I believe I have already made clear – in the context that you wish to portray it. What I did was valuable work – your choice of "crusade" shows that you under-stand as much – but it was never about the Jews, no matter how desperately you would like it to be.'

The man's arrogance, his implication that he understood Freddy on a personal level, grated across him. Freddy could feel his temper rising, but he couldn't afford to let Bayer see even the slightest loss of control – whatever Brack might believe about who called the shots, the balance of power in the interview room was still a delicate thing and, so far, Bayer was holding it. He shrugged and tried to pretend the gesture made him look unim-pressed not awkward.

'Then what was it about, Herr Bayer? You don't seem to be a man who acts without purpose.'

It wasn't meant in any way as a compliment, but that was how Bayer heard it. He sat back and looked suddenly fuller.

'You are correct, I am not. I had a very clear purpose, and I am glad that you asked for it. The men I killed were a stain on Germany, Inspector, and that is why they died. It is not a compli-cated thing. They dressed in soldiers' uniforms – uniforms that should always be worn with pride – and they dishonoured them.

And now you are frowning. Perhaps I could use Majdanek to illustrate my point. Do you want to know about that? It seemed to matter to you before.'

Freddy didn't want to hear about it at all – he had no desire to hear the kind of detail he knew Bayer could provide about the horrors that had happened there – but he had no choice and he nodded.

Bayer drew up his chest as if he was preparing to deliver a lecture.

'Majdanek was the pinnacle of the military's disgrace, and it was my starting point. There was no legal basis for what happened there, you see. And the soldiers who were ordered to carry out the task that was given to them were not trained or equipped to properly complete it. It was a shambles of planning and execution, and the officers who ordered it – who brought the army and therefore Germany into disrepute by their actions – should have been tried and convicted of crimes against their country. If they had been, if the trials at Nuremberg had done what was asked of them and punished those who had forgotten what it meant to be a soldier in an army that has always been run by the strictest, most chivalrous of codes, well...' Bayer spread his hands as if the decision to murder had been taken out of them. 'We would have got our honour back, Inspector. Germany would have been able to stand proud before the world again.'

Detail would have been better. Hearing about the screams and the blood and the overflowing trenches and how revolted Bayer had been by all that would have been better than this clinical disinterest and this nonsense about codes. Freddy knew all he was doing by asking questions was giving Bayer more air in which to indulge his peculiar take on the war's brutalities, but he couldn't help himself.

'What about the victims? At Majdanek. At Dachau and everywhere else the SS experimented on the innocent. And what about the millions consigned to the ovens? Was none of this ever about them?'

Bayer's face was such a blank it was hard to look at it and not shiver.

'That is a rather emotional response, wouldn't you say? There are always victims when a regime wishes to change the way a country regards itself, which is what the Third Reich set out to do. This is not about them and how they were treated; this is about the legal framework that enabled that treatment. The measures imposed against the Jews in 1935 were enshrined in the statutes and, therefore, their use, in whatever form that took, was both just and justified. Everything that came next should have followed that pattern. There were, however, no laws governing what the army was asked to do in the war and there was, therefore, no honour in the army doing it. That was what has damaged our country in the eyes of the world. "To Help, Defend and Heal" is the German army's code, Inspector, did you know that? And that is mine too. If I have a "crusade", as you call it, it is to help, defend and heal our army's reputation in the world, by removing the men who ruined it. My only regret is that I couldn't complete my work, because, as you say, you stopped me. Given what those men did when they were alive – which seems to matter so much to you and some of your team – I wonder if you regret that as well.'

The measures were enshrined in the statutes... they were both just and justified.

How many times had Freddy heard the same sentiment echoed in the shrugs and the 'it's not my fault; it's the law' that had excluded him and his family from the shops and cafés that had once welcomed them in? He forced himself to push the past away and focus on the present, although the line between those two states felt hopelessly blurred.

It would have been very easy to dismiss Bayer as mad – on some level, he undoubtedly was, but he was also frighteningly clear in his explanations and as much of a zealot as the men he had killed. And he was unrepentant. His voice was calm – it had only hardened when he used the word *stopped*. Apart from in those fleeting seconds when he remembered that his 'work' was done, his bland expression barely flickered. He was – and always would be – in his mind, a moral and honourable man. He also had more insight into Freddy than Freddy could bear, although Freddy had no idea what he meant by 'some of your team', unless that was Matz, and he had neither any idea why Bayer thought Matz was interesting nor any intention of pursuing that.

He got up, ignoring the perfectly levelled use of *regret*. He didn't have the stomach to hear any more.

'Would it have mattered?'

Walk away – don't let him get any further under your skin.

Bayer's voice, unfortunately, was sharper than the one in his head. Freddy stopped halfway to the door. He knew what was coming; he had no idea what Matz's pen would make of it. He asked the question anyway.

'Would what have mattered, Herr Bayer?'

It was the first time Freddy had seen the smile that had made Hanni's skin crawl. The longing to be a man in Brack's mould, to be comfortable beating any trace of emotion off Bayer's face, almost overwhelmed him.

Don't touch him – don't hand him such an easy victory.

Bayer took it anyway.

'If my motive had been the one that you wanted, would that have made a difference? If I had said that I killed the men I did because of what they had done to the Jews, would that change how you view me? Would you plead for leniency on my behalf? Would you find a loophole to let me go free again, to let me carry on? Your background and your sympathies aren't hard to determine, Inspector. I didn't need your hesitation at Pommernallee to tell me those. I imagine I wouldn't have found a record for your Party membership at the Centre if I had gone looking.'

Bayer didn't drop his smile or his gaze. Freddy couldn't answer him; he couldn't breathe another ounce of the same air as him. He slammed out into the hallway and crouched down, stuck his head between his knees and tried to stop the world swirling.

When he was finally able to pull himself up again, Matz was waiting.

'I didn't write it down. Brack can go to hell.' He held out the notebook which had less than half the interview recorded in it. 'I only included what incriminated him – the rest of it was poison and it doesn't matter. You got him, Freddy. He's confessed his guilt; it's done.'

Except Bayer saw the truth in me, and so did Brack. And I wasn't the hero here at all – that was Hanni.

Matz was still holding out the notebook and his voice was pleading. 'Did you hear me? It's over. It's time to move on.'

He needs me to be normal; they all do. He needs me to be happy.

Freddy managed to follow Matz back to the incident room and to nod at the clapping and to smile as if he really believed that 'it's over' was true. He didn't manage that because of Matz's praise-filled speech or because Brack was forced to join in the congratulations and to raise a glass with the rest of the team. He managed it because the first person who stepped forward to shake his hand, the one who stayed by his side as if she was holding him up, was Hanni.

CHAPTER 21

29 MAY 1947

'Is it done?'

Hanni slid onto the bench beside Freddy, keeping the distance between them that they always kept now.

He nodded. He didn't turn to look at her. He kept his eyes on the water splashing over the rocks. 'Yes. This morning, at eight o'clock.'

He doesn't fit in here, not today.

Viktoriapark was in full bloom. Fragrant purple lilacs fringed the narrow waterfall; the last drops of the spring's cherry blossom hung pink and sweet from the trees. Their vibrant colour only served to highlight Freddy's lack of it. He had received a commendation after Bayer's arrest, but he had never got his bounce back. His face was hollow, his skin was grey: he looked less like a man who had witnessed an execution and more like a man facing his own.

He should never have gone – or not alone anyway. The whole case still weighs too heavily on him.

As soon as Hanni had discovered that Freddy had decided to be in attendance at Bayer's last moments, she had come looking for him, thinking she could somehow soften the ordeal. Now that she was with him, she couldn't think how to begin.

'How was it?'

The question came out so clumsily, she expected a sarcastic dismissal. He continued to stare at the tumbling water rather than at her, but he didn't bite.

'As empty as him. There was no one there except the officials who had to be – and me. He delivered a speech about dying with honour, but nobody listened or cared.'

Which should mean, please God, that he will be quickly forgotten.

It also meant that she was safe. That if Bayer had worked out her connection with Reiner the way she feared that he had from his smile, the knowledge had died with him. Hanni knew she should be grateful for that, but she was too worried about Freddy to care.

She picked a spray of blossom from an overhanging branch simply to have something to do with her hands. Bayer was gone from the world, and he needed to be gone from Freddy. There had at least not been a trial – the judge had decided that his confession and the weight of the evidence, including all the completed cards found at Bayer's lodgings, didn't merit one. There had, however, been a leak to the newspapers and headlines filled with outrage about the killer 'the Americans have allowed to stalk Berlin's streets'. Even Freddy's hero status had almost toppled under the fury that 'betrayal' unleashed at the Document Centre. And the ripples the leak had caused were still coming. As Captain Cooper had succinctly put it, anyone requiring help from American sources in the future 'could go whistle'. So forgetting Bayer was the best thing for everyone, except she wasn't sure that Freddy could.

'Why did you go? The department didn't need anyone there, and you didn't owe Bayer any show of compassion.'

She had expected to see sadness or defeat when he finally turned round, but it wasn't there. Instead, there was a warmth in his eyes that reminded her of the man she had first met.

'But that's the thing, Hanni: I did. Bayer made me face up to myself. He made me realise I'm not some kind of superman, with all my memories and my pain safely locked away where it can't reach me. He made me realise that I'm human, with all the chaos that state brings with it.'

Now it was her turn to watch the water without seeing it.

'And is that what you want? To be so raw?'

To her surprise, he laughed. 'Of course not, who does? Isn't it easier to live your life with your secrets well hidden and feeling untouchable? Isn't that what you prefer?'

It was the first question he had asked her since she'd told him he no longer had the right to ask any. It was the first real conversation they had managed in weeks. They had been skirting around each other since March, working the same cases but avoiding direct contact.

Two more murders had happened in the two months between Bayer's arrest and execution – both of them with a clear run from killer A to victim B, as Freddy had once put it, and both of them quickly solved. Freddy and Hanni had worked them like the most distant of colleagues, passing each other without comment at the crime scenes and in the incident rooms, keeping their communication to nods and impersonal notes. But she had still run to his lodgings when she feared he might be suffering and run to the park when his landlady pointed her there. And it was still far safer to answer his question with another, rather than blurt out that, no, she didn't prefer it and it was the burden of kept secrets that was ruining them both.

'Do you regret joining the police, given everything that happened with this case? There were rumours a few weeks ago that you were thinking of leaving. Are they true?'

His laugh this time had a harder edge.

'They were Brack's rumours, not mine. He would have the flags out if he could get rid of me. But, no, I'm not leaving. I still believe what I told you when you asked me why I joined up in the first place. I care about justice; I want to be a part of how we reshape that. And as for this case – Bayer helped me there too. He showed me what the alternative to proper police work is:

crusades and vigilantes and moral ambiguity. That's not the world I want to be living in, even if I thought for a little while that it was. So I have no regrets about joining the police, but I do have regrets. About us.'

They had never been in a more perfect setting. Hanni could see the shot as clear as any she had ever taken: the waterfall, the lilacs, the blossom and the birdsong – it was a backdrop staged for lovers. And as for the players who would fill it: his arms were barely a stretch away from hers; his lips a handful of seconds. Nobody could look at the two of them through a lens and mistake what this image meant. It would be beautiful in every aspect.

And it cannot be.

Hanni stared at the waterfall's rocks and tried to reshape them into bomb sites and rubble. She stared at the boughs drooping over the water and tried to recast them as bent and broken limbs. To remember who she was and what she had come from. To remember that Reiner was still out there. That she hadn't defeated him, or released herself from him, or revealed his true face to the world, but had stirred him up instead, leaving the fight against him still there to be fought. That she still had no explanation for his 'hearts and minds' speech. None of those images were what she wanted, but – if they would stop the voice in her head which was begging her to see only beauty, which was begging her to say nothing in response to his regrets but 'me too' – she would hold on to them as tight as she longed to hold Freddy.

'I don't love him, the man who's been standing between us all this time, who is still there. I don't love him at all; I hate him, but I'm not free of him yet. He has caused terrible harm and he needs to be made to answer for that. And he could cause still more, to you and anyone else I am… close to.'

She heard his sharp intake of breath and the sudden rush of words she pushed away but crystallised around 'let me help'.

'It's my battle, Freddy. I will deal with him: I made a promise to do that, and my promise still stands. But it's my fight, and I can't let myself love anyone until it's done.'

She stopped before the weight of everything she couldn't say smothered her.

She closed her eyes. She concentrated on the water's gurgle, on the breeze stirring the blossom, on anything that would block her thoughts and block whatever arguments he used to persuade her that there was a different way.

Freddy, however, said nothing. The silence widened and her head became harder to fill. And then she felt it, the shift in the air as he moved.

She opened her eyes, expecting to see an empty space on the bench. He was still there. He was still looking out at the water. But his hand had bridged the distance she had placed between them, and it was waiting, palm open – in a gesture she had to tell herself was born purely from friendship or reject and lose him forever – for hers.

She didn't speak; she didn't look at him, but she took it. Their skin met; their fingers curled.

Hanni closed her eyes again. She let the sunshine and the warmth of Freddy's presence wrap itself around her, and she breathed.

A LETTER FROM CATHERINE

Dear reader,

I want to say a huge thank you for choosing to read *The Commandant's Daughter*. If you did enjoy it, and want to keep up to date with all my latest releases, just sign up at the following link. Your email address will never be shared, and you can unsubscribe at any time.

www.bookouture.com/catherine-hokin

Although this is a complete novel in itself, it is also the first in a series of four which will follow the story of Hanni and Freddy as they try to navigate their way through the shadows of World War Two into a more hopeful future. Writing a series is a first for me, but it is proving to be a fascinating experience and I have grown very fond of my two central characters. The continuation of their story will take Hanni and Freddy back to Berlin and to Theresienstadt, but there will also be new locations and challenges facing them. I really hope you will join me with them on their journey.

I also hope that you loved *The Commandant's Daughter* and, if you did, I would be very grateful if you could write a review. I'd love to hear what you think, and it makes such a difference helping new readers to discover one of my books for the first time.

I love hearing from my readers – you can get in touch on my Facebook page, through Twitter, Goodreads or my website.

Thanks,

Catherine Hokin

www.catherinehokin.com
goodreads.com/author/show/14552554.Catherine_Hokin

 facebook.com/Cathokin
twitter.com/@cathokin

ACKNOWLEDGEMENTS

Hanni and Freddy are not real characters, but the times and historical events I have immersed them in were. As readers of my previous books will know, a huge part of my writing process involves research, and this one has been no different. If it takes a village to raise a child, it definitely takes a library of resources to write a book.

I cannot list every source I have used, but some are too important not to mention here. Those I would like to single out are: for post-war life in Berlin, *Berlin: A Modern History* by David Clay Large, *Berlin Days* by George Clare, *The City Becomes a Symbol* by Donald A. Carter and William Stivers; for the Nuremberg Trials and post-war guilt and denial, *The Anatomy of the Nuremberg Trials* by Telford Taylor, *The Mark of Cain* by Katharina von Kellenbach, *A Nation of Victims* ed. by Helmut Schmitz; for Theresienstadt, *The Terezin Diary of Gonda Redlich* ed. by Saul S. Friedman, *The Theresienstadt Deception* by Vera Schiff, *As if it Were Life* by Philipp Manes.

I owe thanks to so many people, and I hope they know that, just because I always mention them, that doesn't mean I value them any the less. To my editor Tina Betts who always has my back and an eye to the purple. To Emily Gowers my incredibly insightful editor who has, in this book as she always does, made me a far better writer. She will still never see draft one. To the Bookouture marketing team: you are wizards. To my son and daughter, Daniel and Claire, who are unfailing in their love and support, and to everyone in the writing community who continues to believe, as I do, that rising tides lift all boats and cheer on every success. Jane Anderson, I am especially talking to you. And last, but never least, to my husband Robert who gamely pretends that he can remember all the plots and who I could not write a word without. Much love to you all.

CPSIA information can be obtained
at www.ICGtesting.com
Printed in the USA
LVHW040531190122
708837LV00003B/189